OF GODS STRANGERS AND MESSENGERS

F. D. Brant

F. D. BRANT

GRESHAM, OREGON

Books Written by F. D. Brant

Science Fiction Adventure

Survival Trilogy

Time of Isolation

Desperate to Survive

A Taste of history Past

The Harsh Lands

Post-Apocalyptic

Unexpected Unplanned and into the Unknown

Contemporary Christian Fiction

The Woman in the Snow

To be released at the end of 2017

Post-Apocalyptic

Discovery Trilogy

The Ones Before

Discovery

An Ancient Fire

CONTENTS

PROLOGUE 7

A TALE OF THE PAST 19

AN UNWANTED ADVENTURE 37

THE HUNT AND HISTORY 59

TIME – NEVER ENOUGH TIME.....................81

ENERGY, WE MUST CONSERVE ENERGY 103

ALL IS NOT WHAT IT SEEMS 129

TIMOTEE – CARAOLYN – CHANGES.............161

TIME IS AN ILLUSTION, BUT THERE'S NEVER ENOUGH..189

SCIENCE? DON'T UNDERSTAND IT, I JUST USE IT..223

THE PAST, A NERVOUS PRESENT, AND AN UNKNOWN FUTURE.................................255

SOUTH, SHOULD IT BE SOUTH? 281

PENETRATION AND FIRST CONTACT 311

SUSPICIONS PUZZLES AND RAIN 343

TIME WAITS FOR NO ONE 375

TO THE MOUNTAINS WE GO 429

EPILOGUE 451

PROLOGUE

Young TimOtee was returning from his day of classes at the teaching center. He was named after his great grandfather who lived with the family on their farm. For someone so old he seemed to get around okay. And he had great stories to tell now and then. But today TimOtee's mind was on other things. He was frustrated as one of the instructors from the learning center required a many paged report on their past history, and of the time when the gods had visited their world. He remembered, when younger, thinking about such a time and the adventure it had presented to one's imagination. But that was the past and he, for one, did not believe in such nonsense. So why would he have to write about it?

As he came through the door he sighed deeply and looked up, since he was actually looking down at the time, and saw his mother standing there with her hands on her hips smiling at him. He heard her ask, "So what's wrong little one?" *Little one*, how he hated that pet name for him. He knew how he had come by it, but that was a lifetime ago and should have been left behind once he was no longer the runt of the family. Still once a name stuck it seemed one was stuck with it forever. Shaking his head with a disgusted look he said, "I've a required report on the time when the gods came to our world, but it's all a tall tale as far as I'm concerned. Nothing like that could really have happened."

She shook her head slightly and held a slight smile on her face as she looked down at her fourth son. Yes they who farmed had a tendency to have large families and theirs were no different. She and her mate had eleven, and while TimOtee was actually number seven in the line of siblings it meant he had a lot of competition. "Well then *little one* I suggest you talk to your namesake. I think you will find some insight into those times. And maybe get enough to do your report. You might be surprised what you will learn. I must admit that I was when I had to write the same report a long time in the past. After all he is my grandfather, and at the time your great grandmother was still alive, may the gods protect her soul. And she confirmed much of what he stated to me. And believe me the stories he told seemed too fantastic to be real. Yet, they were consistent.

"Who knows for sure if what he passes on is accurate or not? And one thing for sure, there's no one alive today who can dispute what he says. And it's surprising, considering his age, his mind is still sharp. It's only his body that is failing him now. So before you go in and bother your namesake, wash. The mid-meal is just about ready and he will be out to join us anyway. And to be polite I suggest you wait until the meal is done before asking him. Do I get an okay from you, young man?"

TimOtee brightened and smiled up at his mother before running out to wash up. Maybe things wouldn't be so bad and he had to admit he was hungry. He remembered his mother commenting that he had to have a hollow leg for all the food he put away. But what was one to do? He was hungry all the time. And mom always put together such mouthwatering meals. So wasn't it polite to put away as much of this good stuff as one could? He thought so anyway.

* * *

It was after the meal and he knew that before his conversations with his great grandfather he had chores to do. Besides he knew that after a meal his grandfather would take a nap. All he could do was shake his head at that idea. After all naps were for babies and he was anything but a baby. So why would a full grown person need such a thing? It was all well beyond him. Well, he had lots of raking, filling the water troughs, and making sure the beasts had their fodder. Then it would be hauling the manure out to the edge of the fields, with his siblings' help, of course, as they all worked. And there was always more work than the time the sun would provide light. And shirking one's duties was something that wasn't tolerated, and if caught one would find the punishment severe including missing meals. And one thing for sure, he had no desire to miss any meals. Heck he found that even between meals he'd be starving.

Then, once it was all finished, all to the satisfaction of his father and mother, it would be time to clean up. After all working the stalls and such left one covered in all the refuge, and stepping in a fresh patty took a while to remove from one's bare foot. And it left a telltale odor that gave away the fact that you had been careless enough to not watch where you were stepping. And as the sun was setting he and the rest were finished for the day and they headed over to the place that sat outside of the house where they could do a cursory cleaning. Later it would be baths before bed – again this was in the bath house which was attached to the main house.

The first allowed in that place were all the girls. He didn't understand why they had the privilege but they did. He remembered complaining about that a couple of times only to be put in his place. And once that had happened he never asked or complained about it again. He had been told, too many times, that it was only manners that the females or girls went first. He seemed to remember his dad mentioning that somewhere in the past when the world was a much more dangerous place that the males or men would guard while the females would clean up. Then the males would clean up in shifts. After all, it was reasoned, that once the females were clean, they wouldn't allow the males inside unless they cleaned up too.

So, as far as he could figure, the whole tradition came from that time. It wasn't that he had a problem with it, only at times he had been so tired that he just wanted to get it over with and go to bed. He remembered being told that when he was very young, and all of them could vouch for it, as they all had been informed that it applied to all, that he had bathed with the females. It had been a shock to learn this, and he was sure his younger sisters thought it was wrong too. But then again, it was something from the adult world that he, as of yet, did not understand.

Still this was considered the normal day-to-day routine but with this report, (He seemed to remember others getting this same break in the past and it had bothered him then.) he was allowed to take a break from part of this required work and go work on the report. And as in anticipation there on their covered porch sat his great grandfather, again the one he was named after. This was another mystery since he couldn't see anything special, or anything about himself that could be compared to this one, still one didn't have a say what would be their name, and to be honest he didn't know if one disliked their name, where sometime in the future, they could change it. Mentally he shrugged. It probably didn't matter anyway. It was like that hated nickname he had, once it became a part of you, you were stuck.

As he approached the porch he saw the old one smiling, although he didn't appear to be looking his way, but instead he stared out into the distance like he was remembering some past happy memory. Well, TimOtee was sure he had many of those. So trying not to interrupt he quietly stood next to him waiting for the old one to be aware that he was here. Yet, as the time passed there seemed to be no change. *Is the old one deaf or blind?* He cleared his throat hoping to get his attention. Suddenly with a speed that surprised TimOtee, the oldster turned and faced him laughing. "Ha, it took you long enough. Been watching you and was thinking about your brothers and sisters, and the times they came to me for this same information. And I suspect if I'm still around when your youngest sister AnnOtee has to face the same report she will come see me also.

"Still what I have to say, what you need to write in your report is important. I know that your mother, my granddaughter by the way, has said that there are no others who are from that time, or who are alive today, but that isn't entirely true. You see I'm not the only one who faced these gods and lived to tell. Still, at the time, with the chaoses that were happening all around me, and yes our world, I wouldn't have given me a chance to be here, to live long enough to see my children, and grandchildren grow up healthy and strong. And now not only children and grandchildren, but you and the rest of the brood all being great grandchildren, and so I feel really blessed. Of course at the beginning it was only me, and your great grandmother wasn't with me as of yet. But, I get ahead of myself. Go get your papers, and your writing tools. Pull up a chair and get something to put your paper on because you must take notes.

"Get comfortable, and understand what I will require of you. You see it will take you at least five days to write this, and after each day I will require you to write out what we have discussed, and then show it to me. So in the next five days we will be meeting here, unless it rains." Here he laughed once again, "Yeah, I don't see that happenin' anytime soon."

His namesake turned to him and with a serious look asked, "So what is your opinion, and thoughts about this stuff?"

TimOtee was caught off guard. He didn't expect to be asked a question, especially *that* question. He knew what he thought about the subject, but never had put those thoughts into words. "Ah, I don't know

. . . Ah I think they're not real . . . Ah, you know, kinda' like the games we play where everything is how we think it might be, but for us is only a game, and nothing is really there other than in our heads."

Nodding his head, the old one smiled again. "I can understand that. In truth, if I hadn't lived it I probably would have figured it is all manure, all that stuff you rake out of the stalls or accidently step in when they're hot and fresh." Here he laughed again, "Yeah, I've stepped in my share of them, and each time I always vowed I'd be more careful, only to have it happen again. So go get your materials, and have your mother step out for a moment. I'd like to ask her something, if you don't mind." The old one watched as the young one continued to stand there. Shaking his head he asked, "So, TimOtee, why are you still standing here? We have much ground to cover and only so much time to do it in."

"Ah, sorry sir, I thought you had something else you wanted to say." With that TimOtee headed inside the house yelling, "Mom! Your grandfather wants to see you. He's on the porch!" And after yelling this headed to his shared room to get the necessary materials.

TimOtee, the oldster could only shake his head. "Youth! Was I ever that young?" His granddaughter stuck her head out the door and he could see she was shaking her head also. "Did you need anything?"

"Yes, I was hoping you could bring me out something to drink – maybe a pitcher since all this talking is dry work."

She smiled at him saying, "No problem – maybe some fresh fruit juice?"

Nodding his head enthusiastically he said, "Yes, please."

As the senior waited, for both his great grandson, and the drinks, his mind drifted back to the beginning of this part of his life. He needed to put things in order, and how he would present the facts. After all, he had done this too many times to count. Yet, he found, in his own mind, to be something important. It seemed that when one was further from the event, whether it be distance, or time, the less important or real it seemed or became. And in this case it was time that became the culprit. And he was seeing the results of this passing of time in the way his great grandson viewed that time. It had become myth.

It truly wasn't that far in the past when one looked at the overall scheme of things. So what would it be like, say in ten more generations? A time when there would be no one living who had been there . . . When all of it – this history – would simply be in the writings with no proof, other than those same writings. He mentally shook his head. He could see that soon there would only be disbelief, and the myth theory would become the predominant view. Well, he couldn't do much about that. So it came down to the ones he could influence. No he wasn't trying to bring them to his way of seeing things. And yes he realized that time changed and colored things. Plus one only saw and interpreted things from their own point of view anyway. So he knew that even though he tried he would still be putting himself into what he said. It was then he realized someone had been standing there – actually two someone's. Looking up since they were standing and he was sitting, he smiled a sheepish smile. "Sorry, was lost in thought about how I would be approaching this." He could see his granddaughter about to say something about his last comment, but with her son standing there, she refrained. Still the two of them had a great relationship, and her tongue and humor were really sharp – one of the many things he loved about her.

He reached up and took the glass of cool juice and smiled a thank you, and had her place the pitcher on the small table that sat next to the chair. He had his namesake pull of a chair that faced him. He cleared his throat before speaking, and at the same time leaned forward. "I see you are ready, but am I?" Here he laughed, before turning to his granddaughter, his namesake's mother. "I think we'll be okay for a while. If you could check every once in a while it would be nice. I know when I do this, or have done this in the past; time has a way of getting away from me. And I know there're things that have to be done." He watched as she smiled and withdrew gracefully.

Again, inwardly he smiled. She, his granddaughter had always been one of his favorites.

Sighing quietly, he turned back and said, "Okay, now the way I'm going to present this is probably different than you expect. What I mean is this: First off when any of us tell a story we usually tell it from our point of view, and if one wants to be honest, that's probably the best way. But that would limit all that was happening at the time. Instead I'm presenting this history to you as if you would be on top of a mountain. And from there you, through some miracle, could see and hear all that was happening. I guess kind of like it would be if you were one of the gods."

Young TimOtee wondered how that could be since his namesake could only see what was happening around himself. But at this moment he refrained from asking. He'd give it some time, and if he had questions he would ask then. "I don't know what you mean, but I guess."

"Oh, I think it will be a better way. Because you see there was a lot going on, and if I kept it strictly to only me, then much of what happened as this unfolds wouldn't make any sense. Okay then, are you ready?" He saw the youngster nod. "Well, it all started when I was about eighteen. And soon I thought I'd be ready to go find a mate and begin my or our own farm, but fate intervened. And I was out in one of the fields . . ."

CHAPTER ONE

A TALE OF THE PAST

TimOtee stood on the sloping hillside overlooking the valley below. It was a warm day, but the breezes were cool. He knew he couldn't remain here long. He had lost his pursuers a short time in the past, and it wouldn't take long for them to pick up the trail once again. Around him sat large rounded boulders. In fact he was standing on one at this very time. The soils were yellow in color with evergreens scattered around. The bushes were sparse, so different from the valley below him which appeared to be covered in green.

In truth it was hard to tell, but his heart reached out to that valley. It had been where he was born and had grown. He and his family owned – past tense – a small farm and on that fateful day when his family and the farm were lost forever, he had been working one of the far fields. One of their beasts had become separated and lost and he was out trying to find it and bring it back. It was then he heard the sounds which caused him to pause. Turning around he looked back towards the farmhouse just in time to see indistinct figures close to the house, followed by the shimmering wall that went up, forever separating him.

Nobody knew who the attackers were; let alone what this shimmering thing was. The only thing that was known lay in the fact that if anyone touched it or got too close, it meant instant death. So, all avoided these opaque barriers like the plague. The rumors flew stating that the ones who were always seen before this barrier went up seemed to be bipedal like they were, but that was all that could be stated. No one from the other side of these barriers had ever returned to let the ones on the outside know. So the only assumption was that any on the inside were as good as dead even if they were not.

He remembered running away in a panic when he saw this, and hoped beyond hope he hadn't been seen. Eventually he worked his way into the foothills, followed by the lower slopes of the mountains. Here he had joined one of the many refugee camps, and eventually had moved into an established rag-tag village where all tried to keep each other's morale high, even though it was close to impossible. He learned that there were many such places like this village scattered across the ranges, and many had been established a long time in the past, and the ones who lived there considered the areas where these new villages were springing up to be trespassers in their territories.

Any, who were not from these established villages, and within what they considered their land, would be attacked if seen. So most of the time when they left it would be in groups for protection. And unfortunately for him he had become separated, by no fault of his own and then had been spotted. And thusly why he was alone, a long way away from where he was staying, and taking this brief stop to overlook the valley. He really needed to move. He knew he wasn't far from another's territory so if he could cross over then it should stop the pursuit from the ones behind him, but open him to danger in the new territory.

Still what could he do about it? Nothing really, nothing at all. At least there would be a possibility he could pass through the next claimed area unseen and work his way back to where he was staying. Still, when he returned, if he did, he would be coming back empty handed. Food and necessities were in short supply, and that was the reason he and the rest had left. Unfortunately he didn't know the fate of the other ones he had been with, but suspected that at least some died when the rivals attacked. *Better get moving,* he thought. He could hear voices in the distance and they seemed to be getting closer. Maybe the best way would be to move down into that valley, be close to that shimmering danger, and then work his way back.

Whatever his decision he needed to move now. So quickly looking back he slid off the boulder, and down into the underbrush where he knew the trails. After all, even though it had been a while since he'd been here, he was on familiar ground, giving him a slight advantage. And at this time, any advantage was needed. There must have been at least twenty chasing him, running him down, and trying to push him towards some trap ahead. But he had expected such and had circled around and avoided their out runners. So with care and as much speed as he could safely make he headed down into the valley.

"Where'd the turd get to?" The leader of this patrol screamed. Looking around at the rest he could see them cringing and not making eye contact. He spit on the ground yelling, "You worthless bunch of, well I don't know. If we lose this one there'll be hell to pay once we get back, and you all know it." Whoever this was seemed to be able to continue to avoid them leaving nothing to follow, no trail, and he seemed almost to be a ghost, but there were no such things. When he saw he wasn't going to get any response from the ones with him he shook his head in disgust. "Just don't stand here. Spread out and see if any of you worthless worms can find him. If you find anything alert the rest of us so we can form up and get him."

TimOtee slipped silently down the hillside keeping the brush and trees between him and the ones above him. At this point he left the known trails and began to work his way parallel to the hillside trying to spot any of the pursing members. He never got a good look at them so he really had no idea which one of the many in these mountains and hills they were affiliated with. He suspected it was the ones who claimed this, but it could be as easily another coming in to attack instead. Well, he had no plans to find out. If he did it meant he was too close, and with the only weapon he had at this time being a small knife, it wouldn't provide much of a defense, let alone be a great offensive weapon.

He could see ahead of him the small stream that seemed to be a break between the valley and the beginnings of the hills. Shortly he would be entering a marsh like area, while not large, would be a great place to lose the followers. There was quicksand, and while it had a reputation as a killer, it usually was the elements that did the killing. The quicksand simply trapped one. Plus there were areas where the brackish waters ran deep with buried limbs and debris making it easy for one to become trapped and drown. It again was an area he knew well, and he planned on using this place as his offensive. He could use his knowledge to either cause the attackers to break off their attack, or to whittle their numbers down by the natural traps that existed throughout this area. His real worry would be that they knew of this place also, or that they would surround this place and keep him isolated and wait him out.

Still he suspected that wouldn't happen simply because they were too close to those shimmering barriers, and all the dangers associated with them. And even though he had never been close to the chasers, he felt if he had known any of them he would have been able to recognize them from a distance. So he felt they would be on unfamiliar ground. Adding to the pressure on them would be the fact that this valley would be considered out of their claimed territory, and belonged to the ones behind those barriers.

He found he was breathing hard, and his lungs burned from the exertion, but he really had to keep moving. Chancing a glance behind he saw, in the distance, the first of whoever they were pull out of the brush and become visible in the grasses of the valley. At this point it was only one, but just as he thought, he heard the whistle that would alert the rest that he had been spotted. He smiled, even though there was no humor in it. He had them, and they didn't know it. In only a short distance he would enter the trees he saw ahead. They were the very trees that marked the entrance into the marsh, and its myriad of traps, hiding places, and even many hidden damp caves, where the moisture dripped continually. Not a comfortable place to remain – this marsh – but better in one of those caves than be captured by the likes of these.

He reached the trees, stopped and turned around, looked right at the pursuers, smiled, pointed at the one he suspected was the leader, making it appear to be a challenge and disappeared from their sight. He had plenty of time. They were still far back and he would be well within this dangerous place before they reached the point where he entered. *Now let's see if you are brave enough to come inside after me.* In a way he hoped so. It would be time to whittle them down a bit, to make it a little more equal. Still whether they would take his challenge, or take the bait and enter, he really didn't care. Once he was inside they would have lost and would need to return unsuccessful.

In truth this place wasn't that far from the farm, and his family had built a safe area inside one of the many caves. It was here he would be heading once he determined what the ones behind him were going to do. Now he could catch his breath, and watch or spy on them without he ever being seen. He was in his world now. Now, if only he had a home to return to, but at this time it lay behind the barrier, and the place he had been living since then was a long way away at this moment. So he would have to use this place, a place of last resort, for a while. He had hoped he would only need to be here when he had come up with some way of passing through that barrier and learn what had really happened to everybody he had ever known.

He heard them approaching, and their heavy breathing, but they stopped. He could hear the leader screaming, and see the others cowering. Again he smiled and shook his head. All of this wouldn't change a thing. He wouldn't become their victim today, or become their prisoner either. After a while he got tired of listening when it became obvious no one would be entering. In a way he was disappointed. He really wanted to return the favor, but it wasn't going to be today. So silently he slipped away, heading deeper into the marshes looking for the landmarks that said it was safe to pass this way, and eventually found the hidden pathway that led to the family refuge.

Before entering he studied the surrounding area, the ground for tracks, and for other sign stating someone had been here. In a way he hoped to find his family here. He had come here a number of times since the barriers, but no one had ever arrived, no one had used what was here, and today was no different. So sighing quietly he opened the hidden entrance and entered into a dark area where he fumbled for a candle which he lit. He then headed deeper inside went into a worked side tunnel and sat down heavily in a makeshift chair, setting the candle on a small side table and watched as the flickering light cast shadows. He breathing eased, and somewhere during this time he fell into a troubled sleep.

* * *

"Well Colonel, what do you think? Wasn't I right? This has gone even better than I predicted." General Pertion smiled because Colonel Jamison was always the one who would demand caution. But this time it wasn't necessary.

The Colonel shrugged, "True, but we're a long way from taking control of this planet. I must admit the admiral did a great job of losing our pursuers, and that loop back feint followed by rising above the plane of the system was sheer genius. Still, I'm waiting for the other shoe to drop. Everything has gone much too easy so far. Yes, I know, this planet is primitive in comparison to us – but, so what. It wouldn't be the first time a primitive society beat a technologically advanced one."

The General laughed, and shook his head. "Ever the pessimists are you? I'll admit I was a little surprised by the ease, and success so far. But, I don't worry about such things. If it changes then we'll adjust. It's that simple." The two continued their tour of the captured area, and so far what natives they had were cowering in fear. There were still a few running loose behind the energy barriers, but it wouldn't be long until the last few were rounded up and put in the camps, followed by stasis. Before stasis they would decide what to do with them. For now they'd be kept together. After all, these primitives could provide the manual labor necessary to get things set up. He didn't know how long they'd have before the ones who were chasing them caught up. So the pressure was on to dig in and be prepared. Time definitely was not their friend.

* * *

"I don't know sir. One moment they were there, and I really thought we had boxed them in, and the next they were gone. Unfortunately from here there are a million places for them to go. And yes I know, we've got to track them down and end this." Here Lt Jacee sighed, as he shook his head. "I really thought we had them this time."

Looking into the eyes of his navigator Captain Samuels said, "Yeah, me too. But these are very good at what they do. And the one thing you can always expect from them is the unexpected. So I guess it's back to square one." Shaking his head, he continued, "Time to send out the scout ships once again. We'll set up somewhere in the center of this sector and do it all over again."

* * *

TimOtee awoke with a start. He had a crick in his neck from the awkward angle his head had been in when he fell asleep in the chair. But, what had awakened him? He took slow deep breaths trying to clear the cobwebs in his mind. There was a metallic taste in his mouth letting him know how deeply he had been asleep. *Where am I anyway?* Nothing at the moment seemed familiar. It was then it all snapped back into focus. And then in the background and what he figured was probably some distance away he heard a scratching sound – subtle and different from the natural sounds. He figured it was what had awakened him. As he listened he could hear what he suspected was some sloshing followed by distant voices. Still, he couldn't be sure. It was like the sounds were being carried by the winds, and when they either quit or changed direction the sounds would drift away.

Carefully and quietly he lifted himself out of the chair. With no idea how close the ones making the noise were he didn't want to alert them to his presence. He slowly worked his way to the hidden entrance and peeked outside to see if he could see anybody close. His location was on a small island somewhere inside this marsh, and like so many of other such pieces of dry or semi-dry land it was totally uninviting. He worked his way through the low scrub brush and high grasses and did a quick circuit trying to locate the source, but came away empty. The voices he had heard never made an appearance again. The one thing he did notice was the fact that the winds had picked up tremendously and from the opposite direction of the prevailing wind. He suspected a front was moving in, and from the speed of the wind it had to be a strong one.

He didn't know how much time he had but suspected that shortly it would be raining. He would be safe where he was, but wanted to be sure there were no others around and still searching. So with care he worked his way to the edge and made a slow circuit around the marsh, remaining within it at all times, using the cover the marsh provided to remain out of sight. As he worked the side closest to the shimmering barriers he found a bunch of strangers, dressed in strange clothing standing in a circle and while he couldn't understand anything they said, he could tell there was a heated discussion going on from the animated way they moved. *What's this all about?*

It was at this moment he realized that these strangers were very different from him and the rest of this world. He remembered the rumors stated that the ones who had placed these barriers were bipedal like them, but there never had been any proof. He caught his breath, because at that very moment he realized that these strangers were the very ones responsible for what was happening to their world, and to the people who lived here. Did he dare move closer? *No, that would be stupid. If these are the ones, then there's no way I'll understand them. It's obvious they have ways far and away above of us – which could mean they have ways of sensing others close to them.* A possibility since they seemed to be standing out in the open and not really paying attention to the surroundings.

Were they that arrogant that they had no fear of an attack? It really appeared to be the way of it. Why? Heck he had just escaped from that rival clan, and yet, these, how many, maybe five or six, stood out in the open without an obvious care in the world. He watched, fascinated by their lack of awareness, and . . . stupidity? It seemed so to him anyway.

* * *

"Sarge, you are aware that we are being watched, right?"

"Yeah, and so what. There's no one here who can do anything to us. What we've seen so far consists of primitive, and I mean primitive weapons. And there are not even the beginnings of chemically propelled weapons yet. Only knives, bows, and such, so, I have no worries about any of them. And if I read this right it's only one, and whoever it is, is in that swamp. No place I have a desire to go. But if you want to, go right ahead."

"No, no", the private responded, "Just thought I'd let you know, not that you didn't, obviously. So why are we out here? I mean, as far as we are aware we got completely away, and there's nothing on this world that can harm us, so why the patrols?"

"Hey, like you, I take orders. I know they could do a flyby and use other things like an orbital or something, but we were told to do it the old fashioned way. I'm guessing here, but other than the energy fields we are using to isolate us; the ones in charge don't want to put out too great of an energy signature. You know something that would give us away. Besides it gets us out and away for a while. And I prefer this to the busy work they would find for us."

The rest couldn't disagree with that.

* * *

Staying where he was TimOtee watched, from his hiding place, as the strangers headed off and back towards those barriers. He needed to decide whether to follow them or to head back to his personal sanctuary. He really wanted to see how they got across those barriers that kept him and every other one who lived on this world, from entering. But before he could even leave the marsh he watched as they disappeared through the barriers by simply walking through. How was it done? He knew death awaited any who touched them. Were these bipedal ones, who appeared to be like them, immortal? Or was it something else? Well he had no answers, and he really needed to decide what he was going to do. One thing for sure he couldn't hang around here. So standing on the edge of the marsh he made a decision and decided he would head back and at least warn the camp or refugee village of what had happened to them.

There was a smell of old smoke in the air. Yet, TimOtee still had a little distance to go before he would enter the narrow canyon entrance to their refugee village. Something didn't feel right, and with those feelings he slowed his approach and decided to study the area for a while. He looked up towards the top of the sheer cliffs that came off the mountains here, and helped hide the valley on the other side of the trail that split these cliffs. The sun was getting low in the sky so he needed to move, needed to make a decision as to what to do. After some time had passed and nothing moved he carefully approached, and headed inside.

The passage was bathed in deep shadows, again nothing unusual since the canyon walls were so steep. But, this time, because of the lateness of the day, it was dark enough that one couldn't see the normal obstructions, rocks and such, that one needed to avoid when approaching their camp. Yet, the deeper he went the more alarm he felt. By now he should have heard something, anything. But the only sounds were the normal dusk and evening sounds. This slowed him down even more. And with a growing unease he stopped at the entrance to the valley and saw only darkness. It was as if there never had been anybody here.

He knew in that instant, like the farm where he had grown up and subsequently lost, that this place had been attacked and wiped out. Thusly leaving the smell of old smoke in the air that he had smelled as he had returned. The realization made him sit down heavily right then and there. Now in a short time not only had he lost his family, but now this place where he had made new friends was also gone. Both had happened in too short of a time period. He suspected that this place was attacked after he and the others left to find those needed supplies. And furthermore, he suspected it had been the reason they had been attacked while on the trails. It had to have been the clan or village that claimed this area as their own. At least he thought so, as it made the most sense.

Sucking in a great quantity of air he let it out slowly, stood back up and slowly worked his way into the burned out village. It was dark enough that he could barely make out anything even with his strong night vision. And after working the whole area he now knew that all who had lived here were either dead – from all the bloated, dead bodies still here – or were captives of the ones who attacked. To be honest he never knew how many lived here, but from his initial survey there appeared to be too few bodies. Although, because of the darkness, he was sure he had to have missed a few. *Now what?* He thought. He had to admit he had no answers. He had expected to come back and hopefully be able to explain what had happened, but, and obviously there would be no need now.

Should he stay the night, or should he retreat to somewhere else? Shaking his head he was undecided. *Still it's full on night, and moving around in the dark is not the best thing to do. So I guess I'll stay the night, and move out in the morning. Again, now that this place is gone I really have no idea where to go, or what to do. Maybe in the light of day I can make a better decision.* Moving as far away from the entrance as he could and up against one of the walls of the canyon he built a small fire. With only what he brought with him he settled down for a long and uncomfortable night. Tomorrow would have its own problems. He'd faced enough for one day.

Little one: "Wow! Did all this really happen to you? I mean it seems like . . . well, it must be made up right?"

GGF: "I know it can sound like a tall tale. And from what you know of me it doesn't seem possible that I could have lived this. Do I have it right?"

Little one: "Ah yeah!"

GGF: "Well, let's give it some more time and see what you think then, okay?"

Little one shrugged and nodded. After all what else could he do? One thing for sure, he hadn't expected this.

CHAPTER TWO

AN UNWANTED ADVENTURE

The air smelled fresh and clean. The storm he sensed coming in had been a quick one. It had dropped showers through the late afternoon throughout the evening, and by morning was gone. It was now pushing the zenith of the day and TimOtee was far away from his starting point – the burned out remains of the refugee village. With the light of day he was able to get a true understanding of the devastation that lay before him, and it was much too much for one to handle. He had made a quick search of the area to find some food that could have been overlooked, and to find out if any had survived. He might have well just left – shouldn't have wasted his time. The destruction was complete.

So with a heavy heart he headed out. Fortunately he had been able to get a pack from the emergency shelter located in the marsh. So he at least had minimal supplies to sustain him. Still it was way short of what he should have. Yet one did what one had to. Truthfully he had no destination in mind, only to put distance between himself and all the death and destruction that lay behind him. From that peaceful existence of a farmer to this, it all lay heavily upon him. *Why? Why has this happened? Why all this death? Why can't we just get along? Is it so important that it's worth killing someone because they happen to be in an area that you claim?* All that kept going through his mind were these and so many other questions. And he found he had no answers.

He found that subconsciously he was staying in the foothills, and paralleling the valleys watching for those shimmering barriers. He had hoped that these things would only be local, in the area where the farm and village he knew was located. But, so far, they seemed to go on forever. Nothing in the mountains, but the valleys where they produced their foods, where most of the major trading centers, and villages lay, it was here that all of them appeared to be blocked, (It might not be the truth, but it surely appeared to be so.). It left many of the familiar areas places to stay away from. (Of course, since he hadn't been completely around the shimmering barriers he had no way of knowing.) There were many wild clans, bandits, and raiders that used the great mountains as a base of operations. And whoever it was who had placed these barriers had forced most out of the valleys and into those hills and mountains. Leading to many confrontations and with the results being what he found when he had entered that canyon the previous night.

So which does one choose to go against, the wild ones in the mountains, or these unknown invaders with their magic? He stood with his hands out in front of him palms up and in his mind he placed each in his hands weighing them trying to come up with some answer, some solution. Looking from one hand to the other he kept asking, "This one . . ." then he would look at his other hand and ask, ". . . or these unknown ones?" Unfortunately with too little information he had no way to come up with any satisfactory answer. He shrugged, and after this brief break continued his trek out of the area.

* * *

It was five days later and he was camping close to a stream when he heard voices. At first they were too far away to understand anything. Yet, as they came closer he realized once again it wouldn't have mattered. They were the unknown strangers who had placed those barriers, and unlike the few he had seen from the marsh, this time there had to be at least twenty of them. Watching from his hidden position he could see they knew what they were doing. It appeared they were taking a break, and eating a meal – something he'd love to do. At this point he was out of what he had brought with him, and had to resort to hunting. Having to do this slowed his progress, but even still he really didn't have a destination yet in mind.

Watching he could see that they had guards out, and as one finished eating one would rotate out, relieve a guard, who would then come in to eat. At no time did it appear that they were relaxed. He noticed that whatever it was they were eating seemed to be in containers of some kind. Fortunately, or unfortunately, the distance was too great to determine exactly what these things were, but obviously they contained their food. Quietly he pulled further back. The last thing he needed at this moment was to be confronted by these strangers. Again, like back in the marsh, he saw that they remained in the open giving the impression that they had no worries at all about any who would be interested in doing them harm. *How can this be so?* It made no sense to him at all.

TimOtee was just about ready to withdraw from the area, away from the stream and leave it to these strangers when he heard a shout and saw one of those wild clans come out of nowhere and attack these strangers. Looking at the size of the attacking force he felt these strangers didn't have a chance. Yet, before the attackers could reach and overwhelm he saw these strangers react. He had never seen anybody move so fast. They were sitting around, and suddenly they were a blur of motion, and within a couple of blinks of the eye most of the attackers were down, with the rest fleeing.

It had happened so fast, and the death brought down on the attackers had been almost instant, he found he was standing and staring with an incredulous shocked look. He realized what he was doing and immediately dropped back down into the foliage he had withdrawn to. How did they do that? He found he was breathing rapidly, and still wasn't sure he believed what he saw or not. Looking once again at these strangers he saw that once again they were relaxing as if nothing had happened, and all they were doing was walking around in a leisurely fashion enjoying the scenery. *How'd they do what they did?* Well, he had a new question to add to the too many he already had.

He looked closely to see if any of the strangers had been killed or injured, and try as he may it appeared that they took no damage at all. *How is this possible?* He remembered seeing the flight of arrows inbound at the time of the call to attack. Those arrows had been accurate. It was one of the attacks that generally were successful in weakening an enemy. And the attackers had followed up with the immediate ground attack. None of it appeared to be out of sync. Yet, they were the ones who suffered, not the ones they attacked. Were these strangers gods, or did they have some sorcery about them that protected them?

Now with care he pulled even further back. He wanted no part of these strangers and their apparent ability to protect themselves, and to almost negligently, with little or no effort, overcome a force at least twice their size and sustain no casualties. How did one bring these strangers down? With enough distance between himself and the strangers, plus working away from the would-be attackers he withdrew deeper into the foothills. He'd wait out the strangers, and go back later to see if there was anything salvageable from the attacking dead. He suspected the surviving attackers wouldn't be back.

* * *

The patrol was sitting around for the midday meal. As usual the lieutenant had the guards out, and they were being rotated in so all of them would be able to eat something. "This sucks", private Snyde stated. "So why aren't we allowed vehicles or skimmers, or anything. I didn't join to hike this whole damn planet."

The sergeant smiled and only shook his head before speaking. "You . . . all of us do what we're ordered and it's just that simple. The reasons as to why isn't given to our paygrade. So be thankful that we are where we are. After all . . .

"Sergeant", the lieutenant interrupted, "I do believe we have at least one not too far from us. Just wondering if you are aware?"

"Yes sir. But it's him I'm not worried about. Not that there's anything or anyone on this world that can harm us. One of the guards stated he picked up movement from up the hillside so I suspect we are about to be visited. That one you just mentioned has been there since we arrived. I suspect he is someone who isn't interested in us other than normal curiosity."

Shaking his head the lieutenant stated, "I guess until these primitives realize they can do nothing to us they'll continue to try. Are the men ready?"

The sergeant looked at the lieutenant with an evil smile, "Of course sir. We're just waiting for the dance to start."

* * *

The leader of the small army from one of the wild clans looked down on the unsuspecting strangers. It appeared to be an easy thing. They seemed to be completely unaware of their presence. He smiled and signaled the rest to spread out. He had at least twice the numbers of the ones below. *This will be quick and easy. Hardly raise a sweat. And look at what they have. Not sure really but I'm sure we can get great prices for the items in the markets.* He looked around and saw everybody was ready. So with the confidence of surprise and success he signaled for the attack.

* * *

"Here they come", the sergeant whispered. "Close order weapons only. Let's show them how it's done, up close and personal. Now wait . . . wait . . . okay, let's do this." Suddenly the patrol was a blur of motion moving so fast that the eye couldn't follow. In the first few seconds the first line of the attackers were already down and dead being unable to both believe what they were seeing let alone being able to react to it. These supposed victims were doing impossible things. And the attackers found themselves becoming the victims instead. In less time than it took to count to ten at least half of the attackers were dead and not even one of the intended targets was down. The remaining attackers stopped in disbelief, which was a mistake as they too began to fall. At this point the few who remained dropped their weapons, and ran back into the hills in full panic mode.

"Come on sarge, let us go and finish them", one the privates yelled.

"No, not the way. We need a few to live so they can take back to wherever they live that we are to be left alone." The sergeant looked around and asked, "Everybody ready to move out? I think we are done here." *It's obvious these primitives know nothing about power armor.* With a nod from the lieutenant they pushed out and continued their patrol, moving away from where TimOtee hid as if nothing had happened.

* * *

TimOtee watched until these strangers had moved out and beyond where he could see them. He listened carefully but all he heard were the normal sounds and other than that silence. He wasn't sure if he was ready to head back to where the battle had taken place, if battle was the proper term. It was more like a massacre, and not for the intended victims either. He wondered if the attackers would return to at least claim the bodies, or possibly some attempt at a counter attack. Still, considering the turn of events and the total rout he felt they were probably still running.

After what he considered enough time he entered the slaughter zone and was sickened by what he saw. Most of the bodies, on the blood soaked ground, were in pieces – So many in fact that they were barely recognizable as people. Their weapons lay as they fell. He carefully searched through what was here; found a good bow, and a long knife. He thought he might add a few that he could use as barter, or to sell in the trading centers, but he did have to consider the weight. He had no pack beast, and because of this could only carry so much.

After doing a quick and thorough search he headed off in his original direction, watching now for the raiders who had failed in their attack on the strangers, and because of this, might take revenge on any they found, and avoiding these strangers who appeared to be almost gods seemed like a good idea also. No one moved like they did – no one. And to show no injury or death – just who were these strangers, and where did they come from? From the two times he had witnessed them he found he now really feared them. Yet, they were a mystery. As far as he knew no one like them had existed on their world, so where did they come from? Could it be they actually did, and had been living in one of the island kingdoms, who had decided it was time to control the world? No, that just didn't seem like a possibility. Still, where else could they be from – the stars? *Right, as if someone could be from there.* He immediately dismissed it. They had to be from here on this world hidden away and only now were revealing themselves. It was the only thing that made any sense. *Or maybe, just maybe they belong to or are the gods – but no that can't be, can it?*

TimOtee looked up in the sky and realized that more time had passed then he expected. Still, what can one do? He surely couldn't have exposed himself during the attack and rout. It would probably have meant he would be one of the dead now and that really was the last thing he wanted. He wanted to live, after all he had really just started life, and barring some disease or accident he should live a long one. But with this happening around him he truly couldn't say he'd be alive tomorrow, let alone by the end of this day. And why was he witnessing all of this anyway?

These thoughts brought him full circle, and as he continued to push towards the coast, which had been his unconscious destination, he came back to these strangers. Again, who are they, and how could they do what they did with such ease? And those shimmering barriers, what were they really? As he thought these things he continued to cover vast amounts of ground. He had shifted to a trot that allowed him to move quickly. And this was something he could do all day if he had to. For now with the land somewhat open he needed to do this. By nightfall he had to be somewhere where he could find a place to be out of sight, and here wasn't it. Looking around he realized that he was finally in unfamiliar territory, which meant he'd have to be doubly careful. Other than the fact that the lay of the land was similar to what he knew that was just about as far as he could go. *So who are they, and why are they doing what they're doing?* Well, being on this side of those shimmering barriers prevented any from knowing what was happening. So his questions would have no answers. And speaking of those barriers, when would he leave them behind? It seemed, even though he was still running the foothills, they continued in the chain of valleys below him. Who could have such power, such an ability, to do something like this and have it appear almost instantly?

There had been no warning, no hint of anything wrong, no sign of change, and yet here he was on the run, and as far as he knew one of too many orphans. If these strangers were gods, why would they do this? Yet, as far as he knew, even though he had to admit not being overly religious, they didn't fit any of the ones who were thought to exist? Still, did he ever truly study the subject? No, he had to admit to that. So there was no way to know if these, well, whoever they were, fit into the world of their gods. He heard a noise, and immediately stopped and crouched down doing a quick search with his eyes. He was breathing a bit fast and had to wait until he could breathe normally again. Until he did he wouldn't be able to hear the subtle noises that could point him in the direction of where the sounds had originated.

There it is again! He listened harder, and realized that it sounded like someone chopping wood. Slowly heading in the direction of the sound he climbed the slope heading towards the top so he could peer over and look down the other side. And once there he found the vegetation here to be around waste high giving him something to hide behind. He lay flat on the ground so that he wouldn't silhouette himself against the skyline and carefully looked around. First thing he noticed was that the land dropped down into a large bowl like area, and it seemed to be full of trees, and the grasses were green lush and high. Further study also revealed a small lake and a stream that appeared to be coming from the mountains behind. It was a beautiful and hidden area.

He still hadn't located the wood cutter or whether there was something built here. But with the amount of trees that were down there it easily could be hidden among them and no one would see it until they were right on top of it. Quietly he shifted his position concentrating on the bowl. The sounds had stopped a while ago, and he was attempting to figure out where the one who had been doing the work had gone. He heard a sound behind him and turned around quickly to see an old man standing there holding what appeared to be a smoking pipe. "So", this old one asked, "Why are you hiding and looking down at my home?" He had a quizzical look on his face. "In my mind someone sneaking around like this is usually up to no good."

TimOtee, carefully pushing himself up to a standing position, didn't know what to say or do. The last thing he expected was to be caught this way. He had always considered himself to be good in woodcraft, but he had to admit he never heard this one approach, making him feel the amateur. "With what's been happening I couldn't be sure what I faced here."

"Been happening?" The old one asked. "What's been happening?"

"You mean you haven't heard or seen anything unusual?"

"Other than you sneaking around . . . no. I keep to myself and my place. It's out of the way, and if one was looking my way, unless they are on the ridge – like you – this place would be no different than so many others that exist."

The old one had his back turned towards the valleys below and while he appeared to be relaxed it was obvious to TimOtee, that this one could move, and move in such a way that if he made any threatening move he wouldn't have a chance. "Look, I'm from the east of you. And we were attacked by strangers who then put up shimmering barriers that will kill any who touch or come to close to them. I've been trying to get beyond whatever they are and their influence only to run into a couple of the mountain clans. I watched as one of those same clans attacked a small group of the strangers. I thought it was over for the strangers but they had no problem taking on the clan and defeating it. And they did it in such a way that appeared to mean nothing to the strangers. No different than eating a meal, or walking around." TimOtee stopped a moment, "So you are completely unaware of any of this?"

The old one shrugged. "Anything that happens on the outside means nothing to me. I lost my mate a long time ago, and now it only me, the few beasts, and my pet that assists me with the care of the beasts, and alerts me if someone *like you* happens to be close by. And again, why are you close by?"

"I was jogging through the area staying out of the valleys and running the foothills. You mean you really don't know what's been happening?"

"No, and why should I care?"

"I don't know, anyway, I heard a sound that caused me to pause. Eventually I could tell it was someone who had to be chopping wood. So I traced the sound up this hill and found it was coming from that bowl you call home. I was trying to learn more, like who was the one cutting the wood, and was this a temporary camp or maybe something more permanent."

"Well, whoever you are, I'm the one who was cutting the wood, and now that you met me be gone. I prefer my privacy." And with that he turned and began to head downhill into that bowl leaving TimOtee remaining standing, flabbergasted by the immediate dismissal. He followed for a short time trying to come up with something to say, but in the end stopped and stood silent as the old one retreated and disappeared among the trees. He wondered if he should follow him, and at least warn him, but it really appeared that he wasn't interested. Shrugging TimOtee turned and continued to head west. Apparently he wouldn't find help here.

* * *

"Sir, nothing new to report. The scout ships have all returned to refuel, and change crews. CIC is asking what you would like them to do." The communications officer, on duty at this time waited patiently for a response. Personally he knew that this whole thing had to be frustrating for the captain, as well as the admiral who was using this ship as his flag ship. They had come so close to engaging the rebels, the malcontents, these rogues, the ones who were breaking their laws. And what had made it worse was the leaders of this . . . well he didn't have a name strong enough. Anyway they had been trusted members of the military protecting the worlds from piracy, and attacks from terrorists, and such. Yes, unfortunately terrorism hadn't disappeared. It appeared that there were always bad people who could only torture and kill.

He wished they had been able to eliminate the bad element out of their societies, but good wishes never brought anything to the desired outcome. Yet, he had to admit they had come far. Still in the outer rim areas like where they were presently, protection was harder to provide. And there were many places in this universe that had yet to be explored, or had only been surveyed by the advanced scouting, exploration, and discovery teams. And, unfortunately, in this sector very little exploring and discovery had been made. It was literally on the edge of known space. The only thing that could be stated was the fact they were still in the Milky Way galaxy.

He was brought back from his musings when the captain said, "Okay lieutenant, I'll go talk with the

Admiral. I'm sure he'll want the updates as bad as they are." He turned and shook his head. They had been so close to ending this – so close. Here he smiled, *yeah; close only counts in that old game horseshoes, whatever a horse is, fragmentation grenades, kinetic strikes, and those planet buster bombs.* He began to pace the small area available to him. Those seats got uncomfortable after a while, and no matter how ergonomic they were, his butt wasn't.

He headed over to astronavigation and stared over the Lieutenant's shoulder looking at the plot of where they sat unmoving in this sector. Yeah, he could have seen it from his multiple displays at his station, but the screens here were larger and easier to see. Besides his was set up for tactical, and as such lacked the detail this big monitor could provide. *Just where did they get off to?* His force was presently sitting outside of a large asteroid field. While they were searching he had mining and supply ships working the asteroids for needed materials, and others out searching for the ice that was always among the large rocks.

Water was used for the obvious, but also was a source for the hydrogen they used as fuel. So any time they remained in a stationary orbit this work was performed if at all possible. Fortunately, even though it wasn't the best of food, the supply ships that were part of his force could keep them active in the sector for a long time. So if necessary they could outwait and locate the rogues they were chasing down. And once found he hoped they would be reasonable and surrender. But, to be honest, he doubted that would be the case, since only death awaited them. So he suspected there would be a battle sometime in the future. And again to be honest, he wouldn't be surprised if they scattered and disappeared in too many directions. Space is large, and there would be infinite places to hide.

Probably, in the end, the best he could hope for, and he knew the admiral had confided to him the same thoughts, would be to make them ineffective, and maybe in the end, make them no more than small groups of pirates. Every once in a while they would get enough leads to find out where a particular nasty group would be located, and be able to wipe out the nest. But there always seemed to be others to replace them once the one nest had been destroyed. It was like the old territorial thing, or pecking order. Once some nasty had been weakened or taken down, others moved in to replace them. Here he laughed inwardly. *Job security I guess.*

He pushed back up, since he had sat back down, turned around, and headed for the Admiral's cabin, and the flag lieutenant who would be in the small office that was attached to the Admiral's quarters. He'd need to inform him, who would then pass it on to the admiral. In truth this information was nothing more than an update, since nothing had been found. The only good coming out of this so far was updated surveys, and a more accurate representation of the sector. They had other places they needed to be, but until this was resolved here they would stay. Before doing this he informed the Lieutenant to send out the scout ships once again and he'd update them on their way out as far as updated search parameters.

* * *

"How long do you figure it will be until they pick up our trail?" Flag Captain Heraldson, Admiral Sympson, and General Pertion were walking the captured area more to get out and catch a breath of fresh air. Time was of the essence. All of them knew that the ones giving chase wouldn't give up. Still, when they had lost them inside the asteroid belt, laying a false ion trail, going dark, before using stealth to backtrack, hiding their signature inside the trails left by the pursuers, making it doubly difficult to trace, they felt semi-safe. It had been a chance comment by one of the crew that reminded them of a primitive planet in this sector that could possibly be used as a base of operations.

Such a move went against the laws of the commonwealth. Any planet that showed signs of intelligent life was off limits to all, and while these planets could be monitored from space, with satellites placed in orbit, no landfall was allowed. It was felt that all intelligent species had a right to go in whatever direction they went, unless they became hostile to the rest of the universe – then and only then could any intervene, and maybe tweak things a bit, to change the direction of a species. With as much space that existed in the universe there was no room to be unreasonable.

Their own homeworld was proof of that. They had been a warlike species for much of the time they had existed. It was probably the main factor in pushing their tech forward. And as the populations grew then the fighting was due to the lack of resources. This pressure came close to destroying their world. Eventually they reached out to the stars using generation ships initially to move populations out to newly discovered worlds that could support them. The universe was full of them simply because of size. And with the distances between stars they could never know if the generation ships had been successful or not. It wasn't until the development of faster-than-light drives that moving settlers to fresh new worlds became easier. And it allowed them to check on the worlds where they had sent the generation ships. Many had made it, but others had disappeared never to be heard from again.

And on these worlds where these generation ships had reached, their true homeworld was no more than myth. In some there had been regression back to a more primitive state, and others had become stagnant remaining at the level when the ships were sent out. While a very few had actually advanced and were close to the same level as the homeworld. Still, while the faster-than-light drives had been developed, communications seemed to still be limited by the speed of light. It really hadn't made sense. If they could move like they did, why not be able communicate in the same way?

In truth it wasn't that difficult to figure out since FTL travel was limited to a small portion of space-time, while communications would entail all of space-time, limiting it to the laws of physics. There had been small advances, but when one considered the vast distances that exist in the universe, small advances don't do much. Presently it required "mail" to be delivered by small robotic courier ships. So communications over the vast distances were one-way, going to and from, making conversations a long drawn out affair. Kind of like the early days of radio where one could send, wait, change to receive to listen, and repeat.

Still, here they were, and yet they were breaking those very laws of non-interference. If time allowed, eventually they would be dug in and the energy signatures they were emitting would be hidden deep within the planet, and then they could do their own influencing. With the technology they had there were none here who could challenge them. For now they controlled the surface but those energy emissions would give them away sooner or later. So the pressure was on to get set up enough that they could research the landscape, find the area they were looking for, and begin the excavations. Now if only the pursuers would give them enough time, then they would be hidden with their location forever lost.

Little one: "Wow!"

GGF: Laughing he asked, "So is 'wow' your favorite word?"

Little one: "No. But I would never guess in all of my life that you saw and lived all of this. Had to be scary huh?"

GGF: Smiling said, "You know it. Let's get back to it shall we?"

Little one: Leaning forward in anticipation said, "Sure. I can't wait to hear what happens next."

CHAPTER THREE

THE HUNT AND HISTORY

Lieutenant Smyth, part of the small crew of three plus the agent was out and back to searching for the criminals. It was the only name that applied as far as he was concerned – unless he wanted to call them traitors, which might be more accurate. They were traitors to all their civilization and the way they dealt with not only each other, but the many species they had discovered over the millennia they had been in space. While they had been assigned an area to search, he had a hunch, and while it would be just outside of his assigned area he felt it was close enough. Besides, when they had lost them it had been during the time they were traversing the huge asteroid and gas field – an area outside any of the local solar systems.

Looking over at his second who also handled navigation, Lt. Smyth said, "Look, I know what we were assigned, but I have a strong feeling that we aren't going to find anything here. Instead I'd like to take a look over in this section. It's really not that far from where we're supposed to be. Plus it's just enough off from the way we came in here to catch a possible ion trail or something similar that will allow us to at least find a direction they ran in."

The navigator shrugged. He was also the copilot and second in command. So he had just about as much say in how they did things as Lt. Smyth. Still, he knew from experience and years of working with the Lieutenant that his hunches paid off more times than they failed. Still, they had come so close this time in bringing this chase to an end only to have it fail like every other time against the rogue admiral. It was frustrating as hell. "Look, we were assigned the search area for a reason. I say we do at least a cursory scan of the area, and then if we have time before we have to report back, then maybe do as you suggest. I, for one, don't want to face the flag Captain, or for that matter the Admiral. Neither is very forgiving. And one thing for sure they didn't get to where they are by going off and doing as they please."

"You're right Pete. So how can we approach this so that we can move on to where I suspect they went?"

Pete shrugged again. He really didn't know. Still he knew that the assignments had been made so the limited amount of scout craft could maximize the coverage during the search. Again part of the problem dealt with the fact that as they and all the other ships moved around, all of them were leaving new ion trails. And eventually this fact would obscure what they were looking for. Add to it the fact that the ships the criminals were using were similar to their own – not the newer stuff, but still of similar construction, similar power systems, and all, it meant if they did muddy the waters – so to speak – the trail would be lost forever.

It was one of the reasons for him wanting to stay on task. By doing so, and eliminating an area, then anything found in a newly opened area for search could belong to the traitors. And while free thinking was something that was encouraged, he didn't know if this was the place for it. Still, Philip Smyth just seemed to have the knack for finding things where others failed. Yet, was this the time and place to trust this ability? Again he wasn't sure if it was. He thought about asking the marine sergeant for his opinion, but thought better about it. His main area of responsibility was protection, and while he could approach the agent, he knew, from experience, that most of the time, they kept out of this part of such operations. He was responsible for the undercover stuff, and would be the one who would be inserted on a world where none of them were allowed by law.

Glancing over his shoulder, and inwardly he shook his head. He didn't understand how one could do what the agent did. Many times, and this was scuttlebutt, they would be alone and separated for years while they learned the language, the culture, and whether it would be beneficial to make contact. Many were never heard from again. And he suspected they had died a hard and lonely death. But there was no way to know. Nothing official would ever be mentioned. And it would be as if these individuals never lived – had never existed. He shuddered at the thought of this. He wasn't a loner – never could be. So to be an agent took a special person. It was then he realized that Phil had asked him a question. "Sorry sir, was concentrating on something else. Could you repeat?"

Smiling because he knew what and where Pete's mind had been he asked, "Okay, so what do you say to running the perimeter of this search area followed by doing a quick crisscross? That should give us a rough idea as to whether anybody has been in the area. And if we sense nothing then move on next door and check out where my mind is saying we should look."

Thinking it over before answering Pete finally said, "Works for me. So if I have it right you'd like me to plot a course that would get this accomplished as fast and as efficient as we can, then finish at a good entry point into the area you suspect."

"Exactly. So how quick can you have it programmed in so we can get on with it? Those trails they left won't last forever."

Looking at their present position, and overlaying the search area, and adding the area where Phil wanted to search he studied the plot. "Should have it set up within the next ten or so, then you can look it over for your approval."

Smiling Phil said, "Great, let's do it."

Jerod listened to the conversations going on around him, but in truth he wasn't part of the military, and was more of a passenger in reality. One time in the deep past an outsider might have considered one such as he as a political officer. One assigned to the crews to keep them in line with the doctrine of the government, but they would be wrong. Such hadn't existed in too many centuries to count. Then if that outsider was told no, probably the next thought would be, "They're spies. Yes he must be a spy." Again, the observer would be wrong. Yet, and in a way this might be closer to the truth than one might want to admit. Still spying wasn't his job or function either. Yet from the uninitiated's point of view it might appear to be so.

In actuality his job was much tougher than that. He had to infiltrate unknown species, remain hidden, learn their culture, their direction, and their goals. When the species were similar to him it was easier. But too many were vastly different with ways of thinking and acting that any of them would never understand. And in most cases his was more as a hidden observer than a participant on those worlds. This meant, in a sense, he had to be a throwback. He had to be someone from an earlier time, someone who could live without any of the modern conveniences – a primitive, for lack of a better word.

It also meant that he would be up against unknown predators, and unknown dangers that these worlds presented, let alone the intelligent species that ruled there. Any and all of these factors meant that death was often the result, and very few in his profession lived to retire. So far he'd been lucky – if luck had anything to do with it. He'd survived too many encounters with strange flora, and beasts to count and he was still here. Yet, he'd want it no other way. The civilized world was, well, too civilized for him. When one was running for their very lives, or trying to solve some deadly issue that came out of the blue, either you fixed it, or you died – it's just that simple. It meant he felt so much more alive, alert, and mentally sharp. Even these trips around with the scout ships could seem boring, and routine. While, in truth, these flights were anything but . . .

So he listened more with half an ear and kept to himself, as did the marine sergeant. He'd felt fortunate to be assigned to this crew. All of his class rotated around to the different scout ships, and to the different patrols. It did seem that this particular scouting crew did solve more of the issues, located more of the lost or hidden targets than any of the rest. And however they did it; it meant he would have a chance to be on his own once again.

If he happened to look in a mirror, something he rarely did by the way, his appearance would be completely nondescript. Meaning if he was responsible for some incident that would draw attention to himself, after he disappeared, no one would be able to accurately describe him. It was part of what made him good at what he did. He sighed inwardly and his mind started going over the files he had on this rogue splinter group they were chasing.

He didn't understand how this splinter group, which had been part of the elite military guard by the way, had been successful for a number of years of hiding their activity. Yet, it might have been the trust they had. To even become one of the elite took years of dedication, years and batteries of tests – both dealing with one's mind, and of their personal intelligence. And, to be honest, if they hadn't slipped up, and here he felt it had been "Murphy" who had been responsible for that slipup, then they probably would still be working their evil magic from within the empire.

It had happened on a little known and far flung planet under the jurisdiction of the empire. The planet, or the ones living there, really didn't have much to offer. The world was resource poor, and it's location within the solar system was barely in the habitable zone. Yet the ones who lived here eked out a living from large farms. And because of the harshness of the climate the world produced a tree that when cut, milled, and turned into useful items, such as paneling or furniture, had a rare beauty in its fine grains, and deep color. Still, even though this helped the economy, the trees took a century or longer to become useful. And even here where they originated, there were never many. And as result while the timber helped, it wasn't much.

Yes, there had been attempts to transplant the trees, to grow them in greenhouses, attempts to move them off world where direct and daily care could be administered, but all of it failed. For whatever the reason, they only survived in the wild. So, as these facts became known, the ones living here explored their entire world, marking each and every tree they could find. And knowing the rarity and the difficulty of the species, protected them, and would only allow usage when one of the old giants would die, or was close to death, and from the roots of the old tree others would come forth. There may have been sometime in the past they seeded, but now new trees only came from the roots of the old ones.

It was here this elite rogue element set up a hidden base deep within one of the many ancient forests. Here they had dug in, and in the underground had created their base of operations. It was a place to hide the old ships that were supposed to be mothballed, and "parted out" to keep the fleets operational. And slowly over time they built their hidden fleet, and pilfered supplies. And because of the remoteness of the planet, it was here where they would run their legitimate maneuvers. And under the cover of these exercises add to their hidden cache.

It wasn't long after this they began running operations as pirates using disguised ships attacking merchant shipping. And because it would be taking place in one of the sectors where they patrolled it made it easy for them to not find the pirates or be far enough away that they couldn't arrive in time to protect the merchant ships or fleets. Although they did capture enough of these pirates to keep the suspicion off their backs, making it appear they were doing the best they could. Of course there now was no way to know if the ones they caught were innocent and had been used simply to keep the truth from being learned.

It was a freighter that was having difficulty with the faster-than-light drive that dropped out of hyperspace to record the elites actually emptying one of the captured merchant vessels. And it was obvious to the freighter what was going down. He had been in normal space only a brief time, but with the military grade equipment on the other ships he had been spotted. Fortunately, for him, his touchy and temperamental drive decided to would work again just as he was being approached by one of the boarding vessels, and before the boarding vessel could make his systems null, he escaped.

He was sure they would try to trace him, but once in hyperspace it was nearly impossible even for the military to do so. He prayed his FTL system would hold together and they hadn't gotten a fix or been able to identify him. (That finicky drive had need of being replaced for a long time, but that took credits for which there never were enough.) It would be the only chance he had. And he also realized that he wouldn't be able to approach the capital, or any of the major planets since the ones responsible would probably have spies watching all the major space ports. It would have to be another backwater planet, and one they wouldn't expect him to go to. Plus wherever it was he went it would also need a secure communications net. He needed to get this to the leadership, and it had to be soon.

* * *

The operations out here had been going well for the elites, and they left no witnesses. It was easier that way. Once the merchants were captured it simply meant the crews would be breathing vacuum and if the captured ships were valuable enough they would sell them on the black markets, but if the captured vessels would be recognized then they were simply destroyed – a case of a failed drive or some other failure within the ship's system that led to a catastrophic chain reaction. It seemed that the elites had been caught because of that chance encounter, but they hadn't gotten to where they were by being stupid. So they devised a plan – hastily put together of course – that made it appear that the pirates had disguised some of their ships to look like the military patrols, and they would then hide at particular jump points, and demand inspections of the merchants looking for contraband.

With space being so huge it was an easy thing to move illegal goods. So it wasn't unusual to run into these patrols that attempted to curtail such movement. Still the odds were in the favor of the blockade runners since there were still unknown jump points and others that had been accidently discovered that allowed the tramp freighters and crews to come in through a back door. And as long as man had existed, there had always been a demand for anything that had been restricted or outlawed. So the elites felt by using this ploy they could circumvent the damage done by being caught so unexpectedly. So they sent a series of robotic couriers back to operations, hoping to beat the one ship that had seen them and escaped.

In this they were lucky. From the paperwork the agent was reviewing it was obvious that once these robotic couriers arrived it had an immediate reaction where the elites were asked if they needed any other assistance and how was this information obtained. Of course with this long distance communications, this back and forth took place over days of time. And like back on their homeworld where one spot on the planet became the starting point for the tracking of time, their homeworld became the way time was tracked throughout the many colonized planets. Since all had different lengths to their days, different revolutions around their stars, and different lengths to their seasons, without this one point of reference to initiate as a common setting all would be chaos.

In their reply they stated that "They had it all under control and now that they were aware of the new tactics of the pirates they would put more emphasis on covering those points where this could happen." The one thing they hadn't counted on was the fact that while that FTL drive had been a problem, the sensor suite the merchant had wasn't. In fact, in the recent past, and because of the increased incidents with pirates, he had to decide where to spend his credits. He knew the FTL drive needed work, but if he wasn't able to spot possible situations where pirates could be involved, then having an overhauled drive wouldn't matter. After all, there were ways to disable the drives, and destroy the fields before a ship could either initially enter or return to hyperspace.

So being aware of one's surroundings, and he did want to be able to go home to his family, became paramount to his way of thinking. Simply stated, the drive would have to wait. And, again while what he had wasn't top of the line, or new, nor could it be classified as military grade, the suite still was very good. Good enough in fact that it not only identified the ships involved by their transponders, visuals, and identifying marks, it specifically identified members of the elites themselves. The evidence was so overwhelming there would be no way for them to deny their involvement.

It was the sudden silence from headquarters that tipped them off. And soon one of their spies on the inside confirmed that they had been identified as the perpetrators and there would be forces coming in shortly to deal with the situation. And in that very moment, all their plans, all the manipulations, everything they'd worked towards were gone. And in that instant they pulled out taking as much of their hidden supplies as they could. Running further out towards the rim worlds where it was considered the frontier, and where many of the pirate clans hid. It wasn't long after that the taskforce he was a member of had taken up the hunt, found part of the traitors or rogues and had lost them here, and thusly why he was with this particular scout ship team, and if lucky would be prepared for insertion. Still as good as the elites were, the most likely outcome would be a return to their cap ship, a resupply, and a return to the search once again. Still, one never knew. At the same time they could extend if they could find a particularly rich debris field. Then it would be a simple loss of time as the bots harvested the needed raw materials.

With these thoughts Jerod looked around the cramped cabin as silence reigned. He could tell the ones flying this ship were serious about their assignments. And while, at times the teasing and atmosphere inside could be light, giving the impression of nonchalance, and of carelessness, when one really looked it was obvious that these men and women were anything but. Still he was just a passenger, taking up precious space. These scout ships were small, and highly maneuverable. Plus the sensor suites they had was equal to the largest of the ships, and because of their size could become no more than a hole in space – appearing to be no more than any of the flotsam that existed in space. In truth as lightly armored as they were, they had to be. Weaponry was minimal, and was more as a last resort than anything else.

Still, they were fast and could outrun almost everything ever produced except some of the civilian race ships. It was another reason for the lack of interior space. Between the large drives, the maneuvering thrusters, large sensor suite, and the tanks it left little room for a crew, and thusly why the crews generally amounted to no more than three individuals. A fourth could be added, and here he was the fourth, but it made these ships claustrophobic, not that they weren't already. So Jerod attempted to stay as much out of the way as he could. Still, there were times when it was comical as someone had to get around another. In truth the marine had his own small room where he or she remained most of the time.

He sighed inwardly as he stared out at nothing. He needed to return to the descriptions he had. All of it needed to be in his memory. If this scout did locate the planet the outlaws had escaped to – if they had that is, then he would only have the small electronic suite, the standard insertion pack, and some well-hidden and modified weapons to protect himself. And if he died everything would self-destruct leaving no evidence behind to identify him as an alien to the existing population. Anything such as paper, which still had a purpose, even after all the times stated that whatever new device that came forth would finally eliminate such needs, like the cockroach, was still here.

As long as there were bureaucracies paper and paperwork would always exist. He had often wondered, in his spare time – when he had any, which was rare – just where all these reports sat. Did anybody ever read any of them, or were they just filed away never to see the light of day? He imagined that somewhere deep underground bots would have all these reports filter down to them where they would endlessly file them away. And these vast repositories would go on forever, until civilization collapsed under the great weight produced over the centuries. Then sometime in the future when a new society or people came along they would discover this vast network and wonder at the stupidity of their ancestors, or aliens . . . Or maybe not.

It could be that doing such a thing was part of what made them, well – them. Maybe their actual DNA had this need encoded inside, and no matter how often civilization collapsed and was rebuilt, that in the end it would be paperwork that would continue to be the reason for those failures. Shaking his head he smiled thinking about all the time lost because one had to take time out to fill and file some report. It made him wonder if anything ever was truly accomplished. Personally he knew that after returning from an assignment that it seemed the paperwork he had to file, and the debriefings all took more time than the actual assignment. Did it finally reach a point that assignments were never completed because of the pre and post requirements? Jerod laughed quietly at these thoughts, yet had to admit that at times it surely seemed like it did.

His thoughts were interrupted by a comment from the pilot slash navigator who stated, "That completes the bare minimum sweep through our search area – and nothing found. Still I feel there's a couple of areas that have shown up that were a bit out of the range of our sensors and I'd feel better if we at least cleared those areas." Do you want to report our progress back to communications?"

Jerod watched as the Lt shook his head, "No, not yet. I'm getting a stronger feeling that where I suggested we look is where we will find a trail of some kind. Since we're supposed to be out here and searching for as long as it takes, we will wait before we report back."

It didn't matter to Jerod. Whether they moved to another area, remained in the same, returned to the ship and resupplied, in the end, until something was discovered, he would simply be a passenger. Until something was discovered, confirmed, and a location found so he would remain. Yet, once it did happen his role would change and he would be the one in charge until he was dropped. An agent officially outranked any in the military, but they were only allowed to use this ranking when the mission began, and was limited to insertion only.

And the reason for this simply was experience. The military was good at what they did, and he was good at what he did. This prevented problems associated with some officer thinking he knew more than the agent whose life depended on his training and knowledge. The military might know a lot about their ships, the tactics that went with fleet movements, and insertion of the "ground pounders", but for the type of work he and others like him did, such tactics would get the agents killed. And to be honest it had happened when some admiral or general thought they knew better and overrode the orders of the agent.

Of course the said admiral or general would then try to blame it on the dead agent since he or she wasn't alive to defend themselves. But all situations were always recorded and as such even when there were attempts to modify or delete such damning evidence, in the end the truth would come out. The cost of training an agent was astronomical, and the government looked upon the guilty parties with askance, and the punishment meted out usually ended the careers of the said leaders. And in some cases it actually included jail time since it had been determined that these same had been criminally negligent. Still the agents could fail for the same reasons. Trying to command the military to do as they pleased, instead in the limited capacity and authority they had.

He shook his head inwardly, *Enough on these side thoughts*. He needed to get back to the problem at hand. Jerod needed to study the leaders, and not only that he needed to know as much about the systems in the quadrant, and the possible intelligent species that occupied the planets. He had much work ahead of him. Added to this burden lay the fact that little was truly known. This part of space was just too far out on the fringe to have any more information other than what the survey ships had put together back when the area had been opened for possible settlement. In truth those initial surveys stated that of the fifty plus solar systems located out here, only a few had habitable planets, and of those that were available half were eliminated because there were primitive and intelligent species living there. Still that left five or six good worlds available.

* * *

Did this oldster really think these strangers, maybe ones from the stars, the outer islands, or the gods would leave him alone? Apparently, as far as TimOtee could tell the answer was yes. It was obvious that this one wanted to be left alone, and had made it perfectly clear, so TimOtee headed once more in the general direction of the coast. He personally had never been there, and as far as he knew none of his family had been. Still, at this very moment it was at least a destination. And he had been informed there were larger townships and such. Not the smaller villages he was familiar with here where farms dominated the lands. Still if there hadn't been a place to sell what they grew then it would probably be different.

He knew that there were cooperatives that ran and sold their merchandise to, where else, the coast. It was there they could get the best price for the grains, fruits, and produce. And even though he never paid much attention, since, and to be honest, he never had plans to, either join one of the traveling merchants, to go the distance and lose the time it took to reach the coast. The farms lay in a great valley or series of valleys that ran deep into the interior of the great continent. It had been speculated that sometime in the deep past this vast rich farmland had been under water, and this had put down layers of rich soil that allowed the bounty they reaped. Personally he really didn't know if this was an accurate assessment or not.

Still if one could see this area from high in the sky then it would show steadily growing mountains to the north where eventually they reached a height where the snows never melted. And to the south were rolling foothills with many small hidden valleys, streams, rivers, lakes, swamps, and marshes. To the east beyond the great valley lay one of the largest desolate areas. Again, like the valley it lay between the foothills and the mountains with one additional range that sat between the valley and desolation. Again those who thought this way figured it was this additional range that split the continent which kept moisture from the desolation. And it was rumored that beyond the desolation lay another range of mountains, and beyond those mountains which ran east to west, was the other coast.

At least this is what was taught in the learning centers. Personally, until this incident, he had never been far from the farm. There was too much work to keep it operational. Besides he had never been an adventurer – until now, when it had been forced upon him. Well, to be honest, he still wasn't one, but if not he had better learn the ways of one otherwise there would be a great chance of him dying. Just like the ones who attacked that group. It still shocked him at the ease these strangers defeated the superior force attacking them. And, again, it seemed to be more of a rout than a fight. It was like the ones attacked could care less that they were. It was like he taking out a bothersome crawler or such, and once done to move on with whatever the day's assignment had been.

He realized that he had been thinking more than watching where he was going, or what the time of day could be. Both were important if he was to survive another day. From now on he was in new territory and he had better consider the fact that it all could be hostile. Stopping and looking around, he realized that he presently was in an exposed position. Anybody looking over the area would spot him. Shaking his head he thought. *How can I be so stupid? Am I so green that I'm going to trust any and all whot might be around? And am I going to show the world that I have no concerns and will let all see me? Well, stupid if you believe that I'm sure there's many who'd love to sell you some swamp land for a tidy profit, and leave smiling while they go look for another sucker.*

Looking around he could see to the south a stand of trees which probably meant there was a water source close by. TimOtee decided enough had happened and it was getting late in the day anyway. It was time to find a place for the night, and presently these trees were the only thing in sight that possibly could provide shelter. Before heading there he carefully searched to see if he could find anybody watching him, and when satisfied he was alone made his way in that direction. Careful he now was, to be sure he found a safe way to get to this new goal. After all, if he injured himself then he could blame only himself. And if the injury was severe enough it could also mean he'd die.

Little one: "Wait a minute. How do you know what you are talking about? You haven't even talked with these strangers yet."

GGF: "Well, I have to admit at the time I didn't. And right now I'm not telling you how I learned about what was happening especially when I couldn't see or have been in contact. That's for later."

Little one: "If you say so. But this seems . . . I don't know."

GGF: "Let's continue, and maybe you'll find your answers. Ready?"

Little one: He had to admit that this was much more than he was expecting. Looking once again at the oldster it just didn't seem possible he had done all these things. "Sure."

GGF: "And you are taking notes, right?"

Little one: Sighing, "Yes great grandfather."

CHAPTER FOUR

TIME – NEVER ENOUGH TIME

The patrol was returning and it would be a while before they left again. So far they, and from what rumors going around stated, hadn't found that particular hill or mountain as of yet to where they could safely dig in. One of the major problems they faced was the fact they couldn't use the equipment they had that would locate the ideal place. The energy signature would give them away immediately. So they had to do it the old fashioned way. Yes, the energy used would leave from the planet at the speed of light, and as such would take a long time to travel any distance in the infinite vastness of space. But they hadn't lost their pursuers that long ago, and as such, couldn't count on that same vastness to give them time. For all they knew the ones chasing them could be just outside of this solar system at this very moment in time, and they had been here long enough for the signatures of the type of energy they were using to be seen.

The lieutenant reported in while the rest of the patrol headed for the temporary shelter to clean and overhaul their equipment. While they had no problem dealing with the primitives thanks to their tech, a failure at an inopportune time could mean death for one of them. They had enough problems without adding equipment failure to the mix. Right now they had enough spare parts to keep everything functional. But they weren't able to bring all the cached supplies when they had to abandon their hidden base. And in the rush to leave it was simply grab and take with no plan as to what would be critical, or what could be left. Plus they hadn't been here long enough to reorganize what they did bring with them. The lieutenant suspected that the organization of all the stuff wouldn't happen until they were safely underground.

They had half a dozen cruisers, and a number of light attack craft, besides the freighter conversions that held military grade hardware instead of civilian. And all of these ships were sitting on the ground hidden behind the energy barrier – more to keep the locals from seeing them than the hunters. The rest of their fleet remained hidden in orbit or close by monitoring the wave bands for the specific signatures that would identify the pursuers. They had to get all of this underground now. But so far it wasn't in the mix. That energy field they were using, even though they had it at minimum, since there wasn't anything on this planet that could bring it down, would eventually be a signature recognized as a tech level well above this world, and bring in the pursuers like screaming banshees. And the size of the force chasing them was greater than what they had.

Admiral Sympson was worried. All had been going so well when it had gone to hell. Still they had made their escape, and had in the process became outlaws, not that they weren't before. Only now it became common knowledge, where before it was only known to them and the underworld they dealt with. And while he couldn't be sure who was leading the pursuit he suspected it had to be Admiral Williams. And if it was, it meant that their respite would be short. It meant that the Flag Captain would be Captain Samuels, who was probably more tenacious than the Admiral. And both of them surrounded themselves with likeminded crews. They needed to move and it should have been yesterday.

He headed over to where General Pertion had set up his field office. Some of the marines he had with him remained behind the energy barriers guarding the ships leaving the search for their new base to the general. As he approached the temporary building – a prefab construction – he could see that a couple of the lieutenants were reporting in and waited until they had completed their reports, saluted and left. He hoped that what they had given the general was good news. Still from the way the general was shaking his head he suspected it wasn't. He entered the headquarters and watched as the general wrote something down. Yeah even now notes and paperwork never ended. "So Arthur, from what I can see we don't have a location yet."

"No Dave", the general replied, "We've been having do deal more with the natives of this world than actually finding anything suitable. Now don't get me wrong, we can easily handle anything these primitives can dish out. Unfortunately it slows us down somewhat. It seems these mountains are loaded with primitive tribes and clans who consider any outsider an enemy. And as such they feel it is their responsibility to let the trespassers know they are where they don't belong.

"It means we are spending more time dealing with these attacks, more time putting them in their place, than locating a proper mountain to dig into. And we want it to be a place where the natives are unaware of us. And it must be a location completely isolated and hidden – not that you don't know this because you do. Look, just like where we were located before, the mountain or range needs to be solid rock, with the trace elements that will help us hide our energy signature, and at the same time be strong enough to support the weight once we remove what we need to create our base of operations.

"Colonel Jamison had been working hard on keeping the patrols out and moving looking for exactly what we need. But we only have so many people to do this and less technicians who can nail down the actual site. The patrols are attempting to locate potential sites, but until we can get a tech into the area to confirm the location we're stuck. Again, I know you are aware of all of this, still it gives me a chance to voice my frustrations."

Admiral Sympson chuckled, "Frustrations? Really, why would we have any of those? After all, we had a sector nailed down . . . Could do pretty much as we pleased. We had it set up in such a way that there was no way we would ever be discovered. And eventually could retire to wherever seemed like a great place. Only to have that freighter with a failing hyper-drive drop out right in the middle of one of our operations and blow it wide open. Why would we be frustrated?"

Laughing, Arthur stated, "If you put it that way, I guess we shouldn't be, right?" Shaking his head the general continued. "There's been some progress. It's just hasn't been as rapid as we'd like. But that's Murphy once again. He always seems to complicate things. Still I guess we should be grateful that we're here instead of sitting in a prison waiting for the executioner.

"And on a different subject, how's the resupply going, as well as the initial inventories of what we were able to bring with us?"

"Plenty of water so converting it to fuels so we can fill our tanks is almost complete. But we've had to wait on any inventorying since I do not want to unpack any of this stuff until we have our base. Who knows, we may have to abandon this place in a moment's notice. And having supplies lying around would mean we'd have to abandon them. And to be truthful, this isn't something I'm prepared to do. Still, it might come down to it sooner or later."

"Understood. Until we can get all of this underground it's probably better to leave all of it on the ships."

* * *

TimOtee had a bad night. Being in an unfamiliar area, close to the river, and while hidden, didn't eliminate the sounds. So he suspected that he was lucky to have gotten any sleep at all. His eyes burned, and his energy was flagging. It was like after a really intense hard day's work was behind him. At least with the small river – more of a large stream – he could fish for his breakfast, and maybe he would simply stay here today. As far as he knew there was no one around here but him. Besides, he had nowhere he needed to be, and no time to be anywhere. So maybe spending a couple of days here – as long as no one arrived in the area – would give him a chance to recover.

He not only needed to recover his strength, but needed time to think about everything that had happened to him in the last few days. *Is that all it had been? A few days? It surely doesn't feel that way.* Yet, when he really thought about it, the truth was, it had only been a few days. In that time he had seen more chaos, more death, more of just about everything, than he had in his eighteen turns their world made around the sun. It had been maybe a hundred turns in the past when they had discovered this. Until that time it was felt the sun rose and set, and the repeating seasons were just the way of things. Now they knew it was because of where they were when going around their sun. It was something very hard to understand, but the proof was there, so it had to be fact.

Enough on this, he was hungry. So heading over to the water he baited his hook threw it into the rippling waters and immediately hooked a fish. It took only a short time where he had more than enough for his meal. So he withdrew, cleaned the fish, built a small smokeless fire, buried the fish in the coals once he wrapped them in leaves and waited. Later he would catch more, take time to smoke and dry the meat so he could pack it and take it with him. Maybe he would stay more than a couple of days just to resupply on his food. Looking around he thought there would be a good chance that small game might be here also. Then he could do the same with that meat and have some variety. One thing for sure he had no idea what was ahead, or if there would be available game. So he had better do it now.

In the end he actually spent seven days by the small river. During that time no one came by to shatter the tranquility or the isolation of the place. If he hadn't experienced what he had it would have been easy to consider that nothing had changed or had happened. Still, he knew better. It was time to continue towards the coast, and to see if there could be an end to those shimmering barriers. Taking one last look around, he made sure that the area appeared to be pristine, as if he hadn't been here at all. Who knows he might need to use this site again sometime in the future. Sighing, he shouldered his bag, kept his weapons loose and available and quietly left his refuge behind.

As he continued towards the coast he kept himself in the lower foothills. By doing this it allowed him to monitor the valleys, and at the same time stay away from the roving wild clans that lived in the mountains. By being unfamiliar with the areas on the other side of this chain of valleys – to the south – with the many swamps, marshes, slow running rivers, dank lakes, and the often times thick growth of vegetation that existed there he felt it was a death trap he wanted to avoid. As the first day waned, since leaving his temporary camp, and with the sun setting he realized that the shimmering barriers were beginning to swing across the valley. Could it be he finally reached the end of these things? Well, it was too late to do any exploring today. So tomorrow he would see what he would see.

After another restless night, (too many strange noises, hard ground, and such) he, being blurry eyed, moved quietly down into the silent valley. Other that the slight humming sound the barrier made there were no other sounds at all. It was still too early for the breezes to change direction, and the gentle down canyon movement still was in control. In the distance, a little above the bottom of the valley, he could see what appeared to be an abandoned village, and in the great distance abandoned farms. One thing for sure, he couldn't blame them. Still he wondered where the people had gone. Maybe they had gone in the same direction he was heading – to the coast.

It took longer than he thought to reach the valley floor and here he picked up a major trail heading towards the village. On both sides of this trail were trees widely spaced and an occasional creek. With the silence the sound of the running water seemed much too loud. He suspected once the daytime breezes took hold that the winds through the trees would mute this somewhat. Of course with the overwhelming sounds from the water, as it crashed over the rocks and boulders, it could hide other sounds he should be aware of. After all, when something was abandoned like this it usually didn't take long for the bad element to come in and strip anything of value that may have be left. And usually they wanted no interruptions to their deeds.

So he slowed his approach. He had no way of knowing if this was happening, had happened, or everything had been left alone. These barriers were a new thing, and once their lethality had been discovered, most avoided them by staying far away. And this area he was presently in was close enough to one of those barriers that there was a great chance he would be the only one around.

It was midmorning and he could feel the air warming as well as the sounds of the winds as they began to pick up. He saw the grasses swaying in the wind creating waves of motion that caught the eye. He was still a little way outside of the village when he came across the first of the many farms. He stopped by the trail that led to the farm and tried to see if anyone or anything was still there. It seemed even the beasts were gone. He started down the trail to confirm what he saw but half way down the pathway changed his mind and headed back out. His greatest chance to see if anyone was still around lay in the village, not these outlying farms.

Soon, and it was towards the zenith, he was walking down the one main path through the small village. The only action was the twisting dust spirits.

Otherwise the village was dead. It felt as if the place had been abandoned for a long time. Could it be that these barriers began here, and had proceeded towards where he had lived? He had no way of knowing, since he knew no one here, and there wasn't anyone to ask. And he wasn't a scavenger, as of yet anyway, so he continued on through the village, out the other side and continued towards the far end of the valley. He stopped briefly and looked towards the existing barrier and noticed that the side of the village that was closest to the barrier actually seemed to disappear beyond it. For now it meant nothing, but he knew he would be returning this way. At that time he would carefully approach this point and see what he could see. This had been the only place where he had seen the barrier actually cut across a structure. Since the barriers had gone up he hadn't been able to see if they continued on the far side. He had a slight hope that somewhere he could find an opening and be able to enter inside of these things, head back, and find his family. He didn't really expect it to be that way, but until he saw with his own eyes he would wonder.

He felt that had these barriers only been one-sided that the ones who were trapped on the other side would be able to work their way around and meet up with friends and family. But that hadn't happened. So the logical conclusion was that these barriers enclosed this area. And again in truth until he had finally reached the end of the barriers he didn't know or have proof that they did end. Well, it was time to find out. Looking up he could see the day was getting away from him and soon he'd have to find a place to spend the night. At least this area had been farmed so if nothing else he probably could stay in one of the abandoned farm houses. It was a valid thought, but one he wasn't sure he could carry through. He basically was a farmer, and the honor system they lived by stated that the property of others were just that and was to be left alone. And if he entered another's place he would be violating that trust. Still he felt if he only used the house for protection, and a place to sleep leaving everything else alone, it should be okay.

He began to look for one of the outlaying farms since he had no desire to retrace any of his steps yet. He really needed to get far enough to the other side of these barriers to confirm his suspicions.

Eventually in the distance he saw one that gave the appearance of being a large operation. He could see the main house, which was large, and many outbuildings. In fact he thought he could hear the bawling of the creatures that were part of the operation. It surprised him that there seemed to be some of them still around. It made him wonder if this operation was abandoned like the rest he had passed so far. As he approached the path that would lead up to the farm he realized that it wasn't abandoned, but the ones he saw were not the type who would work such an operation. TimOtee stopped in his tracks as he realized what he was seeing was some of the bad element who had taken advantage of the situation and made this place their base of operations in the area. Looking out towards the barriers, which at this point weren't really close, he decided it would behoove him to work towards them and give a wide berth to this farm and the ones occupying it at this moment.

Fortunately it appeared the ones who were there weren't really paying much attention to the main trails that led through the area. He suspected that they were taking advantage of the fact that no one was around and was stripping out anything of value before leaving themselves. It meant they wanted no witnesses, or if someone was discovered, like him, kill them, and leave a little of the loot with the body to redirect the suspicion away from them. Still if any of the real owners would think about it one person wouldn't have been able to take as much as a gang. And even if they had come to the conclusion that it had to be more than one individual the natural outcome from finding a body with some of their property would be, "Whoever this is got what they deserved". Not realizing that like they this dead one had been a victim. One thing for sure he had no desire to become that victim.

Fortunately the winds were quite brisk moving the grasses in waves presenting a lot of motion. Add to this the many flyers in the area and there was continuous motion. So his cautious movement through the same grasses should go unnoticed. Meaning simply it should be no problem to get by them. It burned him deeply that there were ones like these who would violate that universal trust. But, he was well out numbered so there was nothing he personally could do about it other than remember. Unfortunately he was too far away to be able to identify any so they would get away with what they were doing. He hoped that someday they would pay, but he would never know. Eventually he was far enough beyond the farm to continue his search for a place to spend the night, and in the far distance he thought he saw another possible farm. This one was small. Only the house the family lived in and no real outbuildings at all. And while it didn't appear to be a very successful operation, it was obvious the ones who had lived here had taken good care of what they had.

Looking up he could see the sun would be setting soon. *Where'd this day go to?* To him it didn't seem possible that it was this late. Still the sun didn't lie. It made its way across the sky each day in a leisurely fashion. And while its path varied by the time of year, and the length of the day verses the night changed, it was consistent. So, for whatever the reason it was he himself that had lost the time. Still with all that was going on it was no surprise. Looking to his right he could still see the barrier and he was far enough away that the winds and the sounds of the rustling leaves overcame the humming produced by that wall. Looking ahead again and towards the farm it seemed to have disappeared. It was then he realized that it was set back in such a way that it seemed to be hidden, and it was probably the way the light had fallen and his location on the trail that revealed the farm house to him. Still he was pretty good on judging distances, and using landmarks so he continued along the trail until he felt he had to be close and cut to the left and immediately dropped down into a depression that immediately hid him for the main trail.

He hadn't found the pathway to this place but noticed now on his right that the land continued to fall away and in the distance there seemed to be a large slash cutting across the main trail. He suspected there would be a footbridge at the minimum and possibly one that would allow the movement of goods. Again not knowing anything of this area he really had no idea if there were other farms and maybe villages further along the track. The shadows were deepening and it wouldn't be long until dusk would be upon him. He needed to move. Picking up the pace he continued in a westerly direction, more or less, and found that there was a slight rise and then in the distance and more to the north he saw the farmhouse.

He realized he still had a distance to go and suspected that by the time he reached it, it would full on dark. Unfortunately he didn't know if the place was abandoned as most had been. And he didn't know if they had a guard beast either. Still from what little he could determine the house appeared to be empty. Its location was further away from the barrier, but he didn't know if maybe the bipedal beings that had created this barrier had raided the area or not. If they had the ones who lived here would have had no chance at all. Quietly and with care he approached the house and called out to alert anybody who could be here he would be out here and would like an invite inside. He heard no response so he continued up to the door and tapped lightly, gave it enough time, and repeated. With no response he opened the door and entered into a pitch black room with a small amount of light entering from the open doorway.

He pulled out his fire maker and lit it off and found a candle next to the door which he lit. Looking around the house appeared to be empty, and there was a feel of it being that way for some time. Still he wasn't sure what he wanted to do. He knew the light he had just created could be seen from the outside giving his location away. Well, for now he'd have to chance it. Without the candle he couldn't see anything at all. He turned around and closed the door and began to explore this house. The floors creaked a bit, which was no surprise. Very few of the buildings that had wood floors didn't creak. Still it was a sign of the love and care the owner or owners of this farm had.

Many farm homes continued to have only dirt floors using sawdust as a covering that they replaced a number of times through a cycle of the seasons. Well, he needed to find the food prep area so he could fix a meal, followed by heading outside to locate their privy, and then the sleep room or rooms. Tomorrow would be another day, and he felt privileged to have found this shelter for the night.

It was at that moment he heard a creak over his head. He knew that the sleeping areas general were on the second floor. So maybe someone was here. But if there was, why hadn't they answered when he hailed the house? Of course it could simply be the house settling for the night, and again since this was a strange house to him, this could be the explanation. Truthfully it would be smart if he went ahead and checked it out. Looking around for possible stairs he found instead a ladder that led to the upper levels. This was further proof that the owners were not well off. Still through the flickering light of the candle he could see the landing area and railing placed there to keep someone from falling. But that was just about all as everything else lay heavily in shadow.

Now he wasn't sure if he wanted to climb the ladder or not. It would leave him vulnerable to someone hiding up there making it easier for them to attack. Still since that first sound he hadn't heard anything further so maybe it was just the house settling. Well, he'd eat first, and watch this area to see if anybody came down, and if he heard no more suspected movement he would carefully head up that ladder and check out the area.

* * *

Admiral Williams came out and stood next to the captain staring at the different screens and monitors that existed on the command deck. Looking over to the captain he asked, "How did we lose them? I don't expect you to answer, still with the ships they had, and the fact we weren't that far behind when they entered hyperspace, and knowing there would only be a few sectors they could head, we should have been able to outguess them." *Well, it hadn't happened that way. I had hoped to have a surprise for them and wanted to catch them before they entered hyper. But, it didn't happen, and that meant there's a good possibility that General Pertion and Admiral Sympson have someone on the inside – Someone who was able to warn them.*

Captain Samuels continued to remain silent. He and George had known each other for a long time, and while he never wanted more than being a captain, he knew his friend had loftier goals in mind. And, fortunately, he wasn't one who demanded all the formal stuff once they were out and on assignment. The admiral felt it could be too distracting if they had to keep an eye for him when he was out and about. That didn't mean he was slack in how he did his job, or let incidents go, because he didn't. He demanded respect not because of his rank, but because everyone knew he had been there and done it all himself. And like the ones they were chasing he was one of the best tacticians they had. In many ways this would be a chess game between two masters with the outcome unknown until the very last move.

"Well, sir, I know you aren't looking for an answer, but it deserves one anyway. With us here and our ships out patrolling the other sectors where they could have come out of hyper, nobody has found anything as of yet. I know we're under pressure and generally a time limit since we're supposed to be patrolling other sectors to keep the merchants from falling victim to the bad element out there. I know we left a few ships to hopefully fill that need. Still we haven't heard back on your request for some of the reserves to fill in until we can finish this one way or the other, and that's worrisome. Still it will take a while for the communications to go both ways and we are still well within that time frame. So I guess until we get official orders that requires us to return we'll continue to search.

"Of course space is huge, and that adds to the issues we are facing. Plus there's the fact that they may have come out of hyper, reset their systems and went back into hyper. And considering the speed of light if they did that and we are clear across the sector then it would take days before we'd catch the jump signature as they entered the field. Something none of us have figured out how to eliminate. So I'm hopeful they are still here somewhere and we can find some sign of their passing soon before the ion trails dissipate and leave us nothing. Plus we haven't caught any of the gravity waves that are formed when we leave hyper, and again while they take longer to spread and dissipate, it would be nice if one of our scouts could catch one of those hints that we are in the right part of space."

"True. Still we are going against Admiral Sympson and David has always been a little better at this kind of thing than me. Fortunately the small fleet we have with us, and in our favor is the fact we are a little larger than the one he commands, and we have some great minds, I'm sure eventually we'll turn up something. And we have a few days before those orders are overdue. So I'm hopeful they will allow us the time necessary to end this."

"If not sir?" Victor asked.

"Then they will get completely away, and will have dug in somewhere making it nearly impossible for us to find them." He knew that the most likely direction they would take would involve digging deep into the bedrock and building a hidden base using the natural radiation, and solid rock to prevent anyone from scanning them. He was sure that they had to be somewhere at this very moment planet side, looking for such a location. And if this was so he hoped there were no intelligent species there. If there was it meant the breaking of additional laws, and the contamination of a species by a technologically superior race. It was close to impossible to correct such intrusions.

Captain Victor Samuels knew the facts, but sometimes it helped if one talked them out. By bouncing such thoughts off of one another, at times it brought forth new thoughts and ideas that would help them solve whatever the problem or problems there were. He looked over at the communications officer asking, "Any updates from the scouts?"

She just shook her head. There had been nothing. And in this case silence wasn't good news.

Little One: "Now wait, ships? And what ships are these? I mean, well I know that we are supposed to have ships that are out on the sea, but this makes no sense."

GGF: "Yeah, I can see that. I guess if we were to consider the strangers gods then their ships would sail the skies and not the waters. So for now until you know more think of the skies as the home of the gods, although at this point in the story I didn't know anything and had yet to come to any conclusions. So don't jump too far ahead, okay?"

Little One: "How can I do that? I mean what I've heard so far is a surprise. I thought I'd be bored and be daydreaming. Instead this! Okay will I know all by the time you're finished?"

GGF: He smiled. "I don't know if you'll know all. Heck I don't know all, or understand everything and

I've been here much longer than you. Are you ready to hear more?"

Little One: "I guess, but there sure seems to be a lot missing and a lot that doesn't make sense, and a lot that seems like something I'd think up for some imaginary game."

CHAPTER FIVE

ENERGY, WE MUST CONSERVE ENERGY

Admiral Sympson headed into the temporary shelters they had built and went to the section where General Pertion had his office. Entering he saw Colonel Jamison finishing up a conversation, at least that's the way it appeared, since he had just stood up, with the general leaning on his desk. He waited for the General to recognize him, since it was important to have him finish whatever it was they were discussing. After all, it would be his men who finally scouted and located a good site for them to dig in. The information he had was just that anyway. Still things were getting critical and the pressure was on and building fast. He saw the colonel turn to leave and as the two of them looked his way realizing he was standing there.

"So how long have you been standing there David?" Arthur asked. The general turned back to Colonel Jamison saying, "At least the natives are more of an irritant than anything else. Look, as I said, I agree with you, but in the end it means it slows our searching down. And, as you are well aware, time isn't our friend. Do what you have to, but the ones chasing us will not give up."

Colonel Jamison nodded, gave a crisp salute, and headed out of the temporary shelter. Arthur took a deep cleansing breath and turned back to his friend and asked, "Okay, what great piece of news are you bringing me?"

David smiled, although there was no humor in it. "Energy is the problem. We are sending much too much out where it can be identified, and our power cells are heading towards drained. I know when we landed that we had to grab a pretty large chunk of land to insure our own safety. We didn't have the luxury to scout this planet or its people or species. So for our own safety it required that we do what we did. But now we are beginning to see the results from having to maintain the energy fields. Yeah, we have our own generators out and using both solar, and fusion, although the latter in a minimal capacity, since we are having difficulty with overheating. Space is great for keeping them cool. Not so here planetside.

"And the conversion of water to hydrogen and oxygen is going well, but all of them cannot match the overall drain on our systems. Either we pull back our barriers and cover a smaller area or shortly it won't matter and they will come down because we won't have anything left in the battery banks. Truthfully we need to remain on solar only."

"I knew it was bad, but I didn't know it was that bad", Arthur replied. "So how long do I have before we reach the point of no return? The problem we are facing here on the ground is the natives. While they are more of a nuisance than a threat, they still are slowing us down. In fact what I was just discussing with the colonel had to do with that little problem. So far no one has been injured by the numerous attacks the natives have thrown at us. But that doesn't mean it won't eventually happen. Somewhere a piece of equipment will fail, or a power unit will overload and then we will have lost someone.

"I've had to authorize him to increase the size of the patrols. And since we can't get a ship up to survey the mountains, nor can we get ground vehicles out and about, it leaves us doing it the old fashioned way – by foot." Shaking his head Arthur turned around back to his temporary desk and pulled out a bottle. "Care for a little something to relax the nerves?"

Smiling David replied, "Of course." He reached for the small glass he was offered. Unfortunately in their rush to abandon their previous base of operations, much of the booze got left behind. Nobody's fault since it was in a protected area, but that meant they had less to enjoy. Taking a deep breath and letting it out slowly David thought how he would answer the question. "From the discussion with my engineers, and the ones responsible for the maintenance of all that we have, I'd say we are good as we are in the present configuration for at least five to seven days as it relates to this planet's day-night cycle. After that if we either do not find what we are looking for, or find a way to reduce our power usage it's going to come down anyway." He sipped appreciatively the golden fire before sitting down in one of the folding chairs. "My, this is good!"

Shaking his head he wondered how all of this would end, and to be truthful, how he got involved in this in the first place. Well, in the end it didn't matter. He was tagged an outlaw now and there would be no going back. And it would be his friend George who would be pursuing him. *Of course it would have to be that way. Murphy seldom misses a chance to screw things up. If it could be anybody else who is doing the pursuing I'm sure we could outthink and outrun them. George on the other hand is good – very good. Plus we used to run war games against each other so we know how each of us think. It surely complicates things. I really have to second guess everything I do so I'm not doing something or leaning on some tendency that would allow him to anticipate my move.* He realized Arthur had said something, "Ah can you repeat it please. Was lost in thought there for a moment."

Smiling David said, "Yeah, I can understand that. We are kind of stuck between that proverbial rock and a hard place. Anyway, what you've told me lets me know how desperate the situation is getting on both sides of the coin. We're being slowed down by the natives, and your power is slowly draining away with no way to recover if we don't change. Okay, I'll have the colonel and some of the captains begin a check as to where we can reduce our footprint. I know you're doing the same on your side. Unfortunately, as the colonel was relating to me when you arrived, the patrols haven't found what we need. And as they work their way towards the mountain ranges here, they meet with greater resistance slowing them down even further. Unfortunately this is one area where we cannot compromise. Otherwise they will find us.

"Have you thought of maybe sending out one of your scout ships to see if they can find us an alternate location if this place becomes too hot? I think it would be smart of us to find somewhere else in case we are found out before we succeed in burying ourselves."

"Not a bad suggestion General. I've been so busy trying to keep this situation under control that I hadn't the time to think about other alternatives." He put his hand to his chin as he thought. "Maybe we need to find a large asteroid, or maybe a small moon. If we can locate the right one then with the equipment we have we can hollow it out and work from there." He suddenly stood up and handed the empty glass back to Arthur, stating, "I'm going to get right on it. I think it's an excellent suggestion." Deep in thought, he turned and left heading back to the ships and his own office. There was much that needed accomplished and not a lot of time. At least, for the moment, all of them were on the same page.

Still he had to admit that this planet, this world overall was a beautiful place. Yeah, as it usually is, much of the flora and fauna seemed a bit strange, and surprisingly the intelligent life forms here were similar to them, which meant a similar start back in this planet's past. Plenty of water, and with all the farming they had witnessed, at least advanced enough to begin the process to manufacturing and such, later in their future. It really was too bad they had to come here. While he never had necessarily agreed with the "hands off" requirements set by their confederation of planets and worlds, generally he followed them. After all, sometime in the future, once the ones from this planet would be advanced enough they could be approached with the idea of admitting them.

He shrugged. Well it was another crime added to the long list of crimes they already committed. So in the end it probably wouldn't matter. If they were able to dig in and hide eventually they might leave and find a better place – or not. Still if they didn't get underground soon it wouldn't matter they would be found. There was way too much energy signatures being sent out into space. And while it would only travel slowly at the speed of light, thusly giving them time, in the end it would be received and identified for what it was. He could only hope that by the time it was they would have quit sending out the energy readings or signatures and be hidden.

* * *

Lt Smyth came out of the sleeping cabin – not much more than a closet with bunks that folded against the wall when not used. It was time for his shift and so far they had found nothing. Looking over at Lt Drury he could tell that everything was normal, and nothing had changed. Taking a deep breath and trying to clear the cobwebs that seemed to linger Philip said, "Guess it's my turn. Go grab a bite and turn in. I think the agent will be out shortly, and he can be the navigator for a while."

"Yeah, sounds good. It's been so quiet it's been difficult to stay awake. I really hate it when it's this quiet. It usually means things are just about to get interesting. Still we've all ran a number of these patrols in the past and found nothing. It might turn out to be the same. Anyway the bridge, as small as it is, is yours. See you in a few. And I hope you have some better news then I did." Peter slowly pushed his way out of the seating, stretched, rolled his head to clear the kinks in his neck, slid past Philip, and there was barely any room to do this, and headed for the seating area where they ate.

Things were definitely tight on these things. Philip thought about when the navy was a wet navy instead of space bound. He loved history, especially the history of the military and navy specifically. From what he read these scout ships were even smaller than the sea craft, especially when they first began to roam the seas that plied the underwater world. If he remembered right they were called submersibles or something like that anyway. Still as large as those oceans had been they had only existed on the surface of a planet. Unlike space, which seemed infinite, the modern scout ships could survive almost indefinitely. He looked over the charts, and had the computer system play back the previous shift's logs, and as Peter had stated there had been nothing out of the ordinary. *Damn, I really thought we'd begin to pick up something by now. I know we haven't finished doing a fine search of the area assigned, or are we near enough to where I suspect, or have a hunch they have gone, still nothing and that's a worry.*

Looking over the incoming communications traffic he saw that nobody else had found anything either. It was as if the traitors, the outlaws, or whatever name one attached to them, had found a black hole and disappeared forever. Of course this was an impossibility, since the crushing gravity would had destroyed anything entering into and past the event horizon. Still he knew Admiral Sympson was known for his maneuvers, and tactical awareness. In the war games they had played he rarely lost. And generally he would come up with some twist or change of direction that would be completely unexpected. And fortunately the only admiral who had come close to matching him was leading their ships. So if any could find them it would be Admiral George Williams. Now if they could just get a break.

About this time he heard the door slide open from the closet that was considered the sleeping quarters. Looking over his shoulder he saw Agent Jerod emerge looking like he didn't get a whole lot of sleep. Hair was mussed up and the clothes were quite wrinkled. The agent headed over to the eating area and grabbed some coffee. Turning Jerod asked, "Like some, since I'm here?"

Shaking his head Philip said, "No. Too early for me. I've got to be up for a while and actually eat something. Love coffee, even our horrible stuff, but it doesn't love me. Still that doesn't keep me from drinking it."

"Yeah, understood. Still I drink it whenever I can. Once I go planetside there's too many times where I can't get any. So I enjoy it while I can. Still it goes through one much too fast and almost seems to be a waste of effort – still . . ."

Philip could hear the brown liquid enter the sealed cup – all liquids required a sealed cup so to avoid spilling on the electronics. (If that happened the results were usually fatal to the equipment and could strand them. Yeah they had redundancy, but it was easier to avoid the possibility of it happening.) "So Jerod what made you become part of the planetary infiltration division? Yeah, I know it doesn't officially exist." He heard him sip his coffee.

"Ouch that's hot. Still it tastes wonderful – even this stuff, which is probably the next best thing to lubrication oil. Why'd I become part of this dangerous profession? You know I've asked myself that too many times. And I guess I could ask you the same question since you are flying this scout ship. Yeah I know it has some defensive and a very limited offensive capability. Still we both know that even a small capital ship would make this no more than dust, and not raise a sweat. And it's the size of this ship, its speed and maneuverability that gives it the best chance of survival. Yeah I'm required to know the stats on everything out here.

"I don't know, I kind of fell into it. Had been doing a lot of mining – for myself, not with one of the big mining operations you see – and hoped to make my fortune that way. You know kind of like those prospectors of old. Kind of romantic of me I have to admit. Still I've never been the type that can handle routine – you know doing the same thing day in and day out – and it was one of the reasons to try these different things. Yeah, before you ask, mining was only one of the many occupations I tried. Even tried farming once or twice, but I'm definitely not cut out for that kind of thing. Anyway somewhere along the line and while I was out exploring one of the many asteroid belts in the myriad of systems we have inside our confederation, I had a failure. My personal transportation failed. Not a surprise really as I never had enough credits to keep it operating. Still to pay the bills I had to take chances.

"It was a frustrating time. Here I was drifting in space – at least life support still functioned – attempting to make enough repairs that I could get the FTL back online so I could reach one of the small out-worlds – I was out in the border worlds on the rim of what is still considered part of our civilization – when what appeared to be a well-cared civilian ship drop out of hyper and after a period of time where we eyed each other they finally broke the silence and asked if I needed any help. Because of the length of time where I wasn't sure what their intentions were, I kind of was short with them. Said something like, 'Duh, I come out here just so I can break down and see if I can fix the problem before I die', or something like that.

"Whoever was on the communications that day was just about as sarcastic as I was saying something to the effect that if their help wasn't needed they had other places to go and people to see. I knew whoever this was wanted to see me back up a bit and ask, and you know what, what choice did I have? So taking a deep breath and shaking my head and I went ahead and asked for help. The crazy thing was this civilian ship was large. So large in fact that it could take mine into its hold, which they did. Once inside I was informed the deck had been pressurized and it would be safe for me to come out.

"Now the worry was, could they be pirates? Although I have to admit I've never seen pirates in a ship like this. Still this didn't mean it wasn't just because I'd never seen one. Still I couldn't stay inside mine since this wouldn't solve anything. So with some trepidation I opened my hatch to find that the military, our military were the ones flying this boat. It means that this was one of those unmarked vessels the navy and intelligence services use to keep track of things out in the fringe. And now I was aboard one of them. These ships weren't supposed to exist and had always been denied by both the navy and intelligence, yet here was one. Now the worry, once I identified what I was on, was what would they want with me, and why had they picked me up? All good questions and I hoped the answers would be favorable to me.

"After I disembarked a warrant officer came up and asked me to follow him. He led me to the lifts and from there to the mess. It was a quick and direct route and I wasn't allowed any detours to see what this ship might actually have on it. In the mess I met the captain, the commander of the mission they were presently on, and an agent. What surprised me was the fact that there on the table they had a dossier on me, open on the electronic tab so I could see they knew who I was, and all of my history. Like most I'm generally honest, but we've all skirted the laws now and then. Not necessarily broken them, but bent the hell out of them. They motioned me to sit, which I did. I noticed that the mess seemed empty at this moment which meant nobody would to hear what they wanted to discuss. I have to admit that worried me.

"Anyway, to make this story shorter than it can be they offered to repair my ship and in return they wanted me to work for them. They said they had been impressed with my ability to improvise, to be able to think on my feet, so to speak. And it was then as I continued to explore, mine, or whatever that I got a regular paycheck, and as time moved on they offered to train me for what I do now. At first I wasn't sure if I'd be interested, but in the end said yes. And truthfully I'm glad I did. I have to admit I love the work." Jarod looked down at the cup and realized it was empty. He shrugged, turned around and refilled the cup. With his back to Philip he asked, "Now that you know how I came to do this work, how about you?"

Philip smiled. After all it was only fair that he reciprocate. Besides it would help pass the time as they continued their search. "My story isn't that complicated. I come from a military family. Still in a way I'm the black sheep of the family."

Jarod shrugged while smiling. If you are in the military, obviously since you are here, and your family is military how could it make you the black sheep?"

"Good question, but don't put too much in that statement. I think, in a way I disappointed both of my parents. Yeah both had a military career, and both have since left the service to pursue other interests. In fact they are out homesteading on the rim somewhere right now. Couldn't stand civilization, and the boring routine it presented I guess. Still to get back to the answer it simply is the branch I chose. You see all the rest were or are marines while I'm here in the navy. Yeah, in a sense we are still in similar situations since the marines are the fighting force on our ships. But at the same time they are ground pounders and this aspect didn't appeal to me. Space has always been my passion. And yes I could have been a pilot in the marines, but again what they do is more on planets than out here in deep space. Until they are launched to either help defend the fleet with the navy's own fighters and bombers, or support the marines on boarding actions or planet insertions, they too are simply passengers.

"Me, I had no desire to be a passenger. So instead of becoming what has been a family tradition, I pilot scout ships for the navy. It's more to my liking and

I'm no longer just a passenger having to depend on the skill of the captain and their crews for my survival while moving from one place to another. Yeah the danger is still here, but I'm able to take a more active role. I guess in some ways it's no different. Again it probably the way one wants to look at what's going on. We all take our orders, and try to do it to the best of our abilities.

"Oh believe me, we've – my family and myself – have had many discussions, or arguments if you prefer, on the subject. Still here I am, and there they are. I suspect it will always be that way. And yes I do have siblings – three brothers and two sisters – and all of them are in the marines. And yes we are an unusually large family. What can I say, my parents are passionate people and I guess it is reflected in my family's size. And the answer is no, before you ask. I'm single right now with no prospects in the near future, or anybody on the horizon who could be waiting for me." Philip laughed and shook his head, "And no I do not have a girl in every port. Not that I'm uninterested in being physical. What guy my age isn't? And I do have a reputation to maintain since I'm in the navy, and while I don't fly the bombers or fighters that support the fleet, I do pilot a craft. And that seems to mean I'm hot blooded. Still, at this time in my life I'm good. – although I do have an ongoing relationship, but where it will lead . . ."

He paused for a moment looking over the monitoring systems and the ship's controls before turning once again towards Jerod. "Just one last question if you don't mind – and if you won't or can't answer it that's fine. I understand operational security. We deal with it all the time. So why the one name?"

Jerod laughed. "No problem with that. And before you add anything else like is this my real given name I'll tell you no. Once we become full-fledged agents our birth names are kept in our personal files, but from that time on we have a simple and single name given. It can be changed, but from what I've learned it rarely is. Jerod is it until the time I leave this service. At that time I'll recover my birth name and Jerod will cease to exist, as he hadn't existed before I became him. Do they ever use a name more than once? To be honest I have no way of knowing. Still, I suspect the obvious answer would be no.

"Oh don't use the idea of the position of the alpha to try and determine how many agents may be out here in the real world. It really means nothing. And I have no way of knowing either. I overall know very few – and you could count them on one hand and have fingers left over – agents. Simply it's this way to protect the agency, and other agents. We really aren't spies. Although I'm sure there have been times when we've been used in that field. We deal with newly discovered worlds – make sure we can add them to worlds available. In a way it leads to a higher death rate than even what happens to our marines, or army, or any of the armed forces. I'm speaking of percentages of course. Our division if we included everyone wouldn't come close to one branch of the service.

"Yes we do as much scouting and analyzing of these worlds as we can with the satellites and probes that we use. But in the end and from these tests there's always something missed. And that's where I come in. You know sometimes there appears to be some sapient species on a world, but you'd be surprised how many times it turned out not to be so, or visa-versa if I want to be honest. You'd be surprised what we've turned up. Still with our hands-off policy most of what we've found is in classified records and the locations of these planets are also in those same files. Accessible by you guys, for example, if you happen to be in one of the sectors of space where the planet exists.

"For example, in this sector of space, even though it has been lightly surveyed, we've located at least two solar systems that have sapient life in them. Again I can say this because we, all of us here, are operating in this sector at this moment. If we hadn't I wouldn't or couldn't tell you about it. Let's hope the ones we are pursuing will obey our laws on this subject." Taking a deep breath and looking down at his cup he found it was empty again. "Enough of this stuff. I have to limit myself to two cups after I arise and two cups before bedtime. Otherwise I pay a price for overindulgence."

* * *

TimOtee heard the house settle a couple of more times. Nothing unusual about that, as far as he knew most buildings did just that. It made them seem like they could be living beings adjusting to the changes in the daytime to the night time temperatures. Like they were great beasts hunkering down to keep warm. Still that one sound from the second floor seemed to be somewhat different. Still he hadn't heard any more creaks or squeaking floorboards so maybe it was just this house settling. He had just finished eating his jerky and drinking some water and headed out to the gathering room to think about what he wanted to do on the morrow. His original plans had him heading for the coast. Again he really didn't know the distance, what lay between him and the coast, how safe the travel would be, or how long it would actually take.

Still, this trip wasn't a requirement. It originally had been a goal simply because he couldn't think of anything else to do. And he figured there was a good chance to get some help in those areas where there were more people. But now that he had come to the end of the barriers he wasn't sure. Yeah to find out if they truly did encircle the area they encompassed was important to him. If there was a weakness somewhere he wanted – needed to find it. He knew he wasn't alone dealing with the chaos and loss, still it felt that way. Sighing he wasn't sure what to do. *Maybe tomorrow in the new light of a new day I'll have a better idea.* Soon he'd head up that ladder, check out the upper floor, and probably sleep in one of the rooms. For now he'd stay here and look out one of the windows that faced in the direction where the gang was located.

* * *

Captain Heraldson headed towards where they were keeping track of their supplies looking for the chief petty officer responsible. The admiral had contacted him earlier and made a really valid suggestion which he planned to put into action. Still it could only come about if in the rush to leave the items necessary hadn't been left behind. The suggestion, and he thought it had probably come out of the meeting between the admiral and general, simply stated was to seed the many moons this planet had with stealth monitoring arrays. By doing this it would allow them to monitor space, and to possibly get an advanced warning, if one of the scout ships from the pursuers came close. Of course by then it would mean the scout had honed in on their energy signal. Still any lead time they could get would be critical.

All the supplies and such were still held on the freighters. Other than what they needed to survive or for shelter, was kept aboard so that they could abandon this planet with a minimal loss of time. After all, their adversary was very very good at this game of war himself. Even though Admiral Sympson had bettered Admiral Williams it had been close most of the time. And in those fleet maneuvers some of the skirmishes had been won by Sympson. And while the overall outcome generally was in Sympson's favor, it may have come down more to the support staff than the admirals. It really was that close. He was happy – very happy indeed – that this time they had won the first round. Still with all this energy bleeding out into space their signature should be found and recognized soon. The only hope he had, which was two-fold, was that their pursuers were on the other side of the sector, meaning that even with the speed of light it would take a long time for the signature to reach them. And secondly they would be able to find the mountain they were looking for, and get dug in deep within the range where the actual rock and soil would eliminate any chance of detection.

Pressure was on, and time wasn't their friend. If Murphy hadn't raised his mighty head back where they had been working their scheme – quite successfully he added – then none of this would have been necessary. He knew that both the general and admiral had thought such a day would come by and had been searching for an alternate base of operations. Heck if they hadn't then most likely they would have already been caught and facing the consequences of their actions. He knew they had been looking for a second base for quite a while and had sent probes out here in the frontier regions where it would be easier to get lost. And with the discovery of their little scheme the admiral had immediately headed for this part of space.

Yeah it wasn't a direct route that would have given their destination away. There had been quite a few close calls, feints, misdirection's, and a few scattering of their ships with points marked to come back together. So far all of it had worked, and for a short time they would have this respite. He hoped it would be enough. If not they'd be on the run again and it wasn't something he was looking forward to. *Now if Murphy will only give us enough time.* He reached one of the freighters where there was a tent pitched out in front of it. This was the temporary office of the supply CPO. At the front entrance stood a couple of marines, who were obviously on guard duty. Yeah, they had marines who were all in for the loot and such. It didn't matter the branch of service, there were always bad apples that were looking for an angle, or willing to take advantage of whatever the situation provided.

He had to admit it had taken a lot of time to bring in the ones of like mind, and to keep the discipline among the ranks. The problem when dealing with the ilk they had was many didn't take well to discipline. Still, after some examples were made, and a few were forced to breathe vacuum, it brought home to the other malcontents to conform. So far the rewards had been worth it. He stepped inside the tent and received a salute from the CPO which he returned. The CPO was behind a makeshift desk made out of some of the supply crates with paperwork spread out. It was obvious he had many of the ones who worked under him reorganizing what they had been able to grab. The CPO asked, "So what can I do for you sir?"

Smiling even though there was no humor in that smile Captain Heraldson said, "Chief I need you to locate and then pull those sensors. And it needs to happen as fast as we can get it done. Once located have them delivered to me. We need to get these things placed on the moons of this world so we can begin to monitor the space around us. And that means the necessary power supplies also. They'll be in stealth and passive mode so the power requirements won't be as great as normal. Yeah and I know by doing that it means we won't have as great of coverage as we'd like. But at the same time it reduces the chance of them being discovered and leading them directly to us.

"Oh and on that subject we will probably be pulling back our energy fields soon. I've been informed that the power requirements are exceeding our abilities to keep them up. Again we haven't had the time to work in other sources of energy, and really can't anyway. At least until we can dig in and begin to build proper – and finding that location is in the general's hands. And he's stated that they've been having issues with the locals, which I guess should be of no surprise. And before you ask no, the locals haven't been able to inflict any injuries or pain upon us. With the way we're being attacked it's more of a nuisance than anything else. And it's been slowing down the searching as the patrols have to watch out for ambushes. I would guess that the ones in the mountains where we need to go are a bit more aggressive than the ones who are farming the valleys. I suspect that they are probably territorial and most likely have been fighting each other for whatever good land might exist in these mountains. And unfortunately we are no part of any of this.

"The worry comes down to whether we pose a big enough threat that they band together under some, for lack of a better word, clan or the leader of one of the clans that have dominated the area. If this happens it will make it much more difficult, and slow us down even more. As you know, part of the problem lies in our energy signature. Even though this part of space has only a cursory survey, it still marks out the energy sources, and levels of tech a planet might have. And this one doesn't have anything like what we are using. So we are telling them exactly where we are unless we can dig in and hide all of this energy usage behind lots of rock.

"Unfortunately we'll be creating an even larger energy signature when we begin to bore. Still if we can get it done quickly enough and shut down most of what we've been using going stealth ourselves we should be okay. It'd mean that they would probably come and check out this planet because that's where the emissions would have been coming from. Still if we can get underground and the energy signature is gone they probably will do a search from space – because of the fact of leaving an intelligent race alone – and once they find nothing to move on and look for us elsewhere. Yeah, I know it's a bunch of 'ifs', still it's all we have at this moment. And if we can get those sensor arrays placed they should give us warning in time to either continue with our plans or abandon this place."

The chief listened quietly and leaned on his makeshift desk while looking down, "Sounds almost impossible sir."

The captain chuckled, "Yeah doesn't it? Still we've been able to lose them. And who knows we still might win this round."

"One can hope. I'll get right on it. In fact I think I know exactly where those particular items are." He saluted again and headed out to grab a couple of the enlisted barking orders as he did.

Captain Heraldson turned and headed out and went to talk with the admiral they had much to discuss, and much to plan. Including the possible abandonment of all they had put together here in the short time that they had been on this world. Dawn wasn't too far off, and he could feel the weariness, it was time to go catch a few hours if possible. That, of course, would be after his meeting with David.

CPO Fredrickson cursed under his breath. *Yeah, I think I do know where those items are. And because we didn't figure we need them they are still aboard the freighter and buried all the way in the rear. It's going to take most of the day just to unload what's in front of the sensors, and then we have to immediately put all of it back. Isn't there enough going on?* He sucked in a lung full of air while he turned to the crew of enlisted who he had under his control. "Okay let's get to this. We don't have all day, or night, even though it's going to take all day!" *Now if I can keep the captain off my back. Pressure's on all of us and this just sucks.*

Little One: "But you said you didn't know what's going on beyond that shimmering barrier. So how could you know this?"

GGF: Laughing lightly. "I know it's a lot to take in, and all I ask is that you stay with me. And yes at this time in the story I didn't have a clue as to what was happening behind that shimmering barrier. And, truth be told, I was desperate to find out. So you think you can wait a little longer to find out how I learned this? I really don't want to reveal the answers yet as it wouldn't make much sense."

Little One: He lifted one shoulder in a shrug. "I guess, and I really suspect I don't have a choice, do I?"

GGF: "No. No you really don't. Shall we continue then?" Seeing little one nod his head he smiled. "Okay, here we go."

CHAPTER SIX

ALL IS NOT WHAT IT SEEMS

TimOtee moved about the farm house remaining on the ground floor. Through the curtained windows he peered out towards the farm where the outlaws had taken over, but could see little activity. After being out and about all day and then consuming a meal he could feel the weariness washing over him. It was time to head up that ladder and to the second floor and see what accommodations awaited him there. Tomorrow, with the rising of the sun, it should allow him a chance to see the overall situation in this area and then make his decision from there. He went from the window and over to the ladder bringing the small candle with him. One thing for sure he didn't want to fall because of a misstep caused by the shadows. He slung his pack over his back and holding the candle in one hand and using the other to hold on to the ladder carefully maneuvered himself up the five rungs. It wasn't easy, and they creaked in complaint.

As he reached the top and in an awkward position he set the candle down on the flooring and finished hoisting himself up and sat on the same floor. He swore that he had heard that floor creak once again, but then it could have been the ladder since it made complaining sounds. Still he needed to be careful. After all this wasn't his home and in a sense even though he had found no one here he was a trespasser. So if one of the owners were still here then he had some explaining to do. Still it might be some small beast. Well, until he went through the doorway, which was simply covered with a hanging cloth, which reinforced the financial situation of the present owners, he wouldn't have an answer.

Turning to his left since he was sitting with his legs dangling over the ladder, he pushed up and pulled the cloth carefully back extending the candle forward to light his way. As the candle lit the area in a soft flickering light, casting shadows in the corners, he saw a room that had one large bed, some homemade cabinets, knitted rugs, and shelving that the owners had built into the wall. On one of the shelves he found a lantern which he lit. Once lit, it brightened up the room. He had his back to the rest of the room when he heard movement. Turn rapidly and pulling his knife, since he didn't know what he heard was a threat or not, he saw a young woman who couldn't be any older than he. She showed fear and her eyes were large. He could now hear her breathing which had become rapid. And like he she was holding a knife for protection. The large bed was between the two of them and she was leaning slightly on it.

Shocked for a moment TimOtee didn't know what to say. Tipping his head to the side he finally asked, "Are you the owner of this place?"

She remained silent for the longest time. Then she slowly shook her head. She didn't move remaining in a position that would allow her to protect herself.

He realized that he was blocking the exit. In the uncertain light of the flickering lantern he thought she was pretty, maybe even beautiful. But she seemed to be partially covered in dirt and there were smudges on her face. He carefully moved away from the door but still remained between her and the exit. Trying not to put on a threatening front, and yet at the same time remain protected he slowly approached the bed. "Okay, if you're not the owner I guess that puts us in a similar situation, because I'm not the owner either."

She finally spoke a bit loud and with some sarcasm, saying in a voice that was just downright musical to his ears, "I know that."

"How could you know that, unless you are from around here? Still other than that group that has taken over that other farm back from the way I came, there's been nobody at all." He paused thinking, but he found no ready answers to what he found.

She dropped her head and shook it slightly before answering. "Yeah, I'm from around here. In fact I'm from that farm you just described. That scum moved in quickly and there was nothing I could do to stop them. I was lucky to escape with my life. If they had seen me I'm sure after they got through working me over, they'd have killed me. They seem the type that doesn't like witnesses." She stared at him and asked, "You aren't one of them?"

"No, even though I could be lying and the rest could be outside. But I can't do that to you. I'm from an area that is further east. It's the barriers that forced me in this direction. Just like the barriers here that is outside of the village and just east of these farms."

"No", she said, "I'm sure you're not part of them as I watched you approach from a distance and you were alone. I can't really see the main trail from here, but it appeared you came from that direction."

"Yeah, that's true. And when I saw who was on that farm I gave it a wide berth. I wanted nothing to do with them. I've dealt with enough of those types already in my travels. And whoever the ones are who placed these barriers I've even run into them. And to be truthful they scare me more than the others who are at that farm."

Still wide eyed, she asked, "Are you saying you've been on the other side of the barriers?"

Rubbing his neck and shaking his head TimOtee said, "No. But they – the others – have been outside of the barriers and what I've witnessed makes me believe they could be gods, or at least something like them anyway. I watched as a clan that outnumbered them at least two to three to one attack them. I honestly thought these, whoever they are, were in trouble. You know how wild and strong the mountain clans are. So I suspected that the battle would be over in short order. And it was. Only it was the clan that lost. I've never seen anybody move like these strangers did. And while I was hidden it was obvious to me that these strangers knew I was there."

CaraOlyn put her hands on her hips with derision in her tone stated in no uncertain terms. "You expect me to believe what you just said? Really? Do you think I was born yesterday? All I can say is what an imagination you have." She shook her head and didn't say any more. *I really don't like this situation. He's between me and my way out of here. At least I have this bed between the two of us. Still . . . I don't know. What he just relayed to me seems to be a tall tale, a falsehood. Maybe an exaggeration of the facts, and by making them larger than life, makes him feel good. I don't know. The only thing I do know is I don't like this at all.*

Silence grew between the two of them as TimOtee stood there trying to understand her unbelief. It had happened just as he said. Of course he was the only one there. Well, himself, the strangers, and the attacking clan. And one thing for sure the remnants of the clan weren't going to collaborate his story. And as far as the strangers went he doubted they spoke the same words so there would be no help from that direction. Still with all that was happening around both of them it was obvious that they were living in unusual times. Some might even say exciting. Exasperated he asked, "What's the problem with what I told you? It's all true." TimOtee pointed out towards the barriers asking, "And do you think those things are part of my imagination also? I watched someone die coming too close to them, and I watched the strangers go right through unharmed. I expected to see them die also, but it didn't happen."

With sarcasm in her voice she said, "More fiction, more stories to scare the young. You really expect me to believe all this excrement you're spouting?"

It was his turn to be frustrated. *How could one be so dense?* "Oh then what's been happening here, the barriers, the abandonment, all of these changes didn't happen and we just happen to live here having this nice conversation in *our* bedroom just before we sleep for the night. Are you always this dense?"

This brought a quick anger to her that he saw flash in her eyes. "How dare you say that to me! I am the daughter of the owner of the largest farm in the region. I do not take that kind of abuse from any let alone some traveler and teller of tall tales. You can apologize right here and now!"

He smiled, even though it wasn't one of humor. He shook his head, "No, I don't think I will. I've said no falsehood, nor have I told some tall tale to entertain or scare the young ones. Everything I've told you is the truth including who you appear to be from my point of view. So we can either begin to talk and discuss our situation or we can go on calling each other names. And I really don't think we will do each other damage from throwing those types of weapons around. It might make us mad at each other, but I think we will survive." He remained where he was. In this uncertain light he could tell that once again she was nice to his eyes, but with the shadows he had no way of knowing if she was armed beyond the knife or not. Still he suspected she had to be. With what had been going on it would be stupid not to be carrying some protection. And with her alone she would be a prime target for ones who had taken over the farm where she lived.

Her shoulders slumped and she looked down. "Look, I'm sorry. It's just that this has been really tough. First those barriers went up, then one of the villagers went over to investigate what they might be. We had farms on the other side that disappeared behind that thing. When he came close it killed him . . . it really killed him! All I know is that from that point it panicked all of us. It seemed the barrier was wavering and it moved and approached the village. Who'd have thought such a thing could move, let alone exist? I surely didn't. We could hear it and that alone was enough to scare anybody.

"We had a hasty meeting in the village . . . although; with the sound of the barrier in the background we all were very nervous. It was hastily decided to abandon the village. Some thought we could move back to some of the larger farms, like ours, but others wanted to leave period. And to only return to our farms and the village when it was safe. We never saw anyone, only the barrier. And the real issue other than it scared us to death was the fact that no one could see through it or beyond it. It seemed to go on forever to the east.

"My family decided to leave. I realized I had left something I needed back at the farm and while the meeting was still in progress, and knowing what we would be doing I snuck out and headed back. Unknown to any of us we had been watched by those outlaws and when we left they moved in. I stupidly confronted them and almost paid the price for that stupidity. But they weren't organized yet, and I knew the area better than they did and escaped. I could hear the frustration and anger from them. I'm sure they had anticipated a lot of pleasure from me, against my will, and as if I would have had a choice anyway. And that's how I ended up here. Unfortunately I do not know where my family went, or if they returned to find what I did. All I know is that I have been hiding out here now for too long, but didn't know what to do.

"At least here I was safe – safe until you showed up. Then I feared you were one of those. And shortly others would show up. It really scared me since the only way out of this house is down below. Yeah, I thought about climbing out one of the windows, but if you look there isn't much of an overhang. In fact that way is downright dangerous. Still, probably, in the end, I would have tried. And if I fell to my death at least it would be better than the way I would die at their hands."

"At least you won't have to worry about that for the moment anyway. I'm not them, and I come from a farm myself – one of them that are on the inside of that barrier. Oh, I'm TimOtee by the way, and you are?"

"Sorry, it's just been crazy. I'm CaraOlyn."

"So CaraOlyn since you can't stay here forever, what are your plans?"

"Plans? Who's had time to make plans? I've been living day-to-day just trying to stay out of sight, and to avoid being found."

TimOtee smiled. "I think it's a little late for that. After all you have been found, and found out. You mean all you were going to do was stay here and wait it out? Doesn't sound very smart to me." He could see the anger forming once again.

"That's twice you've insulted me, and in a very short period of time. I'm of the mind to throw you out of here!"

He laughed, and when he did he could see it made her angrier. Now he felt maybe he should tease her a little. Maybe she was used to getting her way, and probably had other family members to back up her threats. But right at this moment it was only her. He was curious to see if she could pull off her threat. He rather doubted it and if she tried, well, it wasn't like he hadn't dealt with tougher and more dangerous situations. Besides it might be fun. It had been a long time since any of his siblings and he had wrestled. He was the last at home with the rest of his family on their own farms close to their sires. Unfortunately all of them were inside that barrier. "Let's see you do that. And understand if you do try I will no longer consider you a female and take whatever response is necessary." He saw that stopped her.

"Why would you do that? I am a female and deserve the respect that is due."

"It was explained to me a long time ago that respect is due as long as it is earned. And if the female is unknown that respect is given until she shows herself to be otherwise. Then and only then those rules will no longer apply. And the way I look at it if you do what you are threatening to do then you are declaring that you no longer are protected. Yeah, if I was one of those others you ran from, or someone attacking you then all bets would be off. But none of that applies here. So please come on and try to throw me out of here. I haven't wrestled with my siblings in too long so it might be fun." Once he had stated what he had he sensed some reluctance in her but waited.

"You . . . you wouldn't do that would you?"

"And why would I not? You are the one being aggressive here. The one who seems to be like rotten fruit, one who is demanding something she doesn't deserve, someone who looks down upon others. Not good in my way of thinking. So once again, let's have at it." He motioned to her inviting her in and kept a mocking smile on his face. In a sense even though he was playing along – although he wasn't sure she was also – he, after all that had been happening, was beginning to tire of the whole game. He'd rather be back at home thinking about the future instead of wondering about it. He could see a bit of doubt in her stance and continued to wait. He figured she wouldn't carry through those threats.

Suddenly she darted across the bed trying to outflank him and head out that door. He didn't know why since it was quite dark out and there was nowhere for her to go. And while she might see him as a threat he really wasn't. She came off the bed in a single motion and he grabbed her by the waist which threw both of them in a circle. Using the momentum from the rotation he threw her back on the bed and jumped on top straddling her and using his weight to hold her down. At the same time he grabbed her arms and began to pin them down to the bed also. She fought like a wild beast, but his strength and speed was greater than hers. Besides this had been something he'd lost too many times against his older siblings. Being the youngest one learned a thing or two over time.

Both of them were breathing hard but no matter how she tried she couldn't throw him off of her or unpin her arms. He could see desperation on her face as she continued to struggle. It was obvious to him at this point that she was truly worried that this was going to go much further and she'd not like it. For a brief moment it became a real fight as she fought to throw him off of her, but his greater size and strength prevailed, with her finally giving in and breathing heavily. There was sweat on her forehead and he could see that it was the same for most of what was exposed. It made her skin slick. "Look", he said as he too was breathing hard, "Let's end this. If I was what you are presently thinking, and yes it's obvious to me what you are thinking, then we'd already be at that point. We're not, and we won't be. So I'm going to get off of you and maybe we can be civil. And don't try to run again. It's not smart, or maybe I should say it's a stupid move.

"Yeah I know, when one is in what is a perceived danger, one has a tendency to run and once one has taken flight plan only later. Where would you go? It's dark outside and there are too many obstacles that could hurt you severely." He continued to sit there looking down at her finding that even with all this conflict between the two of them he was being drawn to her.

Looking up at him she had to admit he had bettered her. She had always considered herself both strong and quick, yet this one was quite a bit faster than she. And as far as strength she could tell almost immediately that what she had tried to do was a mistake. Still once she started she had to carry it through. Yeah, she had to admit now, if he wanted to ravage her she'd be unable to prevent it, but he hadn't. And still he remained on top of her. Even though it hurt her ego she stated, "Yeah, I guess. Now will you get off of me."

"Get off of you? I don't know, this is kind of comfortable." He could see she was about to struggle once again. "Okay, so it is possible that you can be polite?"

"Okay. Sir! Can you please get off of me."

He was once again in a teasing mode. Besides he really did have the upper hand right now. "Now, that didn't sound very polite. Let's try that again."

Taking a deep breath and hating every moment of this . . . this inconvenience, or compromising situation she found herself in she quietly said, "Please allow me to get up."

"Only if you promise to not bolt again . . . to be a little more on the level, and to quit insulting me. I'm not your hired help, nor am I some poor sod that you can look down upon and feel superior."

What choice did she have? It was either agree or find herself at this one's mercy. In a subdued and defeated voice she said, "Okay."

Carefully he took his weight off of her, and swung down between the bed and the doorway still holding her arms. Then he helped her off the bed but remained alert. This one had spunk, and a strong feeling of superiority that could still lead to trouble. Still at the moment she remained somewhat subdued. Once standing she headed back to the other side of the bed to keep it between them. She remained silent.

Now what? He needed this impasse to end between them.

* * *

CPO Fredrickson cursed silently. *Why did it seem that anything they needed was always buried in the furthest corner and on the bottom? We're going to have to unload the whole ship just to get at what we need. And, of course, once we do that we'll have to put it all back.* He shrugged. The only thing he hoped was everything was back and locked down before they were discovered. Yeah, they had been lucky so far and had escaped and was presently hiding – well sort of hiding – on this primitive world. And *primitive* was the key word here. It meant their energy signature couldn't be hidden among other energy signatures a more advanced society would be producing. It simply meant they might as well be sending out the welcome mat to the ones who were chasing them.

Looking around at the mess that was scattered about he thought, *Maybe this is a good thing. At least it will give me a chance to do an initial inventory. With the limited time we had when we escaped things were thrown in, tied down, and secured with little knowledge of what was really here.* Turning to some of the enlisted sailors he ordered, "Let's try and at least put a little organization in this, and before we put it all back I want a list of what's actually here."

Meanwhile the Captain had been putting together the scheduled flights necessary to place the sensor arrays on the moons. Still he was limited in comparison to the ones who were pursuing them. He had only three scout ships available and to fly them he would need to take the flight crews from their capital ships. So it left them vulnerable if they were discovered before the arrays had been placed and the crews were still out in the scout ships setting up the arrays. Still if push came to shove, any of them could take the small capital ships back into orbit, and if there was enough time to take the scout ships back on board and disappear once again. Still if things went their way none of these preparations would be necessary. Once they were dug into the bedrock they should be hidden and safe.

While the plans had never been to set up in this sector, if nothing else then this place could be a hidden base for use sometime in the future. And here they could use the base as a place to go to in emergencies – sort of like now. Unfortunately he, and the rest of them, really didn't know if there would be enough time to do what they needed. Again they couldn't hide their energy signature, or could they eliminate what had already left the planet and gone into space. The only thing they could hope for was the time to get dug in. Then, and if the signatures were discovered, they should be well hidden and with other false trails laid they should be good to go. *Better head into that meeting with the flight crews so they know what we are facing, what they need to do, and the care they must take. Add, of course, a rendezvous point in orbit if it all falls apart, and hope by the time the meeting is complete that Chief Fredrickson has the arrays aboard the scout ships.*

* * *

Lt. Smyth came out of the cabin where they slept and saw his second and the agent staring down at the sensor suite. Curious he approached as close as he could. It was tight for two of them let alone the three. He really couldn't see what they were studying but took a deep cleansing breath and let it out slowly. "Okay, you two, what has your interest?"

Jerod turned around and smiled saying, "Oh a possible ion trail. It's faint and dissipating rapidly."

He pulled back to give Philip room to replace him. "Here, you study it. I'm sure you're better at it than I am."

Replacing Jerod he leaned down next to Peter and began to study the sweep. *Yes, there is one, but it's tenuous at the best. But is it what we are looking for, isn't that the question?* Looking back at Jerod and then the second lieutenant he asked, "So when did this show up?"

"Actually just a short time ago sir. We thought about waking you up but realized you'd be out here shortly anyway. And we really have no proof, being how weak this trail is, whether it has the proper signature or not. I was just running tests to confirm it with Jerod watching when you came out."

Lt Smyth could see how poor the sample was and wasn't sure himself. Looking at their position they had finished the outer and inner sweeps of the assigned areas and had moved close to where he thought the renegades had headed. Sure enough it was in one of the possibilities that he had a hunch about. Still what was here could be natural. "Okay, do we have a possible direction of where this trail leads? I know by coming into it where we have that we have two possible directions. Still if we ignore the one that heads in the direction of where we lost them and go with it in the opposite we should be able to see it either strengthen, or if we are going the wrong way, weaken. Send a message drone back to the unit and let them know we are pursuing a possible trail. Give them all the data we have at this moment, and let them know we are down to only a couple of message drones, so unless this lead actually pans out, the next contact will be when we return for further orders. Or if we are able to confirm that we have found what we are searching for, then it will be by drone."

"Yes sir. Will get to it as soon as you take over."

"Okay then, I've got the con." *Maybe, just maybe we finally have a direction. Hmmm, we are in the vicinity of one of the systems that have intelligent life in it. Hopefully, if this is their direction, they didn't compound their crimes by landing on the planet. Still, I guess, with what they've already committed adding this to the list would be minor – to them anyway.*

"Sir", the communications officer stated, "we've just received a communications drone from one of our scout ships."

Captain Samuels turned and nodded. "So is it good news? If, I guess, we can consider chasing one of our own as good news."

"Well, an overview of the communique says they have found a possible ion trail. Tenuous for sure, but from everything we know at this moment it's more than we've had. It went on to say that they only had a couple more of the drones so they wouldn't let us know more until they knew one way or the other."

"Which scout and where are they?"

"It's the one commanded by Lt Smyth sir. Basically they said they had searched the area they had been assigned and before returning to resupply to follow up a lead." The communications officer walked over to the navigation console, pulled up a 3D representation of the surrounding space and pointed to the sector where the scout was searching.

Nodding his head, Captain Samuels said, "Okay, it shows a system where one of the survey teams had located an intelligent species. Thanks for the update. Go ahead and disturb the admiral. I'm sure he'll be interested." He watched as the communications officer left the bridge. Turning to the rest of the on-duty crew he stated, "Let's find out as much as we can about that system. Where the planet is located that has the sentient life, what their level of technology, and whether there's been any satellite activity to update our information. We need to know as much as we can about them.

"I suspect, in the end, if they are primitive it will come down to the agents working on the planet's surface. We cannot afford to pollute a primitive culture. And if our adversary has done just that we cannot add to it. This simply means our hands will be tied further." He watched a few moments as he saw the officers get to work. He needed to head down to research this himself. It wasn't that he didn't trust his crew, only, which for him any and all, and that included himself, needed to look over the data. With so many eyes looking at it there was a good chance they'd catch most of what was important. *Oh yeah, need to compose a return message, and limit what they can do if they do find the trail. Can't have them barreling in and break the law even if they are pursuing the bad guys. Of course with an agent aboard that shouldn't be an issue. If someone does need to go down to the surface it will be him. That's, of course, after he has a chance to study the indigenous species so he can make the necessary mods to blend in. Better him than me, that's for sure.*

* * *

Sucking in a lungful of air and letting it out slowly TimOtee didn't know what to think or where to go from here. Yeah she gave in, but he suspected it was because she really had no choice. He was bigger and apparently faster than she was and when he had her pinned under him she probably felt helpless and feared what he might do. After all, she didn't know him as much as he didn't know her. So as far as either of them went, both could be lying. He hadn't the opportunity to look at the other rooms that were on this floor so he had no idea if the owners had children or whether they were simple storage rooms. "Look, when I arrived here I hailed the house, knocked, and there was no response. I guessed it had been abandoned like every other building, other than the one farm that I passed. So why didn't you respond or something?"

Exasperated she replied, "Isn't that obvious? Or are you that dense?"

If he wasn't careful she could make him angry so he kept tight control on his emotions. "No, it isn't that obvious. If it had been the ones I avoided they wouldn't have wasted their time on hailing the house or knocking. They'd have busted in and taken what they wanted including you. I'm not that way. I've disturbed nothing, other than you, and planned on staying the night out of the elements before heading south and then east on the backside of this barrier." He put his hands on his hips and shook his head. "Are you always this insulting or is there a nice person in there somewhere? If I was one interested in you, your sharp tongue, and attitude would end such thoughts immediately."

"Good! Why would I be interested in one like you anyway? And what's wrong with my attitude?"

"I'd guess you're close to my age, and for many females, or younger females, by this time they have mated, or are close to becoming mates. Yet, from what I can see I suspect you've probably had a few suitors but even those left. Nobody likes to be continually looked down upon. And in an intimate relationship it is something that will cause it to end quickly."

Anger flared, "How dare you insinuate that I'm a shrew! I can have any male I want!"

"Right."

"And what's that supposed to mean?"

"All you've presented is words. And words alone mean nothing . . . anything at all. It is actions that point one in the direction they are going. And your actions speak volumes of who you are and what you really are worth. Nobody wants to deal with the likes of ones like you. Life is too difficult to have to come home to one who complains and looks down on them. Home is the place where the two of you defend against the rest of the world. It is not a place to fight day-in and day-out. It is not a place where one tries to get the best of the other, or a place where one becomes the master and the other a slave. And that haughty attitude says that's exactly what it would be.

"Look, I came up here to sleep, but obviously I'll have to look elsewhere, unless you want to. You can decide what you want to do, but I think it would be better if you stayed in this house for at least tonight. With those bad ones not far from here they may decide to raid other abandoned farms and properties. Although I suspect that this one will be ignored. It is obvious that the ones who worked the land here are not well off. It's obvious they love the land, and took loving care of what they have. But it's never been a lot. To me they have struggled to maintain what they have.

"So what's it going to be? Are we going to at least cooperate while the two of us are here? Or are we going to have problems? On that it's your call." With that he shut up. TimOtee couldn't remember the last time he had spoken this much. He could still see the anger in her stance, but could care less. Again it was obvious she had never had to do much herself. Definitely she was a daughter of some rich farmer who had been waited on hand and foot, never having to do anything for herself. Thusly developing an overly large ego where she was better than the rest.

CaraOlyn was at a loss. How dare he speak to her that way? She couldn't really be as he had just described could she? All she knew that since her world had gone crazy and everything she had ever known was gone, she wasn't sure what to think or even what direction to go. And it had been a few days since she had eaten, more than a mouthful. Add to this was this male who had put her in her place. And she had tried to get around him, tried to defeat him. But he turned out to be too quick, and too strong. It was also obvious he wasn't stupid. And, she had to admit, once it had become obvious he could overwhelm her, he could have taken advantage of the situation. Yeah, she was sure she would have fought back, but from what she had experienced she still would have lost in the end. And if she wanted to admit it to herself, and she wasn't sure if she did, he seemed to be sort of good looking too.

Not sure what to do or how to approach this standoff – well not a standoff in reality – she knew he was waiting on her response. But what could she say, or do? When she had escaped the farm where she had grown up, just ahead of those bandits, and had become separated from the rest of the family and workers she found she was really scared. A couple of times she tried to tie back in with her family but the bandits were harassing them pushing them further away and trying to take the family and villagers out. There was no way for her to get back to them. Yeah they had a place to go if they ever became separated, but it was now on the other side of that barrier. She had gone into the village but there was no one around. The sound and the feel of the barrier close by made her jumpy and nervous. So she withdrew and went past what she knew and could see the bandits ransacking her home. It made her mad but she knew she was helpless.

Eventually she had worked her way further in and while she knew generally where this poor farm was located it had taken her awhile to find it. And like the rest of the surrounding area, the owners had left for their own safety. It had been a few days since she had arrived, and had found a few scraps of food, but barely enough for a single day, let alone for the time she had been here. She heard the hailing of the house and the knock and almost panicked. She was afraid to move and worried it could be the bandits. Instead it turned out to be this one. And he had already proved he could take her any time he felt like . . . yet he hadn't. She guessed that this counted for something.

Still she was at loss as to what she should do. "Look. I'm sorry. My world, my life that I've always known is gone. I haven't eaten in a couple of days. I have a great fear that I'm going to be another victim of those thieves and murderers. I hid here because it's the only thing I could think to do. So please understand . . . I don't know what to do, where to go, how to protect myself against their kind or any honestly that want to do me harm or take advantage of me. So what do you expect? How should I act, how should I protect myself, again I don't know."

Not sure how to respond TimOtee shook his head slightly. "What am I to do with you? First you put forth this superior attitude, and now you're saying just the opposite. Which one is you, and it makes this moment that much more complicated. Can I believe anything you're saying? Or is it all some type of game where you are trying to take advantage of another farmer to get your way? You tell me."

She leaned on the bed almost pleading. "Look, growing up we have always been told that a female does not go around alone. There's too much bad in the world and too many of us disappear forever leaving the families to grieve and never knowing. I'm alone and in that situation now. And I have to say it scares me to death. What is it that I need to do to convince you I'm sincere? I know that I kind of came on wrong, but then again what did you expect? I'm here, alone, and very vulnerable. I have to try to keep me safe, and right now it's obvious I've failed miserably. If you had wanted to take me, I'd have fought, but I already know I'd have lost. And we both know what happens too many times when that happens to a female. She dies soon after, or is hauled so far away from her home and all she knows, she then is used by all the males and there is nothing, nothing at all she can do about it other than eventually die.

"I know that none of us want to talk about such things, but unfortunately it's still part of life. I guess this is a roundabout way of getting here, but I really don't know what to do." She could feel her emotions beginning to overwhelm her, and could feel the tears beginning to form in her eyes. The last thing she wanted to do was to cry in front of this stranger, to show more weakness, but it was becoming harder not to break down.

TimOtee thought a moment. It wasn't like she was the only one in this situation. Yeah he was a male so he had a better chance. Still it really didn't even the odds for survival. Looking close she didn't appear to be starving. If she hadn't eaten in a couple of days it would be too soon to see those kinds of results. Taking a deep breath, and breathing out loudly he shook his head. He honestly didn't know what to do. One thing for sure he was having enough problems keeping himself safe. The last thing he needed was a female to really complicate things. He, truthfully wanted to get back to his farm, the one where he had been raised. He had hopes, once he reached the end of the barriers that he could swing around the backsides and find an opening. He was still a long way from learning if this was a possibility. Looking her in the eyes he stated, "Well, I guess we are at an impasse for the moment.

"Look, I'm not the type to take advantage of a lone female. At the same time I cannot afford to take one with me."

Alarm flared. *Why would he want to take me with him? I'm not one who will do such a thing. It means, no matter what he is telling me that somewhere I still could be raped. So far I've avoided such a thing and I'm going to try and continue to avoid that horrible outcome.* "Go with you? Why would I want to do that? We haven't talked about anything like that and I have no plans on leaving the area, thank you. My home is here."

Exasperated he said, "Look, you said yourself you don't have any food, and you are alone. Two things that say you aren't doing very well on your own. I'll give you some food, but you really can't stay here. At this moment your home, like mine is lost. So you have to decide whether staying here is worth your life. The trek I've taken so far hasn't been easy, but I've only had to worry about me. If I had another male with me it would still make it harder. Still adding a female could make it almost impossible. And that, my dear, is exactly why I stated what I did. So you have to decide tonight what you want to do. One way or the other with the sunrise I will be continuing my search for a way inside the barrier so I can find out what has happened to my family and the farm."

He reached down to grab his pack and saw her jump. With an incredulous look he asked, "And what was that all about?"

She shrugged, "I was worried you were getting something to make things worse for me. What did you think I could be thinking? I'm still a female, and one alone and not in a good situation. Again, we do not know each other and as you said we both could by lying. What you have said could be meant for me to lower my guard at which point you will take advantage of me. I really don't want that."

Tipping his head to the side and turning his palms out he said, "Yeah, I guess it could be that way, but all I was doing is getting some of the dried meats out to give you some of it." He picked up his pack and set it on the bed, opened it and pulled out a packet of dried fish, looked at it and tossed it across the bed in front of her. "I have more, so go ahead and eat this." He could tell she wasn't sure. "Now what?"

"I have no way of know if this is safe, or whether it is laced with something that will put me to sleep making it easier for you to take advantage of me. I've heard about such things happening."

"Oh, really, and for the god's sake, toss it back and I'll take a bite to show you it's safe. In the end if you don't want it I'll take it back and with me."

"No . . . no, that's all right." She reached down and grabbed the food and carefully unwrapped it from the cloth it was stored in. She could tell that it had been cured properly and gingerly took a bite. The flavor was outstanding and she could feel her mouth watering. It tasted wonderful. In fact she hadn't tasted something this good in a long time. She quickly put the rest of the piece she had in her mouth and began to chew hungrily. She whispered, "Wow, this is good."

He stood and watched as she devoured all that he had passed on to her. It was obvious she had been telling the truth. The way she consumed the dried and cured fish spoke of one who had missed a few meals. "I can see by the way that disappeared you weren't lying about not eating. So, once again where do we go from here? I had no plans, when I entered this home, to do any more than spend the night. And don't get any ideas about me going and saving your farm. I'm only one person and I'm already on a personal quest to save the one I grew up on. Look, I'm going to head for one of the other rooms that are on this floor. I saw the privy on the outside when I came in. I think you know where it is. If you need to use it let me know. That way I'll know it's you going out and in the door and I won't have to worry its some intruder. I'll do the same for you. Maybe in the morning light we can both head down the ladder and discuss what we are going to do around their table. Until then, good night – I think."

He grabbed his pack, turned and headed back out through the doorway and worked his way back down the platform to the second door that was on this level. Pushing back the cloth that covered the entrance he entered holding the candle for light. Once inside he found that indeed it was a store room – although there was enough space to lay out his sleep sack. Shaking his head he had to admit that he had been looking for a good night sleep on a real bed. But now that option wasn't available. He really began to wonder what he had gotten himself into. Mentally he shrugged. He had to admit he really didn't know. Maybe things would be clearer in the light of day. TimOtee, once he had the sleep sack lay down, blew out the candle and drifted off to sleep.

Little one: "Wow! There's a lot happening. And who is this female great grandfather?"

TimOtee: Smiling he said, "I'm sorry, but I cannot reveal that to you yet. But I think you will find out as time goes on and you hear and learn more. And yes there's much going on that I was unaware of at the time. Shall we continue or is it time to take a break? You see once I begin to tell this story I kind of lose track of time."

Little one: He looked around and realized that the sun was beginning to set. Had that much time already passed? He looked over at the door and saw his mother standing there smiling. "Ah yes mom?"

Granddaughter: "I think it's time to take a break and continue this on the morrow. Food will be on the table shortly and I think your great grandfather can use a break anyway. So go clean up, put your stuff away. You know after eating you still have chores."

Little one: Sighing said, "Okay." He turned back to his great grandfather and shrugged. "I guess we are done for today. When do you want to meet tomorrow?"

GGF: He could tell that the one named after him had gone from reluctant to enthusiastic. He smiled, "Oh that's up to your mother, and the work that has to be done. Now head on in. I'm sure you want your share of what your mother has worked hard to prepare." He watched as TimOtee grabbed his materials and run into the house. He shook his head. "I guess the mention of food is all it took to get him moving." He heard his granddaughter laugh and knew she agreed.

CHAPTER SEVEN

TIMOTEE – CARAOLYN – CHANGES

"Okay, where'd it go?" There was frustration in his voice as Lt Smyth studied the monitors. It seemed the ion trail or trails, since they were dealing with multiple capital ships, had disappeared once again. Turning to 2nd Lt Drury he said, "Okay let's slow down and begin a detailed sweep of the area. It could be we are following another false trail laid down by the admiral. I've been in a couple of exercises being on the opposing team, and he has always been a great tactician and could find ways to keep one on their toes." He had been standing and he leaned over the monitors looking for some pattern – anything to give him a hint to what had transpired.

He pushed back up and began to pace the really small deck area inside the scout. "Darn. There's just not enough room to give this justice. I need more room. How am I going to think this through if I can't pace a bit?"

Peter laughed lightly. "So why'd you decide to become a scout captain if you need the room? And, I can see that Allie has been after you to clean up your act."

Shaking his head and smiling Philip said, "You know the why of it. I love this action, this freedom. Well, at least as much as any in the military can have. Still one has to give up things no matter what one does. And why would you say that?"

Shaking his head Peter replied, "Oh come on! You always were a great one for using cuss words when things didn't go right. Now it's darn? And until you and she started dating no one has been able to get you to change."

Philip smiled a sheepish smile. "Well she and I did hit it off rather well."

Jarod sat back behind the two of them but didn't say anything initially. "So, if you need more room, I can always fold this seat out of the way become part of the wall and make like a fixture. Then all the room that is will be available to you. And who is this Allie you keep talking about?" This brought a chuckle from the two officers.

Smiling Philip said, "No, no that's alright. I don't know but for some reason pacing helps me think, and right now I'm trying to outguess one of the best at this. I know if I ever feel like I'm getting too big of an ego I can always bring up past exercises against this guy and be immediately placed where I am. Still he and his ships have to be somewhere. Oh, she and I met probably a year ago, and her name is Alicia Stokes. Father retired from the marines so she's quite aware of this lifestyle. In fact I asked myself why she wanted to date someone in the military since she has full knowledge of what would be involved." He looked back over the scans, both the ones presently being run, and the ones stored trying to see some pattern. He shrugged. There just didn't seem to be any. This guy was good and every time he and the rest went against him it was always reinforced. After some additional time had passed he asked, "Have we gotten a return COM yet?"

Peter shook his head, "Nothing yet, but that's no surprise. It's going to take time to go both ways, and once the packet comes back our way it has to locate us. We were only able to give a general location. In fact, not that you don't know it, but once it drops out of hyper it will do a quick scan trying to locate us and if it can't find us then it will signal and we'll have to go and retrieve it."

"Yeah, and I suspect it will be the retrieve option. Look let's move a little closer in towards that inhabited system and see if we can find some additional traces. I'm sure that it's just another feint, but maybe we can find something else that will point us in the right direction. Unfortunately any of the other scout ships aren't close so we will be on our own for quite a while. Besides, until we actually find more than this trace, they could have gone somewhere else and we are the ones following another false trail."

Jerod continued to listen and waited until they completed the routine. "Must be nice to have someone waiting, still I know the rep of you navy types. You know a girl in every port. Well that's what it was called when the navy was a wet navy. Now I suspect it's a girl on every planet, or maybe more than one."

Both of the officers turned and faced him with Peter saying, "I guess that reputation will always be with us. And probably for many of the sailors it's true. And with that I'm sure there are many that visit those houses that service the military, both male and female, and thusly why we have a line up outside of medical to cure those social diseases that have always been with us, especially after what is still referred as shore leave."

Laughing himself Jerod said, "Yeah, funny thing about that. You'd have thought by now that such things would have been eradicated, yet STD's are still around, and most likely will be until our species is no more. Actually, if I thought about it, I suspect they will outlive the human race and find some other species to infect."

"Yeah, probably so. Philip turned back to the monitors and Peter sighed, "I don't know but now and then a little companionship is nice. Hell, it happens aboard the larger ships. I guess anytime we mix the sexes it's bound to happen. It's a natural outcome of the way we are built. And, yes I know, it's frowned upon but it still will happen."

"True, so very true", Peter said softly, as if he was only half listening. "Still somewhere along our time here we need to find that other who can put up with us and maybe add to the population."

Jerod laughed out loud. "I've never heard stated that way, but I guess it's the truth. Usually when we find that other, math doesn't add up anymore."

Philip turned around and asked, "What do you mean math doesn't add up anymore? Its math that gets us here and keeps us moving around space, and allows us to do pretty much everything we do."

Smiling Jerod replied, "Yeah but in relationships one plus one doesn't necessarily equal two. It's usually three or four, or who knows how many." That brought a chuckle from the other two.

Philip shrugged, "I guess I can't deny that one. Even with all the ways to prevent such a thing it still happens. If it didn't none of us would be here. I guess, in a way it's the favorite past time of man . . . and woman." He took a deep breath and let it out slowly. "Guess we had better get back to what we're here for. So Jerod, any ideas?"

"Unfortunately nothing that would help. It seems you and your ships have gone up against Admiral

Sympson before, and I only have the information that is available to agents. I think hands on experience are far better than me just reading something in a report. I do know that the exercises has their parameters, things that limit what is being tested, but here there are none and he will take advantage of his full knowledge and experience to defeat you. And that's just about the best I can offer."

"Actually you are right. I didn't think about that aspect. Yeah the war games always have specific rules and goals, and if I really think about it, limitations. Out here there is none other than space itself. This immediately increases the challenge – if challenge is the word to use. In fact we were lucky to have followed him here, and even though we were able to do that he's still disappeared." He paused a moment looking down at the deck. "Wonder why someone like him would change and become an outlaw? I mean look at what he accomplished before he turned. He was one of our greatest tacticians."

"Yeah, but he wouldn't be able to go much further, and probably soon would have been offered a role in the academy. It might be, and this is only a guess on my part, he was beginning to get bored. And with the prospect of either retiring or ending up an instructor looming on the horizon he just plain didn't like his options. By doing what he has done it has taken the boredom out of the picture and possibly made him feel alive and challenged."

Peter had remained quiet throughout the conversation finally stating, "You know I've never thought about it to be honest, but you could be right. He was only a few years from reaching the highest he could have gone and that might not have appealed to him. We haven't been at war – which is a surprise considering how often we've been in the past – in probably a century. Yeah small skirmishes, something that involved the marines more than the navy, other than transporting and protecting them, so what is someone who is ambitious and part of the military supposed to do? Of course the last thing I expected was for the admiral to go rogue."

* * *

Admiral Sympson sighed, as he shook his head. *How did it get so crazy? Everything had been going so well when it all came apart. Just a little longer and I, with the rest of the likeminded, would be out of here and on the way to set up on our own.* He had a cruiser hidden behind one of the many moons this planet seemed to have captured. And if he had the time – and the credits to be honest – he had found a mothballed carrier that he would have added, picking it up through the black-market. It would have officially shown up as broken down and sold for scrap. Then he would have outfitted it with scout ships, and a few of the old fast attack units to help secure the area of space they had been planning to occupy. Well, that was in the past now. Somehow he needed to get his people out of where they had infiltrated the supply chain. The last thing he wanted was those who were loyal to him to face a military tribunal for their part. Of course he had others loyal to him that had infiltrated much of the military.

Still, until they could either secure a hidden base on this planet, or be on the run again, there was little he could do. He looked around and knew that the few ships he had on the ground were exposed and vulnerable. This operation needed to be complete yesterday, and at the present they hadn't located a site to begin their tunneling, followed by hollowing out the bedrock and shielding it. Right now they were sending tons of emissions into space saying to all who were interested, "Here we are. Just follow our signal and you will find us." Pressure was on – of course once they had been discovered that it really had begun then. And of course, it had to be Admiral Williams – an old friend who now was the enemy – who was almost as good at tactics as he. George had come close in a few of the exercises of besting him, which meant he needed to be on his best game if he was going to win this round.

Looking over where the merchant ships or freighters were being unloaded he really didn't like that happening either. Still he understood the why. They needed to get those sensor suites placed on the moons and put in the passive and stealth mode so that they couldn't be discovered by the ones searching for them. In this situation they needed as much of an advantage as they could. The only factor in their favor at this moment was the fact they had gotten a jump on the situation. Still they had left a lot behind. He was still of the mind to have some of his units go back and try to recover what they left. Yet that was something for the future. They hadn't truly gotten away as of yet, and he didn't want to begin heading for the area in space where they had planned on setting up. Until he was sure they had gotten away there was no way he wanted to leave a trail for them to follow. Fortunately that location was clear across known space and actually had some initial work performed. The tunnels and chambers had already been worked and shielded, and a couple of the smaller moons had been hollowed for use as a space station to be used as a repair base for their ships. In fact much of their stolen goods had already been moved. They had only about half an earth year left to get the rest moved.

CPO Fredrickson glanced over and saw the admiral standing in the distance and more or less looking his way. He knew what had to be going through his mind. They had to empty the whole cargo hold to get to what they needed and that left them open to losing more of their supplies. Well, he'd get this done as quickly as he could. He only hoped that the teams that were out searching for the proper mountain would find it soon. They had been exposed much too long as far has he was concerned. Still if they could get the arrays set up then it could ease things a bit. After all, not knowing anything was harder on one's system then knowing. Even if that knowing meant the pursuers were closing in. At least they would know where they stood.

He also realized that they were not recharging their power units as fast as they should. So far they had refrained from using the fusion reactors, knowing full well that the signatures and emission those babies put out would draw the others in like bees to honey. But the solar units just couldn't keep up. Soon they would either have to chance it, or reduce the size or area of the energy fields. Not that they were covering too great an area now. Again when they landed the fields were set up with the idea of just getting them up and integrated. Now comes the fun of having to use more power to set up intermediate units so we can shut down and pull in the outer ones. Shaking his head he thought, *One thing at a time chief, one thing at a time.*

* * *

General Pertion and the colonel sat inside the command tent. At this moment it was silent as both men were lost in personal thoughts. Things had continued to go badly. The further into the foothills and mountains they went the more resistance they faced. And at this moment it appeared that no matter how many of the natives they slaughtered they continued to pour out of the canyons and hidden valleys. While it was more of an irritation, the fact was it delayed what they needed to do. It might actually have to come down to fly overs with subsequent scans to find the specific bedrock formation they were looking for. Still this was the last thing they wanted to do. It meant additional energy signatures would be emanating out into the surrounding space, further identifying their location to the pursuers.

Looking at Colonel Jamison he said, "This is really getting old. And soon, if we aren't digging in it won't matter. I know that our soldiers are doing everything they can to expedite your orders, but all this fighting is taking time, slowing us down, and using supplies for which we are limited. When we looked at the surveys for this area of space and the initial results of the culture on this planet it seemed a simple thing. Do as we have, put the ones who are inside our barriers in stasis, find the geology we need and dig in." Here he laughed, even though it was a bitter one. "I guess no matter how you think it will go it rarely does. And when it does I guess it's time to be looking over one's shoulder waiting for the hammer to drop, or the surprise that Murphy has waiting."

Smiling Colonel Jamison could only shake his head. Yeah this operation had gone into the tank when they had been discovered. And since then all it had done was go further into the crapper, and in truth, he had expected to be well on their way underground by now, being able to hide their energy signatures, and be free of the ones chasing them. Instead here they sat on their collective asses with larger and larger groups of natives out of the hills ambushing and attacking them. So far, other than some really minor injuries they hadn't lost anyone but with the heavy use their equipment was taking it would only be a matter of time before something failed and they lost someone.

Their original plan had been to keep from killing any of the natives of this world. *Ha like that happened.* As soon as they began sending their squads into those mountains the attacks began and they hadn't let up since. Leading him to wonder why there appeared to be farms and farmland – land under cultivation – and an apparent peaceful existence. Well obviously looks could be deceiving. "Yeah I guess so. And from what we've seen so far Murphy must be really laughing at us right now. Yeah I know that those early surveys have sketchy info in them and make general conclusions, but before we landed here we monitored things and it seemed consistent with those early surveys. Who'd have thought those mountain – and I guess we can call them clans – natives would be so protective of what they consider theirs?

"If they only understood that once we find what we need they wouldn't see us again. It's like talking to the proverbial wall. Their language or languages aren't that hard for our translators so we know what to say, and understand their replies, but these clans, what can I say? Look if this doesn't let up soon – and how many can there be in those mountains anyway – we're going to have to take a chance and send out one of our scout ships to do the hard work for us. The ships we have orbiting this planet has to remain stealthed otherwise we could use them to do a deep survey and know immediately where to go. It might be, in the end, with what's been taking place here, we may have to do just that. Unfortunately the moment we do it we will be sending out a beacon saying 'all who are out there welcome, here we are, so come join the party'. But each day we delay we're saying the same thing while we maintain these barriers. I don't know . . . at this moment I'm at a loss as to what to do."

"Understood. I Talked with Admiral Sympson and he is just about as frustrated as we are. In fact he's got the chief unloading a series of sensor arrays that will be placed on the moons and be operating in a passive mode to help hide their signature and monitor the space around us so we will have a warning if one of the scout ships, or worse the group that is chasing us come into the local neighborhood. Unfortunately, and you can see for yourself, those arrays are in the back of the freighters requiring the complete unloading of those ships. It adds another layer of vulnerability since it will take a while to put all back.

"Look somehow in the next few days we've got to start drilling. Also, we will be pulling back the barriers. We've taken in too great of an area and the power drain is too much. So you will need to keep a couple of squads tied in with the teams preparing to move the barriers. As you know, such a change always leaves a few holes until the new units are integrated into the system. Yeah we all knew that when we first set up that we took in too much area, but thought we'd be in our new base by now and it wouldn't matter. Well, we aren't and it does. I know it will reduce the patrols around our existing perimeter but nothing can be done about it.

"Once the arrays are loaded into the scout ships and they head out then the sailors and our combat engineers will begin to make the adjustments. So I need those squads to tie in with our engineers and coordinate the move."

"Yes sir, I'll get right to it." He took a deep breath and let it out slowly. "Here's to hoping this is only temporary and we can disappear."

"Amen to that colonel . . . amen to that."

* * *

TimOtee awoke. Something was happening and through the grogginess of his sleep filled mind he couldn't quite determine what it was. His mouth tasted of metal saying he had been really deep when he was abruptly wakened. Well, it was no surprise that he had slept this deeply. It was the first time since all of this started that he was back inside a building. He could hear the female CaraOlyn moving in the bedroom. It became obvious that she had heard it also and it wasn't a bad dream or something similar. Breathing deeply he felt numb – another sign of how deep he had been. *Not smart to be that deep. It means anybody could have come in here and I wouldn't have heard them at all.* There were no windows in the room and while there was no door, only a cloth hanging over the framing, it seemed to be pitch-black. It had to be the middle of the night. So what was it that had awakened them?

He wasn't sure if he even had the energy at this moment to push himself out of his sleep sack but could hear the stirring in the other room increasing. Whatever it was seemed to be bothering her. So with care he pushed himself to a sitting position leaning on his arms shaking his head to break up the kinks in his neck. He then pushed himself up and stood, feeling briefly dizzy. He looked at the cloth or curtain across the doorway and it appeared to be somewhat lighted. How could that be? Curious, he pushed aside and the house seemed to be lit up with the interior showing a soft glow from the light seeping in. At that moment he jumped as he heard the sound of those strangers and shouting. Most of it seemed distance but how was it that it could be that bright outside?

He looked himself over to be sure he was at least wearing something. He normally slept with little to nothing on. Still during these times he had taken to remaining fully dressed. One never knew when one would need to move immediately, not giving one time to dress. He slipped his footwear on and headed for the ladder. As he approached the ladder he could see a frightened CaraOlyn standing in the bedroom doorway. "What's happening?" She whispered.

He shrugged, "How would I know? The room I'm in has no windows, no way to see outside. You have to know more than I do." She just shook her head and said nothing. She had grabbed the curtain that hung across the bedroom doorway and was holding it in front of her as if it would protect her. *Useless!* Was the first word that came into his mind – *she's worthless.* "At least get yourself together and if you aren't dressed properly get that way. We may have to move at a moment's notice and I really don't think you want to have to leave in your night clothes, if that's what you are wearing right now. I'm going to go down the ladder and see what I can determine, okay?" He could see she was wide eyed with fear and seemed frozen to that spot. He shook his head, she really wasn't his problem. If she wanted to stay and fend for herself – more power to her.

Exasperated he headed down the ladder and into the food prep area and the windows that faced where the brightest light seemed to be filtering in. Once he reached the windows he realized that they were too dirty to be able to see out. The light source was reflecting off the heavy grime and allowed him to see absolutely nothing. One thing for sure that light was bright. In fact he couldn't remember seeing anything this bright other than the sun, and wasn't sure if the sun was as bright. *How is this done?* He really wished he knew. It was another sign that they were dealing with those strangers. He turned and started to head for the front door only to run directly into the girl. He hadn't realized she had come down and was directly behind him. She let out a scream as he desperately grabbed her and they both fell to the floor in a heap.

Shaking his head and with some sarcasm he said, "For the god's this is a strange way to say you want to get close to me."

In a haughty voice, "It is no such thing. And why would I want to do that?"

He began to laugh, even though it wasn't the kind of situation where one normally did. He closed his eyes and shook his head. "Well, here we are and whether it was your intention or not we seem to be very close and on the floor. So do you want to dance, or are you looking to get closer than that?" He saw the anger flash in her eyes and then it was immediately gone.

Suddenly CaraOlyn realized the ridiculousness of their position and where they were. And while the statement he made angered her, she suddenly realized that the way they were this moment could easily be interpreted just as he had asked. She was silent for a moment, and then slowly she began to laugh also.

He pushed himself off of her since he was on top. Being this close tasting her scent, and touching her brought forth ideas that no young one should have – well maybe not the truth, after all youth always fantasized about such things – for one of the opposite sex. He blurted out, "Hey you smell good. Ah, sorry, I didn't mean that . . . ah that doesn't sound right either."

She smiled because she knew what he was trying to say. "So are you planning to get off of me anytime soon? I thought you said that you wouldn't do that again."

"Yeah, I guess I better, but this does seem to be becoming a habit. And I have to admit it is rather nice."

"Okay, enough."

He rolled over to the side, pushed back up, and then helped her to her feet. "Look, I'm going to head outside briefly to see if I can figure out what's happening. Please stay here where I know you are safe – well as safe as you can be in times like this. Once I determine what it is I'll come back and let you know."

* * *

The sergeant yelled at his squad, "Move! We've got to cover this area and not allow any of the natives past! The swabbies need to pull back the emitters and this is going to take some time." Darkness surrounded them, although it wasn't something that affected them. Their night equipment turned night into day and it was more to be alert for the natives of this planet who would or could be working their way through the tall grasses and brush that seemed to be everywhere. In the distance they could hear yelling, and knew there was a chance, like other patrols that some of the locals could be getting rambunctious, needing a reminder to leave them alone. Still so far these natives seemed to be thick headed and kept trying to defeat them.

"Okay you grunts, make sure you have the motion sensors activated, and I want a heavy weapons pit set up in the middle with the rest of you worthless slugs spread out anchoring off from the pit. I'm not worrying about any warning shots this time out. It hasn't worked in the past. So if you have confirmation that they are approaching take them out. We have no time for fun and games. The quicker we get this done, the quicker we can be behind the barriers."

TimOtee could hear the yelling as he quietly made his way out the door. He looked back to make sure the female remained inside. It was then he heard, in the distance, yelling and understood what they were saying. It sounded like the criminals back at her farm were coming to investigate all the action that was happening close to where he was. *Great! Not only do*

I have to worry about the ones who are close to the barrier – those strangers, but now the outlaws are heading this way also. He realized he wasn't far from the doorway, turned around and headed back. He opened the door and quietly informed CaraOlyn that the outlaws were on the move also and to be aware and be careful.

He headed back towards the deep ravine where the bridge spanned the depths and quietly approached from that direction. In the direction of the barriers he saw moving lights, heard heavy rumbling sounds he had never heard before, and could see the strangers moving in the grasses. Well, more or less. It was after all dark and it was simply the unnatural movement of the grasses that said something was moving through it. Besides, now and then he could hear the garbled voices drifting on the winds. He glanced up where the barriers were and to his surprise the one closest to him dropped and disappeared. *What's going on? And why has it disappeared? Is this the reason the strangers are here?* Well, he could ask himself all sorts of questions but he knew he wouldn't be getting an answer.

He heard the outlaws getting closer and suddenly the night lit up with streaks of light. This was followed by a chattering sound. Then came the screams as the ones from the farm began to take the brunt of the weapons fire. Suddenly he jumped and fell down hard onto the ground. There was a large explosion, followed by a bright flash of light, and then some flames ignited the grass in the direction where the outlaws had come from. The flames only lasted a few moments and then burned out. He found he was breathing hard, and had remembered the grasses leaning heavily over away from the direction of that blast. He also remembered that there was a flash of heat preceding the winds that pushed the grass over. *What do these strangers have that can do such a thing?*

He heard someone coming through the grasses behind him and worried that it might be one of the outlaws. But there was no sounds coming from the direction they had been. He suspected that whatever weapon the strangers had used had either wiped them out, or in silence the outlaws had retreated. So who could this be? Suddenly, she was beside him. He could hear her heavy breathing and she quickly came beside him and lay next to him. He could see the fear and waiting until she got her breathing under control and asked. "So, why didn't you stay where it is safe?"

"Safe? With whatever that is? I don't think any place is safe."

So, instead of getting further away you came closer to the danger?"

With a bit of frustration in her voice she said, "Well, what did you expect? While I really don't know you well yet, you are the only one around here where I might feel somewhat safe."

"Safe? Against that? How can I be safer than the farm house?"

"I don't know. I just felt like I didn't want to be alone."

"Okay, I can understand that. Look I know we can't see very well because of the time of night, but it sounds like these strangers may have solved your problem, or at least some of it."

"What do you mean?"

"You heard that explosion . . ."

"Ah", as she interrupted him, "yeah. That's exactly why I'm here instead of there."

"Okay, I guess that makes sense. I believe the strangers just took out that gang."

"You mean they killed them?"

"That's exactly what I mean. So I think in the daylight you can probably sneak over there and check it out. If it's safe you can return to your home. And for me, with this opportunity that's exactly what I'm going to try and do. For whatever the reason the barrier is down here and my home is inside of it. So please go back to the farmhouse. Wait out the night and go check. I've got to go while the strangers' attention is drawn away from here. I'm going to attempt to go inside before they put the barrier again – if that's their plans. And . . . I need to do this on my own. Good luck, and if things go well, I'll come back to you and see how it has worked out." He could see her nervousness, but he couldn't wait. Time was against him.

"I . . . ah . . . are you sure it's safe?"

Shaking his head he flatly stated, "No! In fact I suspect it's anything but. Still I believe this will be my only chance. Good luck!" With that he moved out leaving her behind. He had to do this on his own.

She remained on the ground lost for words. What did he think he was doing? Now she, once again, was alone. She had to admit that she hated it. While at first she was terrified of this TimOtee, in the end he had turned out to be quite nice. And again, if she wanted to admit it, and she wasn't sure she did, he was nice to the eyes, and she found she had been drawn to his quiet confidence. Now he was gone and she probably would never see him again, even though he stated he would be back. With the sounds of the fighting still off in the distance she pulled back and worked her way back to the farmhouse where she had been staying. There really wasn't much else she could do at this moment. She stopped for a moment as the words he had stated came back to her. What was it? Something about the ones who had taken her home were the ones fighting and were losing? If that was right it meant she could sneak over in the light of day and see what may actually be taking place.

Once TimOtee pulled away from CaraOlyn he headed for the top of the ravine and ran along its edge using all the cover he could find. He hoped the fighting would continue. It meant that all the attention would be towards where the action was. With what he had seen in the past he knew the ones who attacked these strangers were going to die. Whoever the strangers were they were ruthless when attacked. Yet, at the same time, if left alone, they didn't go out of their way to go after anybody. He knew he was taking a really big chance by trying to get by this skirmish line, but this might be his only chance to get inside of the barrier and find out what happened to his family and their farm.

He heard movement and stopped, froze in position and waited almost holding his breath. But there were no additional sounds. Maybe it was the winds, or some small night creature. Taking a careful look around and seeing nothing he continued to work his way through the tall grasses and bushes. Eventually the sounds of the fighting lessened and became distant. Unfortunately new sounds and lights were now becoming prevalent. What were these things he was seeing? Again he could only work his way to the edge of barrier that ran east and west. It had been the north-south barrier they had dropped. And one thing for sure, he wasn't going to get too close. He knew what it could do. From his hiding place next to a large tree surrounded by the same tall grasses he stared out in awe at what he was seeing. At this moment he had to wait. There was too much activity ahead of him and too many of these strangers.

As he stared at them he realized that these were dressed differently than the ones he had observed when they were outside of the barrier. So, who were these strangers? He knew it was something he had asked himself a number of times, but at this moment there were no answers. Plus, if he wanted to be honest, there truly was too little information to make any conclusions at all. Still with what he had witnessed they seemed all powerful, and that attack made by one of the mountain clans, and not one of the strangers fell, and the way they moved . . . Then tonight to see the power they seemed to control. It was like bringing fire from the skies, controlling the streaks of lightning and directing it wherever they wanted. There was only one thing that would match what he had witnessed. They had to be their gods. There was no other explanation.

Still, he had no proof, nothing at all. And while he watched he began to worry. If the ones ahead of him didn't retreat back deeper inside the barrier he'd be trapped between the ones he had found a way around and the ones ahead of him. No sooner had he thought this when behind he heard movement. *For the gods – now what?* He crouched further down behind the tree and knew from what he had witnessed, again from the past, there was a good chance they would find him. He was at a loss as to what to do and pulled back closer to the barrier that was behind him. He could feel his hairs stand up from the energy emanating from it and knew he could go no closer. He lay on the ground and made himself as small as possible. With the way they were sweeping back to this other group of strangers he was afraid they would find him. But, there was nothing he could do. He was trapped.

CaraOlyn spend the rest of the night back at the farmhouse, nervous, afraid, and restless. *Why would he do such a thing? Doesn't he know it's dangerous?* Obviously, but he took off anyway and left her alone. *Funny, in a way, when he was here I didn't feel so scared, and if I want to admit it, maybe safe.* Now he was gone and she felt really bad, tired, drug out, and miserable. *How dare he leave me alone!* Then again, she really hadn't given him any reason to stay either. Through blurry and burning eyes she looked out and could see the devastation caused by the fight the night before. *What could cause such damage and destruction?* She had to admit she didn't have a clue. Knives, bows, and such hurt and killed, but that was just about their limit. This . . . well, whatever it was, not only killed, but destroyed the very ground.

She turned around and sat in one of the chairs that were around a table. She leaned forward with her arms folded and placed her head on them. "For the gods, I'm tired", she whispered. Taking a deep breath she let it out slowly and blinked a few times. Her eyes were really burning. Eventually her eyes closed, her breathing eased and she fell into a troubled sleep.

Little One: "Looks like those females can be trouble, huh?"

GGF: Staring out at nothing and smiling, "Yeah, it can seem like it, but you never know."

Little One: "I guess with what you saw I probably would have thought the strangers might be gods too."

GGF: "I surely did, but then again I still didn't have any real proof. Shall we continue?"

Little One: "Yes! Yes, please."

CHAPTER EIGHT

TIME IS AN ILLUSTION, BUT THERE'S NEVER ENOUGH

Philip listened as the conversation continued between the three of them. "Any of what we've said could apply. Still, it's a bothersome thing when one of our best goes rogue. And to think he volunteered to lead our forces out on the rim – the area where there'd be the most action. Maybe when he first got himself assigned there it was for legit reasons. After all, he has refused reassignment a number of times over the years. Of course this meant he had time to build his forces with likeminded individuals. And from the size of the force he took with him when we began this chase it's obvious we have many more rotten apples than I imagined. Yeah I know that when we look at the size of the military it's still a small percentage – a very small percentage to be honest.

"Not to change the subject, but to change the subject, we need to find some ice. While we aren't desperate yet, our fuel is becoming an issue." Turning to the agent he explained. "We need to convert the water to its base elements so we can fuel the engine, and refill our oxygen tanks. Yeah I know we don't use much of what's in those tanks since we have the scrubbers and converters, still some is used and I always feel safer when they are as full as we can make them. It won't delay us too much, but out here failure generally means death and I have a lot of years ahead of me right now." He turned to Peter and asked, "While I know we've been concentrating on our search, do you remember seeing any of the belts that we need?"

Peter looking down at the electronic map of the region of space they were in, and with a cursory glance saw nothing close by. Still they were heading for a solar system that had many planets and usually out on the edge of such systems there were always the rocks and such they could use. "Nothing close, but we are heading towards that system so I suspect it's our best bet anyway."

"Okay, then we'll continue on this heading. We'll add the search criteria to the ship's system. For now it's the best we can do."

Jerod needed to get back to researching what they knew of the worlds that existed in the distant solar system they were approaching. He knew, as did the crew of the scout ship, that there was intelligent life on one of them. If the rogue Admiral had set down on it then his job just got more complicated. He really hoped it wasn't so, but one didn't survive by hope alone. But before tackling the information on his reader he asked the two, "Have either of you heard anything about the system we're approaching? The information I have on it is old – the original survey stuff – and many times the navy has done their own surveys later that never make it into the official reports. You know like you guys out on patrol making scans of such worlds to be sure pirates or others haven't landed to take advantage of the situation." It was silent for a moment, but in the end both of them shook their heads. "Thought I would ask – thanks anyway."

Lt Smyth replied saying, "No. There's been no reason for such patrols. As far as I know there's been no reason to be out this far. This is literally on the edge of known space. While we, as a species, are expanding deeper into space, opening new planets, inviting people to settle, this area is at least a century away from even being considered."

Jerod nodded his head, "Yeah, that's what I thought, but it doesn't hurt to ask." He turned back to the reader and continued his research.

* * *

"Get those arrays aboard those scout ships now!" CPO Fredrickson yelled. With the two operations running at the same time personnel were thin. Both were critical and both needed to be completed yesterday. With the arc lights keeping the area in bright light, turning night into day, it made the job so much easier. Still those scout ships needed to be in the air this night. He turned back to the forklift operator and with exasperation in his movements he signaled him to move it. He was left with just this one unit as the others had gone to move the emitters as they reduced the area the barrier surrounded. He saw the forklift skid and almost turn over. Yelling he said, "Careful! Those things are delicate and break easily. Watch it! If you break this one, we don't have another available."

He looked out beyond the lights to the west where the other crews were working. He hoped there would be no issues there. Still the nights didn't seem long and he'd been moving for the last eighteen hours with no break. *Soon, soon I need to get some rest, but when that's going to happen is anybody's guess.* He looked longingly at the area where the mess was set up and thought about breaking long enough to get some of that strong coffee. It had been rumored that it could float an old wet navy battleship – whatever that was.

* * *

Lt Smyth monitored the situation as Lt Drury made the EVA. Jerod watched from his own monitor. They had found a large ice field and had sent the equipment out to begin the process of gathering the ice, and converting it to fuel, oxygen, and refilling their water tanks for their own use. They would be here for at least the next twelve hours doing the conversion work. If they had a tender with them the process would have been less than an hour. Still all the ships had the capability to do this on their own. Time was the difference. It had surprised all of them to find this field but it was welcome. And what helped was the fact it was on the way, saving time overall. Still it was a delay. "Peter, I have you clear. Do the checks and get back inside. Once the process starts I don't want you out there in case something catastrophic happens."

"Not a problem, Phil. You know how I love doing this – not!"

Phil laughed, "Yeah, me too. Like you it's one of my least favorite things to do. Still we both qualified for it and know there are times when we have to. And, unfortunately, this is one of those times."

"Yeah, you don't have to remind me." Peter returned to running the checks. It would probably take another thirty minutes before the task was complete.

Jerod stared fascinated by what he was seeing. What the sensors had found left him wondering what had happened to cause this. Yeah, he knew from the analysis that the event that had caused this floating field of debris had happened millions of years in the past, and it hadn't happened here. The debris was still drifting. He suspected that if the time was available they could backtrack the debris and find the area in space where it had taken place. Still that was what the survey teams did. And yes sometimes he did ride along with them. But for now this would be just some added data for this sector of space.

Sometime in the deep past this had been a planet, and from the amount of ice he suspected that there was a great possibility it had been covered in water, with a deep rocky core. Still whether it was close enough to its star to be liquid or too far out and be a frozen snowball he really had no way of knowing. Again if they had time, they could bring samples back and have them analyzed to determine if the world had an atmosphere or not. Well, all they could do was mark the area on the star charts, and if sometime in the future a science team wanted to explore the questions raised by the debris then it would happen. If not then it would be no different than so many other areas that were unexplored, or slightly explored. It would simply be a footnote and nothing more.

It took being in space to put things in perspective for him. He, and he suspected most of his race, felt special, important, and ones who were to rule. Once in the depths of space it didn't take one long to realize that they were just a mote, nothing of importance, one of the many species that rose on their particular worlds believing they were it. And while they had only been traveling in space for roughly a thousand years . . . yeah years, such a concept . . . they had barely touched the galaxy their solar system and star had been born in. And in that time they had found a number of species at different levels of technology. Not only that but a number of worlds where there had been such only to be extinct in the present. These worlds were havens for the archaeologists, and the many theories that they put forth. Who knew? Maybe someday some alien race would visit their world wondering what had happened. Especially since the signs would say that at one time there had been an intelligent species here, but now were gone.

He wondered, *would we kill ourselves, or whether it would be the depleting of resources that would force us onto other worlds?* As destructive as their species had been, they still could go extinct. Still they, as a species, were pretty spread out. So if something happened to them on their homeworld, out there somewhere others would survive. It left him wondering if such did happen would they remember? *Oh stop it Jarod. Stop being so remorse. All any of us can do is what we can while we are here. Anything from the past is unchangeable, and anything beyond my lifetime is beyond my ability to influence.* Still, seeing this broken world – chunks of rock and ice – always sent him into introspection.

He heard the airlock cycle and knew that Lt Drury was returning. Had that much time passed? He looked at the chronometer, smiled, and inwardly shook his head. He'd better be careful. Such introspection on alien worlds could lead to one's death. He looked over to Lt Smyth and asked, "Everything on schedule?"

"Yeah, as much as such exists out here." He shifted so that the cameras that were monitoring the work could be observed by Jerod. Phil pointed at the small craft heading for the closest chunk of ice. "See, it's about the grab the first chunk, haul it back and place in the processor. Now it's pretty much routine, and BORING. It's simply monitor and be sure it all works right. We'll be powering down, keeping things at a minimum, so the processing machinery can use as much as necessary – not that you don't know this." He turned towards the inner door to the airlock and watched as the LED turned green signaling a complete cycle and waited as the inner door slid open. "Glad to have in back inside Pete."

Pete smiled saying, "No more than me. I know there are many who love being out there, but this is as close as I ever want it."

The time began to drag. With the ship powered down so that it could be redirected to the processing equipment there was little they could do other than monitor the progress and the surrounding space. And this portion of space seemed as dead as the fragments that were once a world that surrounded them. "So how much longer", Jerod asked.

"Oh, however long it takes. There's never an exact time since each time we do this the circumstances are different. Such things as what's available, the quality of what we are collecting – you know, such things as purity, contaminates, and such, all have an influence." Lt Smyth shrugged, "It's all hurry up and wait. Still until everything is topped off we're here. Never know when you will need every drop you have in this business."

"True, when you state it that way I guess it was a stupid question. Still . . ." At that moment an alert sounded. Lt Drury turned and looked at the console stating, "Looks like we have a return message. At least it will give us another message drone once it has been refurbished. And since we are recharging at this moment I think it can be added to cache to be serviced since the equipment is out and in use." He monitored the approach and sent the" accept" signal – all encrypted of course. How any of these drones found their targets was beyond any of the crew. Still it was rare that a message drone got lost or didn't find its intended target. Once aboard both would have to confirm identities before the message would be uploaded to their ship. If the identities proved to be false the unit would self-destruct leaving only a bit of debris behind.

It took a while for the process to take place, but with nothing really happening it helped relieve the boredom they had been facing. Eventually it was decoded and the three of them took turns reading the message : TO SCOUT SHIP ALPHA CHARLEY SIX TWO NINER ZULU GOOD WORK. SO FAR YOURS IS THE ONLY SHIP TO HAVE FOUND A POSSIBLE DIRECTION. THE FLEET WILL REMAIN WHERE IT IS PRESENTLY LOCATED. UPDATES ARE NECESSARY WHEN YOU CAN EITHER CONFIRM OR DENY THE DATA. GOOD HUNTING – ADMIRAL WILLIAMS

"At least we know our packet got there", Lt Smyth stated. "I hope that the direction we are heading will bear some fruit soon." He looked over at the fuel levels, and sighed, "Looks to be a few more hours." They were still a few light years out from their present target.

* * *

CaraOlyn awoke with a start. Yes it had been a bad night, still to have fallen asleep at the table, well this hadn't happened since she was a child. She felt almost embarrassed about it. Still with all that had been happening she felt that it was to be expected. Absolutely nothing had been normal once that barrier had arrived. And, if she wanted to admit it, last night was crazy. She still had her head on her folded arms and was simply staring towards one of the walls when she heard someone clear his throat. She sat up surprised that someone could be here, and mad at herself for not being aware. Sitting across from her sat TimOtee. She thought he might have made it to wherever it was he had been trying to go, but obviously not if he was here. She rubbed the sleep and sand from her eyes, took a deep breath, and tried to focus as her vision was somewhat blurry. "So, when did you get here?" She found her voice to be somewhat gravely, and she cleared her throat.

"Actually quite a while ago. I actually went back up to the room where I had been sleeping and caught a bit of sleep." Clearing his throat he continued, "Thought about disturbing you so you could head back to bed yourself, but thought better of it."

Leaning back and trying to make her mind work as it seemed to be filled with sawdust at the moment she thought. *Guess I must have really been tired – really tired.* As she reached the conclusion she realized she had left herself vulnerable to strangers once again. It was a scary thought. "Okay I can accept that since you are here. But what went wrong? I know when you took off, leaving me alone, you hoped to get beyond the barrier that had come down."

"Yeah, I had hoped that with it down briefly that I would be able to head back to the farm where I'm from. Once beyond the fighting and in the fullness of the night I felt I should be able to sneak past the strangers behind the front line where the fighting was going on. It was crazy even there. They had a bright light and this light seemed brighter than the sun. It turned the night into day and they had these strange noisy beasts that were completely controlled by the strangers. The ones who were controlling these beasts were dressed different than the ones who were fighting. I don't know, I can't explain it. Still it took me some time to find a way around them. They were concentrating hard on what they were doing. As to what it was I have no idea.

"I remained in the deepest shadows and darkness I could find, yet they seemed to be able to tell I was there. Somehow I remained free and worked deeper into the area and continued to avoid the small patrols they seemed to be conducting. Fortunately most of their concentration was directed to whatever it was they were doing. Eventually I got past this second group and felt that I was home free, only to run into the barrier. And we both know there is no way for us to go through one let alone approach one. I remained hidden and watched as the strangers walked, pushed their beasts, and moved through the barrier with no harm at all." Here TimOtee paused and shook his head. "I don't know who these strangers are or why they can do what they can. It left me wondering, once again, if maybe they're gods or something. I mean what they are doing seems impossible.

"When I saw one of the mountain clans attack a small group I felt sorry for them – you know, the strangers. I mean I felt there was no way for them to survive such an attack. Yet, it was obvious these strangers were aware and it seemed like it meant nothing. Meant nothing – can you imagine? If I had seen, which I did to be honest, such a force coming at me and seeing I was outnumbered at least two to three to one I would have ran. There's no way to survive such odds and yet here the odds seemed even greater than that. You would have sworn they were out for a leisurely walk among the fields where it is safe, not where an imminent attack was about to happen. When the clan struck I felt it would be over in moments. And in truth it was. Only it was the clan that lost. I've never seen anybody move like the strangers. And when it was over not one of the strangers were hurt – not one. How is this possible? In the end the clan probably lost ninety percent before they broke and ran.

"I knew, once I witnessed the results, that I wanted to stay as far away from the strangers as possible. Still, as I begin to put everything together that I've witnessed, this barrier and their ability to move it at will, their apparent speed, and ways of attacking from a distance, it all adds up that they might be gods. If they are killing us that means they might be evil – I don't know. Still, if they are gods, there would be no way for us to understand their actions anyway."

Here he fell silent. She looked across the table and continued to wait expecting him to continue, but he said nothing. *I guess in a way what else can he say?*

Gods? Really? That's not possible! No! No it can't be so. Why would gods come down here? She had to admit such thoughts left her shaken. But could his conclusions be right? Still, if she wanted to admit it, from what she had witnessed, what he seemed to be saying made sense. Had they done something wrong to bring down the wrath of the gods upon them, or was it something else? Had there been a war in the realm of the gods . . . Something that had caused it to move here? She had to admit such thoughts scared her. With an incredulous look she asked, "Are you sure? I mean we always considered there had to be gods, and could make rough guesses that some of what has happened was influenced by them, but to actually be here?"

"I don't know. I mean I really don't know. Still if you have a better explanation I'm open to it." Here he shrugged. For now he really didn't know what to do. With his scouting adventure, and being up close and personal to the strangers, he now held more of a fear and respect for them. It seemed as if they could do anything, and seemed immortal. What other explanation could there be? He now had witnessed the strangers being attacked twice and in both attacks the only ones to suffer and die where the ones attacking them. And to put fire in the sky, to make night day, to be able to move like they did, whether night or day, neither making a difference, what other answer could there be?"

Sighing he said, "I don't know, I know I just said that, but I didn't come to this answer easily. In fact it probably has been in the back of my mind for some time now. Still until the fight last night where I saw them taking out the ones attacking with an accuracy that any of us could only dream of, and in full darkness, followed by my scouting deep inside the area where they were working only to run into the barrier again. Add to this those noisy beasts they were controlling, I've never seen anything like them, not that I can say I've seen all the beasts that exist here. Still, these were some of the strangest I've ever seen. And the voices and their speaking and yelling at each other I've never heard or understood a word. And what was even more shocking was the fact I could see one speak close to me, and by the reaction, another so far away that there was no way for them to hear by normal means. Yet, from where I was hidden I could tell they were carrying on a conversation just by the way they acted. I was so in awe with what I was witnessing I almost forgot where I was and how dangerous it was. One of the patrols almost caught me. So, if you have a better answer please, please let me know. If these strangers are gods then we are lost, and it's just that simple."

"Are you sure you aren't imagining some of this?" In her mind she needed to question his conclusions. If they were accurate she didn't know if she could handle it or not. "I mean, I'm not doubting you, only that there has to be some other way to understand all that you've seen. I mean, I don't know what I'll do if they are gods, or if they are why they are here?"

Once again he shrugged and then shook his head. He breathed out noisily and said quietly, "I don't know. I have no answers. And yes, I could be completely wrong."

* * *

"What was that?" Lt Drury asked. All of them had felt what seemed to be an energy or gravity wave moving through space. Both of them looked quickly over the instruments and were at a loss as to what had just happened. Then they both looked out on the operation and the monitoring instruments to see if maybe one of the pieces of equipment had malfunctioned. Yet the scene before them seemed normal. Looking at each other then back at Jerod he could see they had no explanation for what had just taken place. Actually it could have been something that had happened a long time in the past. Something like a star going nova light years away and only now the energy from the destruction of the star had reached them. Still it seemed much too weak for such an event. Plus they would have expected additional waves of energy to sweep over them and so far that hadn't happened. Lt Smyth asked, "Any ideas?"

Jerod shook his head simply saying, "No. Still from the way we moved I know it wasn't my imagination. And if we want to be honest here, space is your expertise and experience. I'm along for the ride so I can apply mine which is infiltration on a planet or the monitoring of such if the atmosphere is poisonous to us. While I know enough to get myself in trouble, it's definitely not enough to explain such events. Just a thought, could such a wave be produced by a ship passing close by while using the FTL drives?"

"Usually not . . . Well I don't think so anyway, but I'm not an expert. After all from what little we can understand about this type of flight and even though we've been using it for a long time, is that we sort of leave this dimension of space-time, and possibly touch the quantum world allowing us to exist in both at the same time and yet be in neither. Think about it. If we remained here with the speeds we maintain it wouldn't take much to destroy us. And such things as planets and suns or stars would be obstacles that could destroy us also. And then we add in the kinetic energy that would be released from such a collision and we'd cease to exist as well as whatever we hit. But if a ship using the drive passed really close maybe . . . maybe."

* * *

"Sir" the communications officer said, "one of our ships in orbit has reported a scout ship approaching."

Alarmed Captain Heraldson stopped. Whatever his errand had been was now forgotten. "Were they able to identify who it belongs to?"

"Not yet sir. But from what they could determine the scout ship has made a direct approach to this planet."

"Okay, thank you Lieutenant. The communications office saluted and headed back to his post with Robert heading in an altered direction towards the command structure, arriving a few moments later, "Admiral we may be in more trouble. One of our picket ships has reported a scout ship approaching from out of system, and I suspect it isn't one of ours. We haven't sent one of ours out any further than the moons. And most are here on the ground with us."

"Damn! We aren't ready." Both of them heard the sound barrier being broken as something approached at supersonic speed. Shocked both of them ran out of the tent to look up, hearing the alert as everyone on the ground ran to their assigned stations. If this was the same ship maybe they could eliminate it and leave nothing for the cap ship it belonged to find or trace. They watched as the auto cannon traced a path and began to follow the target. Suddenly a signal from the craft identified it as friendly and everybody at the temporary base sighed a sigh of relief.

Shortly it landed among the other ships that sat on the temporary landing field and the marines approached it cautiously with weapons on ready. Both the captain and admiral approached moments later with their own personal guard. From the markings on the craft they knew it was from the group that was pursing them. The door opened and a lieutenant looked out and around apparently trying to locate someone. He remained within the doorway and finally spotted whoever he was trying to locate. He looked at both the captain and the admiral saying, "Sirs, I'm part of your spy network within the navy. I can only stay a short time, but will need some fuel before I lift off once again. So when I – we return to our ship the fuel consumption will match our search parameters.

"I suspect it won't be long before you are located. The group is in this sector of space with the caps holding somewhere towards the center. There is a massive search trying to find your ion trails. Apparently whatever you did to lose them worked. Still from what we have learned there is a possibility that one of the searching teams may have found part of that trail and is on the way here presently. In fact I probably passed them on the way here, and another reason to leave as soon as I have the fuel."

"Thank you Lieutenant." Captain Heraldson stated. He turned to the CPO and said, "Let's get what he needs so he can be on his way chief."

"Yes sir."

Turning back to the admiral and keeping the lieutenant within the conversation. "Well, you've always stated that Admiral Williams was good, and it is good we still have a few spies among his ships." He faced the lieutenant directly and asked, "How long do you think it will take you to get back to your search area, and how close is the searchers to this system?"

Scuttlebutt says they are heading towards this system right now. I wasn't sure if I could beat them here or not. And it would have been a little awkward to be found here when we're supposed to be searching another area."

The captain could see that the sailors were topping off the scout's tanks. He stood there in silence until it was done, signaled the lieutenant and all of them backed up so the scout ship could leave. He gave the lieutenant a precise salute, saw it returned, watched as the hatch closed, and heard the engines start and the scout ship lift off and disappear into the atmosphere. The two returned to the command prefab and head into the temporary office of the admiral. "Well Bob, we both knew that our escape wasn't clean and eventually George would find us. I really hoped we had more time. Guess we better get the general in here. He's going to have to find us that area to dig in. And I suspect you're going to have to send out a couple of the scout ships and begin some aerial surveying. If what he said is accurate we are close to out of time and we both know it's going to take time to dig in.

"So I guess the minimal impact I wanted to have on this population has just gone out the window so to speak. By keeping us isolated inside our barrier and minimizing our impact outside to just the patrols, in the end we would become some mythological gods to these people, which is fine. Now we are going to have to reveal more. I guess in the long run it doesn't matter. After all we've violated a lot of laws and regs. Adding one more isn't going to change things a whole lot."

"True. I'll go find Arthur and we can get right on it." Robert headed immediately out the tent and went over to where the marines had set up their command area. As he approached he could see the general standing outside talking with the colonel. Looking directly at him General Pertion said, "Expected you. Once we heard the boom we knew something was approaching and was hoping it wasn't our enemy. Apparently it wasn't since we didn't shoot it down."

"No, but what he came here to tell us isn't good news by any means. The admiral wants the three of us to get together, and I guess if you want you can add the colonel that's fine. I suspect what was told us is already around camp anyway . . . Can't keep bad news from being learned instantly."

"True. It's always been that way. The rumor mill is always faster than light, or so it seems."

* * *

Sighing Lt Smyth said, "I know this seems like it's taking forever, but we are almost there. This is where I really appreciate the tenders and the rapidity of their services."

Smiling, Jerod replied, "Yeah I know, the normal military hurry up and wait routine. You know where the general says, 'I need to troops to be in formation by 0900 tomorrow', and the colonel to be sure pushes the time back, where the lieutenant does it again and when it gets down to the sergeant the troops end up in formation at 0600." Both of the officers smiled a knowing smile, with Lt Drury saying, "Yeah, ain't it the truth."

"So", Lt Smyth asked, "where'd you learn about the 'normal routine' of hurry up and wait, anyway?"

"I wasn't always a civilian. When I became of age it seemed like the thing to do. It paid well . . . at least it seemed so when one is so young and credits don't come around often. And, of course there were the thoughts of adventure – wrong of course. So I served my time and put it behind me." He could see the knowing smiles. "Yeah I know, I went from what you guys are doing, to what I'm now doing – same thing, different department. Although, I think I have a little more freedom." Again he saw the grins getting larger. "Okay, maybe it's all an illusion. I know I'm told what my assignments will be, and there's a chain of command even if I never personally have to see it. Still when I'm on one of the assignments I'm normally by myself, which means I'm in charge of me, not some paper pusher who never has been in the field or has a clue of what it's really like in the real world."

Phil shook his head. "Yeah, I guess if we want to be honest no matter where one is there's always someone above us pulling our puppet strings. I know friends who have never been in the military, and have their own businesses. They state, proudly of course, that they are their own bosses and they answer to no one. Well, I for one don't want to pop their bubble, but yes they do answer to someone. For their businesses to succeed they have to listen to the customers, and whether they want to admit it or not their employees. Even elected officials are supposedly accountable to the voters – although I'll not touch that one at all."

"Good call!" Exclaimed Peter, "I know they, and of course, the citizens are our bosses, still I wouldn't touch most of them – the politicians that is . . . Might get poisoned." Both looked down at the ongoing operation and the instrument suite that kept them up to date. Peter looked at Phil saying, "Looks like we can wrap this up. Let's get the bots back into storage so we can continue."

As they began the recovery operation once again they were struck by a similar series of waves. "Hey", Jerod exclaimed, "we're in a vacuum here. How can it be that we keep feeling these things?"

Phil shrugged. "You got me there. Still space is a fabric and is subject to warping, bending, and I guess if we consider black holes, tearing. Still, this could be the result of a star's collapse millions of years in the past and it has just reached here. As far as I know nobody has been near one when it has gone nova, and if they were they didn't live long enough to let anybody know. I know when the last series struck us I said the same thing, still it's the most logical answer, not that logic in space has anything to do with it. There's still so much we don't know, and somewhere in time our species will die out and go extinct, just like the universe. Oh we hope that we will go on forever, but the odds are really against that.

"After all, the ones who research those dead civilizations that have been found throughout the galaxy pretty much show us our future. From what has been learned there has been a large number of civilizations that became space faring and spread out across the universe only to be gone today, leaving their ruins and the mystery as to why. Yeah, I know that we are trying to learn why so we can avoid the same fate, but can we? After all atrophy is everywhere one looks. Stars are born, then die. And so it is with many of the intelligent life forms that exist. And while there's many a time I don't consider us intelligent because of the really stupid things we do, we are out here and living in many different solar systems and are a space faring race ourselves."

"So", Jerod asked, "where'd you get to be such an expert on archeology?"

Here he laughed. "Oh we all have our hobbies. And no I've never had the time to be part of an actual dig team, but have read much on the subject and during some of my leaves have visited a few of the excavated sites. I have to admit it's interesting what's out here." He looked around, checked the instruments one more time, confirmed that everything was back where it belonged and stated, "Looks like it's time. Shall we continue?"

Smiling Jerod said, "It's about time. And maybe we can figure out what those things were once we have the sensor suite back up and operating at full power."

* * *

Little One: "Wow! Did all of this happen to you? And not only that but all of this other stuff?"

GGF: Smiling he replied, "Yes. I know when you see me today you'd think that all I do is walk the farm now and then, and sleep a lot. But you have to think about how long I've been here, and how over time one begins to wear out. Shall we continue?"

Little One: "Yes please!" This was the third day of the stories and when he had first sat down he never had envisioned any of this. It couldn't be real – could it?

* * *

TimOtee continued to stare across the table. He had some serious thinking to do – not that he hadn't been doing it anyway. With everything that had happened and his original plans to head for the coast he wondered if he should abandon those plans. He still wanted to work around to the south side of the barrier and see if there could be a weak point. Again he didn't know if it would be a waste of time or not. Then there was CaraOlyn sitting there across from him and he had to admit he was drawn to her. It was the only reason he could think of for returning to this particular farm other than it would provide him some additional shelter. Still he wanted to see her safely back to her own farm, but wasn't sure if it was safe yet. Yes the ones who had taken over the farm had attacked the strangers, or gods, or whoever or whatever they were, and had lost badly.

Taking a deep and slow breath he let it out and said, "Look, I haven't had the chance to see or recon the area where the fight took place last night and I want to do that. I might be able to learn something about the strangers, and possibly if there are any survivors."

She leaned forward interested in what he was saying, and at the same time not wanting to admit to herself that this one sitting across from her was becoming more and more attractive to her all the time. She wanted to say it was just the situation they were in that was causing this, but she knew in her mind it wasn't so. "Why do you want to do that? Isn't that placing you in danger?"

He shrugged and asked, "Why should you care? I know that question seems callous, but so far it seems to be the way of it. I mean you are from a higher caste than I am and generally that means you would have no interest or even a desire to look my way. And it has only been circumstance that has placed us together. And I'm sure once this is over we probably will never see each other again. This is partially because I live further east – much further really and rarely travel this way. So it would seem unlikely for anything to come out of this."

She didn't know why but he could always anger her. Still she had to admit it was a valid question, and with what he said after the question made even more sense. "Look, I care because you've helped me, and actually protected me when you didn't have to, okay? And yes when you first got here I acted really badly, and for that I apologize. I just fear that what you have proposed will lead to some harm for you that's all. Am I allowed that sentiment?"

He tipped his head to the side saying, "I guess so. One of the reasons for telling you this is that I would like you to stay here where it seems to be safe. I want to look, to search the area out to learn what the results of the fight were. Then I can make a decision as to what to do next. Look, I still feel that these strangers could be gods. After all, how could they throw fire like they did, or point at someone and kill them from such a distance, and at night? Like the last time I witnessed the mountain clan attacking the fight seemed one-sided. The attackers used bows, short knives, clubs, and such yet in the end it was them that suffered, and as far as I could tell not one of the strangers were killed, let alone hurt.

"It was full on dark making it easier for the attackers. Yes the strangers had their light or lights, however they did that, but the lights only covered what they wanted them to and left much of the area in shadows and darkness. It seemed to me with the accuracy of the return fire, again however they did it, that it might as well been the zenith with a day of sunlight and no clouds. And how did they move the barrier? I know we have no idea how it came to be in the first place, but this is the first time I've seen it shifted. And the strangers only took the one night to make the changes. I have to admit I'm at a loss to explain any of this. So, if you please, let me do this so I can possibly understand more of what's going on.

"I know that you aren't required to do anything I ask. After all, we only met a short time ago and you are your own person as much as I'm my own. Still I feel by you remaining here I only have to worry about myself, and know that if I see anybody moving out there that there's a good chance they are either the strangers, or possibly the raiders who took over your farm. Will you stay?"

"Yeah, I guess so. Still, how long should I wait? If you are injured or killed I won't know."

"I don't know . . . a reasonable time I guess."

"Okay, smarty, what's a reasonable time? For me it would be different than what you would consider it."

"True. Okay, let's say a reasonable time would be the sun beginning to set. If I haven't returned by then, I guess you can consider me gone. Whether I have been killed, or have made a decision to move on. Is that fair?"

She looked down at the floor. She wasn't sure if she wanted to agree or not. So far this place had been safe. Well, more or less safe since TimOtee had shown up. And if he had been one of the raiders then she would have paid a heavy price. "I guess that works for me. Still I will leave it open since this whole thing happening around us is fluid and subject to change at a moment's notice."

He pushed back from the table before commenting. "Thank you. Time's a wasting, and I need to be about it so I can be back by our agreed time."

TimOtee pushed outside and stood by the doorway. He really wasn't sure how to approach this. After all everything that had happened recently was in the nighttime. And things, areas, locations, and such always looked different in the dark. Still he had a rough idea since the attackers had come from the northwest, more or less; coming from the farm they had taken. As far as where to begin, maybe he should head in the direction of the barrier which was now further in the distance. Still it was visible. And if one hadn't been around last night to witness all that had transpired then nothing would seem different. All would seem normal, well as normal is it could be with these strangers and their unknown abilities.

The air was still, crisp, and there was a slight smell of the burning of the grasses and brush in the area. But now it was an old smell saying the fire had been in the past and had nothing to do with now. Unfortunately there also seemed to be a slight acrid smell mixed with the sweetness of the burning smell speaking of death to other than just the vegetation. He remembered watching one of the great wildfires move through the grasslands and foothills. Fortunately the fire had remained away from the farms in the valley. Still it was an awesome sight to witness. He had gone to where the fire had burned and was surprised at how far away it actually had been. The smoke made it appear so much closer – especially when it had momentarily blocked out the sun, changing its light to an orange-reddish hue. And when the winds shifted, from the skies, it rained ash just like the normal rain.

There was a slight breeze adding chill to the air making him shiver briefly. He, with a decision made, headed towards the barrier. He decided that before trekking off in the direction where her farm lay he would see what the ground looked like where the barrier had stood before. He didn't know if it was important, or whether there would be anything there to mark where it stood. He only knew that the only way to find out was to go there in person, in the light of day, and see. As he headed in that direction he heard his footstep crunch on the gravel that made the pathway up to this small farm. It seemed like he was alerting the whole world that here he was. Still there wasn't much he could do about it. It wouldn't be until he was down to the main trail through the area that he'd be away from the rock. Yeah he could have gone through the fields or stayed off the beaten path, but there had been dew the previous evening and everything was wet because of it. And at this very moment it was the last thing he wanted to do was get his clothes wet.

Eventually he reached the main trail, and here he could begin to see the destruction that had happened last night. There were great swaths of burned vegetation, followed by many areas where the grass had been trampled flat. It was obvious that he was now standing on the edge of where the battle took place. Taking a deep cleansing breath he steeled himself up for what he knew he would find out there among the burned and flattened grasses. Still it was why he was here. So he carefully headed into the area and began a careful search. Careful for two reasons; first because he didn't know how many bodies were here, and secondly because the bandits or whoever they were could still be here hiding. And one thing for sure he wasn't here to become another victim. As he stared at the scene before him he thought. *What could do this? I mean, yeah one could start a fire and get the same results, but not as damp as it was last night. If I had tried to light the grasses off the fire was sputter, and creep, but eventually it would die. Yet, here it looks like someone was burning a field after the harvest when the chaff left is dry and burns easily.*

He stood in the middle of one of the burned out areas and just stared. This fire had been hot. Everything was burned down to a white to gray ash that was powdery. Even with the dew everywhere he stepped it raised a small cloud of ash. *They, these strangers must be gods. How else can one explain this . . . this destruction, this damage?* He shook his head as he tried to understand the power and energy expended here. As he thought back he considered those loud, noisy, and stinking beasts the strangers were controlling. He had to admit once again he had never seen their like. As he continued to study the surrounding area he could hear nothing. Even the breezes seemed to have stopped. Looking around he could see no movement. At this moment in time he could be the only one still here. These thoughts sent chills up and down his spine.

Eventually he began his search, and as the day warmed and he searched deeper in this area he found twenty bodies, and areas where some had dragged themselves away from the area. Still even these few he felt probably hadn't survived because of the amount of blood in the trails they left. Looking back towards the barrier where he thought he remembered seeing the strangers defending the area he wondered if he would find a body there. If what he had witnessed in the past held true here, and he suspected there was no reason that it shouldn't, there would be none. And after working through the whole area he found he was right. The only ones he had found had been the attackers. This brought a thought to the foreground. It seemed that these strangers left them alone unless the strangers were attacked. It left him wondering what had happened to everyone who had been trapped behind the barriers. Well, one thing for sure, as long as he was on this side he would never know.

CHAPTER NINE

SCIENCE? DON'T UNDERSTAND IT, I JUST USE IT

"You know I really never understood the science behind these drives. I know it was through a chance discovery within the physics department somewhere many centuries in the past that the understanding came about that allowed FTL flight. I know from what little any layman can understand that the big problem had been the creation of a unified theory that could account for the differences between the very big – you know the great one Einstein had put forth, with help later from theories from Hawking and others. Still, nobody could reconcile the difference from the quantum and its weird world in the very small, to what we understood about the very large." Lt Smyth shrugged as he continued, more or less talking to

Jerod. "Anyway, the unified theory just wouldn't work, and anything that was postulated or put forth in the end failed.

"These physicists are so far above me and as far as the math – well forget that – I know enough to get myself in trouble. Oh don't get me wrong we all have to be able to navigate in three dimensions otherwise space travel wouldn't be possible. But it was that accidental discovery that there was an intermediate between the very small, and very large, and it was this that was the final piece of the huge puzzle. Once they had this part it wasn't long that a provable theory emerged and a revolution in space travel followed. Somehow – and again I only can operate these systems, not understand them – we travel between the world as we understand it, and the quantum world where nothing makes sense. And while there in this 'in-between', we are able to tap into both worlds – ours and the quantum. This makes one of the more important functions of the quantum world available to us – entanglement. It was thought that somewhere this known fact could be used for communications across space. But so far no one has discovered how to take advantage. I'm sure someday it will happen, and then all of this delays we face when communicating across the vast distances will be gone.

"One of the neat things about this trick we use, and I use the word, not the ones who developed this stuff, are that we are able to remain in real time avoiding the penalties predicted by Einstein when dealing with the fabric of space-time. So time remains relative and moves in a normal fashion. Without this we truly wouldn't be able to go through space at all. The time shifts would be too great." He turned to Lt Drury, "Ready to get us back on schedule?"

"Yup. Let's do this. I don't mind the break, but after only a short time with nothing to do other than monitor the equipment, time just drags and I get cabin fever."

Jerod heard and felt the vibrations from the engines as they eased away from the debris field and prepared for the jump into FTL flight. The instant they did he heard both Philip and Peter say in unison, "Where did that come from?"

He stood up curious and approached the tight confines of the command and piloting area and looked over Lt Smyth's shoulders. And there on the sensors sat two strong ion trails. "I thought we didn't have anything but a tenuous trail, what happened?"

Turning around and facing Jerod Lt Smyth said, "Really don't know, but we did feel those, well what we figured had to be gravity waves. Obviously, as we discussed it back when we felt them, they were caused by a ship passing us by. Hmmm, that's interesting."

"Now what could be so interesting?" Jerod asked.

The two lieutenants looked at each other and then back at Jerod with Lt Smyth stating, "The signatures we are reading here are from one of our own scout ships. No not one of the ones the rogues are using but one from our own fleet. Every one of our ships have a special signature attached to the drive – top secret stuff – and even the engineers on our ships have no way of modifying it, and these signatures are tied to particular groups. It makes it easier to be able to trace a group and for the rest of the fleet to know who is where and I guess who it really is. The ones we are pursuing have their own, and that tenuous trail I or we have been following has their signature." Shaking his head, before answering the question that none of them had asked, he said. "That means we have a spy among us and from these trails they have gone to where the rogues are hiding and alerted them, then returned to wherever they were, probably covering their tracks well.

"If we hadn't been among this debris field, and powered down, they would have found us, which would have been a bad thing. It would mean first off we would be curious, but not curious enough to have considered them an enemy. They would probably have some story already available if they encountered another, and because of the fact that most of us who are searching are doing it in a single ship, well we could just disappear – another victim of space. And with the vastness, even with a search we probably would never be found. In a sense I'm glad whoever it was seemed to be in a hurry, and probably kept their sensors passive, otherwise we probably wouldn't be here to follow the trail they left. Now I'm not sure what to do."

Jerod had a questioning look, "What do you mean, what to do? Are we not going to follow this in?"

"Yeah, we are. But now that we know we have some spies within our group, do I send a message capsule informing the admiral of our discovery? If you think about it by knowing what we now know one would think our group should be alerted. Yet, we honestly don't know how many there may be involved with this. So if we send back the message are we going to inform the ones, the spies that we are on to them and put them on alert?"

"Yeah", Jerod replied, "That's a good question. But in a sense with me here you've informed others. Still, I'm not really a part of the navy, and have no real influence here. You know my mission and your involvement in it. It does make one wonder how far the infiltration has gotten, and it makes me wonder if it could be as deep as my department. Thinking this way can really make one paranoid."

This brought out some bitter laughter from Philip and Peter, with Peter stating, "Ah, welcome to our world."

* * *

"Looks like we're going to need to get a survey ship into the air anyway", Admiral Sympson stated. "We are flat out of time, and we need to move this operation into the mountains ASAP. General, I guess we are going to have to push out more of your patrols into those mountains and subdue the natives wherever and whenever they want to try to take us out. Meanwhile, we will be stripping this camp down to the minimum and sending the merchant ships – the freighters back into space to tie in with our cruiser and its escorts, which are still using some of the moons as shielding. Unfortunately the approaching scout ship will be running into our emissions shortly and at the point it will become obvious we are here."

Admiral Sympson turned to his flag captain, stating. "I guess we may need to lay another series of false trails in case we aren't successful in digging in like we planned. Also we will need contingency plans in case we have to leave. Hopefully, if that comes about we will be better organized this time. In fact it might be a good idea to send most of what we have orbiting this planet out to a rendezvous point – somewhere unexpected. That way if we are caught with our pants down, so to speak, we can scatter and meet up later." It was silent for a few moments as the other officers in the room could tell the admiral was deep in thought. Then a smile came to him. "Okay, where's the very last place they would expect us? . . . This, of course, if we have to run." Looking over the ones before him he could tell they really didn't know. "Okay, I have two thoughts on this. First we easily could return to our original base of operations. I'm sure there would be a few ships of the fleet guarding the area, plus some ground forces, but that's probably all. If we could head back in stealthed there's a chance we could grab what we had to leave behind.

"While I don't have the complete plan in my head I think a misdirection to draw off the guarding ships followed by a landing coming from the dark side of the moon, followed by a quick grab and snatch. From there we could easily head for one of our other bases. Possibly the one that's located in that red giant's solar system that has mostly rock floating around in orbit with a single gas giant. Complete inhospitable and perfect."

General Pertion shook his head and smiled. "I guess nobody could ever say you didn't have brass ones. That would be the last place I would go."

"Yes, and thusly why it would be the last place they would expect us. But that's for the future. We still have a chance to be successful here – especially if we can dig in. And with those false trails you will be laying, captain, it should lead to a minimum search here. For one thing they will not want to land and do a close search or influence the ones on this planet. After all, it is against our laws to do this. So if they find a number of trails leading away I'm of the opinion that it will be enough. Okay, any questions?" With none coming he continued. "Okay then we all have a lot of work ahead of us and no time. Captain, stay if you would, I need to go over a couple of things with you.

General you and the colonel have your hands full with these mountain clans. The ones we have in stasis here were simple farmers. I don't know why those mountain clans don't attack the farmlands in the valley but they don't.

"At least when we leave this area the ones we've put under will awaken and have no real memory of what has happened to them. Unfortunately we can't say the same in those mountains. Still if we are successful we will only be myth to any of these who call this planet home." He watched as the rest withdrew and turned to Bob. "Their job is really difficult, but right now yours or ours isn't any easier. The chief has been pushing his crew hard and I know he hasn't been getting much sleep. Still with this latest update none of us will. You need to find your best pilots for laying our false trails. Somehow we've got to make it look like all of us left and then tried to hide our signature. Then at the same time we've got to find what we need yesterday. We only have so much equipment, and very few pilots.

"To add to all of this the general will have to send out all of his marines on those necessary patrols leaving the barrier area to us. With the hasty setup we had to do, and the fact we've had to keep our emission strength down, there's bound to be weak spots in the field – there has to be. Yes, I know once the natives found out that the field is lethal they've stayed well away from it. But I'm sure there are some who escaped the area we've enclosed that are probably trying to find a way back in. I know I would, so I wouldn't expect less from another. In fact as we move our ships out especially our freighters it will shrink the area that we need to protect. So like the operation we did the other night we will need to pull back the barrier, shrink the size and cover less area so we can continue to use solar power instead of bring the generators on line.

"So while you are involved with these projects I've got to put together our action plans for just about an infinite series of scenarios. I really don't think any of us will be getting any sleep soon." He sighed, and took a deep breath while shaking his head. "So Bob how did we get ourselves into this mess in the first place?"

"Good question Arthur. I guess none of us started out with the idea of becoming pirates, rogues or whatever. Still here we are and there's no going back now."

"True, true. Still . . . yeah I know if we knew then what we know now. Okay I guess I'd better let you get at it. Nothing will get done if we stay here and yap."

* * *

"Yeah, the ion trails are fresh and strong." Lt Smyth shrugged. He had to admit this was the last thing he expected. To find there were conspirators inside the command he was a part of was a complete surprise. Still whoever took this chance had to feel it was critical for the traitors or defectors, or pirates, or rouges, or whatever one wanted to call them, to learn how close the pursuit had gotten. Unfortunately there wasn't any way to identify the ship that had warned them, only that it was part of their group.

Neither of the other two said anything. In the virtual world they were traveling the matter that existed in the real universe was simply represented by images created on a screen. In truth there was no windshield like had been used in the past by atmospheric fighters and bombers. There was no need, and it eliminated a weakness in the structure. Instead there was a screen that substituted allowing the pilots an electronic view of what surrounded them. It went back to the wet navy days and submarines. It was learned there because of the pressures sustained that such luxuries could lead to disaster. And while spaceflight didn't involve those pressures it was the opposite problem – keeping the atmosphere and pressure inside.

Without atmosphere the vacuum of space could be just as deadly as deep water dives. There had been a number of failures to systems over time where the subs were destroyed. Death for the sailors most of the time was instant. Others were not so lucky and died a slow death as rescue attempts failed. In space if such a failure happened, unless the occupants had been suited up at the time, or they happened to be in a section that still maintained atmosphere, death also came quickly. And because of this all military space vehicles had solid hulls, and like the old sub, bulkheads, and sections that could be sealed. Still the scout ships were too small, and if breeched, there was only the safety of the suits.

"We will approaching the system shortly so I think we better drop out of hyper, go stealth and see what we can find. You concur Peter?"

"Yes, by all means. Coming in this like this we'll be announcing to anybody who's listening here we are." He looked over to one of the sensor groups paused, studied them for a moment. He then rotated his seat around. "Phil, look at this. I think if I remember right that the sentient species that was found here was quite primitive. Back to a time of animals providing the work, no electricity, or modern conveniences of any kind, yet what I'm picking up seems quite modern."

Phil switched one of the monitors and stared. "Yeah, I think you're right." Lt Smyth rotated completely around and faced Jerod saying, "I think we have proof that our birds have landed."

Jerod came forward and looked at the monitor that Philip had pointed to. And there before his eyes was a number of signatures that could only be attributed to an advanced culture. Nothing in the surveys stating such existed. "Unless they've advanced in a real hurry, I would think you are right. So what does that mean for you?"

Shaking his head, Philip replied. "Not good. We are looking at one of our best, which means he'll have ships out and hidden. Making it almost impossible for us to see them until it would be too late." He was quiet for a few minutes as he thought about what faced them. "Okay, we can be pretty sure they are here. Now we will have to withdraw and send a message to the fleet. Unfortunately they aren't close, and looking at the time it will take for the message to reach them, and then to get the fleet moving we are probably looking at too many hours. Plus we can't go down there, and must remain at such a distance as to not influence the natives. At least any worse than they are being influenced presently."

Once again he turned to Jerod. "I guess we are going to need your services. Now the only problem will be how to get you down there without being discovered."

"Yes, that would be good – not being discovered that is. Look I need as much visual and sensor data we can collect on the population as you can get. After all I've got to become them. I know from the initial surveys they aren't much different than we are. Bipedal, with two arms, one head – I suspect if one was aboard our ship and in our clothing, other than being shorter, we wouldn't look twice. At least that part makes it easier. Now I have to have samples of language, culture and such so I don't stand out too much.

"Once that's accomplished, then it's on to determining where to set down, followed by who I will contact once there. I guess while your work of finding them is complete, mine is just beginning." He turned back to a pack he had been carrying, dug through it and came up with a micro-device that neither lieutenant had ever seen. "I can tell you aren't familiar with this, and most likely this will be the only time you will see it – no it's not classified, but it is very expensive, and only agents carry them. It will assist me on my transformation to be one of the natives. This will hook into your sensor array and record what I need, then transfer everything to my onboard system, so I can integrate it within myself. After all we don't have years for me to gain an understanding of this world and the way it works."

Smiling Philip replied, "Guess that makes sense. And we really don't have lots of time."

Shaking his head Jerod said, "No we don't. And while on that subject here is the second part of this. This will allow communications between your scout ship and me. And the best thing about this is that no one can intercept it, or break the encryption. The encryption changes by the nanosecond so if one routine is broken, by the time they get around to using it, it will be useless. Of course you need to be close enough to get the signal. After all it's only at the speed of light so is kind of slow. And . . . this means you will eventually need to find a place to hide, become a hole in space that is close enough to get the signal. I know that puts you in danger, but there's no way around it. Also this piggybacks on another signal that will be sent to the fleet where everything that is sent, and everything I see, witness, and do will be recorded for a later review." Here he smiled. "Can't get away from 'big brother', that's for sure."

Lt Drury had a questioning frown on his face, "Big brother? Never heard that before . . ."

Jerod laughed, "Just an old reference. Kind of an inside joke between us agents I guess. Look you'd need to go deep into our past at a time where we were beginning to leave our surface. It is a reference from a book written during that time warning what the future might become, that's all."

* * *

TimOtee could feel the day warming further. It would be after the zenith before it reached its peak, but from the growling of his stomach it must be close to the zenith anyway. He reached into his pack and pulled out some jerky and his water container, found a rock to sit on and began to naw on the tough dried meat. The breezes that were blowing seemed gentle with gusts making the leaves in the trees rustle loudly adding to the peacefulness of the area. It almost hid the fact that there had been a life and death struggle here the night before. And as his mind drifted he began, once again, to wonder about these strangers – were they gods or not? He had no answers only what he had witnessed so far.

If they are gods then they would ignore us – I think. And I guess, if what I've witnessed is correct, then they have. They have unless we attack them. Then these strangers, with little effort, eliminate the ones attacking. They seem to control strange beasts, ones I've never seen, and the power they control is so far beyond me, I just don't know – I really don't. From the strangers' reactions they could easily be, but maybe they were from somewhere else here on this world and just knew how to do these magic things. Well, one thing for sure he was simply going in circles and coming up with nothing new, or finding any answers to his many questions.

He looked back in the direction of the small farmhouse which couldn't be seen from here and thought about going back and letting CaraOlyn know what he had found. But at the moment realized he hadn't done everything he had said he would. He got up and headed back to the main trail and went in the direction of the village and of course the farm she was from. It took a while but finally he was back to the point where he had watched the raiders or whoever they were working over her farm. It seemed to be abandoned as the whole area appeared to be. He couldn't be sure since the ones who were there could be hiding. After all they took quite a beating last night, and not many of them, if any, left the area of the attack. Unfortunately the trail up to the house was open and there would be no way to hide if any were still there.

He paused undecided really not sure if he wanted to expose himself that way. Finally after studying the farm for a while and finding no movement he quietly made his way expecting at any moment to be both under observation and then attacked. He could feel the short hairs rising, running chills down his spine. He felt like he was being watched, but saw no evidence of it. As he came closer he veered to the left and headed for one of the barns. Once he reached it, and still went unchallenged, he opened the large doors, letting light in, and immediately wished he hadn't. It was like a slaughter house. It was obvious that not all the villagers had escaped or evacuated the village. There were a number of bodies here, and it was obvious many of them had died a cruel death. Add to the carnage were a number of females, naked and obviously raped before they were killed. The stench was overwhelming and it made him gag. He could feel his stomach become more unsettled and he quickly stepped outside and threw up.

If he had felt sorry for the outlaws that had attacked the strangers and died, he no longer felt that way. In fact he now felt the outlaws had died too easily. They deserved much worse. He left the doors open so the space could air out and headed for the main house. He circled around to the backside and entered through the backdoor, trying to be as quiet as possible. With his anger rising from what he discovered he almost hoped there would be a couple of the outlaws here so he could kill them himself. But the house was quiet – seemed empty. As he looked around and began his search of the ground floor he could see the chaos and mess the outlaws had left. Much of what was here had been ransacked, and destroyed. There was trash and debris everywhere making it hard to move around and remain quiet.

Nothing – and nobody on the ground floor . . . Time to move to the second floor, up the stairs, and then into the individual rooms which all had doors. It was obvious to him that this farm wasprosperous. Everything about this home spoke of quality, although it wasn't as obvious with the damage done. As he made his way up the stairs they creaked, which caused him to lighten his steps. He slowly shifted weight from one step to the next until he was at the top with an open hallway with a railing overlooking the lower floor. He first went to the left, to the first of five doors, and quietly opened the door a crack, peering in and seeing nothing. He opened it wide enough so he could slide in sideways and did a quick look around. It seemed to be a bedroom, and a rather large one. He suspected it probably had been the master and mistress's room with all that had been here. But like the lower floor it too had been ransacked. Looking at the rather large bed he found the blankets and such had been thrown back and it was obvious that this was where some of the rapes had taken place. Plus there was a large amount of dried blood staining the bed and all the blankets. And not only had some of the rapes happened here, but obviously some of the torture also. Again it made him sick to think people could do this to others.

He now wondered what he would tell CaraOlyn who waited back at the other farm. It was tough enough for him. He didn't know how it would affect a female. And if there was a way to keep her from seeing this he would, but knew she'd want to come right back when she learned the outlaws, or raiders, or whoever they were, weren't here anymore. It was then he heard some moaning. Like a creature in deep pain, and barely aware. He listened but whomever or whatever had made the sound was now quiet. He carefully worked his way down the hallway checking the rooms as he went. The next three were vacant and showed the same abuse happening in them that he discovered in the first room. One of them wasn't even a bedroom but a large storage room. It didn't seem to matter to the ones who did this. A room was a room.

He was finally at the last doorway and thought he could hear what sounded like some slight movement. Maybe this was where the sounds had originated. He carefully opened the door and looked inside and again almost wished he hadn't. This turned out to be a bedroom also, and on the bed was a naked female covered in her own blood, and while alive she wasn't too far from death. Again it was obvious she had been raped, and then worked over with a blade in such a way to cause as much pain as possible, and allow her to live though it as long as possible. From the amount of blood around her he didn't know if she could be saved. Quietly he approached the bed and looked down at the female. The first thing that struck him was the fact she was young – much too young for this to happen.

He felt helpless. She had far too many wounds, with many still bleeding. He knew if he didn't do something, and do something now she had no chance. He reached down and placed his hand on her forehead and her eyes which had been closed suddenly flew open with fear showing plainly. She began to try and speak screaming weakly, "No, no, don't touch me!"

He tried to quiet her, to let her know that he was here to help, but she was too far gone in her fear, her pain, and misery to understand. He realized at that moment he would have to hurry back and bring CaraOlyn here anyway. It would take the two of them for this. And even with the two of them there still was a good chance she wouldn't survive. He covered her, and quickly backtracked and headed back to where CaraOlyn was, cursing that he had delayed so long to scout out the farm. Maybe if he had found this female earlier there would be a better chance of her recovering. Now any delay in treatment reduced her chances.

* * *

CaraOlyn was frantic. She thought about that day the barrier showed up and all the chaos and fear it had caused. Then came the time because of the confusion she had become separated from her family, and the ones who worked for her father – followed by her delaying her attempt to find them. Everyone seemed panicked by what was transpiring, and even though she had given it a half-hearted attempt she had made the decision to wait until things settled a bit before trying again. She realized at that moment the family had never made any plans for any emergency that might arise. It meant that if the worst happened, and it seemed to have happened, nobody would know what to do, where to meet, or what they should take.

Until this crisis, for her, and she was sure for her siblings, life had been safe and protected. Yeah they had to learn the responsibilities dealing with the operation of their farm, and the small emergencies that always happen in the day-to-day dealings and workings of such a place. That delay, those decisions had left her alone. Alone and scared to be honest, but then this TimOtee showed up, and for a short period of time her fear had deepened. What were the intentions of this one? Could she remain hidden? And if not, could she defend herself and her honor? And was he one of the ones who had taken over her farm?

Then came that confrontation in the bedroom where she tried to talk her way out of a really bad situation only to lose. This was followed by the struggle where she knew he could have taken anything he wanted from her, but didn't.

This still left her with fear, but he seemed honorable. At least, and if the story he related to her of his past, he was trying to come to some successful conclusion caused by the same strangers, and that wall or barrier. Then came last night. She thought she had been scared before, but this was the first time she had been around this much violence. And when TimOtee led her out – of course it was at her insistence – she was shocked, or at least this was how she remembered the events of last night. Yet he handled it well. She had to admit it seemed like he handled most of the situations he'd been in well. *Who is he? He can't be just a farmer like we are. The way he moves, the way he studies what is happening – making it look like he plans every move, every change of direction. How he tries to take everything into consideration, and into those plans. And even though I've treated him badly he remained considerate to me and my needs.*

The chaos, the confusion, the bright lights in the darkness, the screams of those wounded and killed, the stench, it was too much. She had found herself shaking from fear. Yet when she watched TimOtee he seemed calm, almost separated from what was happening around them. Then came the time when he told her to return to the safety of the small farm she had been staying at – well she almost panicked again, and almost went with him anyway. Yet, she realized that it would be stupid. The things he said made sense. With only him he didn't have to worry about any others. So with reluctance she returned here, and with a large dose of nervousness watched until somewhere during this time she fell asleep only to awaken and see TimOtee sitting across from her. Again, she realized that she had let her guard down. Once again if he had wanted to take advantage of her he could have, let alone any of the bad ones who were in the area. Yet, he remained as he was, still respectful – well in a way – after all she hadn't been to him and he had thrown that back in her face as he should have.

She found she was pacing back and forth in the front half of the house. She was at a loss, and couldn't make a decision whether to leave or stay. Sure TimOtee said to stay. And he also said there was a possibility he wouldn't or couldn't return. He had been gone for what seemed forever. Still that probably wasn't the truth. With nothing happening time dragged and dragged. She knew this from the many times she had looked out the windows to see where the sun was in the sky finding it had barely moved. Still her stomach said it had to be close to the zenith or maybe past it for all she knew. She went back to the table and ate some of the jerky he had left for her, followed by water to wash it down. One thing for sure eating this kind of food required good teeth and lots of water.

With the stress she had been under she found that she was having trouble keeping her eyes open, and before she realized it once again she was asleep at the table. Next thing she knew was TimOtee standing at the table once again. As she came fully awake she realized that he seemed agitated. Letting out a slow breath she asked, "What's going on, and what did you find?"

He was silent for a moment not sure how to answer, but knew if they were going to save the one female they had to move. "Look, your farm is vacant . . ."

Elation! "Vacant! You mean I can go back."

He hung his head and once again paused before speaking. "Look, I have to warn you that the outlaws, the raiders, or whoever they were, were really nasty. It's obvious that they captured a number of the villagers and hauled them back to your farm."

"They did?"

"Yes, and that's not the bad part."

She could feel alarm rising inside. "What . . . what do you mean?"

"Let's just say they had their way with them, followed by torturing and murdering them. Your barn is a slaughterhouse, and your home is pretty much destroyed. I found one living victim in one of the upstairs rooms, but she is in very bad shape. We need to go back there and see if we can save her." Again he paused. "Look I just need to warn you that what I saw is horrible okay?" He watched her reaction and could tell she wasn't sure. Still it was obvious she would go with him. He turned and headed out the doorway waiting for her and together with her trailing him they headed back to her family's farmhouse.

* * *

The scout ship dropped out of hyper and drifted inwards from the solar system's plane. The light, and radiation they were receiving was weeks old, but it revealed much. In a way they were able to see the history of what had been transpiring inside of this system. From their present location they sampled the emissions from the planet of interest and found nothing, no signature of modern energy usage. Visually on all the spectrums they could only pick up what could have been assigned to a primitive society. Carbon dioxide from the burning of carbon based fuels such as wood and such. Still it could easily have been the result of natural fires, volcanos and such on an uninhabited world. Looking at the surveys it pretty much confirmed what they were recording. Still it was the others they were registering that interested them the most. There were numerous signatures of ships approaching the planet and they were definitely the ones they had been chasing. Philip looking over at the other two asked, "You really don't think they went ahead and landed there do you?" It was an obvious question since their traditions and laws forbade such an act.

"If not there, where?" Lt Drury asked. "It looks like they were making a direct approach, and from what we can see it's a long way in the past, and figuring out a rough timeline it must be them. Besides, from what we can see, the surveys, our own readings, those signatures can't be coming from the ones from that planet – that world. I suspect from what we can scan that they are probably early in the Iron Age, or late in the Bronze Age, if we were to do a comparison."

Jerod looked at the two and asked, "Okay, now what? I mean if they've had this much time I suspect, and I'm sure you're already ahead of me here, they've had time to set up, and possibly began to dig in, if that's their goal."

"Yeah", Lt Smyth replied, "Most likely. Not only that but they may have had enough time to set up passive sensors that they will have stealthed so that we won't know about them until they've marked us and alerted them. Of course I suspect they are already aware simply because of what we already know. If we had been able to come up on them without warning there's a good chance we'd catch them all . . . But now, doubtful – really doubtful." Philip shifted gears and looked directly at Jerod asking, "So now what? I know once we are able to get close you're kind of in charge."

"Yes and no. Once we confirm they are they then I have to head down to the surface and finish my study so I can make contact with some of the natives. I'm hoping that it will only be one or two – so much easier that way. I know on many worlds that being a stranger is a death sentence. So as we approach I'm going to need to see as much of the surface as we can. And once we locate a large community to monitor the conversations. To blend I need to speak the local languages."

"You can learn the dialects that quickly?" Lt Drury asked.

"Yeah, crazy isn't it. We've been trained in methods that allow accelerated learning, besides the implanted enhancements necessary. Truthfully, if it came down to it, even though I've flown civilian ships all my life, I could download the necessary information and be flying this scout ship in short order. Larger ships would take a little longer but still possible." He shrugged, "It's all part of what is required to do my job – nothing more, nothing less. Anyway, we have to get close enough that I can use my lander in the unpowered mode. I have to be a rock falling from space so I won't be targeted. The ride is never fun. In fact it scares me – what is the old phrase – *shitless*, to be honest. Still it is the best chance to get down there unknown, and unseen. Pick up is by standard means, once the crisis is over.

"In a sense your job is more difficult. You have to make like a hole in space, get by any sensors they have, find the point where I can leave the ship and begin my descent, and then withdraw without being located, you know withdraw silently, and then make your way back to the command ship. Then, since you are now – well I guess I can say we are – aware of spies in the scout squadron, our part of the fleet, and probably the flag ship, somehow you have to get in and contact the right people and hope they aren't any of the ones spying for these rogues. Then convince whoever it is you are reporting to that what we've discovered exists – and I'm sure whoever they are, the spies that is, they've covered themselves well – and somehow get the fleet to move and make it appear just a change of location so as not to give away the knowledge that you know that they know that you know. Now that's a mouthful if I've ever said it. Still you know what I mean."

Both officers laughed with Lt Smyth saying, "Hey you make it sound easy. Just a walk in the park, a time away on leave when there's nothing pressing, nothing needing to be done – no more than relaxing and reliving the old days." He shook his head and leaned on the console that was in front of him. "Still this approach will be tricky, and we may have to come in unpowered once we get closer. Knowing who we are up against . . ." He paused a moment and looked up the stats on the planet. "Ah yes, it says here there's a number of moons orbiting, so I suspect he'll have ships hidden behind them and much of his passive sensors located on them facing outwards to warn them of ones like us." He sighed. "None of this is going to be easy. Still one thing for sure, and it's this: If we screw up we'll never know since we will be no more than atoms."

Lt Drury nodded in agreement. "I guess we'd better put together a capsule with all the information we have. Set it to head out when we lose signal with it, or it senses our demise, so they'll know what happened to us, as well as what we've learned. I know it won't do us any good, but at least the admiral will know – barring the fact that anything we send could be intercepted and destroyed that is."

Lt Smyth also nodded in agreement. "Actually our way in won't be such a problem. Getting back out is another problem. You see we will use an old tactic to bring us in close. During that whole time we will ride the tail of an asteroid. One we will nudge – so to speak – in the direction we need to go and hide in its shadow. To any station or ship monitoring the area it will appear to be nothing more than space debris. You know as advanced as our sensor arrays and military grade suites have become we haven't figured out how to scan through kilometers of rock and metal. The only real hole in this whole plan is the fact they might have passive sensors deeper out in the system meaning they can see behind."

Nodding, Jerod replied, "Didn't think about that, but then again that's your area of expertise not mine. Still, why not just find one big enough make a hole in it and fly from inside?"

"Hmmm, a thought for sure, but there are real dangers to doing that, and if you think about it they should be obvious. If our sensors cannot see through something like this, we won't be able to see out either. Yeah, if we had the time – which we really don't – we could rig up some of our own sensors and hardwire them back to the ship, followed by adding some maneuvering thrusters so that we could make sure we ended up where we want to, but none of the equipment is available even if we had the time. Sure back with our group there is, but it's there and we are here."

Jerod shrugged, and smiled. "Guess that's why you are here in command and I'm a passenger."

Phil turned to Peter, "Okay, at least from what we know there's plenty of flotsam around us. Let's see if we can find one that will work, maybe already moving in the direction we need to go. Actually let's wait on that. We are still too far out and it would take more time than we have to ride it in. Let's plan a small jump coming out close to that gas giant. I suspect any signature we'd create could be attributed to it. Then from there we should be able to ride the coattails of maybe a comet, so some other large object. Heck if we plan it right we might be able to drop Jerod off and continue to ride it past the planet and back out into deep space leaving them unaware that we were even in the neighborhood."

He looked over the instruments and quickly turned back to Jerod. "I suspect if this works you will only have a brief window to leave so I would put together what you need, and when I tell you, which will be well ahead of when you will need to drop, you can get aboard your ship so that we can do it in an instant." He turned back to Lt Drury and asked, "Plots set?"

"Yes sir. I'm going to bring us out on the backside of the gas giant, and then use its gravity to push us around. I'm hoping they haven't had time to set up anything out there. If they have we're dead and won't even know it."

"I hope you're right. Still with the rapidity of their evacuation from their hidden base I'm sure they didn't get everything they wanted or needed. I suspect they are spread pretty thin themselves and probably only have the approaches to the planet covered, although this is an obvious one. Still I feel we have to take a chance. Plus the fact that we need to add to what we surmise, and make sure what we have isn't fiction but is fact. As good as they are this could be another misdirection. And with all the time it's taking us to make this maneuver, they could be laughing loudly at us as they head deeper into the sector or completely out of the area."

"I didn't think of that", Lt Drury said. "And it would just like them to do just that." He made a few last calculations, setting the destination into the navigation computer, "Sir, we are ready."

Turning around to Jerod Lt Smyth asked, "Any changes, anything doesn't feel right?"

Shaking his head Jerod quietly replied, "No, I think it's probably the best we can do."

"Okay, Pete, engage, and let's hope we can do this. Otherwise we will become another statistic."

Little One: "No, I'm not going to say wow, although I thought I would. Are you sure about this? I mean, well, I'm not sure what I mean, but how can you know this stuff?"

GGF: Laughing he said, "Well, I'm glad to hear that. I was beginning to think it was your only word. Let's just say at the end you will understand. And if you don't at least you'll know how I came to learn about all this stuff that at the time I didn't know." He looked out and could see the sun was setting. "Guess it's time to call it for today. I'm sure dinner isn't far off. So I suggest you go wash up and find out if you can help."

Little One: Grabbing his papers and stuffing them inside his folder he smiled and took off running and headed inside the house yelling, "Mom do you need any help?"

CHAPTER TEN

THE PAST, A NERVOUS PRESENT, AND AN UNKNOWN FUTURE

With a whole lot of nervousness, and she had to admit to fear, she followed TimOtee up the main trail heading towards the entrance to her family's property. The day had warmed considerably and it almost seemed hot. Still the breezes, which were strong, seemed to keep it cool, but with their strength the trees and bushes swayed and moved creating a lot of sound. So much so that it could cover the approach of any of the bad ones that had taken over that property. Still TimOtee moved briskly and seemed unconcerned. Soon they were heading up the main trail to the main house and she began to look around to see what had changed, and in the process hadn't realized that TimOtee had stopped and she literally ran into his back. "Oh, sorry, I was looking around to see what has been damaged."

"Yeah, I can understand that, but I stopped to warn you once again not to enter the barn – at least not yet. What has happened inside the house will be shock enough. Come on we do have to hurry if the one inside is to have a chance." He hurried off again, and she paused briefly not sure if she really wanted to go inside or not. Indecision haunted her for a few moments then she shrugged and followed him inside.

She watched as TimOtee opened and entered ahead of her leaving the door open. She was still leery of what she would find as she came up to that familiar entrance and into the home she had grown up in. As she peered inside she froze and was shocked at what she saw. The place had been heavily ransacked and now looked more like an abandoned house than what it truly was. She gasped in shocked surprise – so much destruction, so much damage, and anything that may have had any value gone. The place stank – odors of uncleanliness, of uneaten food, of blood and urine. *The ones who had taken over had to be lower than the animals,* she thought. Realizing that she was lost in thought and the shock of what she was seeing she hadn't really followed TimOtee, and realized that he had probably headed upstairs.

Not wanting to touch anything for the filth that now surrounded her she gingerly headed upstairs to see that it was worse up here. And the smell of death was even stronger. All the doors were open and she really didn't know which one he had gone into. So she headed for her parent's room passing the open doors to see him out of the side of her vision. On the bed was a female, probably a little younger than herself. She could see TimOtee's slumped shoulders and quietly approached. She looked closer at the one on the bed and realized she wasn't breathing. She turned to TimOtee and could see failure in his eyes.

He turned when he sensed CaraOlyn was behind him. With a sense of loss, even though he didn't know this girl, he asked. "Why? Why does it have to be this way? I . . . I really hoped . . . I don't know . . . I mean I know she was in a bad way, but . . . well . . . I really hoped we could do something for her. You know, at least be here if we couldn't have saved her so she wouldn't have died alone and in fear." He stopped a moment and took a deep cleansing breath and let it out slowly. "Why do the gods allow this . . . this death and destruction?" He shook his head, "I wish I really understood or could understand." He pointed in the direction of the young one who was now dead, "I mean she had a whole life ahead of her, but now none of that will happen."

He looked at CaraOlyn and asked, "Do you have a place where you bury your people when they pass?" He shook his head once again, "I surely hope so because I have, or maybe we have a lot of work ahead of us. From what I could see there has to be at least five or six bodies or body parts equaling that many in the barn. And with the heat of the day they are already ripe."

She was silent, and in shock. When he had stated what he had when he had returned for her she couldn't imagine that it was as bad as he described. Now she knew for a fact that it was much worse, and the shock of discovering how much worse left her unable to act or even think. "Ah . . . ah . . . yeah . . . I guess we do."

He looked at her in surprise. "Either you do or you don't, which is it?"

"Sorry . . . this . . .this . . ." She waved her arms around encompassing the whole area, "I just wasn't expecting this. Why would anybody do such things?"

He nodded in sympathy, "I suspect if we could answer that then maybe we would be well on our way to joining the gods. So, do you have a plot of land where we can bury the dead?"

"Yeah, we do. Do you want me to show you?"

Agreeing he said, "Of course. I've got to get started on the digging. And it would be nice if I could get most of it out of the way before dark. I'm afraid, for the ones in the barn, it will have to be a common burial, and while we can place this one in her own, I don't know her name to mark her final resting place. You wouldn't happen to know her name since you are from around here?"

She wasn't sure if she wanted to look at the body again. It was obvious she had been abused and tortured. Carefully and trying to avoid the naked flesh she looked at her face and shook her head. She realized that this could have easily been her, or any of the ones who had died in the barn. She'd been trying to keep her emotions in control but found it impossible in burst out in tears – tears that refused to end. She felt TimOtee reach out and hug her close and continued to hold her until the tears began to slow. "I'm sorry. I really am, but I didn't expect this or want anything like this to happen. And then to find out what the ones who had taken this over were doing to others . . ." She knew that her life had been shaken to the foundations and remained safe within his arms. It seemed natural, a place she'd want to return to in the future. She could feel the strength in his arms and his gentleness. Such a contrast to what was surrounding them at this moment.

She looked up into his eyes and said, "Okay, I guess I'm good enough to show you where." Still she was reluctant to leave his arms. Slowly she pushed away and headed back out the door, down the stairs and back out the open door. He followed behind and she headed towards the barn. He hoped she wouldn't go inside. She headed around to the backside and there was a smaller building. She went there and opened the rather large door. As he caught up he realized that it was a toolshed. She pointed to the implements and then headed over behind this area and pointed to a small fenced area that had markers from others that had passed. He nodded, grabbed a digging tool and headed to the enclosed area and began the task ahead of him. He turned and faced her briefly saying, "I know this is really bad, but the dead no longer can hurt – only us, only the living. If you can get the body ready upstairs we can put her to rest first, and then move on. And remember, that's what we have to do also – move on."

* * *

"One of the patrols – even with the resistance of the primitives, paired with what one of our orbiting ships reported as a possible site to begin our dig – has confirmed we can start our digging operation." General Pertion sighed. *It had been going so well. If we hadn't been discovered, soon – yes soon – we'd been gone anyway. And it would have only been after the fact all of this would have been discovered. Now .*

. . He shook his head as he looked over at the rest who were in this meeting. The flag captain, Colonel Jamison, Admiral Sympson, and his support staff. They would have to move rapidly now – not that it wasn't an issue before they became aware that they had been discovered. Looking at Admiral Sympson he asked, "How soon can you and yours begin the operation? From what I understand it will be a complicated process. We first will have to drill

through a hillside to get to the point where we can begin the actual operation."

"It won't take too long to set up and begin. As far as how long it will take to make the actual hole I really don't know. I'll have the chief look over what we've got – oh by the way remember we didn't get the big laser drill, but only the smaller units. With that it means we'll have to factor additional time. At least once we get the primary hole cut we probably could move part of what we have here on the ground there. Although overall it would probably be just as smart to leave it here. That way any of the equipment won't get in the way, and we won't be divided between two areas to defend. Still, from what little I know, the area is somewhat isolated. I need one of your squads acting as guards, plus a patrol or two to keep the natives from interfering. Kind of important if we want to get this finished before we have visitors. In the end I suspect we'll be abandoning this area, but . . ." With his statement unfinished he shrugged.

The general looked down at the dirt floor. "Wish you could give me a better idea, but I understand. This whole thing has been a 'seat of the pants' operation since we left on the run. We've finally begun to get organized, but still are far from it, if the truth be known. Oh well, I'll let you get to it. I'll have all the data transmitted to your implants, and to all of our systems so we are all on the same page – or at least as much as we can be. Damn these primitives in those mountains! We've had no problem down here in the lowlands and valleys, and I assumed it'd be easy there too. Wrong! Truthfully I should have known better." He watched as the meeting broke up and everybody head out to take care of the next portion of the operation. *I could really use a drink! Still . . . still that would be stupid. All of us need our wits about us now, and time isn't our friend.*

* * *

The ride into the system and then his dead stick landing on the planet had been harrowing from beginning to the end. The scout ship had ridden in the shadow of the asteroid all the way in, and they had spotted a number of ships, and activity that said the ones who were here were beginning to set up sensors on a number of moons that were here. If they had arrived a little later than they had, then this maneuver would have failed and they would have been spotted. He had hoped to use a small burn, but once they had learned what the rogues had he knew that wouldn't be possible. Now he hoped the scout ship had continued on by the planet undiscovered, and soon would be on its way out of the system and on the way back to the fleet. Still they had a lot of trouble to face with the knowledge that there were spies aboard, and with no way of knowing who they were.

His ride had been bumpy and quite warm. He sweated the drop into the atmosphere knowing that there was a chance they would see through the flimsy disguise that made his single passenger dropship look like a meteorite, and if they did he would never know because he would be dead . . . Or, if they did, maybe end up captured, as they followed him down, and awaited his arrival. Fortunately none of that had happened and he landed safely somewhere in the foothills, and away from any of what appeared to be the population centers. He was fortunate that the ship landed in what appeared to be a forested area. It would have been embarrassing, let alone dangerous if he had inconveniently landed where he would be observed by the native population, who would then come and investigate.

At least it appeared that with what his sensors detected that the natives were involved with the ones he and the fleet were pursuing and not watching the skies for something unusual. Still he needed to get the craft out of sight. And while he could put it into the stealth mode, making it almost invisible, it took energy to do that. And he really didn't know how long this would take, and with the ship in the trees to recharge it with sunlight would be a losing cause. He climbed out after scanning the area and did a quick look around. Right now for any who might be close it would be obvious something crashed here. No his ship didn't crash, but broken limbs and with the ground vegetation, close to where he was, burned simply by the heat of his vessel it could easily draw the curious.

Gingerly he climbed down and for the first time in more time that he could remember he was back on solid unmoving ground. Here he laughed because that wasn't really true. It was an illusion after all. The planet wasn't any different than any of the spaceships he had been in, only larger. Taking in a deep breath of air he tasted the strange air and found it to his liking. Listening closely he heard nothing. It really did appear he made it down without being discovered. Turning around and looking over the area he found that it was somewhat shadowed and felt chilly. It was obvious this was old growth, and even the vegetation that lay under the trees was sparse, further identifying the growth as such.

Well, the first part is complete. Now I need to search the area and find a place where I can stash this thing. He really hadn't paid much attention to the time of day so he really didn't know how much daylight he had left. True with the night vision equipment it wouldn't matter. Still he didn't know what type of predators lived in these old growths. And if he wanted to be honest, he personally didn't want to find out. Behind him there appeared to be a hill, or at least it seemed to be. It was somewhat distant and the land seemed to be running in an upward direction. In truth in the opposite direction the land gently fell away from him. He suspected that the direction where it fell away was to the south, and the hillside to the north. Still until he pulled out the old standby he couldn't confirm direction. Marking the location in his mental map he began exploring the area. He knew that for this day he'd be getting familiar with the area, finding a better place to hide his small ship, and setting up a temporary camp – all critical for his survival. With the freefall method of landing he only had a general idea of where he ended up. He needed to climb that hill, if that was what it was. It would give him a chance – possibly – to view the surrounding countryside and get a better idea of his location. As they had approached and before his drop they had confirmed compasses would function as the planet had a strong magnetic field with north being the strongest. So the compass would point towards the northern icecaps.

It had been found that for most planets where similar lifeforms to them had been discovered that this had been consistent. In other incidences where strange lifeforms had been located, places, such as ones heavily radiated, or with no magnetic fields, or solid ice, or so many infinite varieties where originally it had been thought life couldn't exist, they had been proven wrong. This meant that there would be plenty of existing worlds in the universe for expanding intelligent lifeforms to go forth and populate. It also meant that the way of processing information, of thinking, of culture, of the way anything could be viewed would be vastly different. And in many situations there would be nothing – no similar ground making it nearly impossible to communicate, let alone understand each other. This leading to neutral areas being set up, so the different species could begin the process of learning about each other, and to begin to develop those necessary skills, to talk to each other. Of course this would only happen once each species got over fear, and being suspicious of the other. Even though, and in the end, it wouldn't necessarily be voice that would be used as the method of communication.

Damn! I'm out of shape. Too long aboard ship I guess. Yeah he exercised, but obviously not enough. Heck he was sweating, and when was the last time that had happened? He found, as he climbed the hill, the trees remained heavy. He suspected once he reached the top that he would have to climb one of them to get above the canopy to get a rough idea how deep inside this forest he was. He wanted to set up a passive scanner array also so he could begin to map, not only the area, but what his adversaries were doing. He knew from the signatures that they had energy fields in use – even though they were set on minimal power. It meant that the natives of this world couldn't pass through – in fact it probably would kill them – but anyone with power armor, the modulating code, and shield could move freely through. It made sense since no one on this world had the technology or the understanding. Plus it meant that the atmosphere of this world, the natural radiation, and the magnetic field would dilute their signal giving them more time to accomplish whatever it was they were trying to accomplish.

Eventually he reached the top, breathing quite hard, and with his leg muscles shaking he sat down and leaned back against one of the trees. He closed his eyes and waited while his breathing eased and his muscles relaxed. Shaking his head he thought. *Really? I've really got to do something about this. If this is how I am after tackling such a simple hill, how can I be effective if I go against them, let alone the marines that they have.* Looking up at the tree he was under he could see it would be easy to climb. Even up here on top of the hill the trees hadn't thinned. Shaking his head he got up and began the climb eventually topping out. The branches were much thinner, and he had to be careful. There seemed to be a strong breeze coming from the west and he had to admit, at the moment, it felt good. Carefully looking around he could see the mountains to the north climbing up into the clouds. Looking to the south he could see the valleys and what looked like cultivated fields. And also he could just see the shimmer of the energy fields, and off to the southwest there appeared to be a thin tendril of smoke rising. It appeared to be just west of one of the energy fields.

Grabbing a set of glasses from his pack he zoomed in looking over the area. Closer and towards him he could see what appeared to be a village, and beyond a number of farms. And while he couldn't confirm it, there appeared, close to the energy field, well it seemed to be a blackened area and he suspected where he was seeing the smoke. He couldn't be sure since smoke has a tendency to appear either closer or farther away than it actually is. Add to it that this particular column was almost invisible making it much more difficult to pin its location. *Guess I'll mark that area. From what I can see I haven't seen any movement so it would give me a chance to learn a little more before I make contact with the locals.* He turned back to the tree top and studied it. Found what he was looking for and set up his sensor suite, setting it to stealth and passive, sending the information to his computer on his ship, which then would relay it to his personal implants.

Climbing back down it was now time to do a little more exploring, and set up his camp. The day was beginning to head towards its end and early tomorrow he'd have to get his ship well hidden, and begin his trek towards the area he had marked. Overnight his sensor suite should update not only his map, but give him some great images. For now he had no desire to meet anyone especially the ones he had come here to scout.

* * *

It had been a rough day and looking around TimOtee could see that the day was coming to an end shortly. He was dirty from the graves he dug, and smelled of death, from the pieces of bodies, and the one female he buried. Not a cheerful way to spend the day, but necessary. He straightened up and stretched his muscles. Even with all the hard work he did on the farm he knew he would be sore from this – *different muscles used*. At least it was done. Now he wasn't sure what he would do. He knew CaraOlyn was back at her house, but now that he had gotten her back here he felt that the job was done and he needed to move on. Still both of them had shared a few moments together, and maybe there was something growing between them. Still it could have only been the stress and danger of the moment. He took the shovel and pick back to the tool shed, dusted himself off, and headed towards the main house.

As he did he could hear his footsteps crunching on the gravel that had been laid around the barn and yard area. As he came around the side of the house towards the front entrance he saw that CaraOlyn was standing there in an open doorway. She looked defeated, as if the whole world had come down and had crashed upon her shoulders. Well, if he wanted to be honest, it probably would seem like that with all that had happened. Yeah, he had to admit that once the barriers arrived everything had changed and it hadn't been for the good. Still he had hope that his family was safe, and someday he would be reunited with them. Looking at CaraOlyn he suspected it would be the same for her since she was alone at this moment.

He honestly didn't know how long it would be before the residents and her family returned – if they ever did.

As he approached the doorway he could see that she was wide eyed and staring out beyond him. "Did you see that?" She asked.

"See what? I'm sorry but I've been quite busy with the job I had to do to see anything but here."

In a subdued voice she said, "Yeah, I guess that would be true. I thought I heard something and came to one of the front windows and saw something falling from the sky. Yeah, I know it's something that happens quite often, but for me this is the first time I've seen something like it. I hoped you had so someone could confirm it for me. But I guess it could be my imagination. After all, this has been a hard, hard day for me . . . and oh I'm sure you too. To come back to this, this . . . ah mess, this destruction, and yes death, has shaken me badly."

Tipping his head to the side and smiling slightly he said, "That's an understatement if I ever heard one. Look, not to change the subject, but to change the subject, I think I've done everything I can here and I need to move on. If you remember I originally was attempting to find a way beyond that barrier. And I still need to continue to do this. My family, our farm is inside – not that you don't know this – still I need to continue." He saw alarm rise in her eyes.

"You want to leave? Why? Sorry, that was stupid, yes I know why. Still I need you here. At least until others return. Can't you see that?"

He shrugged and turned his palms out. "Look, the barrier has been moved – moved back and away – and the murderers and thieves, or whoever they were have been eliminated. So you should be safe here until someone does return. And I think in the time we've been together you've learned enough to protect yourself, or to recognize the situation and leave if you must. I know that we've spent this time together, and while the last part has been nice . . ." Here he shook his head when he saw her expression, "No, not the fighting, death, and destruction, or finding what we did here, but you and I. I don't know if anything will come of it or not, since it can all be because of what is going on. So for now I'll consider it part of the circumstances that brought us, unwillingly, together." He took a deep breath and sighed. "Look, I've got to know, just as much as you need to know about your family.

"Once I've found out, one way or the other, then I will come back through to find out how you and yours have fared, okay? When I started this I've seen much too much death already. The first place I stayed was wiped out by one of the mountain clans, and then I watched – as we did here – the strangers take down the ones who attacked them as if they were swatting some irritating crawler. I must admit that it doesn't give me any confidence for those who are inside this barrier. Still what I saw suggested that the strangers weren't interested in us if we left them alone. They only attacked once they were attacked. So with these thoughts I think my family is still alive. Staying here isn't going to let me find out. So I have to go – do you understand?"

Her head hung down in obvious surrender. And in a low voice filled with defeat and dread she said, "Yeah, I can see that. Still . . . I had hoped . . . I don't know . . . I really was hoping you might stay at least a little longer." She shook her head before continuing. "I guess I can understand why." She took a deep breath and let it out slowly looking up into his eyes. Quietly she said, "Okay TimOtee, you win. Be careful out there, and I'm holding you to it. You had better come back and see me, okay?"

"I said it, so unless something prevents my return, I will. Look I'm going to head over to the other farmhouse where we were staying. I'll stay there tonight and then head on to the south and see if I can find a way inside. From what I've seen so far, the chances are small, but until I've had a chance to see for myself I can hope." With that he took her hands for a brief time, turned and left her standing there. It wouldn't be long until darkness arrived and he had some distance to go to reach the other farmhouse.

She watched as he left heading in the direction of the farmhouse where she had stayed for a number of nights. She was at a loss as to what to say, or what to do. Suddenly she felt lonely and lost. She felt something running down her face and realized it was tears. Reaching up and wiping them off, she slowly and quietly closed the door. She was home, even though it had been almost destroyed, but found that she would rather be with him. When those thoughts entered her mind, she first denied them, attempting to push them away, but after a while she knew the denial was false. Maybe if she ran after him she could ask to go with him, and with that thought reopened the door to only find an empty pathway – he was gone, and it hurt.

* * *

Jerod finished his primitive camp and knew that soon, from what shadows he could see (it was almost impossible to tell the time of day inside this ancient forest) dusk was just around the corner. At least with his small fire and his skimmer he would be safe. Later, once he was sure he was safe, he would see what data his sensor array would provide. It would be preliminary since it had only been placed a few hours in the past. Still anything would help. Even with the data he had before leaving the scout ship it could only be called general. Until he developed a more complete image of the overall situation he wouldn't be able to act. And somewhere along the timeline he needed to make contact with a small group of natives, and truthfully he would be more than happy if it was only one. While his implants had assisted him in learning the language, from the samples they had captured, it was still incomplete. He suspected the first time he began to communicate with someone from here he would sound like an idiot. It was that way every time they landed on an unknown world.

The tests he had run since landing had shown the vegetation compatible to his metabolism, so he wouldn't have to worry about carrying vast amounts of food, or a small processer that would render foods safe for his consumption. That, in itself, would simplify things tremendously. Still not knowing what was poisonous or deadly could be just as dangerous as having someone discover a processer he might have hidden on his person. As dusk deepened into night and darkness replaced the gray skies he found he was staring into the small fire, mesmerized by the dancing flames. *Hey stupid, don't do that. It leads to night blindness. And I really don't know if the local predators are fearful of fire or not. Yeah, on most worlds they are, but the moment I would make such an assumption would be the time that these predators use fire.* First nights on new worlds – well, new worlds to him – were always uncomfortable. Strange sounds, strange rustlings in the surrounding brush and trees, the way the plants moved with the wind – all of these and so much more were new.

Still, like moving somewhere new, where the house was different, where the traffic patterns varied from what one knew, and the strange sounds of a home, or the fact that one didn't know the location of any store or whatever made the area appear to be much larger than it really was. It always surprised him when he finally became familiar with a new area how suddenly it shrank in size. He remembered on one world he had been working a series of dirt roads, working his way through the local mountains on these many pathways seeing a huge map in his mind, when suddenly by traveling an unknown road or path that tied the areas together, the map inside his head would suddenly shrink, and those blank, unknown areas would suddenly fill. And he knew at that moment he could see the whole area as a bird flying high making it easier to move and plan. Still until that happened the regions were open, unknown, and large. Even with the general layout he had from the images captured by the scout ship, there were still too many unknowns.

Like, for example, this ancient forest he was presently in. Yes what was given him from the captured images spoke of an unbroken forest, but it didn't present him with the fact it was old growth, dense, or where the way out of it would be. At least this was on the north side of what looked to be similar to the rift valleys of the African plains. If he had landed to the south it would have been a real mess. All the images showed was kilometers of swamp, small marshy islands, the growth that is common in those areas, and he was sure all the traps that such areas held. *Better here than there, that's for sure.* Still each area held its own dangers and he had yet to learn what those dangers were.

This brought to his mind the way of this world. It seemed to have one major continent which was longer than wider – with most of it lying above the equator. What did lie on the equator were the swamps. Below and to the south were thousands of islands surrounded by one large ocean that bordered on the vast continent. The poles had the standard icecaps, and since they didn't take a deep survey there was no way of knowing if there was landmasses underneath the ice or not. If they ended up remaining in the area long enough and satellites were sent into orbit around this world – which could happen – then the surveys that would come out would answer those questions. With this or these series of rift valleys running down the center of the continent, it had a tendency to bring storms straight through these valleys, where they helped keep the valleys fertile. The storms then had a tendency to push north dumping vast quantities of rain and snow on the mountains. At least from the forecast he had received before landing it should be a dry night. From now on he'd have to depend on his sensor array. But one by itself wouldn't be the most accurate.

Maybe, if time allowed, and he put enough distance in he could set up a couple more. Still he suspected that it wouldn't happen . . . yet . . . And while these units were small – fitting into his backpack in reality – he really had no desire to explain them away to the natives. So, most likely, he wouldn't be bringing any with him. Still, maybe if he remained for a day here in this old growth forest he could set up a small triangulation that would give him far better and accurate data. And, he had to admit, the campfire was really nice. Inwardly he laughed. Here they were basically a spacefaring species, and he had to live like his primitive ancestors. Speaking out loud and looking at the darkness he said, as he laughed. "Here be monsters!" All he could do was shake his head at such thoughts. *Here be monsters indeed. And just who are those monsters?* He shrugged because he knew the answer. *Yeah, in the here and now it is us.* Still in the silence and soft breezes of night the warmth, light and the crackling of the burning wood seemed comforting. *Let tomorrow bring what it may.* Now he grabbed a ration, and settled down for the night. It would probably be the last quiet time he'd have while he was here.

Little One: "So how do you know about this one?"

GGF: Smiling, "I know it's hard to believe, but at this moment back then I didn't. It is later where it was revealed. And now isn't the time."

Little One: Frowning and shaking his head. "Why? I mean there must be something that happened."

GGF: "Yes, but before it can be revealed, much more must happen. It is only once the other happens that this can be understood."

Little One: With some doubt in his voice. "Okay, if you say so." He had to admit that this story was so much more than he expected. In fact, if he wanted to be honest, he felt that it would be boring and it would be difficult to keep his mind on what was being said. And in the end he would be daydreaming and missing something important. Instead he found he looked forward to it, and to his surprise the days were flying and soon he would need to write it all down in his own words and let his great grandfather read what he wrote before turning it in to his instructor.

GGF: Looking up and shifting in his chair, "Looks like another one is just 'bout over. We'll break here. I'm sure your mother can use some help in setting the table. Dinner is close at hand and I'm ready for some of her great food, how about you?"

Little One: He had to admit that mom put on good food, and lots of it. He watched his ancient relative and smiled. *Who'd have thought someone old like he is could have such adventures?* "Okay, I'll go help. Ahhh, are we going to continue this tomorrow? I know I've been excused from my chores for this, but we are in the middle of the work time."

GGF: "True, but if you think about it, your older brothers and sisters were excused also. I know you were probably too young to remember, but I think if you really think about it, they had the whole time off when they had to do this report. Now go help, then you won't feel too guilty about not helping the others."

Little One: One thing for sure, one didn't ignore what one was told to do. He smiled at his namesake and headed through the door from the porch where they had been each day and yelled, "Mom, great grandfather said I need to help!"

GGF: Shaking his head and smiling, he stared out across the farmland. He honestly didn't know how much time was left to him, but he had to admit he enjoyed his extended family. Sighing he thought. *Now if you were still with me, CaraOlyn this would almost be perfect.* Still, she hadn't been with him when he had received this gift from the gods. *Oh, well. There must be a reason.* With care, he pushed himself off the chair. It had become harder and he needed to move. And he had to admit moving was becoming more difficult each day. Even with that gift he knew his time left was short. He only hoped that he would get a chance to tell his story to all of the great grandchildren before his time was through. Still, if he wasn't granted that time he knew the love of his life waited on the other side of the veil for his return and their happy reunion.

SOUTH, SHOULD IT BE SOUTH?

TimOtee could only shake his head as he reviewed, in his mind, all that had happened over the days since the shimmering barrier had arrived. He began to wonder if what he remembered before that time was no more than illusion. Still if it hadn't happened he wouldn't have seen all that he had. Not that some of it he'd rather forget. Still he had met CaraOlyn and while the beginnings had been anything but cordial, as time had passed he found that the two of them had grown quite close. Still she had her life and he had his, and right now what he planned didn't allow a female in his life. He needed to do this on his own, and he still needed to move around the south side of the barrier to see if there were any weaknesses there. One thing for sure, he had witnessed the fact the barrier could be moved. Again who'd have thought something like that could be moved? He guessed, if he wanted to be honest, before it was there, there was nothing, and suddenly it was there. It meant that it had to be moved to be set up. Still it wasn't something he had honestly thought about.

It would be dusk before he reached the farmhouse where they had witnessed the fighting. And while the results were as he expected, since he had witnessed other such fights, it had at least freed up CaraOlyn's home. Although what the ones who had died in the fight had done to it and the captured villagers was a crime in itself. They were definitely scum of the worst kind. And in reality their death removed some of the vermin. So in a sense these strangers (he still wasn't sure if he wanted to tag them as gods) had performed a service by removing them. Well, in this instance good riddance. He unconsciously looked in the direction of the moved barrier and the location of the battle as he walked the pathway towards the house. He'd stay tonight and move out in the morning. If, after working some of the swamps, if he survived, and he was unsuccessful in finding a way through the barrier, then he would retreat back this way before heading towards the old growth forest. Some of the lower mountains lay within that forest. It would give him a chance to get up high enough that maybe he could tell how large an area this barrier covered. And maybe he'd get lucky – as if such could be said – he'd find a weakness. Still he honestly didn't expect to, but by not trying he'd never know for sure.

He entered through the door into an empty house, and it felt empty. How could it be that way in the short time the two of them had been together – more or less – that he missed her? He smiled at this thought. He was sure as time went along that both would forget about the other and move on with their lives meeting others in the future. And somewhere in that future they would look back individually on this time and wonder what it would have been like if they had become mates. Shaking his head once again he thought. *Hey, becoming nostalgic are you? One nice looking female comes into your life and turns your head and you're already thinking of the future with her.* These thoughts brought a smile to him. *Yeah, right.* Taking in a deep breath he let it out slowly, looked over his surroundings once again, and knew that it would be his last night here. And he felt with the change in the location of the barrier that the owners would be returning soon. After all it made sense.

Better think about leaving it in good condition. I know if I had strangers staying in my own home I'd hope they would have the manners to keep things neat. And with those thoughts he looked around in the failing light and saw that overall they – the two of them – hadn't disturbed too much. He lit a candle on the table, and knew before he left in the morning he would straighten up as best he could. After all it was only right. He reached into his pack and took out a meal, and while doing that realized that he'd need to replenish soon. At least the swamps had plenty he could use to replenish his supplies.

Going over to the table he sat down and leaned on the table realizing he was tired. It had been a full day of physical labor, and emotionally it had been draining. Learning what the ones had done had been a shock, and seeing how she had reacted didn't help either. Still, he had to admit that in the end, she held up pretty well. He knew it wasn't easy to learn what those thieves and murderers had done. Suddenly he awoke and realized he had better put out his sleep sack. This time he would put it here on the bottom floor and leave it at that. He wanted to do a quick clean and be out and on the trails by the time the sun began to rise above the hills.

* * *

The morning air was crisp and his fire felt wonderful. Jerod didn't have the best of nights. Still being on a strange planet, with strange noises, sounds, and smells could do that to one. And even with what technology could provide, the ground was still hard. Even the sleeping arrangements in a scout ship were better than this. Shaking out the cobwebs still in his mind he reached for a cup of coffee. It might be the last he had for a while since this was something that was unknown here. He decided to work both east and west and set up two other arrays. The triangulation might be small, and be wanting, but it still would be better than the single one. And overnight the one had updated his implants via his ship. As he visualized what it had given him he wondered why the rogues had encompassed such a large area. It didn't make any sense to him. *Unless . . . Unless what? I wonder if they are planning, or were planning on bringing down the cap ships.* Thinking about it, it was the only conclusion that made sense. Still from the images he had from the scout ship as it passed by and the updated ones he now had, it appeared they had reduced and pulled back some of the western portion, somewhat towards the south end of the barrier.

He'd have to keep in touch with the sensors. If the rogues had done that he needed to know if they were going to continue to reduce its size. Of course there could be a number of reasons for them doing that, and while he could speculate, in the end, that's all it would be – speculation. Putting out his fire and confirming he was alone Jarod headed out to the west to find another high point in which to place his next array. At least with this being old growth and because of the deep shadows not much grew under the trees making it easy to move. In the end it took him half a day to get the other two arrays set up. At no time had he come across any trails, or heard any of the local animals that must exist here. At this moment he could have been the only one on this planet, and it was only the vegetation that existed. Still there always seemed to be a symbiosis between plants and animals. In all the planets discovered that could support their kind of life this was the common theme.

Yes, a time or two in their history of exploration there had been rare finds where it didn't initially appear to be the way. Yet, in the end, and even though what was discovered turned out to be almost microscopic, there still were microbes that could be considered animal that helped these plants survive. Plants by their nature were sedentary. And while they depended on the winds to spread their seeds so they could expand, or extend their root systems so others could grow where the roots ran shallow, overall the plant kingdom was more successful when it used animals to spread their seeds. He suspected it would be the same here, and with the proof of a dominant species it overall seemed to be a good world. Still not hearing anything, other than the winds through the trees, could make one wonder.

After setting up the arrays and updating his implants he began to get a much sharper image of the local area and knew that from what he could estimate that by the end of this day he'd be on the edge of this forest. He decided that once he reached the edge he would do a bit of scouting then pull back inside the old growth, camp for the night, and use that time to formulate a basic plan using the updated data from the hidden arrays. At least, if someone became suspicious of him at this time, and he became a captive, what he now carried would not give away who he really was. Although his height would be a problem He suspected that he would be at least a head taller than the average male. And on this world females had a tendency to be shorter. He hoped his first contact would be with only one individual. Better yet, if he could avoid contact and find a way to the barriers he'd be able to test and see if they had been coded to only let certain ones through. He really doubted it since this planet was somewhere in the Iron Age.

If the barriers were coded he would have to take the time to find out those codes, which he could capture from the power armor of the marines, who were patrolling outside the barriers. If not coded then he would pass through the barrier and scout the compounds inside. At this moment they had put up enough of a distortion shield that when the scout ship had passed over nothing could be identified within the enclosed area. So he would be going in blind. Not the first time for sure, but it always made it easier to know at least something. Once inside he'd be placing his own stealth sensors so he could gather intel on the whole operation. And as in any of these operations time was short. He hoped that once the scout ship returned to the fleet that they would be able to get pass the spies within the command and alert the admiral as to what they had discovered. Still all of what would be happening there was well beyond his control. He'd be in enough trouble here.

Unfortunately he hadn't been concentrating as well as he should have been and suddenly realized the trees were thinning and there was growth beginning to show under the canopy. This meant he would be emerging from the forest shortly and he needed to be more alert and not try to plan out everything ignoring everything else. *Okay, Jerod, let's pay attention. Looking at the shadows I don't think there's a lot of daylight left so let's make this quick, pull back, and set up for the night.*

* * *

TimOtee was beginning to wonder why he wanted to go south of the valleys. Yeah close to home there was something akin to this area but so much smaller. And because he was familiar with the dangers and traps within that one he felt he had enough knowledge that he could avoid the dangers in any of the swamps and bogs and be okay. Well, he now knew this wasn't necessarily so. And the heat with the amount of tepid water made one feel like they were in an oven filled with boiling water. It sucked! And the crawlers – flying and otherwise – he had never seen so many. And he was finding many here he had never seen before anywhere. And worst of all most seemed to be blood suckers. His body was covered in welts raised from their successful attacks on his exposed skin.

And that shimmering barrier *remained* without any breaks. It was becoming obvious that whoever these strangers were weren't going to let down their guard at all, and this southern side would be as protected as the other sides had been. *I think that this has been a mistake, a really big mistake. Everywhere I look all I see is pools of standing water. And the smells are awful. And I can't tell from the stench whether it's rotting vegetation or dead creatures. And the mud . . . what can I say, it's all like a sucking trap. What islands I've seen seem to have no bottom either . . . Yeah, another trap to draw in the unaware.* He shook his head as he stood with his hands on his hips and looked around in the distance in every direction. Disgusted with the decision to head in here he took a deep breath, almost chocked on a crawler he inhaled, reached up and unconsciously wiped the muddy sweat off his brow. He had enough.

The problem he faced now was time of day. There was an island in this desolation that was close to the exit of this really horrible area. He didn't know if there'd be enough light to reach it or not. One thing for sure he needed to push through to it. Even if it required that he continue in the twilight. Still, he was sure it would be a fool's errand if he tried to move through these dangerous waters in the dark. He was close to exhaustion, but there was no place close by to spend the night. As wet as everything was he doubted he could even light a fire or make a torch. One thing for sure once he left this place – if he did that is – he'd never return. There seemed to be nothing here that could have any value at all. He shrugged. Maybe someday someone would find something worthwhile about these southern swamps – good luck to whoever that would be. He realized that he had been standing and staring. *Hey stupid, standing here isn't going to get you where you need to be, other than trouble.*

Other than the crawlers and rotting vegetation, a few sickly plants, and weird trees he hadn't seen any other living thing. He looked at his clothes which were soaked, mud covered and from what he could smell had picked up the odor of what was around him. He wondered if any of this could be washed out of his clothes and maybe himself personally. *Okay, let's parallel the barrier and get out here. Maybe if I can reach the island by dark I might be able to push on in the dark by keeping the sound of the barrier close at hand, and by doing that not get myself lost. Still I need to see what shape I'm in once I get to my first goal before I decide.* He immediately pushed off back in the direction he came. Back west, and the worrisome thing was the fact the sun was well on its way to the western horizon, before changing direction and heading north. He didn't have a lot of time left, and he had no idea what nocturnal creatures might roam these swamps. One thing for sure he didn't want to learn or find out personally.

It was twilight and well towards dark when he finally spied the piece of land he had wanted to return to. And he could see that it would be full on dark when he reached it. Eventually he could feel the mud under his feet becoming firm and he knew he was almost to the island. He remembered that this was one of the reasons he had continued deeper into the quagmire. This area gave the appearance he was more familiar with. The one he knew, but as he had gotten deeper within the swamp all changed and there seemed to be little solid ground. Still he had hopes. In the end they were dashed as it continued to get worse. And by not knowing anything about these swamps he had no way of knowing if it improved. Finally he was standing on what would be considered dry land. Although even here there wasn't any dry soil anywhere. A few scraggly trees grew and he suspected it was their root systems that held this piece of land together.

He found that he wasn't moving once he stood again above the waterline. Every muscle in his body ached, and his mind was clouded with fatigue. He had to admit he was asleep on his feet. Did he dare move on and try to get away from this place tonight? Or should he spend a really uncomfortable night here on this poor excuse for an island? Neither held much hope or promise. One thing for sure either way he did this, once out, he suspected he would be spending a couple of days in a camp recovering from this little jaunt into the southern swamps. If he remembered correctly he had seen some dead wood under those trees when he first passed through here. Maybe he could get a fire going, eat something, and then decide if he wanted to chance it in the darkness.

It was then he realized that some of the vegetation here began to glow in a blue-white luminescence. He stood shocked by this sight. It sort of lit the area in a soft glow. Then tendrils started drifting in from a thin ground fog obscuring and revealing the surrounding area. It was an eerie effect overall . . . Giving one the feeling that there was movement being caught from the corner of one's eye. Yet, when he would look fully upon that perceived movement all would be still. It sent chills up his spine. It was almost too much. He needed to get out of these corrupted lands. And it was this more than anything else that made his mind up for him. There was no way he would spend the night here. Whatever the dangers he would encounter, they would be less than the ones he sensed were here. He'd push through and whatever it took, be out of the swamps as soon as he could. And he suspected, once again, he'd never return.

* * *

TimOtee had to admit he was exhausted. How else could it be? At least one of the major moons had risen so he wasn't fumbling around in complete darkness. The torches he had made had been of poor quality reflecting what he had on hand to make them. In truth they were no more than morale boosters since the uncertain light created by them ended up creating more problems than solutions. He suspected that half the night must have gone by him by the time he realized he was out of the swamps. And once he did he looked around for a safe place to camp, *enough is enough,* he thought. Finding a small boulder field and without building a fire he sat down and leaned against one of the larger ones and before he realized it was asleep.

It was his own snoring that awakened him, and he realized what had happened. He found he was chilled and his pants legs plus his footwear were still wet adding to him being cold. Fortunately the breezes were slight and didn't add to the chill. Carefully he laid out his sleep sack, and wet or not climbed in anyway, and while initially uncomfortable he eventually fell into an uneasy sleep where he was chased by the shadows he had witnessed in those swamps.

The sunrise broke bright and cheerful although he was anything but. He hurt, and the clothes he was wearing stunk. He ached, needed some food, and a warm fire would be welcome. He leaned again that rock he had the night before when he had first fallen asleep and felt like he hadn't slept at all. If he wanted to admit it moving was almost too much an effort. At least he learned what he wanted to and that was the fact the shimmering barriers continued unbroken and whoever these strangers were had completely enclosed the area. He found, even now, that he would doze and awaken when his head would drop. He had no energy or the desire to move. Finally with a lot of effort he got up, gathered enough fuel to build a small fire. He needed something hot to drink, and eat some of the trail food he had prepared.

He was at a loss as to what to do. Maybe it was time to head back and find out if anything had changed. Yeah when he had first headed out to the west he thought he might go as far as the coast, but after all this time on the trails decided it probably wasn't worth it. Dejected, and feeling down TimOtee really felt lost. Maybe he would simply follow the barrier back around and stay far enough away so he could see it but not accidently die from some stupid accident or fall into it. He looked up through blurry eyes and realized that more time had passed and it was close to the zenith. He needed to move. Where he was wasn't the safest or best place to be camping. It simply was an area where his flagging reserves had tapped out. Then a random thought entered his mind and it was about CaraOlyn. Why had that happened?

At this moment in time this was the last distraction he needed. In fact he suspected that she'd go her way and in the end he would go his and their time together would just be a simple footnote to their lives. That's if they had any lives. At this point he really had no idea who these strangers were, what they wanted, or if they were interested in any of them. One thing for sure, if he did follow the barrier around he would pass close to where she was, and maybe he could stop and update her on all that had happened. But, if again he wanted to be honest with himself, he was first, attracted to her, and second, it would probably be smarter to not make that contact, although he remembered he said he would stop. Well, he had time to decide since he was still far away from there at this moment. *One thing at a time, TimOtee . . . One thing at a time.*

* * *

Again, it hadn't been one of the best of nights. Still Jarod wasn't surprised. He was on this strange world and he hadn't adjusted to any of it yet. And soon he knew he would probably make contact with some of the natives and before any of that happened he was always nervous as hell. Since one never knew how it would go, his mind would always present the worst case scenarios, which rarely happened. Yet, no matter how hard he tried to keep his mind reasonable, or try to be logical since he had been involved with such contacts in the past, it never worked. At least from what he could see, from the arrays, and the scans before he arrived, the natives, overall, had pulled back from the barriers so the chance of running into a large group was small. He really hoped that he could find only an individual so he could hone his skills. So far he hadn't even seen any of the written language so he really didn't know any of the structure or how names were pronounced or written. He'd need to hide, to listen, and interpret.

Yes, he could speak it, but he suspected that he would be doing a poor job. And only time close to where the natives lived and spoke could he refine it. Usually this was something that took time, and this was something on this assignment he didn't have, increasing the pressure of that first contact. *Isn't that the way of it?* He smiled inwardly. Today he would be approaching the barrier for the first time and with the equipment that he had to determine whether it had been keyed or not. If not then he would have no problem passing through the energy barrier. But if it did, then he would need to take the time of finding the correct passkey and frequency. He needed to get inside as fast as possible. Maybe, if things went well, he'd be inside before running into any of the natives. It surely would simplify things somewhat. He knew, once inside of the barrier he would be facing overwhelming odds and problems, and that would be enough complications. *Better get to it. One thing for sure sitting here isn't going to get any of this solved or me back off this backwards world.*

He had nothing against the natives or where they were technologically, only that he preferred where they themselves were. Yeah, in many ways he was a throwback to earlier times, but not these times here that he knew for sure. Making sure his fire was out and he was dressed and packed as close to the way of the natives of this world, he headed south out of the old growth forest and soon entered the lower foothills that led into the rift valleys. Using his implants he zoomed in on the surrounding countryside studying the area for movement. As far as he could see nothing moved. He still hadn't seen any large animals even though he knew that there were domesticated grazers here. *I guess the energy field has chased everybody and everything off. At least it should make it easier for me. Still I suspect both the admiral and general will have patrols out. I know I would if it was me.* While he had briefly considered this before, he now, for the first time, was out in the open, making him much more vulnerable.

As he looked at the map he knew that there were a number of small settlements inside of these valleys, and far to the west larger settlements that could be considered small cities. It appeared that when the ones they were trying to bring to justice landed they chose a place of little population. Meaning they were trying to keep the impact of their arrival down to a manageable means, and make as little fuss as possible. Still when one erected energy barriers in a world where such didn't exist there was no way one could avoid the impact and panic such would create. He wondered what myths would come out of this. He honestly didn't know, but it was enviable that something would. He noticed that towards the west end of the area where the barrier stood there had been, if it was still there, a village. As close as the barrier was to it he suspected it to be abandoned. And from what his arrays verses the images from the scout ship he could now confirm that the barrier had shifted inward.

Okay, I guess the question would be why? First off I don't know why they enclosed such a large area in the first place. From what can be determined they ended up with a large number of farms on the inside. So what have they done with the farmers? He suspected they had been put into stasis. He didn't think the rogues were the type to murder them. Still, until he was inside of the barrier and had a chance to recon the enclosed area he wouldn't know. On top of the energy barrier they had been running a slight distortion field so that anything inside couldn't be identified accurately. Once again he zoomed in on the surrounding areas and with a decision made headed southwest towards the west end of the barrier. He figured that where adjustments in the barrier had been made would be a good entry point. With all the chaos, the changing of the perimeter and all the equipment tearing up the vegetation there would be plenty of areas to find concealment.

Nothing moving . . . Okay, let's do this. Moving from his place of concealment he headed out of the foothills which appeared to be mostly grasslands with scattered trees. And the further he headed down into the valleys the heavier the grasses became with the trees thinning out further. In certain areas in the distance he could see stands of trees and places where there had to be running water by the way the trees grew. Using what cover he could he continued to watch the lands around him, and again he seemed to be the only thing alive. Yeah, a number of times he thought he had caught movement but in the end it turned out to be the breezes moving the grasslands in waves giving the illusion of something out there. As the day progressed the winds increased almost to a point where the only thing he could hear was the roar of the wind. It was cool with a taste of salt and at the same time there was a tinge of warmth. He knew the ocean was not close so either there was a salt swamp close by or there was nothing to block the ocean breezes.

Unfortunately the maps were far from complete and so he had no idea which was causing what he sensed. Most of the grasses were at least waist high, and did a great job of hiding obstructions, holes, and such from sight. He found he was tripping often, and had fallen a couple of times. Maybe it would be smarter to pick up one of the trails. The last thing he needed to do was injure himself. Yeah with what was in his system he would heal fast, but again he was up against time. He didn't have the luxury of taking time out to heal. They needed to capture the ones behind the barrier and get them off of this planet. Picking himself up for the Nth time he shook his head, *okay I think I've just about come to the conclusion I'll have to chance it and take the trails. That last fall hurt, and that road rash still burns.* He remained sitting, which put his head about even to the top of the grass, as he looked around. Somewhere further to the west there appeared to be a possible trail. This last fall decided it for him. He'd have to risk discovery by the natives and take the safer, albeit more exposed, route.

Standing up and with a quick look around he headed west closer to one of the streams. He looked back at the way he had come and saw a meandering path through the grasses. He laughed at himself since he thought his way through had been rather straight, but it was obvious that it was anything but straight. Looking up at the sun he realized that it was approaching what would be the zenith or high point. So he decided to head on past what he considered might be a trail and go up to the stream, test the waters, so to speak, and eat his midday meal. He was approaching this valley proper, and it was obvious from the distance he still needed to go that most of it appeared to be farmed. Again, from what he could see most appeared to be abandoned. He suspected that once the chaos caused by the rogues was removed that much would return to normal. Well, as normal as it could be after such an incursion.

* * *

It was late in the day and Jarod had gone through an abandoned village, although he suspected since the barrier had been withdrawn somewhat from the proximity of the village that soon the residents would be returning. It meant he needed to move and see if he could cross the barrier before that happened. He could see the line burned into the vegetation where the barrier originally stood, and in the distance where it stood presently. He decided to continue to move to the south. He hoped to find a place that was somewhat isolated where he could set up his base of operations – the fewer who knew of his presence, the better, as far as he was concerned. Upon a gentle sloping hill to the west sat what appeared to be a successful farming operation from the size of the buildings he could see. While it was some distance away it still meant that it wouldn't work for what he wanted to do. So he moved on.

He looked at the sun and knew time would be running out shortly. So he picked up his pace and continued down the trail. Shortly he slowed as he came to a torn up area. It was beginning to approach dusk and the light was becoming uncertain. Still with his implants this would be of no issue. He stopped and surveyed all that lay before him and realized that he was witnessing the aftermath of a battle – one sided for sure. The grasses, the brush and even some of the trees showed damage. Looking down at one of the bodies that was beginning to bloat from being here for as long as it had, he could see that the weapons were no more than bows, arrows, arbalests, pikes, a few crossbows, and little else. And it was obvious the return fire consisted of mounted plasma guns, probably personal laser pistols and rifles that used the plastic smart ammo. The primitives didn't have a chance.

As he worked over the site he realized that the attack had been originated by the natives. *Why would you be so stupid? I mean, really, wasn't it obvious that the ones you attacked had something that outclassed every weapon you carried? And yet . . .* Yeah, and yet you continued to fight until I suspect all of you were killed. As he got deeper into the area once again he could see where the original barrier had sat. Maybe this was the reason for the attack. Maybe the natives figured that once the barrier had come down they could get inside. Still it's obvious that when they pulled the barrier back and repositioned it they had planned on a strong defense. Further proof, in his mind, that the two in charge were no idiots. Soon the many bodies he had found would become riper and it wouldn't be the best of areas to be around. He suspected that the smell would probably bring in the scavengers looking for a feast. And from what he had discovered there would be a feast for many days.

Maybe it would do to move a little further south away from this area. Yet, even though it would stink, the area held some appeal to him. Not this side of the energy barrier, but the other. He figured that once they had reestablished the barrier, confirmed it all worked, and patrolled the area in case someone had gone through before it was active that it would be lightly patrolled. In fact since it was the last to be established he suspected they had added the necessary breech sensors and left it at that. He knew the approximate size of the force overall, and knew from what little they were able to discover when passing through the system that the cap ships were still in orbit leaving a smaller force here on the ground. Meaning overall they would be spread pretty thin. Again he didn't understand why they had enclosed such a large area. Maybe the answers would be revealed once he had a chance to infiltrate.

But for now he needed to pull far enough away from this area to get away from the corruption, and find a place to spend the night. He needed to plan his actions, and he wanted to get close enough to the energy barrier that he could run tests to see if it had been coded or not. Yet, from what he could surmise from what he saw here he really suspected they hadn't worried about that aspect at all. Why would they, when the natives only carried weapons that could be attributed to the Dark Ages of their own world? Sighing and shaking his head he realized that the sun had set hours ago and he was beginning to hear what he would consider insects on his own world. He hadn't realized he had spent this much time going over the battlefield. Reluctantly he withdrew back to the main trail and continued in a southerly direction. He'd give it some distance then he'd find a place to camp.

* * *

TimOtee, sore from his trip into the swamps, feeling really dirty, and noticing his clothes weren't in much better shape headed towards the one farmhouse he had spent time in. He knew he'd pass a couple of streams and decided to use one of them to clean up. In fact with the time of day he figured that once he did this, which included washing his dirty clothes that this would finish this day. And if he wanted to be truthful it would give him a chance to rest. He hadn't realized how difficult it had been to move through that swampy area, besides the heat and humidity and small creatures that assailed him and his senses. He had never been so on edge in his life. He'd thought the time in the mountains, and the running away from one of the mountain clans had kept him on alert. But even there it wasn't so in comparison to those swamps.

He had to admit that he had been stupid, overconfident because of his past experience. Yet he had forgotten one important fact that had eluded him. And that fact simple stated; he knew the one by his farm. Knew where the dangers were, and where the traps lay. He knew the islands, the caves, and all the hidden trails. In the southern swamps he knew nothing and it had almost trapped and killed him. *On the morrow I should be able to reach that farm just across that large ravine. Once there I'm going to have to decide what to do. I suspect that if it hasn't happened yet, that soon the village folk will return to pick up the pieces. And being a stranger to most . . . well, all except CaraOlyn, will make them suspicious of me. And with all that has happened can I blame them?* He had to admit he figured he would be – suspicious that is. He remembered crossing two streams on the way and decided he'd go as far as the closest to the small farm. That way he'd only have a short distance to go before being back on familiar ground.

It ended up taking longer to reach that second stream than he thought and the sun was close to the horizon with the temperatures dropping predicting it would be a cool night. Now he wasn't sure if he wanted to bath in that cold running water or not. Still he could barely stand himself and felt if he ran into any others that from the odor they'd keep their distance. Then he remembered he thought he had seen an entrance to a small cave close by. He hadn't taken the time to investigate at the time since he had other priorities at that moment. There had been a small hillside close to where the stream ran and right now he wasn't too close to it. So getting his bearings he went generally west and in a short period of time was rewarded with being back on familiar ground. Well, familiar in the sense that he had passed this way when heading towards the southern swamps.

Dusk had arrived and in the failing light he couldn't find what he had first observed when traveling in the opposite direction. At least it appeared to be warmer by the hill. *The heck with it! Guess I'll gather a bunch of wood, build a roaring fire and just dunk myself including the clothes into that water. Then I'll try to get most of the stink and dried mud off my clothes, then head for that fire.* There was a breeze beginning to build suggesting a weather change, and the idea of being wet with that wind didn't appeal to him at all. He worked his way around the hill until he was on the lee of the winds finding an area that was almost calm. Here he built his fire, and reluctantly headed for that fast flowing cold water, stood there looking at it, really not sure, but knew he really didn't have much of a choice.

Still trying to catch his breath after his immersion in the water he shivered uncontrollably. He kept slapping his arms around his body trying to get his circulation flowing. To say "it sucked", would be making a mild statement. Still in the semi-darkness he thought he got most of the mud and smell off of him. He looked forward to the change of clothes he had warming by the fire. He could still hear the water dripping off his soaked clothing as he came around the hillside and his welcoming fire. *On the morrow I should be back close to that last farmhouse. Maybe I'll go check in on CaraOlyn and see how she's doing. I don't know really, since I really haven't a clue how the day will go anyway.* He reached his hands towards fire, and added more wood. He had to admit the heat was wonderful. As he warmed he could see steam rising from his clothes. He stripped them off which made him cooler. Still he appreciated the heat and quickly climbed into his warmed dry clothes. He was still shivering but slowly the heat was penetrating all of him and soon he'd be as comfortable as one could be in this circumstance.

* * *

Jerod kept his fire small, and was thankful for the synthetic materials that helped keep him warm. Yes what he wore appeared to be what was common among the natives, but all of that was an illusion. While the force field it contained wasn't as strong as what existed in the power armor, it still allowed one some protection. The biggest being that it kept one warm and dry no matter what the weather threw at him. The only real issue was the need to replace the power packs on a regular basis. So that meant the extras had to be disguised to look like some common item. Fortunately they were small, and on this outing away from his small ship where he had spares, he only carried three or four looking like pretty rocks. Since he was alone and from his personal sensors could not locate anybody close he took out one of his last field rations that he had brought with him. Once finished the fire he had would consume all the scrap. Then it would be foods similar to what was common here – especially for a traveler like himself. Like stuff that would be called jerky, back from where he was from. Again, it was fortified with what was necessary to keep him healthy and full. He had taken a chance carrying a few of the rations as it was, but now there would be no issue as all the evidence that he really was a stranger here would be gone.

He stared into the fire – a mistake he knew. By doing this it destroyed his night vision. Still he counted on his implanted sensors to alert him to danger. And the blades he carried, while appearing to be locally made, were of modern materials. The blade would never dull and it was honed down to the micro level. It was the same for the bow he carried. Of course he did carry a concealed stunner. It was a last resort weapon, and one he would need if he came up against any of the patrols, or once inside if he was discovered.

Well, tomorrow – if things went according to plan – he'd try the barrier and see if it was coded or not. Again with the force field he had, if it wasn't, he'd be able to pass through it unharmed, and probably not set off an alarm. Now all he had to do was keep from being seen by both the locals and the rogues and there should be no problem. The only worry at this moment in time was the fact that everything had gone right, which meant that somewhere soon Murphy should be smiling with his plans set well in place just waiting for them to start fouling everything up. He shrugged, and finished eating his meal, throwing the scraps of waste into the fire and watched as the colors of the fire changed as it consumed the bits he had added. Taking a deep breath and letting it out slowly, he pulled back from the fire and climbed into his sleep sack. Tomorrow all the fun and action would begin. He hoped it would go without incident. After all, that's all one can ask or hope for.

Little one: "You mean you've been in those swamps?"

GGF: Smiling and with a distant stare said, "Yeah. And once was enough for me. In truth I went there thinking that since I worked the ones close to this farm that it should be easy. Now that's stupid I admit that, but youth sometimes thinks we know better. Still if I hadn't learned anything from or taken that trip, which could have killed me by the way, and then you or your mother or others who are part of the generations after me wouldn't be here if you think about it, then I might have been stupid enough to try again."

Little one: Silent for a moment. *What did he mean by that? I'm here, how could it be that I wouldn't"* Inwardly he shrugged. He had always heard how nasty it was in those southern swamps and until this very moment hadn't known his great grandfather had been there. He had always thought him an old man and one who had never done anything in his life. Still who was this other he keeps talking about? "So who . . ."

GGF: Interrupting, he said as he smiled, "Now it won't be long before you will learn who this one is. But you see we haven't met yet."

Little one: In awe he was silent again. "You mean you met whoever this is?"

GGF: Smiling he simply said, "Yes".

CHAPTER TWELVE

PENETRATION AND FIRST CONTACT

Jerod awakened after another less than restful night. Blurry eyed he huddled over his small fire. He was cold and couldn't wait for the sun to rise so he could soak up some of its heat. It seemed that the fire wasn't producing too much at this moment. He looked regretfully at his empty cup. He knew until he was back aboard his flyer this was the last cup of coffee he would have. Yeah it was instant and tasted terrible when one compared it to the brewed stuff. Still it could still be called coffee. He really wondered how, after all this time, instant hadn't been made better. He had also finished his last ration and from now on would be using foods that would be similar to what was used on this planet. If things held true, and he couldn't see why they wouldn't, then these manufactured fakes – full of nutrition and vitamins of course – would be bland, tasteless, and almost impossible to eat. Until there was time to test the plants and animals on this world he would have to consider everything else off limits. And on this foray into the unknown there would be no time to do such tests. Still, if necessary he'd do it.

In the distance and almost on a subconscious level he could hear the hum the energy fields created. Once he got warm and felt somewhat normal he'd need to cross that barrier and begin to recon the camps inside. At least, at this moment in time, he hadn't had to deal with the native population. And that was fine with him, since his hands would be full dealing with the ones behind the barrier. He knew if he was caught by them he would be dead since they couldn't afford to leave any witnesses behind – especially one like him. He really needed to get moving but at this moment there didn't appear to be enough energy to do that. Instead sitting and staring into his fire seemed more appropriate. Shaking his head and sighing he finally pushed himself up, and carefully extinguished his fire. Looking to the east he could see the first signs that the sun was about to climb above the trees that surrounded the area he was in. *Yeah, mixed trees and meadowland . . . Kind of a nice place to camp if one is into such a thing,* he thought.

He policed his campsite to make sure he hadn't left anything that would identify him for who he really was. And once he was satisfied he used his implants to search the surrounding area. Not that it could be perfect since there were all these trees and such. Still, as it had been since he arrived, there appeared to be nobody around. He quietly headed into the direction of the closest energy barrier. The sooner he accomplished this the sooner this operation would be over one way or the other.

The hum became stronger as he approached and shortly the shimmering of the energy field became visible. *At least they set it this way. I know for a fact that there are ways of using this system that changes it from the obvious to almost undetectable: Meaning that the primitive people here on this world could have easily died in the droves because of their ignorance. At least I'll give the rogues this they made sure that this wouldn't happen. Although I suspect that in the beginning a few died trying to breech this.* He began to run sweeps on the field as he approached it. And while he had his sensors running on minimum they sensed no encryption, or remote sensors monitoring the field. *Well, this is a good thing for me. Still, and maybe because of the short time they've had to work – I don't know – it's the reason for none of this.* One of the things the energy barrier did do was distort what could be seen beyond making it difficult to determine if there might be regular patrols around the interior, or whether they set up sensor arrays inside. From where he stood on the outside there was no way to determine this because of the interference of the field. The only way he would know would be after he passed through the barrier making this the worst part on his nerves. "Well, I'm not going to know until I get on the other side . . . here goes."

He reached out with his personal field strengthened and touched the barrier. He could feel the slight tingle as the energy from the barrier flowed over his personal one. There was a soft blue glow that surrounded him. For the moment it appeared he was safe. So he stepped forward and through the barrier. It was now or never.

* * *

TimOtee finished a meal of dried meats washed down with fresh water. It had been a cold night which kind of surprised him. He really wasn't that far from those southern swamps and felt that the heat from them should have kept the area somewhat warmer than it turned out to be. Still he had to admit he had been exhausted and had found muscles he never knew he had. He was stiff and it took some time to work out that stiffness. Soreness permeated his being, and this didn't help his mood. Other than traveling to the coast and the larger settlements that existed there, his most immediate goals had failed. With that failure he had almost decided to head back into the areas he knew and forget about the rest of it. Still he was in a quandary, because of this shimmering barrier, he couldn't go home, or to any place where he had friends. All of that lay inside of the barrier.

Making sure his fire was extinguished he returned to the trail and headed back towards where those farmhouses were located on the outskirts of that particular abandoned village. Here he smiled. He had realized that he had never asked CaraOlyn what the name of the village was nor had he noticed anything that identified it when he had gone through. He suspected that he may even have seen the name but with all that had been going on at the time had simply ignored it. In a sense it wasn't really important anyway other than a way to say, sometime in the future, "I was here". Maybe he could stop by CaraOlyn's farm and ask her. Still, he suspected that there was a good possibility that people would be returning and he was an outsider making it an uncomfortable situation. And he suspected with all that had transpired it would make him suspect as far as the locals would be concerned – especially with those deaths and looting.

He came around a copse of trees that had sat next to the trail and had blocked his vision of what was around the next corner. He thought he had smelled the smoke of a campfire but it wasn't fresh. It could easily be a traveler like him, or maybe some more of those outlaws. He had paused and carefully searched the area and found nothing to raise his suspicions. He then went into that copse and looked beyond while remaining hidden – again, nothing. The day was warming and the breezes were beginning to increase hiding the smaller quieter sounds behind the waves of grasses and the moving rustling leaves. The campfire smell was now completely gone as if it had never been. He turned around and looked behind him and again there was nothing. Shaking his head he thought, *Guess I'm getting too jumpy. Still out here it pays to be careful, especially if one is alone.*

He shrugged, returned to the trail, and being as quiet as he could, he continued on down it searching out the areas all around him for any sign of danger. In the distance he could hear the humming coming off that shimmering barrier and unconsciously looked that way. It was at that moment he caught movement from the corner of his eye and stopped. Trying to find the source of that movement he finally saw, in the distance, a stranger like himself, dressed no differently, although if his eyes weren't deceiving him, this one had to be close to a giant. Still it could be an illusion since there really wasn't anything or anyone close to compare him too. He watched this one move quietly and carefully through the area. While he didn't quite have the movement of someone from the mountains, there was a flow to his movements that said he was quite comfortable in forests and surrounding areas.

Alarm arose as he watched this stranger approach the barrier. *Doesn't he realize that this thing will kill him?* Apparently not as he continued to carefully approach the danger. TimOtee thought that maybe he should run towards this stranger and warn him, but then thought he personally would have misinterpreted such an action. With indecision riding high he began to work his way towards the stranger. Somehow he needed to warn him of the danger before he was killed. What surprised TimOtee was the concentration of this stranger. It was like he was studying the barrier. No, that wasn't right. No, what it appeared first off was the fact he showed no fear. Then it seemed as if the stranger was familiar with this. How could that be? Until it had arrived, no one, as far as he knew, of this world had ever seen anything like it.

He stopped behind some of the tall brush that had been slowly invading the meadowlands here in this area. Here he would be hidden from sight. He watched fascinated and almost yelled out a warning when he saw the stranger reach out with his hand towards the barrier. What happened next almost caused him to turn and run. It wasn't possible, yet as he stood there he saw the stranger make contact with the barrier with his hand and suddenly he was surrounded by a strange blue glow. The stranger continued to stand for a few moments concentrating fully on the shimmering barrier. Then suddenly he simply walked through it and disappeared. Shocked and surprised he stepped out of his temporary hiding place and stared. It wasn't possible. There was no way what he just witnessed should have happened. And yet, it did, and he witnessed it.

He suspected that this stranger had probably picked this area because of its remoteness, and hadn't expected anybody to be close enough to witness what he had just seen. Now that it was in the past he began to doubt himself. It had to be his imagination. Carefully he approached the barrier keeping his distance. Looking down into some of the soft soils here he saw tracks so he knew what he had seen had happened. Still, and even from the distance he presently kept himself he could feel his hairs standing on end and knew if he approached any closer he'd die. How this stranger survived was beyond him. Now what? Did he keep it to himself, or did he announce it to the world? He realized that if he tried to convince others and because there were no other witnesses he would be tagged a lunatic, crazy, and full of imaginings. So he decided to keep it to himself. With his half formed plans forgotten he decided that he would remain in the area and see if this stranger would return and come back out where he had passed through that barrier. Of course he had no proof that whoever this was would exit at the same point where he entered. Maybe he found a weak point in the shimmering barrier and had simply used this weak point to pass through.

As he stood there staring he couldn't discern anything that would constitute a weak point. He stood there with his hands on his hips trying to recall exactly what he saw and exactly where the stranger had passed through the barrier. Unfortunately where the barrier stood at this point the grounds were marked with burn lines from it, and the grounds appeared to be hard holding no impressions. There would be no way for him to know exactly where the stranger had gone through. Taking a deep breath and letting it out slowly he once again shrugged. He realized that he had been standing out in the open and staring – probably not the best of ways to survive. So he turned around and began to search the area for a place to wait. After a short period of time he found where the stranger had camped, and found that whoever this was knew how to pick a campsite. He decided he'd use it, and maybe if the stranger did return where he entered, he'd come back to his old campsite. TimOtee set up his own equipment and began to wait.

* * *

"The fleet should be here." Lt Smyth turned to Lt Drury and asked, "Are you sure we're at the correct coordinates?"

Peter smiled as he shook his head. He knew that what Phil was asking was just the frustration showing through. Both of them knew the coordinates were correct. In fact they had found their message capsule waiting patiently here, which meant that the fleet would be unaware of what they had discovered. "You know the answer, and with our capsule here it's further proof. So what do you want to do?"

"I don't know. After all, this is the last thing I expected. And to further the mystery we weren't sent anything to let us know of a change of location. Not only that but we've left the agent hanging. Eventually he'll need support, the support we were to get from the fleet, and we have no way to inform him either. I guess all we can do is to remain here, but not in the open like this. We'll pull back to one of the asteroids and continue to monitor this part of space."

"How much time should we give it?"

"I guess whatever it takes. We have enough supplies to last, and with the raw materials close by and the bots we should be able to stay here indefinitely if it requires. We're so far out from our home system that our ship isn't built to handle those kinds of distances. Yeah I know it's been done, but I don't like those kinds of odds."

With care they maneuvered their scout ship into the asteroid field, found a large one that they could use the gravity to help hold their position, powered the ship down, and began their wait. Knowing both the flag captain, and the admiral, they felt that soon the fleet would either return or one of the smaller cap ships would return so that the scout ships would know the new location. Both knew that shortly other scout ships would be returning to this area. Part of the problem they faced lay in the fact that one of the scout ships had traitors aboard and when it had passed them on the way to the planet where the rogues were presently located, they were never able to identify the ship, other than the fact it was one of their own. They hoped the wait would be short.

* * *

When Jerod came through the barrier he immediately crouched down and surveyed the area. With his sensors on passive so as to not give himself away, he visually scanned the area while he waited on the report. He found he was in the open which he didn't expect. There had been plenty of vegetation on the outside to hide behind and as such expected it to be the same here. He moved to the south where a large ravine ran parallel to the barrier, finding lots of brush and a few trees here. He knew from the overflight that further south began a large area of land that was all swamp. This he wanted to avoid as much as possible. He had an assignment in the past that had placed him on a planet where it was all swamp and he had hated it. So much so that he made it clear he wouldn't accept another such assignment in the future. He hated high humidity, and even now after all this time the smell of rotting vegetation remained permanently within his mind.

Looking around he found some of the equipment that was used to set up these energy barriers parked and abandoned at this moment. It made sense that they should set up a motor pool area somewhere that was some distance from their main camp. Once again he suspected that the residents within this area were in stasis. Other than wiping them all out this was the easiest way to take care of the problem. As the information began to pour in from his sensor scans he began to develop a map of the area. He had time, and as long as he wasn't discovered it would be important to see all that was here. It would be easier to plan, and to move once he understood the layout, and how many were on the ground. With the pass through by the scout ship they knew that a number of the caps ships were hiding close by or in orbit around this world. Still they hadn't been able to make an accurate count, and by him finding out how many were actually here they'd have a better understanding and overall picture of the operation.

He still was uncertain what the rogues' plans were. He was sure it was something they had come up with after losing the fleet that had been chasing them. Well, he needed to learn that also. It would help in the overall understanding. He searched the ravine and found that it ran generally east to west and remained somewhat deep. If he was careful he probably could move a little closer to the "headquarters" area. He looked at his developing map, and wondered why he wasn't seeing much movement of the ground troops. They should be showing up as red dots. *Why are there no bodies showing up, and what are they up to?* Jerod knew the rogues were running patrols outside of the barrier, but as to the whys he had no answers. And the silence was overwhelming. It seemed that most if not all the equipment had been shut down – not that much of what they had produced a lot of noise anyway. Still with it this quiet it almost sent chills up and down his spine.

As he looked around from the ravine he felt like he might be overlooking an abandoned forward base, and that didn't make any sense to him. He quietly advanced through the underbrush following the ravine as it generally ran in an easterly direction. He still wondered why they had decided to enclose such a large area. And as he studied the area and its general layout it suddenly dawned on him as to the why. Yes he had thought it a possibility still . . . *Oh my, they were planning, or maybe are still planning on bringing down the larger cap ships.* He shook his head. He really didn't want to believe that, yet the evidence before him said it was so. He was so shocked from this conclusion that he almost stood out in the open where anybody could see him. He immediately ducked back down when he realized what he was doing. *Now that's stupid. Are you trying to get caught or something?*

He continued towards the main camp area and still found no one around. *Must be sensors or something else set up. It's the only thing that makes sense. Yeah, they don't have to worry about any of the natives infiltrating their camp or the energy barrier, but they can't be that confident. They have to know they've been found out, and with their location set . . . unless.*

Unless what? He knew that there had been a deeper infiltration into the navy by the rogues. Maybe those unknown few had been able to convince the admiral and the flag captain to search a different sector. He shrugged. There was no way of knowing what was happening back with the fleet. In fact until the scout ship returned he would know nothing at all. It was at that moment that movement caught his eye and he crouched deeper in the underbrush. He watched using all the implants he had at his disposal. He recognized the ranks and realized that these were some of the navy enlisted. No officers in sight at this moment. Still they had to be somewhere.

He needed to get as close to the temporary buildings as possible. He needed to plant some of his stealthed bugs so that everything here could be recorded. This included everything that had happened up to the time he planted his bugs. In this time period, especially in the military, everything was recorded. He hoped that the infection hadn't gone deeper than the navy. If it had gone far enough to have spies inside of the department he worked for then all of what he would be planting would be located and destroyed. He watched as the personnel headed back inside, exited his cover, and quietly approached the temporary building he suspected was the command structure. Carefully on the three sides that were visible to him he hid the bugs, withdrew and carefully worked his way to the other structures planting more until he was satisfied he had the area covered. Silently he withdrew, retracing his steps, almost holding his breath. It had gone too easily. Usually when something went this well it meant something had been overlooked. Once back close to the barrier where he had first entered he paused and went over everything he had done since he had entered and couldn't come up with anything he had missed.

He looked down at the chronograph and realized hours had passed since he had entered. He looked up and realized the sun was well towards setting. *I really don't get it. How can so much time pass? I mean it feels like I was here only a short time – less than an hour really, but . . .* He heard movement and realized that in the distance not far from where he was hidden a patrol returned. Fortunately they never looked in his direction. *Guess once they are inside they feel safe. Makes sense really. The natives have no way of breaching the energy field so they have no reason to expect anybody inside other than themselves.* He watched as they headed away from his location and back to the main encampment. He waited until they were out of his immediate sight and carefully moved up to the barrier, reached out with his hand making contact, waiting while the energy flowed over his personal shield and stepped back through. And once on the other side crouched down, did a quick search with his eyes and implants and froze. Someone was out here and from what he could determine appeared to be either close to where he camped, or was actually in his old campsite.

* * *

Chief Fredrickson had been reading some paperwork as he crossed between the buildings. Shaking his head he thought, *Paperwork! It seems to me that somewhere I've read that when computers became common that they were supposed to eliminate this stuff. Right, and that's why I seem to see more and more of it every day.* The pressure had been increasing since they had learned that they had been discovered once again. Now all he could do was hope that they could dig in before the arrival of the ones who were chasing them. In a sense it was frustrating. It wasn't that long ago that they had established this temporary base, had unloaded all the materials from the freighters, assembled the buildings – after erecting the energy barrier of course – and then made them livable. Now they were going to have to disassemble the whole mess and be prepared to either move the stuff to the new location, or send it back to the caps ships, or be ready to flee once again.

It was at that moment as he was concentrating on the list that he thought he had caught some movement out of the corner of his eye. So he stopped, with some curiosity, since even the general and admiral were out inspecting the location where they were planning an initial cutting into the mountainside. Because of being discovered it had pushed the timetable up and the cutting operation was about to begin. He didn't know if they had the time, but if they didn't start or try there definitely wouldn't be enough time. Looking carefully around the compound and out towards the barrier where there were some fields and brush between him and it, he studied the area carefully and came up empty. *Maybe it was only the breeze blowing some of the grasses around, or some small creature. Anyway whatever it is or was I don't see it now.* He shrugged. He really didn't have time to go chasing some small creature. His crew was awaiting further assignments, and he was the one who would be doing the assigning. Again he shook his head. "Guess I better get on with this or we'll never be ready to move."

* * *

As the day had moved on TimOtee became bored. Staying in the camp and staring at the barrier with little to no change other than the time of day wasn't conducive to staying alert. At times he found he would doze, which was no surprise. When he would awaken he'd chastise himself for his stupidity. He was alone, and while the camp was well hidden, he had found it, so there was no reason to expect others wouldn't. Still, and after his adventure in the swamps, he found he truly hadn't recovered fully. So this down time was probably a good thing. And, if he wanted to be honest, other than possibly touching bases with CaraOlyn he really had no place he had to be, and no specific time he had to be there – wherever "there" was. Still he was beginning to doubt himself. Maybe what he saw wasn't what had actually happened. After all, he had been quite a distance from the barrier and it had only been luck when he saw the stranger appear to walk through the barrier. He hadn't found any proof when he had approached as close as he dared, so maybe it was an illusion, and the one he saw had simply moved along its edge making it appear he had passed through.

The shadows were lengthening, and he could see the sun moving to the west. It wouldn't be long before he'd need to gather some additional wood since it now appeared he'd be spending the night here. Again he chastised himself for not doing it earlier. He had been here all day. Well, not really, but close enough to be considered all day. He stood up and was about to get this chore out of the way when movement close to the barrier caught his eye. He froze in position as he stared. On this side of the barrier stood the stranger and he was looking directly at him. Chills ran through him as he realized he had been seen. His immediate reaction was to crouch down, but realized at that very moment that by doing this he'd be moving making it easier for the stranger to see him. It would too late now since he had already moved. Now the problem lay in the fact that he had brush, and tall grasses blocking his view. He'd need to stand back up to be able to see and he wasn't sure if he wanted to do that.

As far as he knew there was nobody from this world who could do what this stranger had just did. And now he knew that he had to have done what he had witnessed earlier. And while he hadn't seen him emerge, it was obvious to him that the stranger had to have come through the barrier since there was nothing close to hide behind. He was at a loss as to what to do. He shrugged as he came to a decision. It was obvious the stranger had seen him so he might as well stand back up and see what he would do. It was too late to hide now anyway.

* * *

As Jerod had stood on the inside of the barrier he was unaware of how close it had come to him being discovered. As far as he knew he had been unseen and had pulled off the planting of monitoring devices successfully. While the military had advanced equipment – necessary, of course, for their line of work and defense – the department he worked for had better. And because of this there was little chance of what he planted being discovered. And if by some accidental chance it was found the data collected would be worthless to any except him. The data used quantum encryption making it as close as "to impossible" of breaking the code.

He took another careful look around being sure he was alone. Even with his implants there was too much distortion to be able to see clearly what lie on the other side of the barrier. So carefully he reached out and once again touched the barrier letting the energy flow over his shield. Then once equalized, stepped through. Immediately he orientated himself and while not expecting to see anybody he realized that in the distance where he had camped stood one of the natives of this world. *Damn! It's been going so well. Wonder if he saw me come through the barrier. If so how can I explain that away?* He stood there undecided. At least the first part of the operation had been successful. He had his equipment planted, and the information would be sent to the arrays, which would then relay the information to him and to his ship where it would be stored for later usage.

He could see that the native had dropped down trying to hide, meaning that the native knew he had been seen. Then a short time later stand back up. Inwardly he smiled. It was obvious that the native was dealing with the same indecision he was. This native reacted by trying to hide, and then realized that there were two problems with this. First off he moved making it easier to be seen, and secondly once he had dropped the native wouldn't be able to see in which direction he personally decided to go. Inwardly he shrugged. Eventually he knew he would have run into someone from this world, and that would be a nervous time. He preferred to spend some time studying the natives before making first contact. The one thing he had learned was the fact what was recorded or viewed over the monitors lacked reality. It was only after studying others from the ground that a true picture or image would emerge. *Well, not this time I guess. And I suspect that this might be the best I can hope for. Instead of just one . . . at least I think there's just one. Hmmm, better not assume such.* With that he began using his implants and scanned the area. And other than a few of the native animals the scans came back negative as far as others.

* * *

TimOtee watched as the stranger remained planted where he stood. It was obvious the stranger was aware of him but couldn't understand what the stranger was doing. He didn't seem interested in getting to cover, to find a place to hide. In fact he didn't appear to be panicked in any way. He could almost see him concentrating on something, and began to wonder if there was someone else here. With those thoughts he looked all around and could find no others. Maybe that's all the stranger was doing. Like him, wanting to make sure there were no others. Now that brought a worrisome thought. What if this stranger was hostile? By being alone like this it meant he would be an easy target. Yet, almost as soon as he thought it, he dismissed it. If that had been the case then the stranger probably would have already attacked, or at least would have found a place to hide. Neither had taken place. So what were the two of them to do? Should he carefully approach the stranger or should he wait and see what would happen?

He looked down briefly trying to decide, and when he looked up he saw the stranger had finally moved. And he was moving in his direction. Well, it was obvious the stranger had made his decision. And by the way he was approaching it was more along the lines of caution, and yet he remained in the open, leaving himself vulnerable to attack. *Why would anybody do that?* This really made no sense. After all, there was no way the stranger could know whether he, TimOtee, was hostile. Was the stranger taking a chance, or did he have some type of protection like the ones who had placed the barriers? This stranger was dressed like any of the low-landers – farmers and such. Not anything like the ones who left and entered the barriers. Could he be one of them, or something else? He felt his nervousness grow. It would still be a short time before the stranger was close enough for both conversation, and to be able to recognize any of his features.

With whatever the ones who had placed the barrier wore, which he had witnessed in the past, there was no way to see their features, or even determine if they looked like them. It was like they were hiding behind whatever it was they wore. Were they that ugly, or strange? Was there something that would be scary to this world, or would it be something that would make them immediately known? There was no way to know since any of the attacks made against the strangers hadn't even injured any let alone killed one.

TimOtee took a deep breath and slowly let it out trying to shake off the building fear. As the stranger approached he seemed taller. TimOtee knew he was one of the taller people and was used to looking down on others. Yeah he had met a couple over time that was his height, and one of two who were slightly taller, but most of the males came to his nose, meaning they had to look up to him. Yet, as the stranger approached he realized that he would be in the same situation as the shorter ones. He'd be looking up. This increased the nervousness. Still he willed himself to stand there.

* * *

Jarod finally decided that he might as well get this over with and began to approach the native. He knew that there was little chance that the native had anything that could harm him. Still, he had no way to know for sure. He knew from the reports and brief studies made that the population was in the early time of the Iron Age. Meaning they had nothing available to harm him or any such weapon from an advanced technological society. He remained in the open and tried to make the approach as casual as possible. He felt a little nervousness arise. Well, that was only normal. Heck in the world he was from there was always nervousness the first time one met someone new. And until they talked it would remain that way. As he got closer he noticed that they were definitely shorter, meaning he would be looking down upon this one. He had no way of knowing whether the native represented the average, was shorter or taller compared to the general population, since this was the first one he encountered.

Jerod needed to watch his footing as he hiked, and at the same time watch the native for his actions and reactions, followed by trying not to appear hostile. He had stumbled and almost fell when he had hooked a hidden exposed root with his foot. *Now how threatening would I be if I fell while coming to meet this one?* Inwardly he laughed as he imagined how it would look. Any fear this one would have had would probably have turned to laughter. Again, inwardly he shook his head. He still had a short distance to go before they would be close enough to speak, and he was trying to decide how to approach this. He really needed the native to identify himself so he knew how to pronounce his own name, and make it sound like he was from these parts. Maybe not close to here, but at least appear to be part of this world, and culture.

* * *

The stranger was almost close enough now that shortly they'd be able to talk to each other. Other than that small stumble, which could have happened to any of them, after all there was always something to trip over, he hadn't done anything to alert himself as dangerous. Again as he got closer he could tell that his first impressions had been accurate. This one was definitely taller than he. The stranger continued on like he was unconcerned about his personal safety. Or did he know something, or had some protection? TimOtee had to stop this as he knew he was only guessing. And the one thing he had learned over time was the fact when one guessed in the end one was usually wrong. So, okay, how was he going to approach this personally? When the stranger reached the point where greetings normally were made, unconsciously he reached out both of his arms in the greeting of the day. If the stranger replied in a similar fashion he could assume he was simply a stranger to this area.

* * *

Jarod was close enough now and hesitated for a brief second and saw the native reach out with his arms with his hands down. For a moment he thought it might be a sign of surrender and then realized that it was a form of greeting. And since the native had initiated the move with his hands open and down it meant he should return the greeting by reaching out with his two arms and hands up so they could grip each other's forearms. Even back on earth this had, sometime in the past, been a form of greeting. So he reached out and could sense relief from the native. He had guessed right. They held that grip momentarily, and as soon as the native released his grip Jarod responded in like. Jerod had made sure that his personal shield, at this point, only covered his head and torso. He didn't need the native to feel the tingle from the energy field.

TimOtee smiled and said, "I'm Tim-OH-tay. And may I ask your name?"

Inwardly Jerod smiled. By this one taking the lead he didn't have to figure out how to make the native introduce himself. Now he knew how he would have to modify his name. "And I'm Jer-ODE-da. And I'm a stranger to this part of the world."

TimOtee smiled since in a way he was also. *Such a strange accent.* Yeah he really hadn't lived that far away from here, but it was far enough that he really hadn't known anything about this area. Still he was dying to ask if what he had witnessed was what had been what really happened. He knew that in the past he had seen some things that appeared to be one way only to find out that his eyes had been deceived. But before he could ask or say anything this JerOda spoke.

"I see you found my old camp. It surprised me when I came around those trees and brush. I'd been exploring this shimmering barrier trying to find out if there's a way through, but alas it seems solid. Although I don't know how something can shimmer like that and still be solid – it's beyond me." Jerod was hoping that he could convince TimOtee that what he saw wasn't what he saw. Unfortunately he saw a perplexed look on the face of the native and prepared to answer the questions he felt were coming.

There was silence for a moment as TimOtee tried to gather his thoughts and how he would word his question. After all, they had just met, and JerOda seemed willing to talk. He didn't want to have him shut up and not say anything. So maybe . . . "Look, ah JerOda, I've been trying to find a way beyond the shimmering barrier myself. In fact I've just returned from the great swamps to the south. I honestly thought with my experience that I'd have no problems with them . . . wrong! I was heading back towards the abandoned village that is north of here when I caught a movement somewhere close to this barrier. Of course it could have been any of the wild ones who inhabit the glens and forests. Yet what I thought I saw was you. And you were reaching out and touching the shimmering barrier. I thought about screaming and warning you about the danger of that thing. We've had people killed who had either gotten too close or had touched that thing. So we all avoid it now." TimOtee paused, not sure how to continue. He didn't want to make it sound like an accusation, yet he was almost sure of what he had witnessed.

"I know that I was quite a distance from the barrier, back on the main trail through this area. Yet, I'd swear you reached out and came into contact with the barrier, and there was a blue light surrounding you. Then, and to my surprise, you stepped through and was, as far as I could tell, unharmed. Of course you disappeared from sight. No one can see through that shimmering barrier – no one. So I had no idea if you had been killed and simply had fallen through, or whether you were alive and now were on the inside. So I decided I find a campsite and wait and see if you came back – and you did."

And here I thought I was alone. Jerod thought. *I even scanned the area . . . yeah there's a lot of vegetation here which makes the scans less accurate. Still . . . well . . .* He inwardly shrugged. Jarod knew that eventually he'd have to make contact with the natives of this world. Still this was awkward. How did one explain this away? "Are you sure? I mean I don't recall personally getting too close to that thing. I could feel my hairs standing up on end as I got closer. And I only went as close as I felt safe. I mean I could feel something there, and I could feel chills running through me warning me to stay away.

"In the past I witnessed the strangers – ones I've never seen before – dressed strangely – passing through the shimmering barrier without anything happening, and yet I witnessed a panicked animal run into it and die immediately. It shocked me. I mean, how could it be both ways? How can the strangers walk through unharmed, yet anything else touching it die? So I thought there has to be a trick to it. Word had come to me that some of the mountain clans had attacked these strangers to no avail. It was said that the attacking force was much larger than the strangers they attacked, but in the end, the strangers emerged unharmed. I thought, impossible. How could a superior force attacking a small group who was out in the open not kill them all?

"Then came the strangest rumor, at least to my mind. The ones passing on this information said that suddenly the strangers moved with such speed that it made them appear to be blurring. And in only a really short time the attacking clan had lost, and had lost badly. Again I thought, how can this be so? We all know how fierce the mountain clans are. So I first chalked it up to the telling of tales with much exaggeration. But I had run into others who supposedly had witnessed one of the attacks. I heard, as time went on, that the clans had made a number of attacks and none of them were successful. In fact not one of the strangers ended up with a scratch. Again, I thought impossible. How can it be so when one is in a battle? With arrows flying, long knives being used, and even large rocks being sent down the hills into the enemy, how could there be no injury let alone death?

"At that point I dismissed it as fiction. After all, it is impossible, right?" Here Jarod shut up. He knew that there had been a number of engagements initiated by the mountain clans, and that the patrols were looking for something, but not wanting to engage the natives Anyway one looked at it, it was an unfair fight. Any one member of those patrols could have easily defeated a whole clan – men, women, and children, and not raise a sweat. This information had come to him and the scout ship by energy leaving the planet, plus information gathered from the transmitters the patrols used, and captured by them as they approached in the scout ship.

As TimOtee listened he heard what would have been his own story. He had witnessed one of those attacks, and was surprised by the outcome. And because he was close he was surprised that the strangers hadn't come after him after the attack. But what JerOda said that the strangers only defended themselves, and again, it was what he witnessed. And like what JerOda said the strangers weren't interested in following up on their attacks, and none were hurt in the slightest. Still this didn't answer the question he asked. Again he was sure he had watched JerOda pass through the barrier and return. Yet he had no proof, and this JerOda might be telling the truth. Again here in this camp and back on the trail the distances to the barrier was pretty substantial. So he could have got it wrong. He had to admit that as soon as he saw this JerOda disappear his mind began to doubt what he had witnessed. Still here before him stood this tall stranger.

What to do? What to do? I can't stand here and accuse him of lying. And I have nothing to prove it one way or the other. Yet, I know what I saw. "Are you sure? I mean I happened to be close to one of those patrols, I'd guess you'd call them, when they were attacked by one of the clans . . ."

With excitement in his voice JerOda asked, "You were there? You actually witnessed one of the attacks? Was it as the others described it? Were they exaggerating or were they telling it like it were?"

For a moment TimOtee was taken back. He hadn't gotten around to the real question he wanted to ask before being interrupted. He needed to keep his train of thought so that once he answered these questions he could ask the one he really wanted. Talking softly he simply said, "Yes."

"Yes, what?"

"Yes, what? What do you mean?"

"Yes, it is exactly as I described it, or yes, they exaggerated?"

Smiling TimOtee said, "Oh, I see what you mean. Yes, it is exactly as they described it."

"Really? I didn't think it was possible to be honest."

"Well, you had to be there. And it is true. The strangers waited until the attackers were almost among them before they moved. It was like they were drawing them in, making them over confident, making them believe they had the element of surprise. Then, the strangers moved. I've never seen anybody move that fast. In my mind I kept thinking this is impossible, yet they did it – just like you going through that barrier. I know what I saw."

Jerod stood there thinking. Somehow he had to convince this TimOtee that it wasn't that way, even though it was. He looked up and realized the shadows had deepened and the sun had almost set. He smiled. "Look we can continue to talk about this later. The sun had just about set, and we haven't got the camp set up for tonight. Let's get some firewood, and put some food on the fire. We can discuss this over a meal, and the companionship of a warm campfire."

Little One: "Okay, so you met this JerOda, who is he really?"

GGF: "Well, as you can tell I had my suspicions, but no proof. Let's just let the story continue, and I think you'll have the answer you're looking for. Is that okay?"

Little One: He could feel frustration riding high. But it was obvious his namesake wasn't going to give anything away. At this point it all seemed almost too fantastic to be real. "I guess I don't have a choice, do I?"

GGF: Smiling and slightly shaking his head he quietly spoke, "No, not really. You see it's important to follow this just as it happened. And this IS just as it happened. So bear with me on this and I think once you have heard the whole story you will have all . . . well I hope all of your questions will be answered."

Little One: "Okay, I guess."

GGF: "Good! We'll take a small break here before we continue. And, remember I want to read your report before you turn it in."

CHAPTER THIRTEEN

SUSPICIONS PUZZLES AND RAIN

That possible movement that the chief saw kept bothering him. It would be a while before any of the command staff, let alone the atmospheric ships and their crews, and of course all the ground forces returned. They were being kept in the loop by radio. For him, at this moment, he had a skeleton crew, so what they were doing in the overall scheme of things was minor. Yet, anything they did to load the freighters would be less that needed to be accomplished later. Finally after some additional time had passed, he could no longer keep his mind on the subject at hand, excused himself and headed out towards the area where he had thought he had seen the movement. Two things entered his mind, first he wasn't quite sure how far out the movement had been, and secondly he knew that most of this area was farmland, and on the edges lay the wild vegetation. Meaning that there was a good chance that there would be nothing to show him anything or anybody had been there. Still until he had checked it all out he knew he wouldn't be comfortable.

With what he now knew, their timetable had gotten tighter. Somehow, and he knew it would happen eventually – the ones chasing them were too good – they would be located. He also knew that the one scout ship that had landed here to warn them had been sent back to assist in laying another false trail. They'd contact the ones aboard the command vessel and between them get the fleet to head out and check another sector of space. It might buy them enough time to get all of this underground. But he knew that this was something he or they couldn't count on. So it was the reason they continued to break things down and repack the freighters. It would take, at a minimum, a terran week, but more than likely at least two, but he suspected he didn't have that kind of luxury. Yeah they had been here on this planet for a while now, but it had been too busy to establish the length of a day, so they had been operating by the standard time schedule. It made it simpler that way.

He went out beyond the actual center of operations towards the southern barrier edge where very little happened. He knew that sensors had been set up to keep the area under surveillance, and to set off an alarm if something unusual happened. And there had been nothing from them. He pushed beyond the edges of the plowed ground to where the weeds began to take over followed by the native brush that was tough. Underneath much of this were the wild grasses, some having razor-like edges that could cut if one weren't careful. Past this the grounds became rough and then just before the barrier edge there was a large ravine that paralleled the barrier, running east to west. He figured that it had to have been in this area where he caught that movement out of the corner of his eye. He turned around and looked back at the compound trying to visualize where he had been standing when he caught that movement. Unfortunately there were a number of areas where he had been that would have worked.

He stood there staring when one of the sailors, (It was funny that even after all this time away from the wet navy the enlisted were still called sailors.), watched him. He could see the sailor was curious as to why he was out here, but refrained from asking. CPO Fredrickson knew he needed to get back to what had to be accomplished, but first he would finish this. He knew that word would get back to the rest of the enlisted that the chief was probably going crazy. Still until he was satisfied he'd search. Heading down into the ravine he first followed it to the east until where he might have been when he had caught that flash of movement couldn't be seen from his present location.

He then searched to the west, and found nothing. Yeah, he had to admit that this was something he wasn't good at, but just maybe he'd find something. He also knew he probably should turn it over to one of the marine ground scout units they had, but at the present they were with the rest.

He climbed out of the ravine and began to search the area above, but in the end shrugged. He found nothing. And unfortunately it hadn't relieved his feelings about this. He would head back, and continue the packing job, but once the teams came back he'd see if he could get one of the better scouts to inspect the area. Maybe they'd have better luck. Dusting himself off, he headed back to the compound. Dusk wasn't that far off, and while the ones outside of the barrier wouldn't be back until sometime close to half way through the night, that didn't mean he'd have any down time himself. Now he hoped that if there had been anything left to be found he hadn't destroyed it by searching the area himself.

He'd been looking down and when he looked up he realized one of the sailors had been watching him once again. And from what he could see the one who had been watching seemed to have a questioning look on his face. "Is there anything I can do for you?"

The sailor smiled and shook his head, "No chief . . . nothing at all."

"Then why are you just standing there?"

Again the sailor smiled, "Oh no reason at all. Just was observing someone out in the fields. After all we were ordered to keep a sharp eye out beyond the compound just in case someone infiltrated the energy barrier."

"True, but now you know it was me, let's get back to work."

"Will do, chief." And with that he headed out towards the mess hall. Chief Fredrickson stood there with his hands on his hips and watched him retreat. *Yeah, that's exactly what you were doing. So how long before any of this gets to the rest and they think I'm crazy. And they will never say it to my face.* He shook his head once again and headed to supply. It was where he had been originally going when he had caught that movement. If things continued on schedule it shouldn't be too much longer and they could begin the process of breaking down that building and have it packed and prepared to be shipped to the new location. The sun would be setting shortly and it would be time to get the area lit. There would be no time for breaks now. Pressure was on – not that it wasn't before – and this whole camp had to be disassembled as quickly as possible.

* * *

It had taken the two of them well into dusk to get enough wood gathered for their camp, get the fire going, and begin to prepare a meal. From the way the breezes were blowing TimOtee suspected they might have showers tonight, but held his peace for the moment. He was beginning to suspect something but again like seeing this JerOda go through and return from the other side of the barrier he had no proof. JerOda was stirring the pot of stew they had put together with each contributing to the ingredients. (Jerod had unobtrusively tested the food and found it safe.) And TimOtee, without giving the appearance of really studying what JerOda contributed found, in the end, that what JerOda had added was common stuff. So there wasn't anything here to confirm his thoughts.

Jerod looked across the fire at his unexpected companion, and he had to consider him so, and was still trying to come up with some way to detour TimOtee. He suspected that if TimOtee had only seen him either enter or return then he'd be able to find a way to make him believe it had been his imagination. But to have actually witnessed all of it made it doubly difficult. Inwardly shaking his head he thought. *Am I getting that careless, or is this TimOtee that good? And if he's that good, then I've got to be a lot more careful than I've been. Still I know I ran the sensors, used my implants, and I saw nothing. Yet what he described is accurate right down to the blue glow as the energy flowed over and integrated with my shield, allowing me to pass through. And if I think about it since this is what he described, I was quite busy at that time and he could have come around the corner, so to speak, at that very moment when I would be more interested in the integration then what was happening away from me.* As he added his share to the pot he added something that would insure he'd remain healthy, just to be sure. "So why are you out here anyway? When I came through the village back there to the north it was abandoned. I mean I can understand with it being that close to the shimmering barrier, although it really wasn't that close. Still it would have scared me. And all the farms seemed to be the same. I have to admit that not seeing anybody was quite a surprise, but . . ." Here he tipped his head slightly raising his eyebrows letting his sentence trail off.

TimOtee leaned back on his arms and remained silent for a moment. In a sense it was exactly what had happened to him as he had followed the barrier around coming from the east and heading down to the south side. But in his case, and at the time when he passed, the barrier had almost touched one of the houses that sat on the east side of the village. And what JerOda had just described stated he had to have come through later when the shimmering barrier moved further to the east. And that involuntary lifting of the forehead what was that meant to convey? Doubt? Possibly, since JerOda didn't finish his sentence. It added to the strangeness. "Are you one of the gods?" TimOtee blurted out, surprising even himself.

"Gods? Why would I be one of the gods? And why have you come to such a conclusion anyway?"

"What else would you call it when these strangers are able to do what they have done? No one here can create a shimmering barrier that kills when touched. No one here can move like those strangers did. And no one here, when attacked by an overwhelming force, can rout that force and come away with no injuries or death. And while it's taken some time to come to this conclusion, I think the facts speak for themselves. I suspect that for whatever the reason our gods have come down to our world."

Inwardly Jerod smiled. He had to admit everything TimOtee said made sense. Maybe he could use this conclusion to his advantage. Still he would have to be careful, since he didn't know their mythology. Maybe with care, he could coax the information out of him. Still it simply was the difference in tech that made it appear to be so. Then he realized that he'd have to be even more careful since it went against everything that was in the rule books. Still when one was in one of these operations, many times, the rule book had to be ignored, and he suspected this would be one of those times.

* * *

The chief looked around; it was time to get the arc-lights going. Watching his crew he yelled, "Let's keep this going, we've got to get at least half this building disassembled and into the freighters before the general and admiral return. So let's make this as easy as we can. I need two thirds of you involved with emptying the unit, followed by releasing the pins, stacking the materials, and the rest helping the fork trucks in getting the stacks safely tied down inside the freighters. And unfortunately it's not going to be a fun night. Sleep . . . you can forget about that. We are up against a really tough timeline, and from what the radar shows we are in for some heavy rain tonight – not that what we have to do isn't enough.

"Start with the mess. We can always eat in the open. Then move on to the supply shelter. If what the others are doing is successful then we will be moving into new quarters soon, and should be able to avoid any confrontations with the ones who are chasing us. Right now the others are beginning the tunneling operations to set us up where we can't be found. Besides, if we do have to run again, and unlike when we had to abandon our first hidden base, I don't want anything left behind. We've lost enough as it is. Do I make myself clear, gentlemen and ladies?" He got the answer he expected and watched as they headed out to make his orders a reality. He knew he would be in the middle of it also. They didn't have enough personnel to simply have one stand aside and oversee the operation. It would be "all hands on deck", and so be it.

* * *

TimOtee was almost mad at himself by making both the statement and accusation that this JerOda had to be one of their gods. Now he wished he hadn't, but he couldn't take it back. Still, from what he witnessed how else could it be? He was facing the shimmering barrier, and what made it seem almost alive was the fact that at night it glowed a soft blue. During the day this glow wasn't visible. During the day it simply was that shimmering that gave away its location. And there was that humming that warned any and all to stay away. It was the same blue light he had seen surrounding this JerOda just before he passed out of sight through that barrier. And again he thought he had caught sight of it when he reappeared just before the end of the day. And now he suspected JerOda was silent because of what he' blurted out.

At that moment he realized that there had been a change in the direction of the wind, and there was a taste of moisture in the air. Looking up he could see the stars disappearing and reappearing as the clouds scooted across the night sky, "Looks like we're in for a miserable night. Rain's on the way."

Jerod was still trying to come up with some way to take advantage of what TimOtee had thought and hadn't really been paying attention. His back was to the barrier so he really wasn't aware of anything that could be seen there. Although with the shimmering effect, there wasn't much that could be seen anyway. "Rain? Really. Sorry wasn't paying much attention.

It's be a crazy day of confirmations and revelations to say the least."

TimOtee had been looking down and trying to avoid staring into the fire. It could easily lead to night blindness and out here, even though they weren't that far from some of the farms, such could still lead to death and injury. He looked up towards the barrier and realized that it seemed like darkness meant nothing. It appeared to be lit up almost as if it was day. Not realizing he was speaking out loud he asked, "I wonder how they do that?"

With a questioning look, Jerod asked, "Do what?" (With each conversation he was beginning to nail down the language.)

"Oh sorry. Didn't realize I had spoken out loud . . . still this is beyond me, and as far as I know there's no one here that can do this."

Jerod was still looking across the camp at TimOtee. "Again, do what?"

TimOtee smiled and lazily pointed towards the barrier. "Oh that. You know, turn night into day. Even when we bring all of our candles, and lanterns together we can't do that."

"Jerod turned around and realized that there seemed to be a lot of activity going on inside and they seemed to be running the arc-lights. *Yeah, that would make it appear that the ones behind that barrier could be the gods*, he thought. "Wow! How do they do it? You're right. I haven't been around this thing at night.

Does it do this every night – you know glow like this? And those bright lights inside . . . impossible, yet there it is. Do you think it could be an illusion or something like that?"

He said bright lights, TimOtee thought. *To me it looks like only one light. Could it be more than one, and how does he know it to be more than one?* At that moment and in the distance he heard some thunder. *Didn't think we had the right weather to create this kind of storm. Still been kind of busy dealing with other problems, so haven't really been paying that much attention to the weather. Still when this one lets go we're going to get a lot of rain.* He looked up and saw lightning dancing between the clouds lighting the clouds up briefly. And as he observed this happening the first few drops began to fall. He looked around for somewhere they could go to get out of the coming deluge, but could see nothing that would help. Yeah there were trees close by, but with the lightning they wouldn't be safe. At least where the campsite was located they were in a low spot. Still, being in a low spot wasn't necessarily safe either. It could easily fill with water. "We may have to find some place to wait this out. The trees won't be safe, but where we are might be under water shortly. And we aren't close enough to one of the farm houses to be able to use them for shelter. So I guess it's a wait and see, what do you think?"

"I don't know how much rain we'll be getting, so I don't know."

"A good answer I guess. But I suspect it will be more than what we want."

Jerod could tell from observing TimOtee that he had probably given something away, but hadn't a clue to what that might have been. What bothered him wasn't that fact, but the fact he had caught, far in the distance to the north towards the mountain range, another set of such lights. And being with TimOtee he had no way of heading out and scouting this new light source. It was obvious they were up to something, but what was the question. Right now there were other problems that had to be dealt with – like this rain for instance. Again any of the information on this world was sketchy. Once it had been determined that there was an intelligent species here it became protected and off limits. So all he had was the initial survey results, and what they had discovered when the scout ship passed by just before he left in his own small ship.

It was also apparent that the one scout ship that had passed them while they were refueling in the asteroid field must have made contact with the ones who were here illegally. So everything that was transpiring had to be a result of being warned. Still it was all conjecture on his part. His stealthed devices he had in their camp hadn't updated his arrays, and it would be a while before they did. To remain hidden they would only do burst transmissions randomly and for micro-seconds. Meaning that it would take time for all the data they had collected to be gathered, organized, and be complete. He looked over at TimOtee and saw a shocked look on his face and wondered why. The rain had finally let loose and it definitely was a heavy downpour. At that very moment he realized that he still had his personal shield on and the rain was simply touching the shield and running off leaving a halo effect revealing that he was being protected from the rain. *Damn! Screw up. I should have shut this thing down, or at least set it to minimal. But with everything going on, trying to convince TimOtee that I'm one of them I simply forgot.* He reached up to wipe away some of the water, at least which was the appearance he wanted to present, and reduced the force field allowing the rain to reach his clothes. Still with the modern clothing he was wearing he's still remain dry and warm.

Pointing, TimOtee asked, "How'd you do that?" He saw JerOda reach up to wipe some of the offending drops away and then whatever he had just witnessed disappeared. This was becoming crazier as time went on. This JerOda seemed to be able to do things that were impossible. Was he some type of magician or something? Maybe he was one of their priests, or maybe like he had thought earlier, he had to be one of the gods. He could feel his nervousness grow.

With a perplexed look Jerod asked, "Do what?"

With what he had just witnessed gone, all TimOtee could do was shake his head. Was JerOda playing with him? He seemed honest in his responses, but wouldn't it be that way if the gods had come here? They'd be superior in everything. He realized that for the moment this train of thought would have to be stopped. It was raining harder and if they didn't move then where they were would be under water. "Sorry, but we have no choice, we need to move our campsite. Might be better if we just pack up and head back to the trail, work our way north. There's a farm not too far from here that has been abandoned like everything else around here. While it's still not close, it's the best solution to what we are facing here. This will be with us for a while. So we might as well be miserable while trying to find better shelter then staying here and find ourselves under water."

Jerod shrugged, "Works for me. Since you know where you are going, lead on." He could see that their campfire had almost been extinguished from the rain anyway, and the area was beginning to develop deep puddles. They quickly gathered their wet equipment and by the time they were ready to leave the fire was out and the site was starting to fill with water.

TimOtee pointed back to the trail and almost had to yell over the winds and downpour, "This way. Funny thing, by morning, once this thing has passed, and the rains have stopped, you'd never know that it had rained. The soils here really soak the water in."

Jerod kept track of the time as they traveled the trail heading generally north, and it was hours later when they finally reached the point where TimOtee turned off the main trail and headed down a minor pathway.

* * *

Admiral Sympson, General Pertion, and Colonel Jamison stood back from the teams workings, watching the work proceed. They were at the site where they had finally decided to dig. They had the laser drills operating, and the drills were advancing rapidly through this first hillside. Once through this one they'd begin the actual cutting. If things went well, and all three had to admit at this time that it hadn't, then in less than a week – earth time – they'd have their initial work complete. Then they could move the freighters into the newly created deep caverns. This initial dig would provide temporary quarters for all of them and they could leave the farmlands where they presently were. And here it would much easier to defend, leave a smaller signature, and with the energy barrier, cover a much smaller area, thusly saving energy, and send out less of an energy signature. Other than line of sight transmissions they were radio silent. Again something that would be picked up as the signals traveled at light speed away from the planet.

The advantage of the laser drills lay in the fact that as they cut the circular tunnel the heat generated melted the soils, and rock forming a natural support for the walls once it cooled. All of them knew that their time was almost up. Meaning if this wasn't completed soon then they would probably have to abandon this location and head out into deep space once again. The admiral had the flag captain working on that part of the plan so that if this should fail they'd be able to rapidly transition into the backup plan. It was another reason for breaking down their camp, their present base of operations. Unlike when they had been first discovered and were not prepared, this time they'd not have a repeat of that fiasco and avoid another SNAFU like last time.

The rains had been heavy and it was easily visible in the work lights they had set up. Without them – yes they had their night vision equipment – it was just about as black as it could be. Only when the lighting danced between the clouds or struck around them did it light the area up. In a sense they were happy about the rains. With them being this hard it probably meant they wouldn't be harassed by the natives living in these mountains. And they also hoped, with the failed attacks, and less happening that it would mean they'd learned their lessons and would stay away. Still they had no real hope there. It seemed that the natives from these mountains would continue to try to ambush the patrols – even with a one hundred percent failure rate.

They had to give them a failure as far as learning anything from their attempts, but a passing grade on their tenacity to continue to find ways to wipe them out.

Again all three were expecting Chief Fredrickson to have the camp well on its way to being broke down and loaded into the freighters. One thing for sure the chief was good at what he did, and his people were quite loyal to him. So while it was a worry, in the overall scheme of things, only a small one. They suspected that by the time they returned that at least half of the buildings would be broken down and inside the freighters. And with all proceeding well here they decided to head back to the encampment they had set up close to this operation. With the noise being produced no one would be getting any sleep, but there was hot coffee, and something to go with it back there. And with the rains, winds, and even with the modern protection against the elements they were becoming chilled. So the break would be welcome. And once they had taken theirs, they would make sure all the others out here could come back and warm up; get something hot to drink, and a little food to sustain them.

As they hiked back to the tents that had been set up in the temporary camp the sounds from the construction began to diminish, which was a welcome relief. By being there by the operation one got used to the noise, and only by leaving did one become aware of the difference. All three could hear their ears ringing. They passed one of the many patrols that continually worked the area. They weren't going to take any chances with this operation. And once they were able to make the move, then all the emitters would be shut down, and all the natives they had in stasis would be released unharmed to return to what they were doing before they were captured. Of course they wouldn't awaken until after they had made the move out of the area. And for most they'd awaken where they had lived, making what had happened to them a mystery. And that was the way the Admiral, with the General behind him completely, wanted it. The less the natives knew the better for all.

As far as refreshments went all they had were the standard rations. Coffee always and that was just about it. At least the waste materials from the operation were being used. They were converting it to fuels, and needed supplies that had been used up during their flight from their original center of operations – a place they could never return. Admiral Sympson said, to no one in particular. "I'm a little more positive that we might just get this accomplished and be moved in before the fleet arrives. And with the false ion trails we've been laying outside of this world there's a good chance we will be able to cover our tracks and make this one of our bases of operations sometime in the future. Yeah I know it's so far out that it could only act as a supply depot, but it will give us another hole to hide in if we have the need."

Shaking his head inwardly General Pertion wasn't sure if they'd make it or not. Yeah, after the period of time they'd been here they had finally located the type of bedrock they needed, but it could easily be too little, too late. Especially since they had been alerted to the fact the fleet wasn't that far away. Still the plan that the admiral had put into effect might delay the arrival and still give them the necessary time. "I don't know if we will or not. You're in charge of moving us around, and I and my marines are responsible for keeping you and yours safe when we are on the ground. And these mountain natives have been tenacious to say the least. Making it difficult to do what we had to do. More slowing us down as they continued to come up with new ways to try to kill us. Still here we are one step closer to wrapping this part up. Still, and we, and all of us know it, we are up against an almost impossible timeline here. Yeah from what I can see here of the operation our chances look good. Still, knowing who's after us I have to admit that it means I'm always looking over my shoulder expecting them to be here at any moment."

Colonel Jamison sat in one of the camp chairs and just listened in. He had no desire to talk. Their situation was dire, and that old clock kept ticking away. Inwardly he smiled. He had never heard a clock tick, and it was an old phrase anyway that refused to die. All time pieces were synchronized to the command ship and that included any that they personally carried, along with the internal time pieces that was part of the HUD inside of the armor or tied into their personal implants. Right now they had patrols working the surrounding area and keeping in contact with this command tent. For now, and he suspected because of what they were doing, the natives were staying away. In fact once they began the drilling operation the locals that had been shadowing them had simply disappeared, and that was a relief.

He was about to take another sip of coffee and realized his cup was empty. He looked down at it longingly, but knew there would be no time to refill the cup. Looking up he realized that the staff was silent. Had he missed something? Then listening he heard over the radio network the chief, back in the primary camp, commenting on something he'd found. He listened carefully and if he heard what he thought he heard it sent chills down his spine.

* * *

As the two of them approached a small farmhouse Jerod froze in his tracks. His arrays just alerted him to the fact that something was seriously wrong with the devices he had set up inside the encampment. And there was a great chance because of what was happening that at least one of them would be discovered compromising the whole network he had established there.

TimOtee had just reached the farmhouse and had opened the door preparing to go inside when he turned back to JerOda and saw him just standing in the rain and wind staring at nothing. It appeared he was looking out into the distance and witnessing something, but the only thing that was here in the direction that JerOda looked was the farmhouse. What was going on? Then he heard him say something that he didn't understand, but chalked it up to the fact that the winds were pretty strong and so loud he could have misunderstood. He waved at JerOda trying to get some response and it was like he wasn't even here. He shook his head and thought, *If he wants to stay out in the rain that's his business, but I prefer to be inside where it's dry. So if he wants to stand there that's all right by me. I'm ready to start a fire, dry out, and get something warm to eat.* He tried once again to get JerOda's attention and still failed. So he turned and went inside closing the door behind him figuring that when this JerOda was ready he'd come inside and join him.

Once inside he put together the kindling necessary to light a fire, and shortly had a good one going. As it warmed the heat felt nice and he could see steam rising off his clothing as the heat began to dry the moisture. If he had a looking glass he suspected he would look like one of those small furry creatures that had been caught out in the rain that looked completely helpless and miserable, and to the females adorable. Because JerOda hadn't entered yet he went back to the door, opened it and saw that he hadn't moved at all and was still staring out at nothing. He was becoming concerned and almost decided to go out and lead him in thinking that something might have happened to him physically or maybe mentally to have caused this. Still there wasn't anything around that could harm him so he decided to let a little more time pass, and as he was about to close the door again he saw him shake his head, refocus, look up in surprise, smile, and begin to head in his direction. TimOtee wasn't sure if it was okay or not, but let JerOda in through the open door, closing it once he was inside. He watched as JerOda approached the fire and held out his hands to the warmth.

"Ah that feels nice . . . Sorry about that, but something came up, and I had to deal with it." Jerod smiled to himself as he realized that what he had just stated made absolutely no sense at all.

To TimOtee this statement was totally weird. *Deal with it? While one is standing staring and in the rain no less, right. Am I crazy or is this one the crazy one, or are my feelings and thoughts about who I think he is true?* "Sorry, you lost me."

"I can understand that. Sometimes I have to stand like that and think something out. So don't be surprised if you happen to see me do it again, okay?"

TimOtee didn't respond as something else caught his attention. He remembered his clothing steaming as the heat began to dry them out, and this was the normal thing that happened when one was caught out in the rains like this. And yet, when he looked closely at JerOda's clothing, and while it seemed impossible, they were dry. Dry? *How could they be dry?* Then he realized that JerOda's hair was dry also. This was really becoming stranger by the moment. "So tell me how is it that your clothes seem dry and you look to be the same? You were still standing out in the middle of that heavy downpour much longer than I and yet you and your clothes appear . . . not wet?"

Jerod realized that very moment that he hadn't completely shut down his personal shield or that the clothing he was wearing while appearing to be native was made of the modern materials that shed water. Between the two he could have walked across a stream or river that came up to his neck and emerged dry. It meant that here was something else that could tag him, as this TimOtee had concluded, one of the gods. He realized that for whatever the reason, on this particular mission he was making too many mistakes. At least these mistakes hadn't been against the renegades. "Are you sure? I feel wet, and every time one of those cold drops ran down the back of my neck it sent chills through me."

* * *

The admiral was silent for a moment. "Are you sure chief? No, don't answer that. Of course you are."

"Yes sir, and I'll answer it anyway. One of the crew I had working to break these prefabs down brought me a device that fell off one of the buildings. I've never seen anything like it, and I've only heard rumors that such equipment exists. It's supposedly only available to the spec-ops of a department that doesn't exist within our government. The stuff is superior to any of the military grade that we normally handle. And from what little I can determine this stuff usually is pretty tough. Still, like anything manufactured, if something is hit just right it will break. My feeling is we've had an agent infiltrate our operations, came through the barrier we've set up, and probably left the same way.

"I was suspicious earlier when I caught a movement out of the corner of my eye, but when I went to investigate I found nothing. Still it bothered me, and when one of the patrols that are with you came back I was going to ask one of the scouting units to do a thorough search since it's not my area of expertise. But now I don't have a need since this piece of hardware has shown up. I don't know how many he or she planted since they become what they are attached to making them virtually invisible. Most of the time, until an operation is destroyed because of the intel these things gather, no one has a clue that they've been compromised.

"I really have no idea how many agents we may be dealing with, but with this attack coming from the outside, so to speak, I suspect that we are safe within our own. Still, again it's just rumors, if the agency has more than one working, the others will not know. So if one is compromised he or she cannot identify any others, or even know if there are any other agents working inside."

"Okay. Look, change of orders then. Yes, load all the prefabs on the freighters as you are doing now. But instead of sending them into orbit to await our command to return to the planet and join us here, I want them to offload everything on the cruiser. By the time you've sent the first that way they will be waiting. I want everything we have there on that cruiser ASAP. And once you've got the prefabs moved, then shrink the field back and get those emitters up there also. It will take a few hours once the stasis field is removed before the natives recover, so that is the last thing for you to perform. Got it chief?"

"Yes sir, I'm on it and should be accomplished by the end of tomorrow. Will keep you updated on the progress, sir."

"Can't ask for more than that. So get to it . . . and chief, thanks for the heads up." The admiral broke the connection and looked over at the staff he had with him which included the general. "Looks like we've been found out, or compromised much earlier than we thought. Yeah, the one ship that came here to warn us didn't think they were this close, but obviously they are. Okay, let's organize things so we can pull out in a moment's notice if necessary. Let your patrols know what's going on, and we'll keep the troop carriers here on site so we can withdraw as close to instantly as we can. Anything that we don't need I want aboard the cruiser. As you know it's sitting behind one of the moons and is just inside the gravity well of this planet. So it won't take much to get everything off of this rock."

He turned back to the radio operator. "Get my flag captain on the line. He needs to get moving on one of our fall back plans."

"Yes sir. It will only be a moment." The operator turned to his task and in short order had the captain online. "Admiral? What's happening sir?"

"To keep it short, we've been compromised once again. And no, before you ask, it's nobody within our command. I need you to send out our three destroyers that we have sitting on the opposite side of this system and have them lay a false trail out of here. Use Charley Delta Five Six as an operational guideline. Then we need to begin to set up for our own exit if it becomes necessary. I'm going to leave all that in your capable hands while we continue to work on this. We may just make it, and with those false trails, run our pursuers completely out of system and allow us to disappear completely. It's my hope anyway.

"I think we need to look at returning to our old stomping grounds, at least somewhere close. I know we had shut down a pirate operation on one of the larger asteroids, and it may be a good place for us to run. After all, everything has already been set up, and while it is now abandoned, it wouldn't take much to make it operational again. So look to setting up a roundabout route that will take us there. I'm hoping that the spies we have within the pursuing fleet can keep them running after ghosts for a while longer. If so, it should give us the time. If not, then we are out of here."

"Okay sir, I'm on it, and I'll update you as I can."

"Expect it to be no other way, Admiral Sympson out." He turned and faced the rest of the staff who was with him in the tent, "I know you heard some of that, but it looks like we have much less time than we thought. Apparently one of the agents, who don't exist, has somehow arrived on this planet, infiltrated our basecamp, and then began to bug it. It is only because we are in the process of dismantling the camp that we have discovered this fact. So we need to be set to move at a moment's notice. Either in the cavern we are carving out here, or back on the run into deep space. Get the orders out and get everything loaded that we don't have an immediate need for. That way if we have to abandon our operations here we won't lose anything like we did when we were caught unprepared." He looked over the ones with him, shook his head, and headed back outside. The information needed to be passed on to the ones at the construction site.

* * *

The array began an information dump and Jerod knew that he had been compromised. He hadn't realized when he had planted his bugs that the renegades were preparing to make a move. Still the equipment he was using was supposed to be tough, and remain hidden and stealthy even if they happened to be hit, or roughly treated. Still anything manufactured could eventually fail, and here for whatever the reason one did. From the other bugs he could see the prefabs coming down, being packed up, and loaded into the freighters. Something major was happening, and while all the conversations were being recorded for future use, the only thing it did for him now was confirm his worst fears – *they knew*.

TimOtee observed that suddenly this JerOda had quit speaking and was now staring out in the distance as if he was concentrating on something. He looked around curious as to what he could be looking at but could only see one of the walls that constituted the interior of this home. What was it he was either thinking or concentrating on? At least they were out of the rain. So while he waited for JerOda to respond he went over and built up the fire. There still was a chill in the house, and his wet, but drying clothes didn't help him get warm. Yet, this JerOda didn't appear chilled at all. It was something he didn't understand either. They had been in those rains for a long time. At least a quarter of the night if not longer, and yet it appeared that he had just returned from a leisurely walk around the property, not from the storms, winds, and cold they had just faced. Inwardly he shook his head. *This just isn't possible. For me it would be easy to lay down my sleep sack and sleep half the day away. Yet, this one who is with me seems fresh and ready to tackle the day. He has to be one of the gods even though he denies it. And while I cannot prove it I know what I saw. Add to it what I've seen so far and no matter how hard I try it still is the only conclusion I can come up with. Yeah, later I might laugh at being naïve, if something shows me how wrong I am, but until that moment I'll believe what I can see.*

Jerod knew he was digging himself in deeper and probably confirming this TimOtee's ideas. But a crisis had just taken place, and he was in the wrong place – no surprise there – at the wrong time, and no way to fix it. He wondered if the scout ship he had been a passenger on had made contact with the pursing fleet, and even now they were on their way here. Still there was no way he could count on that. And being only one – at least he thought he was the only one – it meant that overall there was little he could do. He knew that the arrays he had set up were recording everything they caught in the many spectrums that existed. It meant that everything that was taking place here was being recorded for future analysis. And anything that didn't apply would be dumped. Even with the filtering software in place the amount of data was huge. And it was one of the reasons he was only updated a couple of times a day.

TimOtee went to one of the windows that looked towards the shimmering barrier. There had been a change in the sound coming off of it and he was curious as to why. Still from here he could only sense it more than see it. Where this farm was located was sort of a hollow, putting it below the surrounding lands. And with that canyon and deep ravine to the south, and the southerly wall being higher than the northern side of the farm house, it blocked distant views in that direction too. He turned and saw that JerOda had yet to move and he continued to stare out at nothing. Maybe he should go over and touch him or something? Taking a deep breath and letting it out slowly he decided against it. Instead he went into the food prep area and began to fix a meal. The one they were going to have back at the campsite had been interrupted because of the storm, and he found that he was hungry. Maybe the smell of cooking foods would bring this JerOda back to reality.

Little One: "How can you know all of this? I mean, at least you said you really knew nothing about who this JerOda is?"

GGF: "I know it seems a little weird, but I really didn't know what was happening around me at this time. Again later – and I know I've said that a lot – the answers and understanding will be there. So you'll just have to stay with me and believe what I'm showing you. Remember, none of us has the ability to see everything that's happening around us. It's impossible, yet to understand what is happening, and as I tell you the story, you must see everything. Otherwise it doesn't make sense."

Little One: "Okay . . . I guess." He stood up and stretched. Looking out he could see another day was ending. *Where'd the time go? I mean I thought we had only passed a little time since the midday meal, but my insides are rumbling telling me it's time to eat again.* "Great grandfather, where'd the time go?"

GGF: "Can't answer that one. It always goes fast for me."

TIME WAITS FOR NO ONE

After the conversation with the admiral Chief Fredrickson turned to his crew and pushed them harder. He suspected the orders he'd receive were exactly what he had been ordered to do and had planned accordingly. Still this meant the turnaround times would be greater. And instead of being able to take a break between the planned storage areas where they were presently tunneling, now they would need to bring the whole camp down, organize the parts, set the stacks up in areas so when the freighters returned from their outbound trips they could load them once again. If it went as well as it could – and generally that was an impossibility – then once the freighters were loaded for their second trip everything, other than the emitters would be out of here. They had a number of smaller ships they had planned on using for loading of the emitters.

Now those emitters presented a problem in themselves. First they'd need to set up an inner barrier shut the outer ones down, pull them back and repeat until they were ready to bring the whole barrier down . . . Then came the final item – the stasis field generator. It had to be last since the ones who were under the stasis field would begin to recover as soon as four to five hours later, with the rest as far out as twelve. With that final shutdown and loading there would be nothing left to show they had ever been here other than the trampled vegetation, and of course the burn marks where the fields had been. And all of it would recover rather quickly, meaning after a short period of time there would be nothing to show they had ever been here. *Guess I need to organize a team that will deal strictly with the emitters and the stasis generator. That will reduce the size of the crew that's disassembling the prefabs, but I don't have any of the marines to assist.* Even with the pressure on he smiled as his thoughts about the way the marines handled things entered his mind, *It means more pressure on us, but less broken items. Oh well, it's always a tradeoff.*

He looked at the organized chaos that surrounded him, and knew it was going well no matter what it looked like. Over half of the structures were down, and with the forklift operators the designated piles were growing. Maybe they still could pull this off. Still, only time would tell, and not knowing the location of the pursuing fleet didn't help. And while he was sure that movement he had seen just a short time in the past, had been the agent he really had no proof, and in the overall scheme of things it wasn't important anyway. They were fortunate to discover that there had been one that had infiltrated their operation setting up his bugs to monitor their operation. And these bugs were really sophisticated. He knew that one couldn't open any of them to learn how they were constructed. These devices would self-destruct the second any intrusion into the inner workings happened. He had to admit even the ones the military used would do the same. Still, there were workarounds for some of the older stuff.

This led him to thinking that maybe the equipment they used for the same function – infiltration, and such – came from this agency and was simply their older equipment. When this one had been turned over to him it appeared to be a smaller, and obviously a better unit than the ones they were using. Still, it could simply be that the function dictated the form the equipment had to take, and as such meant that in general all such devices looked similar. Part of the problem he faced was the fact that there had to have been more than this one and the others had yet to be located. And with this knowledge it meant there was a possibility that the signals they would send out in burst transmissions could still compromise them and their location. At this point he turned back around and headed back to the radio and asked the operator to contact the cruiser where all of this equipment was being offloaded. And once the contact was made he talked with the officer on duty, and had the officer tie him into security so they could have a three-way conversation. He explained what had been found and his suspicions for which they agreed, and after signing off felt better about it.

He knew that up there the freighters were just now approaching. And once they docked, unloaded what they had, first it would be scanned, and even if nothing was found, there would still be a great possibility, with the sophistication of the equipment they were up against, they'd still miss something, so as a result, all of it would be placed inside an isolation field that would keep any signals from escaping. This would be followed by monitoring that would attempt to catch any burst transmissions. And if this happened, then using triangulations pinpoint those points of transmissions and eliminate the problem. And if this failed then everything they had taken up to the cruiser would be first decontaminated, then recycled and reconstructed. One way or the other, they would destroy those bugs. For now he'd keep the one, at least until they left the area. There wasn't any way to know if the unit was still active, and he couldn't take the chance by taking it with him. So here it would stay. At least with the equipment they still had onsite he'd do as much analysis as he could. Yet, he suspected it wouldn't matter. The important part was awareness, and they had that now.

* * *

Jerod continued to monitor the incoming data oblivious to his surroundings. Normally such information, unless it was an emergency, and again this qualified, would only be updated late at night where activity was minimal, and there was less chance of discovery. Unfortunately this took all of his concentration no matter how many or how powerful his implants were. Somehow he needed to learn more, and the one thing he didn't have, which suddenly had become a rarer commodity, was time. He had hoped he would have had more of it so he could scout out the surrounding area, and become familiarized with both the people of this world, and the extent of the infiltration. Plus he wanted to know how far and deep their crimes had gone. He knew from just what he had observed and what they had recorded and captured in the escaping signals that while the rogues had broken many of their prime directives that they seemed to be uninterested in hurting any here, unless they were attacked. And that at least spoke of some good still existing. Still and in the end the rogues' visit here would be influencing these people maybe forever – who knows?

Unfortunately with his time inside the energy barrier he hadn't been able to determine what had happened to the ones who were living there. From what he could determine the area encompassed by the field was all prime farmland, and giving the appearance that it was being worked at the time the renegades landed and began their operation. He had other questions that he had hoped would be answered by those bugs, but now it was all for naught. With the information coming in he now knew the encampment was being dismantled and moved. Moved to where, again it was anybody's guess. Still if he had to do just that it probably would be where those lights in the distance were located. They were far too bright and steady to be anything that could be produced here. So it was obvious they were making a move to that possible location.

This brought him to the present and the situation he faced and with this the sudden realization that he had been concentrating so hard on what he had just received that he had forgotten he was with one of the locals. *Damn! I must appear to be crazy or something like that to this TimOtee. How long have I been doing this?* He looked at his internal chronograph and realized that a good hour plus had gone by. Sheepishly he looked around and realized for the first time he was actually inside one of the structures the locals had built. A quick scan from his implants stated to him that it wasn't much different from some of the ancient farms and the homes on these farms back on his own world. Must be something about form following function making much of this common no matter where one went.

Now how was he going to approach TimOtee? He had apparently watched him enter the barrier and then come back out – something quite impossible. And he seemed to remember that TimOtee had also commented on his clothing remaining dry, and somehow he remembered trying to counter that observation. Now he had been away, so to speak, for some time making everything this TimOtee witnessed harder to overcome. It was at that moment he caught the smell of cooking foods and realized he was hungry. Following the scents he found what he would have called the kitchen, but knew here it was simply the cooking area inside this house. He heard the floor creak as he headed in that direction knowing that he would be heard.

TimOtee turned and faced JerOda and smiled. "So you're back. I don't have a clue what was going on with you, but I know you didn't or wouldn't respond to anything I asked or said. So I decided to come in here and make that meal we missed when the storm struck. So what was going on anyway? I mean I've never seen anyone go away like that. Yeah all of us daydream now and then, and if someone was to sneak up on us at those times and touched us we'd probably scream. But nobody goes away that way for as long as you."

"Sorry about that. Something came up that drew me away. I know that doesn't make a lot of sense, but it's the truth. And I know what you've been seeing may be a little strange . . ."

"Strange? No. Weird, and well beyond anything I've ever seen anybody do, yes." TimOtee stopped a moment and turned back to his simmering foods. "We'll have to wait to continue this. The food is ready, and I'm ready to eat, how 'bout you?"

Jerod smiled, "Yeah, me too. I have to admit it was the smell of the cooking food that brought me in here, and I have to admit to being hungry. Let's see if the smells and your cooking will be worth the wait."

"Now, what I've learned from my life is the fact that if one is hungry almost anything tastes good."

Jerod laughed. "I guess I can't deny that. So how are we going to do this? I mean I have my own bowl, should I be using it? Or is there some other way you are going to serve this?"

"No we can each use our own stuff. Just come over and take as much as you like as I fixed plenty for the two of us."

"Fine with me. Still since you are the one who did all the work I'll let you take the first helping." Part of the reason he wanted TimOtee to be first was so he could observe the eating ritual. Every culture had their own, and he wanted to be sure that he didn't inadvertently defame some cultural ritual. There hadn't been time with the flyby of the scout ship to actually record any of this.

As they ate the food, Jerod had to admit that it really tasted good, and yes, he had been hungry, and yes, maybe it tasted good because of that fact. Still as they ate neither spoke much concentrating on serious business of taking the edge off their hunger. For Jerod there was a second reason for his silence. The data from his arrays kept pouring in. Unfortunately none of it was good news. The arrays confirmed that they were recording all the data that was available including the radio transmissions being made – all good and proper. But it was the information he was receiving that worried him. And with no word from the scouts or the fleet he knew that they were losing precious time. From all the indicators he could receive it appeared that the renegades might be preparing to pull out. Unfortunately much of the radio transmissions were encrypted so he really didn't know what was really being communicated between the different forces and locations.

It was the patterns of the transmissions that led him to this belief. He'd need to come to a decision shortly. There was no way he, by himself, would be able to do more than monitor the situation and give the fleet an update when they finally did arrive. He only hoped it would be soon, and they would still catch these rogues here doing whatever it was that they were doing. He looked down and realized he had finished his food and could see that TimOtee had finished his and had been looking at him expectantly. He realized that TimOtee may have asked him something and he'd been too deep in thought and the monitoring of the data to be listening. Smiling a sheepish smile he asked, "Ah, did you ask me something?"

"Yeah . . . I was wondering if you wanted any more since I could see your bowl is empty."

"Is there any more, and no I'm good, and I guess I should complement the cook, because it really tasted great."

"First off there isn't any more, but I'd thought I'd ask, and thank you. So now what?"

"Now what, what?"

I suspect the rains are tapering, and I wondered what your plans are, that's all. For now I'm free . . . well mostly. My original goal or goals were to first, get inside that shimmering barrier, and second, to get help. I wasn't able to get inside, and I haven't found any help – at least I don't think I have. So this leaves me free for the moment until I can come up with what's next. Besides what I've seen you do still makes me think you are one of the gods."

"Okay TimOtee, I'm not one of your gods, okay?" Jerod had a feeling that he would have to come up with some satisfactory answer otherwise TimOtee would continue to hound him about it. "Consider me a messenger." It was an idea that came to him almost immediately. By being a messenger he could circumvent this "god" thing.

TimOtee smiled. "Ah, I see. So why are you here – messenger?"

"The ones you call strangers, or gods, since you've described them both ways, are what you would call evil. They were not supposed to come down to your world. Where I am from such is wrong. You and yours are allowed to become what you will be, and are not to be influenced by us or our kind. So I came here to correct this problem. If all works then soon the ones who are here will be gone, and all will return to as it was before. Well, as close as we can make it. I know that once our kind has come to a world like this, at this stage of development, there are always influences that cannot be undone. We, and I speak for ours, have laws against such as happened here."

"I guess that makes some kind of sense. Still you are not telling me all."

Jerod shook his head, "Sorry, this is something I cannot change. I can only reveal what is necessary to correct this, if such is possible. Understand that soon there is a possibility you will witness more of the same, but the intention is to remove this evil from your world. And if we are successful, then you will not be bothered again – at least by us."

"At least by *us*? Are you telling me that that there are other 'gods' out there that might 'bother us'?

Again shaking his head Jerod simply said, "You have no idea." He had an idea beginning to form, and maybe it would be a way to insure that the planet remained safe from his species in the future. "Tell you what, if you want you can come with me. If you do then in the end you will learn much that is beyond you and yours. I need to confirm that you can receive what I have to offer. And if so then you can help in the protection of your world. What do you say to that?"

"Wow, JerOda, you're offering me a chance to come along? Do I have it right? As far as the rest I really don't understand . . ."

"Yeah, that's what I'm offering you, and as far as the rest, well if it goes as I hope, then you will have a much better understanding. So are you willing to take a chance and come with this messenger?"

"How can I refuse such an offer, from the messenger, and whether you want to deny it or not, I'll state that you may not claim to be one of the gods, but being a messenger definitely puts you higher up than me. So yes, I will come along and learn what I can."

* * *

It had been a long shift, double shift, triple shift, if he wanted to be honest, but Chief Fredrickson finally could relax. Looking around, and it had only stopped raining a short time ago adding to the misery, other than the beat down grasses, and plants, no one would ever know they had been here. Shortly the last of the emitters would be shut down, and once loaded into the last small in-system freighter, he and his crew would join the skeleton crew that was still working the shaft in the mountains. They'd simply load into one of the troop carriers and be done. In a way he would have loved to stay here. The planet was nice, and because of where the natives were in their development they would be no more than a nuisance. Still, he knew they had no right to be here, and it simply had been circumstances that had placed them in this situation.

Looking over at the crew as they took a needed break he took a deep breath then gave the final orders. "Let's shut the final ones down, get them into the freighter, and then shut down the stasis fields, load them also, and then all of us into the troop carrier. We are out of time!" Briefly he watched, and then joined in. This was a job that required every able bodied crew member. And while he couldn't see it happening personally, he had received the communications from the orbiting ships that the materials they sent had been recycled. It had been decided that there would be too great of risk they wouldn't find every one of the devices that had been attached to the prefab buildings. In the end it simply meant energy used, since the units that were recycled would be prefab units once again. This reminded him of the fact he still had the one that had warned them of the infiltration. He reached into his coat pocket, pulled it out and looked at the innocent piece of metal and plastic, found a rock where he placed the offending unit and then stomped down on it hoping that if not destroying it outright, to have disabled it. He looked at his handiwork and couldn't tell if he had been successful or not, so he did it again, grinding with his heal, turned and making sure all had been accomplished, then joined the crew on the troop carrier. The freighter had left a few moments before, and now that he was aboard he had the hatch closed, and signaled the pilot to lift off.

Even though they would continue to try here, he suspected that they would be leaving soon. There was too much evidence suggesting that the pursuing fleet would be closing in on them soon. And they were well outnumbered, and capture wasn't an option. He, as well as every marine, sailor, officer, and enlisted knew this. So as long as they could stay ahead they would. Space was huge and while there were many sectors that were unexplored, the ones explored still covered vast areas. And in three dimensional space that left almost infinite places to hide.

In a sense this brought him full circle, because at that moment he knew that their network within the military was huge. He wondered what plans the admiral and general had to get these spies out safely. And this was important – critical really – since many of these spies knew many of the locations they used, which meant that these locations could only be used as meeting points now, since there would be a great chance they would be compromised. And all of this was a game changer, meaning that all their familiar haunts and hangouts were a thing of the past. He knew he wasn't as smart as the ones leading them and he suspected that they had already figured out what had just come to the forefront of his own mind. He felt the ship lift off, and he unconsciously reached for the rings that helped steady one as the ship shifted. Then he felt gravity increase as the ship accelerated, leaving a vibration that ran through the ship followed by a deep roar drowning out any conversation they might have been having. In roughly a quarter of an hour they'd be in the new location.

* * *

When they left the farmhouse Jerod looked out and could see the energy barrier was down. It was obvious the rogues were moving fast. *Damn, where's the fleet? I need you here now. We're about to lose them again. And I suspect if we do we might not get a second chance. That Admiral Sympson, with his skills and experience, will simply disappear and we'll be lucky if we can follow him from here. With what's available to him his choices are almost infinite. It's not like we were on a planet like now, where there are only a few choices available. Once in space there are no limitations other than what the equipment places on them, which means there are no limitations.* "It looks like the shimmering barrier has come down. I guess that means that things might begin to return to normal."

TimOtee laughed a bitter laugh. "Right, if anything can return to normal after this. While not a lot of time has passed, enough has that it will affect our growing of the crops, meaning we'll have less available for the time of cold and gray."

Jerod, as they made their way in the direction of the old growth forest, thought about TimOtee's comment. Maybe he could help a little there. He'd have to make a quick study of the foods they were growing, and maybe he could mix it with better ones allowing a faster and better yield. It might be a gift to the natives of this world. Sort of a payment for the damage they were doing by actually being here. "Never know, things might work out fine in the end. I think that soon others will be returning home, and even you will be able to rejoin your family."

TimOtee had an incredulous look on his face, "Really? How can that be? I mean the farm I'm from, and my family was behind that shimmering barrier, and any of us know what happens to any who got too close to that thing – they died. Well, except you and the strangers, of course. But in your case it's understandable. You are *the* messenger and that gives you some type of protection."

* * *

It had taken them a full day and into part of the night to reach Jerod's original camp. His ship was still hidden, and with the darkness it helped keep it out of sight of one TimOtee. Jerod needed to learn if what he planned would actually work here as it had on other worlds. One thing for sure nobody from his people would be remaining behind to monitor the situation. Yes, they'd be placing satellites around the planet to monitor the world. Still, since they were mechanical, with limited AI's aboard it meant in the long run that the renegades or rogues could circumvent them and return here later if they did escape. So he simply needed people on the ground to continue to monitor the situation. And here before him was his first recruit even though TimOtee didn't know he was one.

"You seemed like you knew where you were going. Yet from what I know, and I have to admit as far as this area goes my knowledge is small, very few travel this deep into the forest. From what I know, and again I can't confirm them, many have entered these forests never to return. I was watching as we worked our way into this forest and the first thing I noticed was the fact there appeared to be no trails, no paths to follow confirming nobody comes here . . . yet here we are. And with unerring accuracy here we stand at your campsite." A fire had been built in the previous fire pit, and the flames were both comforting and warming. Turning around TimOtee grabbed a downed log and with effort began dragging it closer to the fire so he would have something to sit on.

Jerod, watching thought, *Why didn't I think of that? Of course I had other important things on my mind last time I was here.* "Here let me help you with that." He went over to assist and between the two of them got it close enough so that they both could sit and keep warm. "Look, I need to take a drop of your life fluid. I need to run a series of tests to see if you and your people can be of some help. You've seen personally what the evil ones can do. They were to never come here, yet here they are. Once we can either capture them or force them to leave, they are to never come back. This world is yours and yours alone for a long time into the future. Later when things have changed significantly then we may be back, but on different terms. Then it would be as equals, so to speak, but that time isn't now, or in your life time, or even in your children's, grandchildren's, and great grandchildren's lifetimes.

"We, the ones I represent, have put your world in the protective status, and are off limits to any. Yet to insure that this will be, and because the universe is so large we must have ones here who will recognize a threat to you and yours. So what I'm offering you, if the tests come out positive, is a chance to see the future, to actually live longer, and to be able to see and understand everything that has happened when the strangers arrived. I know much of what you've seen is beyond understanding, and I'm not promising that you'll understand afterwards. Only that everything that has transpired will be available to you in your mind. Don't ask how this is possible, just know that it is. Still before I raise your hopes too much, I do have to run those tests. And in the end it may be that what I'm offering is impossible. So again don't get your hopes up."

"This is a lot you are asking, suggesting . . . I have to admit I don't understand at all, and am nervous, to almost being scared. What is it that you are offering me JerOda? Are you offering to make me one of the gods, or a messenger such as you?" TimOtee had to admit that he never expected such an offer, but was this what this really was? He really wasn't sure he understood.

"Messenger maybe, god – no. And none of what's happened here has anything to do with your gods. And what I'm offering will not change you overall. You will still be simply TimOtee, and your offspring will be true to you and your mate, with none of what I'm offering you. And I will be offering the same to a number of others here. It is important – critical really that there are at least twelve of you here that can keep in touch with each other, and to be able to reach beyond and alert us if the bad ones return. But what I'm offering will only last this one generation – even though you will find that you will probably live well into the lives of your great grandchildren."

TimOtee laughed. "How is that possible? We only have so long here before we die, and the new generation replaces us. We have seen it time and time again. We are only given so long to live, to do what we must, and then pass it on to who comes after us. Are you saying you can change such?"

Taking a deep breath and letting out slowly Jerod said. "I will not be changing anything of your world. It is part of what we are. You are to continue on your own path, and while it may seem like a great gift I'm offering, it really isn't. In the brief time I've been here I know that you have mates just like where I'm from. So what may appear to be a gift isn't necessarily. What I mean is the fact that you and your mind will be sharp until you pass on. You will have the privilege of seeing your family grow many generations in the future, but that special loved one, your mate will not see it. Meaning you will outlive her, and many times that can be devastating. After all, the two of you have built a life together, grown close because of the challenges of life, and then suddenly she will be taken from you, with you living on. It's not easy.

"Then you will face the fact that you know things others don't and will never be able to reveal them – because if you did, you would be considered touched in the head. And with the memory you will have absolutely everything that has happened to you, from the point of the gift, will remain with you to access whenever you want or need to. So that pain of your mate passing will never dull with the passing of time.

And, for me, most importantly, you will know all that has transpired here. Everything that has been said, all the images will be at your beckoned call. You see all that we, and I'm speaking of me here, do is recorded – even though that is a strange word that will mean something soon – so that we can look at the facts, and our history as it truly happened, and not colored by someone's poor interpretation.

"So this 'gift' isn't really. Again this may not be something I can give you. But I will know by the morning. Then we will perform the procedure – with your permission of course – then. And once complete we will stay the day to give you a chance to recover, and to begin to see the changes. And finally let me say that who you are will remain just as you have always remembered yourself. And let me add this warning. If you or any of the others I do this to decide to use this 'gift' to their advantage, the 'gift' will turn against you and not allow that to happen. So what do you say?"

TimOtee was silent for the longest of times, and Jerod could understand why. TimOtee got up off the log and began to pace back and forth. It was obvious he was trying to assimilate everything he'd just been told. A couple of times he was about to speak and thought better of it, and then walked out of the light of the flickering fire and into the shadows just beyond, leaned against one of the convenient trees, and remained silent. Eventually he came back and sat back down. With a subdued voice he said, "Okay. I have to admit what you've said is a lot to take in all at once. So let's get this straight in my own mind, as far as me, I'll still be me, right?"

"Yes."

"Will I feel any different?"

"No. In fact you might be disappointed to begin with because of all I've said. Much of what needs to happen will take time. And for a while you'll be hungry all the time, and feel tired. All of this is normal. Let's just say that inside you'll be growing, and much of what I've told you will slowly make an appearance. Then one day you'll realize that you know more, and have some abilities that you didn't know you had. At that point the process will be complete."

TimOtee laughed a nervous laugh. "I'm hungry all the time now. Remember I'm young and haven't completely filled out. So that will be no different. Still being tired all the time will be a new experience. I'm usually that way after a really tough day. You are saying that all of this stuff will go away?"

"Again, yes."

He paused, and leaned forward, "Okay, I guess I'll do it. Getting this life fluid, how much are you going to need? I hope not a lot since I need it to keep alive."

Jerod laughed. "You'd be surprised how little. Now hold your hand to me. You'll feel a little prick, and that's all. I suspect you've lost more to cutting your hand to what I'll be taking."

Reluctantly TimOtee extended his hand while JerOda took out a small device that fit over one of his fingers. He felt a small sticking pain and then nothing. JerOda took it off and smiled. "That's it."

"That's it?" TimOtee asked. Really? I barely felt that." He looked down incredulously at his middle finger and could see a small drop forming on the tip. He'd done something similar when he had jabbed his finger into a thorn. "Are you sure you don't need more than that?"

Jerod smiled. "Nope that's all. Will let you know the results soon. And while we are waiting, let's prepare a meal. Look from the food you prepared earlier I'd say you're better at this than I am. So can I ask you to do the honors and be the cook for tonight?"

TimOtee shrugged, "Sure, why not? I guess it's small enough a gesture if what you are offering can be given."

* * *

Both the general and admiral were exhausted. And they suspected that every member of their crews had to be in worse shape. The pressure was rising tremendously and while it appeared that the natives from the mountains had finally gotten the message and were leaving them alone, they knew from their sensors that they were still being watched. This overall was a minor nuisance. It was the fact that an agent had been inside of their temporary compound, and had planted devices that really worried all of them. And since no one had really seen it happen – the infiltration – they had no idea how many agents they might be dealing with, or when they had arrived . . . Or, for that matter, if one of the crew members was one of the agents who had infiltrated their organization sometime in the past.

It had cast suspicion over everybody. Still from what the chief had related to them it could easily had been that movement he had caught earlier, leading to the suspicions he had, and thusly why he had placed his people on alert and then the discovery of one of the devices that only could have come from the agency. Everybody knew it existed, but that was just about as far as it went. Like the fact they themselves had spies within their organizations that had alerted them to the fact they had been discovered for what they were doing, it was easy to have it happen to them. The general turned to the admiral and stated, "Look we need to further strip our teams down. I think we can rotate squads, and their patrols, from our orbiting carrier, that way it means we have very few to withdraw, if it comes to that. And by doing it this way the ones on the ground will be fresher and more alert. It will give us a chance to keep the power armor in top operating condition. And it might come down to it needing to be that way if we have to fight our way out of here. The engineers are doing all they can, but knowing what we know now I suspect we'll end up abandoning it all and need to disappear once again."

The admiral took a deep cleansing breath and let it out slowly. He'd been coming to much the same conclusion. He had been hopeful, when his ruse had worked and they had lost the pursuing force. He knew from the information he was receiving from his spies aboard the command vessel that they would only have so much time to accomplish what they needed before they would either have to run again, or be dug in. While it was common for agents to be aboard, they generally were simply along for the ride. And while the agents did have the authority to override any command given, it never had happened – at least as far as he or they knew.

Ones from the outside who had studied history had compared these agents to the political officers that were aboard military vessels from the old communist countries back when the navy was a wet navy and before interstellar space travel became a reality. Yet it was probably a bad example. These agents were rarely seen, and they were even rarer on the bridge. They had a policy of strict noninterference. They only became known when they joined a scout team to be sent on some lonely mission. And for most this would be the first time they'd be aware of whom the agent was. And they never returned to the same vessels after being revealed. Generally the officers in charge knew who the agent was, but that was as far as it went, and as far as the two of them were aware, no one had informed them of an agent being assigned to them.

And, to be honest, there were advantages, at times, to have the agents aboard. They were always available for added intel in the meetings if additional intel was needed. Of course there were times when they couldn't pass on what they knew because of the security surrounding the information. And one of the things one never did was to ask where the information had originally come from. This was strictly a "need to know", and most of the time it was well beyond their paygrade. "I can't reduce the engineers that are involved in the tunneling – either yours or mine – since it takes everyone involved to make it happen. Oh, I was updated from the chief and he said the site breakdown is complete, and soon the natives we've kept in stasis will awaken and wonder what happened. All the equipment from there is being recycled and reproduced. It was decided that we wouldn't be able to find all the bugs the agent probably planted. And on the flights back to the cruiser they kept all of the material isolated so whatever could be there couldn't signal back to the arrays I'm sure the agent has set up. And once everything has gone through the breakdown and then created again everything should be clean.

"I've ordered the freighters to head for the light carrier and remain onboard. As slow as they are we'd have to abandon them if we had to do an emergency run. That leaves the troop carriers that we need here on the ground to take us out of here if we need. And we still have one designated to handle the drilling equipment we are using, plus all the minor items. If we need to leave I want nothing left behind here to identify us."

* * *

Since they had returned to his original camp Jerod wondered what the renegades were doing in the mountains. As night approached the artificial lights became more visible and were all concentrated in a small area. That the barrier was gone was another sign that something significant was going on and he, with the loss of his devices, which he had no control over, left him blind and in the dark. Using the arrays he had set up he had monitored the camp being dismantled, and now from what little he could gather it would be almost impossible to say that the renegades had ever setup their base of operations there in the valley, and in the middle of the farmlands. In fact, given a season there would be nothing to point to the fact that their laws had been broken and someone had actually landed here and set up operations. One thing for sure both of the rogue leaders were good at what they did.

After another great meal created by TimOtee, both were tired and relaxing allowing the food to do what food had a tendency to do which was to put one to sleep. Still he was waiting for the test equipment to finish its analysis and see what he could and could not do. Any time in the past where such had to be performed, and the tests confirmed it, they had a limited suite of upgrades they could administer. All of them happened internally so there was no outward change. In fact if a population was far enough along to do autopsies then doing such would show nothing to alert any to these changes. Part of what the testing would do, would first confirm it was possible to do the upgrades, then immediately create the proper chemical balance for the ones who would receive *the gift*. Sometimes such analysis could take a long time as the software would check, test, retest, and reconfigure the concoction until it would be safe for the recipient, and other times the results were almost immediate. As he hoped that it would be tonight. Once the concoction was absorbed into the system then the recipient would sleep for a period of time while the magic was happening.

And time was something he had in very small quantities at this moment. With everything coming to a head he needed to have TimOtee alert and coherent since his overall grasp of this culture was still lacking. Plus he needed to give TimOtee time to adjust to the "changes" that would take place. Things like his awareness sharpening, and the fact that he would be able to remember everything, and recall it at any time, and the fact that he would probably feel better than any time in his life, and the fact that there was little chance he'd ever be sick again, and so many little things. Still, the most critical to Jerod was the fact that they would be able to communicate. Once this operation was complete, then they would be placing geosynchronous satellites around their world to monitor the situation, allowing the ones who were given *the gift* to alert them if someone ever returned to their world again.

If things went well, then no others would receive *the gift*, and once these gifted passed away, and there had been no activity then it would only be the satellites that would keep tabs on the situation. As he looked across the fire at TimOtee he inwardly smiled. *Your world is about to change in so many ways, more ways than you can imagine. And while you might attribute this to your gods, in truth it's simply the fact that we are probably at least a thousand years ahead of you. And if left on your own, someday your distant ancestors might come to my world. Who knows if it will still exist, or whether we will still be around? The one thing we know for sure is the fact that there have been other civilizations that arose, went into interstellar space, and have died out. No one species can claim immortality even though we all seem to believe in it. I have studied the records of many of the digs made by our archaeologists and their conclusions. And the only constant they found is the belief of immortality.*

Yes, we've spread deep into space, and found available type 3 planets to develop. And we've found many primitive species just beginning their climb towards space. I guess for most, even if they are not aware of the fact is that we all seem to reach towards that unknown – that deep unknown universe that we can see above our world. It is one of the driving forces behind our curiosity – The "why", the reaching for understanding of all that is around us. Yes, we've seen worlds where, for whatever the reason, nothing has sparked the growth of the intelligent species that dwell there, and they will never reach beyond. Still do we have the right to interfere in any of their lives, their personal development? I say no . . . Although there are times when we've found an especially violent species that we've set up heavy monitoring.

No not even here will we interfere. I suspect when one of the advanced species may have looked down at us during our primitive times they would have come to much the same conclusion. We were, and probably are in some ways still a violent species. Yet, we were allowed our growth. And as far as I know we've had no influences from the outside to redirect our direction. Still, who can say in the end whether it was there or not? Who knows, maybe there were subtle nudges made that pushed us in the right direction. Inwardly he shrugged. He found that every time he worked towards bringing one along to a higher awareness that he became introspective, and always ended up finding himself in these familiar tracks and grooves reviewing his own motives, and what he knew and felt. Suddenly he was brought out of this introspection when a silent alarm in his head alerted him that the tests were complete and the substance was ready.

He looked up and realized that with his introspection that he had been staring out into the night and TimOtee, while he had remained silent, had a questioning look on his face. Jerod smiled. "Sorry about that. But any time I find myself in this situation I have a tendency to drift off and think about what all of it means."

"I'm not going to ask what, 'all of it means', means because you have so many mysteries that are well beyond me."

Shaking his head, Jerod replied, "Only for now . . . only for now. Okay, are you ready to move forward with this? I only ask because once we move on to the next step there is no turning back."

"And you promise this will not hurt or kill me?"

"There are no guarantees in life. We both know that. Still there should be no issue, and the only problem initially will be that you will sleep, and then feel tired for a few days. And I should mention that you will feel like you're starving and can't get enough to eat. All of this is quite normal. Then everything will settle down, and you'll be your normal self."

TimOtee laughed, "Hey, I'm young and it always seems to be the way of the young, as I said earlier,

I'm always hungry. I know in a few turns around our sun it will change, but that's still sometime in the future. Okay, now that we are getting close to when this, whatever it is, is going to happen I find I'm becoming a little nervous. So far everything you've stated has been the truth. Still when one is dealing with the gods", here he smiled again, "sorry, a messenger, one can never be sure that what is being said is being understood. This is because one such as you is so far above me and what is said could have many layers of meanings, and with my limited understanding I could only be seeing it from a point of view that really doesn't understand what is being offered. Does this make any sense?"

"Yeah, completely. But I really am not who you believe I am, and I'm just as mortal as you are. Yeah, I have my ways of protection; I have to admit to that. And I have other advantages that come because of where we are in our time verses where you are in yours. In truth that's the only difference. Someday there's a chance your people will be in a similar situation, and only then will any understand what I and mine are facing. And again this will only be understood if somehow the words I'm saying to you were to survive until that time untouched and unchanged. If I know anything about the passing of time is that we see thing differently the further we get from an event. And there are others who want to take advantage of some past important event and because it's not exactly like they see it, they will change it to make it fulfill the role they see. So there's a good chance that even this meeting as we both see and know it will become something different a long time in the future, if it survives at all.

"Here, at this time, you and I sitting around an ordinary campfire, discussing this and so many other things, makes it seem, well, an everyday event. I know that this time in your history campfires, and such, are an everyday thing – So ordinary in fact that when one is out and about, to see camps and campfires is normal and to be expected. Believe it or not there will come a day when this isn't so.

"I guess that all I can say about your concerns and your nervousness that both are expected. If you weren't then I'd be the one concerned. I guess, in a way what I'm asking of you is selfish on my part. No, don't say anything, let me finish. You will benefit from this, no doubt. You and the others I choose to give this gift. But in the end what I will receive will far outweigh what you and yours get from this. In the end it also is something that will protect your world from the likes of us. You see when such happens, and fortunately it doesn't very often – rarely really if I want to admit it – then it takes resources to insure we can bring about the removal of the ones who have broken our laws. Then once that's accomplished by having you here that means we don't have to be here. It means that I, and others like myself, can continue working on other important assignments. There are far too few of us, and there are always more to do then the bodies to do them."

Here Jerod laughed, "I guess in a way I'm the one complaining, and it's not helping. Look, it surprised you on how little of your life fluid I took to test, and so it will be similar when you accept my gift. Now wait and I'll be right back." With that Jerod got up and headed out into the darkness and to his hidden personal ship. It would be there the vial would be.

TimOtee watched as he disappeared into the darkness and wasn't sure if his doubts had been answered. It seemed this JerOda had said many things about, well, he wasn't sure if he understood any of what he said. Still he seemed to reinforce the fact that what would happen would only make him tired, and he'd been tired before. So he looked down and stared at the ground watching the dancing shadows caused by the flickering of the flames. It was almost mesmerizing. Suddenly he realized that his mind had been drifting with the movement of the shadows. He looked up and JerOda was standing there in front of him. *How'd he get here without me hearing?* He smiled a sheepish smile, "Sorry this is a lot to take in." He saw JerOda was holding a small what appeared to be a glass container which had some type of dark liquid. With humor in his voice TimOtee said, "Trying to poison me are you?"

He saw that JerOda smiled back, but it was a serious one. Then JerOda spoke softly and seriously. "Yeah, I can understand that point of view. And actually when you drink this stuff you'll probably think that's exactly what I'm doing to you. The taste is terrible – really terrible. I'm happy that it's only a small amount because if it was more it'd be hard to choke down. I've never understood how we could do this and not make it taste better. I've had it explained a number of times, but the explanations always leave something to be desired as far as I'm concerned. Anyway, my suggestion is to toss this in your mouth and swallow it as quickly as you can to avoid tasting it as much as you can. Unfortunately the aftertaste is worse so I suggest you have some water ready." He handed the small glass to TimOtee.

TimOtee looked at it thinking, *how bad could such a small amount be?* One thing for sure it didn't look like something he'd normally drink. It appeared to be somewhat thick as he swirled it around in the small container. And while he still had enough bravery he went ahead and did as JerOda suggested and tossed the concoction into his mouth and swallowed it quickly. Unfortunately it wasn't quick enough and the oily feel in his mouth and the burning sensation that went right up into his nostrils made him choke. The taste was about the worst thing he had ever tasted and he could tell his guts agreed. His eyes began to water like he had grabbed some uncut fermented drink, and he immediately reached for his water skin and took a large draught of water. "Whew! You weren't kidding. I'd swear after that you are poisoning me. My guts are still complaining."

"Yeah, sorry about that. And your reaction is typical. And believe it or not, sometime in my past I had to drink my own version of that stuff, and I have to admit it was my reaction also. Shortly your guts will settle down, but unfortunately that taste in your mouth will stay a while – personal experience talking – then everything will return to normal. Other than the symptoms I've already described, you won't notice any changes for a few days. Then you will notice subtle differences, and much of what you are will be sharpened, and your clarity of thought will improve. In a short time that exhaustion I've spoke of will take over so I suggest you get your sleep sack ready because tonight you will sleep a dreamless and deep sleep. Don't worry as I will keep us safe. So until the morning then, when I'll have a meal for the two of us . . ." Here Jerod laughed, "And think it will be then when you will feel like I'm trying to poison you. I've never been the best of cooks."

* * *

Admiral Sympson paced back and forth outside of the tent they were using for their headquarters. Pressure was building and he felt that soon between the two of them – he and General Pertion – they'd need to decide whether to remain and finish this, or abandon the whole operation and head out to their rendezvous point out in space. And it wasn't where he had told everyone they would meet. With the announcement all who were part of his team knew to look to where that really referred. This way if any of the communications were intercepted nothing would be compromised. And now that he – they knew there was at least one agent on the surface who would be actively working against them – also knew that every transmission, every conversation they'd be having or had spoken would be recorded. He'd been involved with trials in the past where he had been a witness and had heard some of those recordings. He, at first, was surprised, but then realized it was the simplest and best way for what would become a case to be accurate.

Yeah, he had always worried that with the technology that what was being presented could be altered. After all, if one could do this, then there would be someone who could undo this also. Yet, every time he had to opportunity he'd compare what he and his team recorded against what would be presented by the agency and their agents, there never had been any difference. And because of this knowledge he knew everything or most of it anyway had been recorded for future use.

Still for now his biggest worry, since the arrival of one of the scout ships and the crew who actually worked for him, was the lack of any intelligence.

Without it he was dead in the water and knew it. For all he knew the pursuing fleet was closing in and would be arriving here at this planet at any moment. Yes, his sensor arrays, and ships orbiting this planet and the ones further out in the system were all monitoring the surrounding space, but they had missed the agent when he approached. In a sense there was no surprise there. He didn't have enough of anything to be able to cover all the areas of approach. Still it had been a surprise when the one single bug had been discovered. It had been an accidental discovery and one he was quite happy happened. Otherwise they'd be moving a little slower than they were presently and could easily have been caught with every ship making a dash for freedom, with a future meeting for any who had escaped.

He looked up into the night sky at the strange constellations and thought how bright and clear the stars were. It seemed that only on planets where industrialization hadn't taken place yet were the skies so clear and bright. *Price for technology I guess.* He knew that if this place followed the norm that someday the skies here wouldn't be so pristine. It would happen so slowly that it truly wouldn't be noticed until they became aware of the pollution they were creating. Only realizing then the damage they'd been causing. With his mind drifting on these thoughts he realized he had gotten off the subject. He needed to see the progress of their operation and come to a decision. In some ways he knew he had already, but needed to confirm his suspicions. Then once confirmed, come back and discuss his thoughts with the general. He had to admit it was nice to be able to bounce some of his thoughts off of someone of equal rank. That way the answer wouldn't be because the one answering back thought it would be what he wanted to hear.

With the decision made he informed his staff and headed over to the drilling site which would take him about fifteen minutes to reach. As he approached the sounds became deafening. He always wondered how lasers cutting through stone could be so loud, but understood that the pressures being generated when rock was immediately liquefied and turned into gas, in some instances, that the rapid expansion would break and fracture the rock around the area where the lasers were directed. Then the equipment that would be taking the extracted material and converting it to the needed components wasn't quiet either. He climbed the derrick they had temporarily set up to overlook the operation and watched for a moment.

He could see that the lasers had successfully cut through the first hillside, but where the real cutting still lay ahead. They should have already been making progress in the final direction. Turning to one of the engineers who were overseeing the operation he asked, "How's it going?"

"Sir, we are behind. One of the laser rigs broke down and required a major repair, and working with what we have left has put a strain on everything, especially the timeline. Plus it means we had to push the remaining equipment to try to make up for the failure which means we've strained them past their limits. We have the broken one back online now but there's no way to make up for what we've already lost."

Shaking his head slightly he smiled, "Thank you. I'll let you and the rest know shortly what we are going to do. With this delay I almost think the decision has been made. I'll need to confer with the general. Still I'm of the opinion that we will be evacuating instead of continuing. Look to that possibility but continue until you hear directly from me."

The engineer saluted saying, "Yes sir."

He returned the salute withdrew and headed back to their temporary headquarters. *Yes, it's time to look at our losses, and be moving on.*

* * *

Jerod breathed deeply and let it out slowly. It had been a rough night, and there was very little he could do about it. He longed to head out and see what he could learn about those lights that were lighting up the night there in the mountains. His bugs were gone – it was obvious now. And the few that were still on site did him no good. (In a short time they'd self-destruct leaving nothing behind.) The prefabs were no longer there, and from what little he could gather had been transported to one of the ships orbiting this world. What originally looked good, in the end failed. Now everything depended on his arrays and while they gathered everything needed, it wouldn't be enough. He had to remain here and protect the native, this TimOtee. Not that he couldn't have placed a force field around him, because he could have . . . still he would have kicked himself if harm had come to him because he had done just that.

Dawn was still hours away and those bright distant lights were calling him to see what was happening. Yeah getting no sleep didn't help either, but the drugs available would overcome the fatigue for a while. Eventually there'd be a price to pay but right now it was necessary. He knew his charge could end up with some complication and this was exactly why he had to remain. Without proper monitoring during this phase one could die if something unforeseen happened. Knowing this didn't relieve the stress. *Where's the fleet?* This question kept going through his mind. He knew that the scout ship he had been a passenger on had successfully headed back out of the system. And there had been plenty of time for them to pass on everything they'd learned, and actually be back. *So what's gone wrong? I really hate being out of the loop this way, but this isn't the first time, and I really doubt it will be the last. Still we have a chance to wrap this up and be done with it. Yet, every moment that passes by that chance lessens.* He heard TimOtee moan in his sleep and he went over to check on him. He appeared to be sweating but other than that, and what the monitors were saying, he was okay.

He found that once again he was pacing back and forth. Jerod finally sat down briefly and added fuel to their campfire, and listened to the surrounding silence being broken now and then by the rustling of the leaves as they were moved by the slight breeze that rose and fell. He had expected to hear the scurrying of the small creatures, but if they were moving about he hadn't heard them. Still where they were was an old growth forest and as such might not have as many such creatures as he was used to. He knew that his other campsite close to the then existing barrier had plenty of noise being created by those native small creatures. He knew from experience that old growth areas sometimes had very little undergrowth meaning no fodder for the grazers and no place to hide for the small ones.

Eventually he could see the gray of dawn, and he knew that TimOtee would be out for another couple of hours, so he took a chance, went to his ship, rummaged around and found some instant coffee. It tasted horrible – yeah what's with that – but at least it gave the semblance of the real stuff. And right now that was "a pick me up" he needed. *I really don't understand. As long as we've been drinking this stuff there has been instant. One would think after all this time that someone would have discovered a way to make it taste right.* He shrugged. He wasn't a scientist, or one who helped in the developing of food tastes so he honestly didn't know what it took to make it right. He felt his eyes burning from the lack of sleep, and could feel the chill of the dawn. *Why does it do that?* It seemed no matter what world he'd been on it was always the same. It seemed just before the sun made its appearance that it became noticeably cooler. He went back to the fire and felt the chill hit his back as the breezes increased, in the anticipation of the rising sun, sending chills down his spine.

Looking over once again at TimOtee, he whispered, "Soon now . . . soon now." Here he smiled because he knew that once TimOtee awakened he'd feel like hell. While TimOtee wouldn't recognize that word he'd recognize the way he felt. Jerod had to admit that once he came out from that first sleep that he wondered why he had ever gone through the process. He finished his instant coffee and rinsed the cup, put the frying pan over the flames and prepared to put together a meal. TimOtee would be starving when he awoke even if he felt like he had a hangover. He turned and watched as TimOtee mumbled something and turned over. *Definitely not long now.* He turned back to a container that had water in it and added a concoction that was tasteless but would replace needed minerals and nutrients that the process stole from the body.

Suddenly TimOtee sat up supporting himself by his arms. "Wow, I feel like I've been hit by one of our beasts. Even drinking too much of the fermented drinks we have I've never felt this bad. What is that stuff you gave me anyway? Truthfully I remember dreaming – I think anyway – but can't tell you anything about any of it. And like the next day after a night of drinking I'm dying of thirst, is this normal?"

Jerod just smiled and handed him the container. "Yeah, I understand. It's the same for all of us. Drink all of this. It will do two things. The first is obvious; it'll take care of that thirst. The rest that it will do is first numb that headache, and the rest of your body that feels like it was run over, and secondly replace what was stolen from your body for what took place inside." Seeing the look he was receiving from TimOtee Jerod laughed since he knew what TimOtee was thinking. "No, there is no taste to this. It will be like any of the water you normally drink other than seeming a little more refreshing."

TimOtee gave JerOda a look of disbelief . . . Although, if he wanted to admit it, so far JerOda hadn't lied. He said that the stuff he drank last night would taste really bad, and it did, and he'd feel it in the morning, which again he did. So, maybe it would be that way. "Okay, I'm too dry to refuse." He reached out and took the container and killed it. It was like he hadn't had anything to drink for a whole seven-day. "So how long will I feel this bad? I know, at times that it takes a couple of days to overcome too much fermented drink to where I'll feel normal. Oh, and I will feel normal right?"

Jerod laughed. "So you tell me, what's normal?"

"Ah, good point. Okay smart south end of a herd beast heading north, will I feel like I'm me?"

More serious now Jerod replied, "Yeah, and I suspect if you've built up some ideas of some miracle or that you'll be someone who is smarter than everybody who lives here, then you are in for a disappointment. In fact and for a while you'll wonder why you drank that stuff in the first place because *you will feel no different* than before you drank that horrible tasting stuff."

"Really. So why did I drink it if there are to be no changes?"

"Now I didn't say there'd be no changes. Only that after all is said and done you will still be you. It will be only after time as your body gets used to what is happening and has happened inside that you will begin to notice a few things which are different – that's all. I think the biggest benefit out of the whole thing will be your health. And no you won't have super strength or be able to read minds or any of those sorts of things. And like I said earlier none of what has taken place inside will become part of the next generation. It will only be a part of you. And while

I've kind of touched on a lot here I'll conclude by repeating and saying you probably will never be sick again. And any injury will heal faster than you ever remember. And while it's a blessing, it's also a curse. I know I've told you this but I'll repeat myself again. You will have a long life before you pass on. Not as long as mine, but much longer than any here."

"Then, ole wise one, why do I feel this way now?" TimOtee was sitting on one of the logs close to the fire with his head in his hands. It hurt to move. He wondered when that stuff he had just consumed would take effect.

"Give it some time I think you'll begin to feel an easing of the pain any time now. And unfortunately all those normal aches and pains will still be with you. After all, it is your personal warning system that you're doing something you shouldn't be doing or 'hey you've overdone it here'. If those things were taken away there'd be too great of a chance that you'd really injure yourself, and that's not what this is all about."

TimOtee smiled a sickly smile. "Okay, still it would have been nice . . ."

They both heard a roar, and a crack like thunder with Jerod saying, "Damn!"

Puzzled TimOtee looked at JerOda and asked, "What? I've never heard that word before."

Shaking his head Jerod replied, "Sorry . . . that just slipped out. Not important. I was just commenting on that sound and what it means."

"So oh mighty messenger, what does it mean?"

"It means that part of the reason I'm here is now history. It doesn't mean that all who came here are gone, but more have now left. It means that there's a great possibility that it will not end here and the chase, or maybe I should say, the hunt continues. Still, until I check the data I'll not know."

"The chase, the hunt? You've lost me there."

"Yeah I guess that would make sense. The ones who are here were once part of us but decided it was better on the other side so they became, I guess the best word to use here is, evil. And we are the ones who are to capture them and make they pay for what they've decided to do. And since I've been here it's the closest we've been. Still the ones we chase are good at this. So I guess it should be no surprise they may be one jump ahead of us once again. Still, I was hoping . . ."

TimOtee realized that his aches and pains and especially that monster headache was beginning to recede. It was then he realized that he was really hungry. "Hey, not to change the subject, but to change the subject, I'm starving!"

Silence and a pause as Jerod shifted gears and brought his mind back on the immediate. "Sorry about that but you will be this way for a few. I think I mentioned that also, and I do have something prepared for you, again it's me cooking, plus I've added a few additional things to help you recover, and like I said I'm not a cook and I'm not trying to poison you." Jerod filled a pottery plate full and handed it over to TimOtee. "Eat this and it should take the edge off but only for a short time. For your next seven-day you'll be eating much more than you can ever remember eating, then it will suddenly drop off and you'll be back to your normal appetite. Oh and another side effect from this, you'll never be overweight – just won't happen."

GGF: When he related this to his great grandson he smiled inwardly. In fact now that he was old, really old, he had doubted that little fact when JerOda had informed him. He had seen many oldsters over his brief time and most had added weight around their middles. It seemed to be the natural way of things. Yet now he could look back and see that once again JerOda hadn't lied. Even now he could eat whatever he desired and his weight remained perfect. He'd been asked his secret, and all he would do was shrug and say he really didn't have one, and didn't know why he had this gift. Yes as he was telling this story the family knew, but they were told to never let it out of the family and it would always be theirs and theirs only. Now it was time to get back to the story as he stated it to Little One.

There was another sharp roar from the distance causing the two of them to look towards the mountains. This was followed by more of the same and from the rising sun came flashes of something in the air as they rose higher and disappeared from sight. Jerod shook his head. It was obvious the renegades were leaving and their window of opportunity for capture had closed. Still he needed to go into those mountains and find out what they were doing. It might give him and the chasing fleet a clue as to their plans. In the end he doubted it, but until he had been on-site then he wouldn't know. Turning to TimOtee Jerod took a deep breath and let it out slowly. "Well, it looks like your gods have left and returned to the sky."

TimOtee was still feeling the effects of whatever it was he had taken the night before and if he wanted to admit it really didn't care right now. Whatever it was that JerOda had given him this morning hadn't totally taken effect yet and his head still felt two sizes bigger than normal. Standing there with the plate of food he found he was automatically eating it, and while JerOda said he was a bad cook, it really wasn't that bad . . . or maybe he was just hungry after all. He did a single shoulder shrug which here simply meant a noncommittal response – neither agreeing nor disagreeing. As far as the gods, until he personally saw proof that they had returned to their realm, he'd hold his opinion. "So I guess that means you, as a messenger, will be leaving too."

Jerod continued to stare towards those mountains before answering. "Not yet. I have much that needs to be done, and I can still use your help. I need to get into those mountains to where they were so I can see why the move. And soon there will be others here who are following the ones who had descended to your world. I then must make a full statement (he almost said report) to the one in charge about what I have learned and my suspicions of where they might go next. And all of this means I'm here for some time. How long I don't know. But part of what I must also do is find others willing to become part of . . . oh I don't know what to call it. Whatever we decide I guess will have to do. I guess we can consider it an early alert system.

"There is no way of knowing whether, as you have called them, strangers or gods, will return here or not. We, and here I'm not referring to you and me, will be putting some protection above your world. And you will be given a privilege that only you will experience. Others who will join you here as part of the system will only get a portion – enough that they will understand both the gift, the importance, the why, and what their responsibilities will be. What you have been given is not free. You are the advanced vanguard of your world to keep it as it is. To allow you and yours to discover and invent in your own time, to learn of the universe and its mysteries, and so much more that lies ahead of you.

"Had things gone as they should you would have never seen the strangers and they would have never come down from the skies to bother you. But it did happen, and it has given you a taste of your possible future. And as time moves on past all of this, much of what has transpired will become myth. From there it will move into the world of fantasy and imagination with most believing that what you have lived never happened – Something to do with time and distance. I've seen it time and time again. And while I never thought such would be consistent I've been proven wrong. It's like it's one of the laws of space and time that it should be this way. Yet I doubt it truly is. I suspect that it's simply a case of the way a society changes over time. And when something, words for example, change over time, then what it meant and its power is no longer the same.

"I know I'm doing a really bad job of this, but I think as time moves past you, and I think you'll learn how fast this really happens, it will only be then you will understand what I'm trying to tell you here. Once the others arrive, then with all the data collected you will have a chance to go into the skies. There you will witness everything that has transpired on this world as far as the strangers are concerned. All of it will be placed into your memories and you will *never* forget. It is part of the gift you've received. You will see it all as if you were one of your flyers soaring over the mountains. You will be privy to all the conversations, all the interactions, all the battles that have taken place here, and while much of it will be beyond your understanding you will at least get an overview of this time.

"You see, in what we call the military, all, with the equipment and other things that you don't understand but will become part of you, it all becomes available. It means that the ones who are in charge can go back and see an operation from all that has been involved making it, yes far more complicated, but at the same time such can point out the weak points, and maybe learn from the mistakes discovered, making a similar operation in the future, if there's such a thing, be more efficient."

Even with his aching head TimOtee remained silent as he tried to absorb everything this JerOda related to him. Then he laughed. "You're kidding right? I mean there's no way what you just said could happen. It's impossible. Even conversations I've had in the past are long gone and I can only remember parts of them. And sometimes in my mind's eye I can see the one I've been talking to. But even here I'm sure it's changed from what it originally was. It cannot be any other way."

Jerod smiled. "Ah, so we have a doubter, do we? Need proof?"

"Well, yeah, proof would be nice."

JerOda reached inside the topcoat he was wearing and did something and suddenly everything that they had witnessed this morning, everything the two of them had said, discussed, and talked about was being repeated. Shocked, TimOtee sat back down on one of the logs. And as he did he noticed the plate was empty and he had never remembered eating it all. "How'd you do that, I mean, really, how did you do that? It's something I've never seen before."

"Let's just say it's a gift or part of the gift. And because you have it, or will have it shortly, you can go back and review it at any time and confirm what you are saying is accurate. Yet, when you first begin to use this ability it won't come easily. It is something you must learn how to use, and it will take time. And barring accidents, time will be something you'll have a lot of." JerOda then did something else and it all went away. "Look once you're up to it I really do need to get to where the strangers were last before heading up into the skies. Let me know when you're able to lead me there."

TimOtee wasn't quite sure what to make of all of this. And he wasn't sure when he'd feel right enough to lead, but to his surprise it wasn't long after eating that he felt almost normal. At least normal enough that he could take JerOda in the direction where the strangers had been.

Little One: "This, ah what did you call him, oh yeah, messenger gave you a gift that you drank. Was it really that bad?"

GGF: Laughing he said, "Yeah it was that bad. And like he told me I'd never forget, and he's right, I've never forgotten. And again he was right when he stated that this gift was both a gift as well as a curse. I think when we forget things many times it's a good thing. Yes, it's great to remember the good, but who wants to remember the bad? Not me truthfully, but it's all there. And he didn't lie. I couldn't believe there would be any way I would still be here to see you. It is something that appeared to be impossible, yet here I am telling you of this time from the past and I can see it as if it just happened yesterday.

"And now you also have had your questions answered as to how I know what I know, and why I've presented this narrative this way. Yeah, I could have told you this from my perspective but then it wouldn't have made as much sense. So this is why I pass it on the way I do, the way I can see it. And I can see it because of the *gift*, one that has been everything JerOda said it would be." Standing carefully since it had become more difficult as time continued to press on him, he stretched. "Ah yes, that feels good. Let's take a break I need to walk out some kinks, and then we'll finish the story."

Little One: "Okay." He knew the story was almost complete and remembering back at the beginning he really thought he'd be bored out of his mind. Instead the days had flown and he couldn't wait to hear what happened next. Still taking a small break now would give him a chance to move, and maybe get some snack from mom to tide him over.

CHAPTER FIFTEEN

TO THE MOUNTAINS WE GO

Both of them stood there in the mountains. TimOtee had been careful in their approach since he had no idea if the mountain clans had returned to the area or not. It had taken them a while to locate the site. And it had been the smell, an odor that said something had happened here. It was a sharpness, a smell, as if rocks had collided and cracked. And there appeared to be a blue like dust lying on everything that became thicker as they approached the site. When they came up through a narrow "V" canyon, at the top it suddenly widened out and Jerod could see signs of where a tent had been erected, and much of the grasses and surrounding vegetation had been trampled down. He could also see where there had been guard posted, and it was obvious there had been patrols out protecting the area – another reason for the lack of any of the mountain clans. They pushed uphill following the obvious route the strangers had taken and came to a flattened area that was covered in rock dust. Here the lands dropped away a little and not too far in the distance one of the lesser mountains began its climb towards the sky.

Between them and the base sat a ridgeline which they both climbed. Before reaching the top of the ridgeline both could see where there had been some type of construction that was no longer there. Jerod suspected it was a small tower where the work, whatever the work was, could be observed. As they pushed forward and reached the top TimOtee stopped in awe with what he was seeing. Shaking his head, "No, this isn't possible. There's just no way for something like this to exist. We can't do it." He turned accusingly towards JerOda and asked, "Are you sure you aren't gods? There's no way one can do such a thing . . . no way at all."

Jerod was silent. How did one explain technology that was so far ahead of the one he was with? With what he was witnessing here, it was something entirely possible and this technology had been used for a long time. In fact it was old tech if he wanted to be honest, and what he was seeing explained a lot. "No . . . no I'm not one of your gods, nor are they, the ones you have known as strangers. I know what you're seeing here could lead one to that conclusion, but it's just the difference of time."

TimOtee tentatively approached what he was seeing and reached out and touched the lower wall of this circular hole cut through this mountain. It had a downward slope and was so large that he could barely see the top. And the sides of this hole, what could he say, they were smooth like the very rock and earth had been melted and reformed as a solid wall showing no cracks, no joints, and no connections. How was any of this possible? He turned to face JerOda once again about ready to accuse him of lying but stopped instead. He could see JerOda staring out in the distance like he had a few times before and knew he wouldn't get an answer.

Suddenly the arrays informed Jerod that the fleet was incoming and to prepare for communications. He then ordered the arrays to update the fleet on everything he had gathered so that the Admiral would be updated and know they had arrived too late. He stood by waiting for the carrier wave to let him know when the connection would be made. It was still obvious the fleet was light minutes away from here it would be half a day before they'd be orbiting, giving the fleeing renegades more time to muddy their trail and disappear once again. He was already aware the destroyers with the rogue fleet had been laying false trails – if what he heard was truly accurate. He suspected by the time the pursuit began again they would be doing more the unraveling of these false trails then actually chasing the renegades. In fact it wouldn't surprise him if they lost them completely and would have to begin again. What was it, or however was it said; Murphy always intervened and fouled up the works, or a battle plan was only valid until first contact? However it went it appeared that this round went to the renegades. Still, from the evidence here he knew they had had their own problems with Murphy.

TimOtee, once he realized he wouldn't be able to ask his questions turned back to his inspection of this giant hole. He touched the surface and it was smooth. So smooth that it seemed translucent and had depth. And it seemed slick. He first thought of trying to walk on its surface but thought better of it. He felt if he tried he begin sliding, picking up speed until he hit bottom either hurting him severely or killing him. One thing for sure he wasn't ready to try to see if what JerOda told him about the gift was true or not. Heading to what he considered the edge of this circular hole or tunnel he paced it off from one side to the other and found it took twenty paces. *Why would anybody need a tunnel this size?* He had to admit it was all beyond him.

Little one: "Are you telling me that the gods made a tunnel in the mountains?"

GGF: "Yes. And to be truthful, even now I don't know how they did it."

Little one: "So why haven't I heard about it? I mean my older brothers and sisters didn't say anything about it. And there's never been anything said at the education center."

GGF: "And there won't be either. What I'm telling you now is one of the things we keep in the family. When I wrap this up I'll let you know what you can report and what is our family's secret. The mountain clans even stay away from it considering it sacred, a place where the gods left their mark. And yes, before you ask, since I've been there I'm allowed." Here he laughed. "I guess in a way the clans consider me blessed by being there, and in the presence of one of their messengers. But no others are allowed."

Little one: He was silent for a moment. From what he could determine there might be a chance he'd get to go and see this, but was almost afraid to ask.

GGF: Inwardly he laughed. He could see the eagerness of his namesake, and yet see that TimOtee wasn't sure how to ask. "Yes, we will be taking a trip there so you can see that what I've said is the truth. Now let me continue."

Little one: "Yes! Ah, yes please."

TimOtee looked over at JerOda once again and saw he was still staring into the distance and seemed to be concentrating once again on whatever it was that a messenger of the gods would, well, be concentrating on. The air still seemed to have that smell of broken rock, and every time a breeze would come up it would create small swirls of rock dust blue-gray in color against the brown of the bare soils. In a sense it had the look of the areas surrounding mines. Only here there weren't the tailings that usually were mucked out of the mines – just this fine dust that seemed to coat anything close by. He kept a nervous watch out since JerOda seemed oblivious to anything happening around them and he worried that the clans would show soon making their situation here untenable.

Eventually Jerod finished his upload and conversation with the approaching fleet, turned and faced TimOtee. "Impressive isn't it?"

Smiling and shaking his head TimOtee had to agree, although impressive probably wasn't the word he'd use, *Maybe impossible, beyond comprehension, or something along those lines – but not impressive.* Still he had to admit that indeed it was impressive. And considering how short of time the strangers were here this shouldn't exist. He'd visited a couple of mines that were close to the farm and had been impressed by the work performed. He had learned, with the help of many workers, that some went pretty deep into the ground. He had asked how long and some had been in operation before he was born. None of those came close to what he was now witnessing – no not one. "So, JerOda, how'd they do this?"

Jerod should have realized it was a question that would be asked, but he had been so busy with updating the fleet, gathering the data and trying to put it into some semblance of order that he hadn't been thinking about what his assistant would want to know. So how to answer that's the question. He inwardly shrugged. Even if he told the truth he knew that TimOtee wouldn't believe him. "Let's just say they used the power of the sun to do this."

Involuntarily TimOtee glanced up at the sun and instantly regretted it as it temporarily blinded him from the brightness. He laughed at his stupidity. How many times had he done that with the exact same result? "If that's true then how can you deny my conclusion that you and the strangers are gods?"

Valid question, Jerod had to admit. Still how did one explain what they knew to one who had just entered the Iron Age? "I know it seems like we must be . . . and I really cannot explain it better than what I did. And I will repeat myself here, we are not your gods, and I am just a messenger. Shortly there will be other strangers arriving so be aware. And yes, I want you here so you can explain your side, what you've seen and witnessed – how this has affected you and the people of this world and how you think it will influence your future. I know it's a lot to ask of you but it's important – critical really. Can you do this for me?"

"Yeah, I guess so. But why is it so important, these facts? Don't you know yourself?"

"To answer you, simply no. I have my perspective and you have yours. And right now yours is more important than mine. After all, we were never to be here on your world. We have a policy of noninterference, and consider that sacred. And unfortunately it's obviously not so sacred that one of ours broke it. Still we need to know what damage may have been done and go from there." Jerod walked over to the newly created tunnel and sent invisible beams down its interior. He needed measurements so he could come up with some explanation as to why. He suspected he knew but until he researched it and had all the facts he wouldn't be able to present his theories.

TimOtee watched curiously but couldn't see anything special about what JerOda was doing. He seemed to be studying the tunnel, which TimOtee would probably add the description cavern, but other than that it didn't appear to be any different than when he had looked in awe at this, this tunnel. Still JerOda continued to do his studying and every once in a while he'd stop and stare like he did when he seemed to be looking at something in the distance. And as the day continued to move with no clansmen showing he found that his aches from earlier were disappearing slowly. So slowly he hadn't noticed it until now. And JerOda continued doing what he had been with that tunnel. He thought by now there couldn't be anything special about it other than its size and how quickly it had come into existence. But there must have been something about it that he couldn't see. So once again with his curiosity piqued he stood beside JerOda and looked once again inside the tunnel, but nothing had changed. So he shrugged and headed back from the tunnel, found a rock and sat down, Until JerOda was finished he knew there'd be no conversations.

As he looked around he realized that close to the opening of this massive tunnel there appeared to be rock that had melted, puddled, and then became solid again. He stood up and went over to one such pile and tentatively reached down and touched it afraid that it could still be hot, but was rewarded with a simple warmth similar to how the sun heated rocks during the daytime. He tried unsuccessfully to pick one up and found it was attached to the dirt it had flowed into. He tried a number of different ones and was finally rewarded with one that broke off and came free. Examining it closely it seemed to have a few smooth surfaces that had a sheen similar to what he had seen on the walls of that vast tunnel. He had been concentrating so hard on the sample he didn't realize that JerOda now stood beside him. It took him commenting to bring that realization to him when JerOda asked, "Interesting stuff isn't it?"

TimOtee almost jumped from the surprise. Catching his breath and slightly shaking his head he said, "Don't do that. I nearly jumped back from surprise. And to answer your question, yeah I've never seen anything like it."

"No surprise. I didn't see any active smoking mountains nearby. If there had been one and you then visited it you would see stuff like this everywhere. It's what happens when it gets hot enough to melt stone and make it a liquid. Now it will never flow quite like water and like water which takes longer to do its work, it will destroy everything in its path. Oh I guess I should qualify that water thing. Normally water as it flows will cut through just about anything in its way but will be slow about it unless there's way too much then anything close will be destroyed. Melted flowing rock does its destruction immediately when it touches something."

"So I guess what you're telling me is that the strangers used heat to make this tunnel, do I have it right?"

"What do you think since you have the evidence in your hand?"

"I don't know . . . This is far beyond me, and are you sure about smoking mountains?"

"I know you haven't seen any here but yes there are smoking mountains on your world. Most are well out in your seas, and a few are close to the top and bottom – we call them the poles, although with the amount of snow and ice nobody lives there presently to witness them." Both heard the crack of sound emanating from above. "Okay TimOtee we are about to be visited by others from the sky. I've had a conversation with the ones who are from above and the leader had taken one of the faster methods of travel and will be here shortly. I need you to tell him everything you have seen, and know. It is important to get the information firsthand. We, the ones I'm a part of, must get as much and as accurate information as we can. And later we'll – you and I – go down to your farm, now that it's no longer blocked by the barrier, and see how your family fared."

Somewhere in the distance TimOtee heard a roar, but it wasn't really too close. And with the trees, hills and such he couldn't pinpoint the location. Shortly it returned to the normal sounds and he waited not knowing what to expect. Coming up the hill from the direction they had come from came three strangers dressed much as the strangers he had witnessed. Seeing them made him somewhat nervous but JerOda seemed unconcerned so he waited quietly. He heard them speak to JerOda but couldn't understand anything being said. *It must be the language of the gods,* he thought. Suddenly the one in front turned to him and addressed him in his own tongue and was surprised. Still the voice sounded different like he was speaking through something giving the voice an unnatural sound. "I'm Admiral Williams, and you are?"

"Admiral? Is that your name? And what is that second? Is that part of your name also?"

Admiral Williams smiled, even though it was something that the native couldn't see. "I guess such would seem a little strange. I've only had a brief time to review what was sent, and no, Admiral is not my name. It simply means I'm in charge of the rest, well except for this one . . ." here he pointed at JerOda, "he is kind of in charge of himself."

"Ah, then, what was that again, or yes, admiral I am TimOtee."

"TimOtee is it? Then I'm glad to make your acquaintance. Come, we have much to discuss, and while I know what I'm wearing might be a bit intimidating I'm required to do this for my protection."

"But, if you are the one in charge can you not change such requirements?"

Turning towards JerOda the admiral laughed. "You told me he was sharp and as usual you're right." He turned back to TimOtee and said, "Like some of the plants you grow for food, there are layers, and it is the same. Yes I am in charge, but only here. No not on your world", here he pointed up to the sky, "but up there. And from where I come there are others who are above me and I must answer to them. Does that help?"

TimOtee shrugged. If they were gods, even though they continued to deny it, he'd never understand these layers. "I guess I'll have to take your word for it. And what is it you want to talk about?"

"Simply everything that has happened when, as you call them, the strangers arrived. Can you do that?"

"Yes."

"Good then come with me. My staff that I brought with me has set up a small area where we can be more comfortable."

TimOtee looked back at JerOda as the admiral led him away. He felt nervous and saw that JerOda gave him an encouraging nod.

* * *

The sun was setting when he returned to where JerOda was waiting. TimOtee was silent as he tried to absorb all that had just transpired. First he saw that somewhere while he was gone JerOda had found a chair to sit on, which meant that it had to come with the admiral. He still didn't understand anything about how these strangers talked over great distances, or how they traveled. Still the admiral and the ones who were with him were real living individuals just as he. But what it was that left him in silence was the fact that no matter the question from the admiral and the one who sat there next to him he had an answer. Not only that but a clear and sharp recollection – almost like he had perfect memory. Was this something the gift from JerOda gave him? His introspection was interrupted when JerOda asked, "Did it go well?"

"Ah . . . yeah . . . I guess. I mean, well I'm not sure what I mean."

"Were you able to recount everything?"

"Yes, and that's the problem. There's no way I should be able to do that so perfectly. Is this part of the gift?"

"Yes, one of the many. I wasn't sure if this would happen as quickly as it did, but I'm glad it has. I know that perfect memory sounds like a great thing, but it can be a curse also. I know, at times, when one didn't have such one usually wished for it. Because of perfect memory not only will all aspects of your life be there to review, but this includes the bad as well as the good. It means one has to learn how to keep certain memories buried, and only reach for them when it is needed. Yeah I know I've said this before, but now you know what I've been saying."

"I hadn't thought about that. I mean this is all new to me and this is the first time I could see everything in my mind. In a sense it was like living it over again. I guess I can see advantages to such, but the other side, I'm not so sure I'm looking forward to that."

"Like all of us, you'll learn to adjust." Jerod stood up and then pointed at the camp chair he had been sitting in. "Here you take this for a while. I've got to go and discuss a few things with the admiral, and while I won't be gone as long as you it will take time." With that Jerod headed over to where the admiral and his staff waited. He saw the admiral was still seated and seemed to be in conversation with his staff. "Admiral?"

After a brief pause Admiral Williams smiled and said, "Sit down please."

"Thank you sir." He sat in the indicated seat and waited.

"That's quite a story this TimOtee related. Did he receive as you agents call it, *the gift*?"

"Yes, although it was only recently and it could have been days before this aspect would have taken. But we both know that once the process begins no one knows which will manifest itself first. And for him it appears to be perfect memory, which for our need is critical. So did you get what you need? And what I mean is between the data I've transmitted, and your interview with the native."

"Yes, unfortunately we were sent off on a wild goose chase by reports of a number of supposed ion trails that had a signature we were looking for. Apparently it was another feint giving them time to get away once again. And I suspect what we have will do us no good anyway. Even though we'll have to check out that location mentioned I suspect we'll find nothing. I'm sure it simply was a code phrase letting all of them knows where they'd meet. And again with all the ion trails in the area I doubt if we'll be able to figure out which are real and which are false. Admiral Sympson is good. Well, better than good and we missed here. Meaning we'll have to probably regroup and try again at a later time. And before you ask, no we aren't finished with this. Space or the universe is large and there are way too many places for them to run or hide. So we'll have to wait and look for the signs of their return.

"I had a look at their handiwork, and I think I now know the whys. From the initial size of the tunnel I'd say they could have carefully flown a cruiser in there. It's far from finished, but I suspect if they had completed what they were attempting then there would have been a rather large entrance door placed on this thing making it virtually invisible. And the only time any would be aware something was here if one happened to be in the area when it was opened to allow something in or out. And by using the planet itself for shielding the likelihood of discovery would be close to zero. And I suspect now that they have escaped our grasp that they will have the necessary time to do just that somewhere else."

"Makes sense. Look I know you'll be pulling the fleet back, re-outfitting, and such, and then following whatever orders the chain of command desires – such is the life of the military – but I'm going to have to stay here a while longer. TimOtee is the first of what I need here. I've got to find at least nine or ten more. Then I've got to work with the agency to get spy satellites set up in this system so we can continue to monitor the situation. And while all that's happening bring the ones I've given *the gift* to a little training session so if the unthinkable happens and the renegades return we'll be aware and able to respond.

So I need one of the four person exploration ships left with me so I can return back to our own space once I'm done. And, of course the flyer I used to get here isn't capable of interstellar flight so needs to be picked up.

"I'd guess that I'll be here for close to one of our years. I really don't have the data on this world to know how long it takes to move around their sun, but suspect by the time I return all of this will be second nature. Oh, by the way have you figured out who are the ones working with the renegades?"

The admiral let out an exasperated breath, "Yeah, but too late to do anything about it. When they felt they were compromised they disappeared with the scout ship they were using. And since a scout ship is really tiny, and they knew where they were going, well let's say like the ones we've been chasing . . ."

"Understood. Okay then, I'll let you get back to what you have to do, and we'll make the ship exchange in orbit around this world. I'll radio when I'm able to do this, and I promise I won't delay you too much." Here Jerod laughed. "After all I know how the military works – hurry up and wait!"

* * *

His great grandfather laughed, "And that's how it all happened. And I have to admit it was an adventure of a lifetime, one I'll never forget – not that I could. Yes, the messenger JerOda stayed with us here for a cycle, something he called by a strange word, 'year'.

And I was brought aboard his method of transportation and there was given the insight to see and understand everything that happened. It was like seeing images in my own mind, but it flowed continuously. Much I still don't understand, and to be truthful will probably never understand. JerOda said it would be that way but it was important that I saw – as well as the rest who had received the gift – everything he had. He said it was because we needed to recognize the signs if the strangers ever returned.

"And we were given special ways of being able to talk to the messenger. And for me this is the strangest of all. As you and I are here face to face, so to speak, it is like that. Only I see his image in my mind. I don't know how, only that is the way of it. At times it could be embarrassing when out of nowhere the messenger would talk to me. He'd be unaware what I was doing at the time, and if it was something private he'd leave muttering an apology and then talk to me later.

"Now remember I want to see the whole report because there are some things I talked about that must remain in our family alone. It is our own special secret. Oh yeah, your great grandmother is the same CaraOlyn I met there to the west. You asked and now you know." TimOtee the senior looked out at the darkening skies and knew the sun had set. But he had need of wrapping this up today so his namesake could work on the report, and he would have the time necessary to read and make the corrections and omissions necessary.

TimOtee the great grandson stood in awe. He had never guessed his great grandfather had ever done anything like this. And to have actually been alive at the time of the gods or strangers, as he also called them, had been a total surprise. And that alone would have been enough, but to also meet and travel with the messenger – what a privilege. TimOtee had to admit that this past seven days had gone by fast. He expected to be bored, and to daydream through this time, but to his surprise the adventure kept him well involved and the days had flown. And now that the adventure was over he was reluctant and a little sad that it had ended.

"So why are you still standing here? I suspect you will miss your dinner if you lollygag around here for too long. I know the appetite your brothers and sisters have and if you don't get in there for your share there might not be any left." He laughed when he saw the panic in TimOtee's eyes. One thing for sure this young one could pack away the food. Maybe it was a good thing they lived on a farm. It might be the only way to keep this brood fed and full. As he watched his great grandson run inside he could only shake his head. In a few moments he'd join them and enjoy the family – his family – and all the chaos that went with growing children.

"So TimOtee it looks like you've passed on the story once again", the voice inside of his head said.

"Yes, JerOda. Yet it is as you predicted so long ago in the past. It seems the further we are from those times the less is believed, and slowly I see it moving into myth. So were you spying on me?"

Jerod laughed. "No, but I like to check up on an old friend now and then. And the answer is no before you ask, the ones who visited your world are still out there somewhere. There's been nothing since the time when we met. And I've been busy on so many other projects. Still you are important to me. I'll cut this short as I know your meal is waiting. And by the way thank you."

"Thank you? Why thank you?"

"For the friendship we've had over time. In what I do such a thing is precious."

Smiling inwardly TimOtee said, "You are most welcome." And after his answer he felt JerOda withdraw. *Yes, who'd have thought our time would lead to a friendship that has covered these many generations – surely not I. I felt that once he left that would be it, unless the strangers returned, which they never have.* He knew on the morrow they'd be heading out, as a family, making the trek to the great tunnel. He also knew that there would be a slight chance he'd see some of his great grandchildren bring forth another generation, and most likely his time would then be done. Again he smiled, he had lived a long life after all, and even with the gift he had received from the messenger, he had been promised this long life, but eventually he'd reach his end. "Soon", he whispered, "soon I'll be home to join you CaraOlyn oh love of my life. If you could only see what our family has become . . . but maybe you can." He shrugged and with care stood up and headed inside. His granddaughter really did put on a great meal and he wasn't one who wanted to miss it. And as he went through the door he turned and looked over the land that was their farm – so very different from the time of chaos and when the gods had visited their world. *Yes, so very different.* He shrugged, the smells of the food awaiting him drew him inside and he could hear the joyful sounds of his family sitting around the table.

EPILOGUE

Jerod had just wrapped up another of the many projects that seemed to always come his way. Now came the part he always hated. He knew from the contacts he had with other agents, and so many others in these circles he traveled that it seemed to be a universal dislike. And because of this dislike he wondered why it still persisted. It seemed, if he remembered his history right, that when computers first came to be it had been thought this would spell the end of paperwork. Well, he, and probably every other worker of this time could attest to the fact that like the common cold they all still faced it. And for him because of what he did it seemed like it took longer to fill out the necessary forms and reports than an actual operation.

He entered through the doors – real doors – of an ancient nondescript building that existed in one of the poorer industrial parks inside the capital city of the now existing empire. In front of him was a standard reception area with a long counter with workers behind doing what they had to do, and a number of guards patrolling the area. The guards looked to be from any number of rental agencies who supplied guard services, but he, as well as everyone who knew what this place was all about knew better. Up on the third floor, which was really down, he had a small office but like any visitor he had to check in first. It was all part of the appearances that had to be maintained. It seemed like a busy morning as he had to take a number and wait his turn. *Funny,* he thought, *this is something else people thought would have disappeared by now. Taking a number, waiting in line or sitting waiting for one's number to be called.*

He had been sitting for quite a while on that incoming flight to here and decided to stand. In a sense it was nice to be here where everything was predictable and so very routine. It was almost like a small vacation, except, of course that paperwork waiting patiently. Finally his number was called and he approached the window he had been directed too. Once he reached the window a young woman smiled at him and asked for his reason for wanting to see the CEO. All of this being part of the way inside for any of the agents. Yes there were privacy fields but with any technology someone would always find ways around. In a sense this was the wars that were fought today – one side always trying to crack the new, while the other tried to keep them from cracking it.

As was always required he had his ID scanned, followed by the standard Bioscan to confirm he was who he said he was. He gave the young lady the code phrase which was an answer to her question. While it wouldn't be obvious to any observer he could see the reaction in her eyes. Still all that would be seen would be her smile. Then she said, "You're appointment is confirmed. Go to elevator twelve, it will be available to you but for only as long as it takes for you to arrive. If you are late then you will have to come back and do this all over again . . . have a nice day sir."

He smiled and thanked her. Again what had been stated was all for show. Yes, every day and many times through the day the elevators would change, all in a random way. If any who were here on regular business, any, including the one for the agents, the elevators would be just that. It was an old mechanical style of system that would move them to their destinations somewhere above. Because of whom he was when he stepped into elevator twelve the bottom opened and he was lowered by gravity lift to the third floor where he'd be spending the rest of this day, and to be honest most likely all of tomorrow. When the gravity lift stopped he exited and like above there was a counter with a number of people working. Only here they were part of the agency and unlike above, the guards here were dressed in military uniforms carrying serious weapons. As far as he knew this location had never been breached or even located. Still, he knew that if such had taken place there would be no knowledge of it happening.

He walked up to the counter and stood in the field which did a thorough scan, and once it turned green he stepped out. He knew that while what was above was the first defense against intrusion this was the second and more serious. He knew if he was an agent trying to infiltrate this place it would be here he would have the most fear. If his disguise wasn't perfect then going through this scan could be fatal. As he left the scan area he approached the counter and one of the workers handed him a packet, smiled and turned back to their work. Most of what he had been handed was on a small device similar to something from the past known as a flash drive. But it was there the similarities ended. It in itself was a complete computing device with enough storage that it could easily hold all the knowledge in all the libraries that existed in the known and settled universe. Still what was on it was totally encrypted and would only reveal itself once he plugged it into his workstation.

He sighed as he entered the hallway that led to his space and without paying attention used the retina scan combination handprint, body scan that would allow him into his space with the door finally sliding open and admitting him. One thing he'd never understand, with this place under continual air circulation from the enclosed central heating and air units, why did this place always smell like it had been vacant? The actual area he worked from was really small. Unlike in the past where there had to be file cabinets here most would be filed electronically. Looking around the Spartan office, he wasn't the type who made such a space personal, he went over to the wall dispenser and got a real cup of coffee made just the way he liked it and sat down listening to the chair complain. At least the chairs conformed to one's body at least making it comfortable to be in one.

While the workstations never were shut down, the units would sleep to conserve energy. And in a way what was here was a throwback to the ancient past. While much could be recorded verbally, there were virtual keyboards that allowed one to enter data if it was of such a sensitive nature that verbalization wouldn't be allowed. He placed the small unit he had been given into the proper slot and waited for the handshake between the workstation and the unit. In the meantime as this was happening the workstation greeted him asking if he would like to listen to any messages that were patiently waiting. He asked that they be given to him from the highest priority to the mundane. He was halfway through the messages when one caught his attention. "Your friend TimOtee is ill." He sat up and had the message repeat. As brief as it had been it still sent chills through him. It meant that TimOtee's time was close. It was the first sign of the failure of the nanobots that kept one healthy and the body performing efficiently. He asked when the message had arrived and learned it had been a couple of weeks in the past. For him this wasn't good. It could mean his friend had already passed on to wherever one went after death. He immediately contacted his boss and once permission was granted immediately headed out. He wanted to be there for his friend.

* * *

TimOtee, the great grandson was out in the fields working when he heard the news. It seemed like yesterday when he had spent that time with him, his great grandfather and learned about the time when the gods had indeed visited this world. He remembered after that week, and once what he wrote had been approved he had been praised for such a good report. And that trip to the great tunnel had been really eye opening. He thought he knew what it would be like and learned that he had under estimated its size by a lot. Now there was a barrier built to keep the wild creatures from accidently blundering into it. Because if they did then they'd die as there was no way to rescue them. He remembered being disappointed by that barrier because it completely blocked the view. Then it was pointed out that just a little way was a platform that allowed one to see the thing in its entirety. Eagerly he had climbed to the top and froze as he stared. There was no way this could be real, but there before his eyes here it was.

He straightened his back and heard his joints pop, yes being a farmer truly is hard work, but he, like the rest of his family would have it no other way. His mate was back at the homestead taking care of their first. And he realized, with regret, that the young one would never get a chance to know his great great grandfather. For whatever the reason he knew that the old one had reached his end. Still he had to smile since this one had lived a really full life. He took the farm beast back and put her in one of the pens, made sure of feed and water, and headed for the house. As he came through the door he could see the worry on his mate's face. He smiled, although it was a sad one. "I guess I better go. You're more than welcome to join us if you like, you know that."

She smiled back reflecting that same sad smile. She had met the old one and had an instant liking for him, and they had become fast friends, but for now she felt it were important that only the immediate family should be there since his strength was failing. And she knew immediate family would be a large group since he had lived so long. "No, no not now. I, with the rest who have joined the family will come later. I think it important that it be only blood right now."

He could understand that but felt that once she had joined the family she was blood. After all, it took two to bring a new life into this world, and they had done just that. In an awkward silent moment where he was undecided he finally let her choice be the one for now. And she did say she'd come later. Before heading out the door and to the main house he said, "Okay, but please come when you are ready." He saw her nod, and he found himself striding across the open lands down towards the main house. Most of the family had built around that ancient old structure and had added to the size of the original farm, and from his vantage he could see others approaching the main house. This alone spoke volumes of what they thought of the old one.

As he approached the main house he could see his mother sitting on the porch. She looked older than he remembered, which made sense since time did this to all of them. He could see the sadness in her eyes, and as the family gathered she told everybody to remain outside, and to be quiet. Then she stood up and with a strange look on her face said something that sent chills through the ones gathered there. It was obvious she wasn't sure how to say it but eventually just stated, "The one your great grandfather knew as the messenger is here and is with him."

A shocked silence ran through the family. They all had heard about the messenger but none of them were sure how real this one could be. And now he was here in person. How did he know? But then, if he was a messenger from the gods didn't they know all?

Shortly a stranger came out on the porch dressed no different than they. And the second surprise was his age. Well, the way he appeared to not have aged. He appeared to be somewhere between their mother and them but that was impossible. He smiled a sad smile, and then quietly said, "His time is almost over. His body is frail, but his mind is still sharp. So each of you go in quietly and see him in this world for the last time. I feel that today is to be his last. And I will be here through the burial then I must return." At that point they could see the tears forming in his eyes before he turned away from them and went back inside.

* * *

And yes this messenger did as he promised. He remained with the family through their time of grief once the old one passed on, and he confirmed to each and every one of them that what he had told them had been accurate. And finally before he disappeared he stated that his time here was to remain as a family secret, and the only time he might return would be if the ones returned, otherwise their world was their own, and they would be allowed to grow as they would, with only a small footnote in the history, which would probably become myth and legend, since the only proof would be a hole in the ground that most likely would end up unexplained.

Jerod smiled one last time as he looked back from the hills surrounding the farms. *Yes, old friend you have done well, and I truly hope you are with your loved one now.* With a sigh he turned back around and headed out of sight and to his small speeder. Mounting it he headed for the old growth forest where this all had begun and to where his ship waited. Assignments awaited and this was more time than he had to be away. Still he felt it important to be there when such an old friend crossed the threshold into the great beyond. With modern medicine he still had half his life to live, and maybe someday when it was his time he'd meet TimOtee, CaraOlyn, and so many others who had gone on ahead of him. But for now that was sometime in the future – an unknown one for him.

He stayed off the trails and headed deep into the woods with so many memories being renewed. Finally he arrived and with a handshake with his ship it was time to be gone, and to close the final chapter here. TimOtee had been the last of the ones who'd received *the gift* to survive. And with the renegades lost somewhere in the universe he suspected he would never have a reason to return, so with much regret he set the ship to leave the surface using as much stealth as possible, took one long lasting look as his ship left the atmosphere and then set the FTL drive and headed for the area inside his ship that he used as an office. Even this trip meant he'd have paperwork. Pausing briefly and staring out at nothing, he said softly, "God speed old friend . . . God speed."

ABOUT THE AUTHOR

F.D. Brant always wanted to write, but life got in the way. Finally after retiring he got his chance.

Storytelling and writing has always been F.D. Brant's passion, but responsibilities took preference. And because of those responsibilities it took retiring to allow those passions to come to fruition. Since retiring he has written 9 books, and maintains a weekly eclectic blog, Words in the Wind.

Growing up in the backcountry he learned the appreciation of "doing things for yourself". Because it was impossible to call in someone to repair anything one either did it themselves or went without. This led to the appreciation of the natural world, and the daily struggles that one faced as nature threw problems at the family that had to be overcome, leading to confidence and self-sufficiency. This led to the strong characters that populate his stories and books. And his female protagonists are strong willed and confident – something that he saw in both in his mother and sister.